GRACE AGUILAR

GRACE AGUILAR

SELECTED WRITINGS

edited by Michael Galchinsky

broadview literary texts

National Library of Canada Cataloguing in Publication
Aguilar, Grace, 1816-1847
Grace Aguilar: selected writings / edited by Michael Galchinsky.

(Broadview literary texts)
Includes bibliographical references.
ISBN 1-55111-377-5
I. Galchinsky, Michael, 1965- . II. Title. III. Series.

PR4001.A45A6 2003 828'.709 C2003-900800-2

Broadview Press Ltd. is an independent, international publishing house, incorporated in 1985. Broadview believes in shared ownership, both with its employees and with the general public; since the year 2000 Broadview shares have traded publicly on the Toronto Venture Exchange under the symbol BDP.

We welcome comments and suggestions regarding any aspect of our publications—please feel free to contact us at the addresses below or at broadview@broadviewpress.com.

North America
PO Box 1243, Peterborough, Ontario, Canada K9J 7H5
3576 California Road, Orchard Park, NY, USA 14127
Tel: (705) 743-8990; Fax: (705) 743-8353
email: customerservice@broadviewpress.com

UK, Ireland, and continental Europe
Plymbridge Distributors Ltd., Estover Road
Plymouth PL6 7PY UK
Telephone: (01752) 202301; Fax: (01752) 202333
E-mail: orders@plymbridge.com

Australia and New Zealand
UNIREPS, University of New South Wales
Sydney, NSW, 2052
Tel: 61 2 9664 0999; Fax: 61 2 9664 5420
email: info.press@unsw.edu.au

www.broadviewpress.com

Broadview Press Ltd. gratefully acknowledges the financial support of the Government of Canada through the Book Publishing Industry Development Program for our publishing activities.

Series editor: Professor L.W. Conolly
Advisory editor for this volume: Colleen Franklin
Text design and composition by George Kirkpatrick

PRINTED IN CANADA

Contents

Figure 1. Engraving of Grace Aguilar by J. Cochran.
Courtesy of the Jewish Museum, London.

Acknowledgments

Contrary to myth, archival scholarship is not a solitary pursuit. Since 1997, when I began work on this edition, numerous institutions and individuals have helped me see it to completion. Thanks to a Visiting Skirball Fellowship at the Oxford Centre for Hebrew and Jewish Studies, I was able to follow Aguilar's paper trail throughout the United Kingdom. Millsaps College permitted me to take a research leave at just the right time, and supported my trip to the University of North Carolina at Chapel Hill, where the bulk of Aguilar's correspondence is housed. The English Department at Georgia State University funded my research at the University of Pennsylvania Center for Judaic Studies into Aguilar's American connections. The librarians at the Bodleian, the British Library, the Newspaper Library at Colindale, the University College of London Manuscript and Jewish Studies Libraries, the Anglo-Jewish Archives at the University of Southampton's Hartley Library, the National Library of Scotland, and the Hertfordshire County Records Office all offered valuable advice and assistance. Special thanks to Michael Dugdale, the great-great-grandson of Aguilar's brother Emanuel, who kindly made several documents in his possession available for use in this volume, and exhibited a great deal of grace under the pressure of a tight deadline. Special thanks also for permission to quote from the Grace Aguilar MSS and from Aguilar's correspondence goes to Jennifer Marin, the Curator at the Jewish Museum of London. Thanks, too, to the journal editors of *Victorian Literature and Culture*, *Jewish Culture and History*, *Literature and Theology*, and *Prooftexts* for publishing my earlier studies of Aguilar and her world. In the process of putting this book together, the editors of the Literary Texts Series at Broadview Press have been unwaveringly encouraging and committed.

Those individuals who supported the project by inviting me to give seminars or presentations include Susannah Heschel, David Rechter, Miriam Peskowitz, and Kathryn McClymond. At Oxford I was encouraged and inspired by the friendship and collegiality of Szonja Komoróczy, Rachel Elior, Ehud Ben Ezer, Elliott Horowitz, Joel Berkowitz, Larry Rubin, Michael Wenthe, and Rebecca Boggs. Particular thanks go to the entire Anglo-Jewish studies crew at Southampton—Nadia Valman, Jo Reilly, Tony Kushner, and Bryan Cheyette—who, along with Bill Williams, allowed an American into their fellowship, and whose excellent taste in Old Southampton's Thai food I readily acknowledge. My colleagues on this side of the water in the small (but growing!) world of Victorian Jewish studies—Meri-Jane Rochelson, Cynthia Scheinberg, Judy Page, Michael Ragussis, and Daniel Harris—offered their time, in some cases their mentorship, and always their welcome suggestions and advice. My department's Works in Progress colloquium helped "wip" the introduction into shape. Grateful thanks go to my research assistants Amy Hawkins, Brennan Collins, and in the home stretch, Laura Carter and Angela Hall-Godsey, who diligently performed the tedious work of tracking down sources, scanning and typing in text, and copyediting, without which this project might never have reached an end.

Finally, my deepest thanks to my family: to my son, Gideon, who reminds me constantly that the Victorians are nowhere near as interesting as bugs, and to Elke, my twenty-first century Woman of Israel, whose love, editorial support, and sacrifice, made this book possible.

Introduction

Significance

By the time of her early death in 1847, at the age of thirty-one, Grace Aguilar had built a multi-faceted career: she was a poet, historical romance writer, domestic novelist, Jewish emancipator, religious reformer, educator, social historian, theologian, and liturgist. As a Victorian Jewish woman, Aguilar managed to produce a body of work that integrated the various aspects of her identity. Her readers included Jews and Christians, women and men, religious traditionalists and reformers. Distributed throughout the British Empire, Europe, and the United States, her books were translated into French, German, and Hebrew. Today, her writings offer students of nineteenth-century British history and culture several rare opportunities: to witness a member of a British minority engaging in an ambivalent encounter with the majority culture, to explore the new literary genres she developed for this purpose, and, through her, to rediscover a minority subculture already in bloom by the middle of the nineteenth century.

Aguilar's writings contribute to a more complete understanding of Victorian literature, Jewish cultural history, women's cultural history, and English national identity. From a literary perspective, Aguilar was pre-eminent among those attempting to produce a new Anglo-Jewish literary subculture that could engage in complex and constructive encounters with broader Victorian genres and traditions. Her novels and poetry both assimilated the forms she drew from her surroundings, and altered those forms to express her particular sensibility as an Anglo-Jewish woman. For example, she assimilated the historical romance form made popular by Walter Scott's evangelical imitators, but her romances, including *The Vale of Cedars* and the tales in *Records of Israel*, turn the evangelicals' representation of Jewish women as uneducated and malleable on its head. As a consequence, her literary works made legible the ideological purposes—whether religious, cultural, or nationalist in tone—often left implicit in novels and poems by her non-Jewish Victorian contemporaries.[1] Her historical romances presented Jewishness as a non-threatening "national" identity that could be assimilated into the "imagined community" of Great Britain while retaining its distinct character. In this respect, she learned from Walter Scott, for she represented Jews in much the same way that he represented Scots. Her poems, too, engaged in complex dialogue with the late Romantic and early Victorian poetics of nature, prophecy, the Holy Land, the myth of the wandering Jew, and biblical exegesis. Her "Address to the Ocean," for example, rewrites the "natural supernaturalism" of Byron's parallel address in Book IV of *Childe Harold's Pilgrimage*, replacing it with what might be called a supernatural naturalism. Critic Cynthia Scheinberg has shown that Aguilar's "Dialogue Stanzas" rewrite the typical Victorian Christian poetics of "prophecy."[2]

In a similar way, Aguilar's essays, poems, stories and novels on women's themes adapted the literary and ideological strategies of the Romantic and early Victorian women writers, whose work was occupied with the developing separation of gender spheres. As its title suggests, Aguilar's *Records of Israel* plays a variation on Felicia Hemans' immensely popular book of poems, *Records of Woman* (1828); her book *The Women of Israel* drew inspiration from *The Women of England* (1838), by the domestic ideologist Sarah Stickney Ellis. As a Jewish woman, Aguilar sought a popular audience in the public sphere by expressing a domestic ideology parallel to that of her Christian female contemporaries. One of the tributes she received acknowledged this tactic and described her in terms Hemans and Stickney Ellis would have recognized as the "moral governess of the Hebrew family." But Aguilar constructs a very different kind of "national" history than her Christian contemporaries do. True, like Ellis's "England," Aguilar's "Israel" is unified by a common language, rituals, historical experience, and above all, sensibility.

---

1 See Michael Ragussis, *Figures of Conversion: "The Jewish Question" and English National Identity* (Durham, NC: Duke UP, 1995) chs. 2-3; and Michael Galchinsky, *The Origin of the Modern Jewish Woman Writer: Romance and Reform in Victorian England* (Detroit: Wayne State UP, 1996) ch. 1.

2 Cynthia Scheinberg, "'Measure to Yourself a Prophet's Place': Biblical Heroines, Jewish Difference and Women's Poetry," eds. Isobel Armstrong and Virginia Blain, *Women's Poetry, Late Romantic to Late Victorian: Gender and Genre, 1830-1900* (New York: St. Martin's, 1999) 263-91.

But unlike Ellis's nation, Aguilar's lacks a common territory, government, military, or centralized church. In other words, Aguilar uses the idea of the *nation* to express the needs of a *diaspora*. Or again, in Aguilar's poem "The Wanderers," based on the biblical account of Hagar and Ishmael in the desert, she used the sentimental tradition of poetry in the maternal voice—which conventionally addressed polemical subjects such as slavery and child labor—to address Jewish alienation from English society.[1] By writing texts that were similar to those of her English contemporaries and yet different, Aguilar could simultaneously make her work appeal to a broader national audience while articulating her particular vision as a Jewish woman.

While addressing Jews' social, political, and aesthetic concerns for the broader Victorian audience, Aguilar was also intent on redressing women's neglect by men within the Jewish community. Here, she assimilated and altered literary forms associated with Jewish men. In *Women of Israel*, for instance, she addressed the limitations of Jewish (male) traditional literature in relation to women—in particular, the limitations of the literature called *midrash aggadah*, consisting of interpretive retellings of biblical events. Aguilar used the *midrash* form, but in a new way, to focus for the first time on Jewish women's needs. For example, in her midrash "The Spirit of Night," she revised the traditional tale of the creation of the Sun and the Moon, in which the female Moon receives only the secondary, reflected light of the male Sun. In Aguilar's revision, the Moon achieves "varied but equal beauty." In *The Spirit of Judaism* and *Sabbath Thoughts and Sacred Communings*, she also adapted the traditionally Jewish male genres of theology, prayer, sermon, and meditation to women's spiritual experience.

In many ways her most significant contributions to Jewish cultural history were diplomatic. She was one of the most visible spokespersons in the struggle for English Jews' "emancipation," which meant seeking to safeguard Jews against conversion efforts, arguing for their full social acceptance, and pleading for the reform

---

1 For examples of sentimental maternal poems with a political edge, see Caroline Norton's *A Voice from the Factories* and Elizabeth Barrett Browning's "The Runaway Slave at Pilgrim's Point," eds. Angela Leighton and Margaret Reynolds, *Victorian Women Poets: An Anthology* (Cambridge, MA: Basil Blackwell, 1995) 80; 142.

of the legal and political constraints on their citizenship. These included the inability to vote, to occupy seats in Parliament, to stand for Mayor or Sheriff of London, to engage in business enterprises in the City, and other exclusions from full civil and political rights. Her essays, in particular, contributed to the cause of Jewish emancipation, including a translation of Orobio de Castro's *Israel Defended*, an apologetic work, as well as her own *Jewish Faith*, a tract on resisting conversion, and her essay "The History of the Jews in England," the first history of that community ever produced by an English Jew.

Besides working on behalf of emancipation, Aguilar also worked for Jews' internal religious reform. Her theological works, especially *The Spirit of Judaism* and *The Women of Israel*, made hers one of the strongest voices in the broader movement among Victorian Jews to alter their religious ideology and practice. She made cogent and influential arguments that prayers should be spoken, and sermons delivered, in English. She opposed the traditional physical separation of men and women in the synagogue and suggested that girls should receive as comprehensive a religious education as boys. She also made one of the first arguments in the English-speaking world for a Jewish vernacular translation of the Bible, in response to which two translations by prominent Jewish men soon appeared.[1] These translations in turn had a significant impact on the style and substance of English and American Jewish religious observance. Thus Aguilar's influence on Jewish reform, although indirect, was profound.

Taking Aguilar's efforts on behalf of emancipation and reform together, we can see that she was an active participant in the Anglo-Jewish variant of the broader movement in eighteenth- and nineteenth-century European Jewish history known as the *Haskalah*, or Jewish Enlightenment. The Jewish Enlightenment followed the European Enlightenment historically and ideologically: beginning in the 1740s in Germany, Jewish *maskilim*, or enlighteners, attempted to replace traditional, faith-based standards of authority within their community with a liberal, humanistic, and secularizing individualism.[2] The English variant, which began in the 1820s, included all of

1 See Galchinsky, *Origin*, 75; 130; 141-42; 186.

2 To compare "Enlightenments" among European Jews, see, for example, Todd Endelman, *Comparing Jewish Societies* (Ann Arbor: U of Michigan P, 1997); Paula Hyman, *The Jews of Modern France* (Berkeley: U of California P, 1998) and *Gender and Assimilation in Modern*

these elements plus a vindication of the rights of woman, which is what makes it unique in Europe.[1] Like her brother *maskilim* in Germany and France, Aguilar was thus engaged in recording and bringing about the complex encounter between Jews and modernity, an encounter that involved European Jews' transition from resident aliens to citizens, as well as the internal reform of their organizational structures, theology, and observances.

Perhaps her most important work as an "enlightener" was to argue on behalf of women's emancipation, both within and outside the Jewish community. During the first half of the nineteenth century, Jewish women were beset by missionaries trying to convert them on the one side, and by condescending and sometimes censorious Jewish men on the other. Conversionists targeted women as the weak link among the Jews, arguing that their oppression by Jewish men, their lack of Jewish education, and their innate spirituality made them natural candidates for conversion. Evangelical novelists like Amelia Bristow and M.G. Lewis followed Scott's *Ivanhoe*—in which the possibility of marriage between the Jewish heroine and the charismatic Christian hero is raised but does not occur—with novels in which just such a marriage succeeds, at the cost of the heroine's Jewishness.[2] Like the conversionists, Anglo-Jewish men

---

Jewish History (Seattle: U of Washington P, 1995); Arthur Hertzberg, *The French Enlightenment and the Jews: The Origins of Modern Anti-Semitism* (New York: Columbia UP, 1968); David Sorkin, *The Transformation of German Jewry, 1780-1840* (Oxford: Oxford UP, 1987) and *Moses Mendelssohn and the Religious Enlightenment* (Berkeley: U of California P, 1996); Marion A. Kaplan, *The Making of the Jewish Middle Class: Women, Family, and Identity in Imperial Germany* (New York: Oxford UP, 1991); *Jewish Women in Historical Perspective*, ed. Judith Baskin, 2nd ed. (Detroit: Wayne State UP, 1998).

1 Major accounts of eighteenth- and nineteenth-century Anglo-Jewish history include: Todd Endelman, *The Jews of Georgian England: 1714-1830: Tradition and Change in a Liberal Society* (Ann Arbor: U of Michigan P, 1999) and *Radical Assimilation in English Jewish History, 1656-1945* (Bloomington: Indiana UP, 1990); David Feldman, *Englishmen and Jews: Social Relations and Political Culture, 1840-1914* (New Haven: Yale UP, 1994); David Cesarani, *The Jewish Chronicle and Anglo-Jewry, 1841-1991* (New York: Cambridge UP, 1994); *The Jewish Heritage in British History*, ed. Tony Kushner (London: Frank Cass, 1992); Eugene C. Black, *The Social Politics of Anglo-Jewry, 1880-1920* (New York: Blackwell, 1988); M.C.N. Salbstein, *The Emancipation of the Jews in Britain: the Question of the Admission of the Jews to Parliament, 1828-1860* (Rutherford, NJ: Fairleigh Dickinson UP, 1982); V.D. Lipman, *Social History of the Jews in England, 1850-1950* (London: Watts, 1954); Cecil Roth, *History of the Jews in England* (London: Oxford UP, 1941).

2 See Amelia Bristow, *Emma de Lissau: A Narrative of Striking Vicissitudes and Peculiar Trials: with Explanatory Notes Illustrative of the Manners and Customs of the Jews*, 2 vols., (London: T.

considered women in their community problems to be solved. In essays, they repeatedly called for female education, on the grounds that, as one commentator put it, women were "the weakness in our camp."[1] But though they called for education, they did not provide it. Moreover, when women themselves attempted to publish texts to aid in the female education effort, the male editors of Anglo-Jewish journals frequently censored or attacked their writing.

In response to both of these threats, Aguilar sought to give Jewish women a proud identity. Her accounts of biblical and historical Jewish women in *The Women of Israel*, combined with her occasional lyrics and domestic fictions (her novella *The Perez Family*, her short story "The Authoress," and the novels *Home Influence*, *A Mother's Recompense*, and *Woman's Friendship*) argued for changes in what women and girls could learn and how they could learn it. Her attempt to lay out a female-centered theology in *The Spirit of Judaism*, along with the sermons, daily meditations, and prayers she wrote for women's use in *Sabbath Thoughts and Sacred Communings*, provided women with a theology and liturgy of their own. These writings provided models of women's full participation in Jewish life and learning, while remaining within the constraints of Aguilar's belief in the separation of gender roles into self-contained spheres.

Her work on behalf of women had significance, not only for Jews, but for Victorian women in general, for these efforts were part of the broader Victorian effort to define separate male and female areas of activity, and in particular were part of the effort to "feminize religion."[2] Along with well-known Christian domestic ideologists from the period, Aguilar participated in constructing and highlighting a female-centered, religiously and morally charged domestic sphere, as well as a range of activities for middle-class women that

---

Gardiner, 1828); M.G. Lewis, *The Jewish Maiden*, 4 vols. (London: A.K. Newman, 1830). For accounts of literary conversionism, see Ragussis, *Figures of Conversion*, chs. 1-2; Galchinsky, *Origin*, chs. 1-2; Nadia Valman, "Speculating upon Human Feeling: Evangelical Writing and Anglo-Jewish Women's Autobiography," *The Uses of Autobiography*, Julia Swindells, ed. (London: Taylor & Francis, 1995) 98-109. For a historical account, see Endelman, *Radical Assimilation*.

1 Abraham Benisch, "Our Women," *Jewish Chronicle*, 8 and 15 Nov. 1861, included in Appendix D below.

2 See Billie Melman, *Women's Orients: English Women and the Middle East, 1719-1918* (Ann Arbor: U of Michigan P, 1992).

could be allied with domesticity, such as charitable work, participation in church or synagogue sisterhoods, and the expansion of women's religious roles.

Aguilar's works offer modern readers a view from the margins of the struggle that took place during the early and mid-Victorian periods over what it meant to be English.[1] By contributing texts that were different from those written by majority writers, Aguilar posed two questions to her readers. What is Englishness? And what are its borders? And while seeming to acquiesce to the borders set for her by others, she often transgressed them. Her double vision, simultaneously assimilationist and resistant, gives her work the double consciousness that makes it worthy of comparison with the work of other marginalized writers, and lends it its Arnoldian quality of high seriousness.

Biography

Grace Aguilar was born on June 2, 1816, to Emanuel and Sarah Aguilar.[2] Her parents were Portuguese Jews who had fled to England to escape the Inquisition. They settled in the northeast London village of Hackney, where Aguilar was born. Emanuel served as the Parnas, or lay leader, of London's Spanish and Portuguese Synagogue, and the members of this family were active participants in the community of Spanish and Portuguese Jews, or Sephardim.[3] For eight years, until the birth of her brother Emanuel in 1824, Aguilar remained an only child. Her younger brother Henry was born in 1827, when Aguilar was eleven.[4] As a child, Aguilar contracted an mysterious serious illness that permanently weakened her and that perhaps left her vulnerable to the other ailments from which she suffered throughout her life. The most serious of these included the measles (at age nineteen in 1835) and her final illness, a spinal ail-

1 For a parallel effort by Scottish and Irish writers, see Katie Trumpener, *Bardic Nationalism: The Romantic Novel and the British Empire* (Princeton, NJ: Princeton UP, 1997).

2 See Sarah Aguilar, "Memoir of Grace Aguilar," preface to *Home Influence* (London: R. Groombridge, 1847).

3 Sarah Aguilar, "Memoir."

4 See Michael Galchinsky, "Grace Aguilar's Correspondence," Letter 5, Aguilar to Miriam Moses Cohen, 30 November 1843.

ment that paralyzed her muscles and lungs.[1] Her almost constant "indisposition," as she referred to it, did not prevent her from keeping a multi-volume journal beginning at age seven, from dancing, or from playing the piano and the harp, like other girls of the English middle class.[2] Nor did it prevent her from some local travel. For example, just after her brother Emanuel was born, her parents took the family on an extended tour of Gloucestershire.[3]

Aguilar's twelfth year was a turning point: her father contracted tuberculosis, the family moved to the coast in Devon for his health, and she wrote her first completed manuscript, a play called "Gustavus Vasa" about a Swedish king (now lost).[4] By this point, her curiosity and intelligence were evident. For years her mother had provided her with a religious education, and by 1830 her father Emanuel was using his enforced rest as an opportunity to educate his daughter in Jewish history.[5] It was not uncommon that Sephardic women and men who had lived through the Inquisition should educate their daughters. In fact, Sephardic women were often seen as responsible for transmitting Jewish culture and history, since the Inquisition had shut down male Judaic spaces such as schools and synagogues.[6] In this way Aguilar received what Rachel Lask Abrahams calls "the Oral History" of the Jews in Spain and Portugal.[7] When, beginning in 1831, she began to write down this history in her historical romance *The Vale of Cedars* and in tales such as "The Escape," her father would serve as her secretary, helping her to preserve and transmit the tales of the crypto-Jews—those Sephardim who, to escape the Inquisition, had pretended to convert to Catholicism only to continue to practice Judaism in secret.[8]

Aguilar proved a ready and eclectic student. She was soon inquir-

---

1 Sarah Aguilar, "Memoir;" and "The Late Miss Aguilar's Case," a German doctor's account of her final illness.

2 Sarah Aguilar, "Memoir."

3 Sarah Aguilar, "Memoir."

4 Sarah Aguilar, "Memoir"; and "Grace Aguilar's Correspondence," Letter 11.

5 Sarah Aguilar, "Memoir."

6 Renee Levine Melammed, "Sephardi Women in the Medieval and Early Modern Periods," *Jewish Women in Historical Perspective*, ed. Baskin, op cit., 128-49.

7 Rachel Beth Zion Lask Abrahams, "Grace Aguilar: A Centenary Tribute," *Transactions of the Jewish Historical Society of England* 16 (1952): 137-48.

8 Abrahams, 138.

ing beyond this oral history into other areas of learning, notably science, religion, and literature. While staying in the South Devon coastal town of Teignmouth, she recorded a series of "Notes on Chonchology [sic]," attempting to contribute to the science of conch shells.[1] Her religious yearnings became powerful during these years. There is indirect evidence that her father taught her to read Hebrew, which was an extremely unusual accomplishment for Jewish women of her day.[2] Indeed, there was as yet no Jewish vernacular translation of the Bible, and Aguilar often felt she could only satisfy her religious yearnings by going to hear sermons in Protestant churches.[3] These visits provided the material for many of her theological meditations, and for one of her most moving and ironic poems, an ecstatic imagining of a revived Israel in "A Vision of Jerusalem, While Listening to a Beautiful Organ in One of the Gentile Shrines." Her practice of attending church would later provide fodder for her critics: missionaries claimed to be able to see in her work the "light" of the gospel; Jewish traditionalists who objected to her individualistic approach to biblical interpretation used the experience to claim she was not authentically Jewish, calling her a "Jewish Protestant."[4] Her passion for literature also made itself clear early on: she produced her first poem during a visit to Tavistock in 1830 at age fourteen.[5] By age fifteen she had begun her first long narrative, a historical romance set during the Spanish Inquisition, entitled *The Vale of Cedars; or, the Martyr.* Written in reaction to Scott's *Ivanhoe*, this romance would take her four years to complete and would be published only posthumously in 1850.[6]

---

1 "Notes on Chonchology [sic]" in the Grace Aguilar MSS.

2 Aguilar later taught boys biblical Hebrew in the school she ran with her mother. In addition, although her biblical translations usually refer to the King James Version, they quite often depart in ways that suggest a reading fluency in Hebrew. The extent of her knowledge of Hebrew is an area for further research.

3 See her "Sabbath Thoughts," notes on a lecture on Psalm 32 by "Rev. R.A." in 1837 in the Grace Aguilar MSS.; also see her poem "Vision of Jerusalem," below.

4 See review of *Spirit of Judaism* in *The Jewish Herald and Record of Christian Effort for the Spiritual Good of God's Ancient People* 2.13 (1847): 39; and review of *Jewish Faith* in *Howitt's Journal* 1 (6 Feb. 1847): 84. In "Grace Aguilar," Beth Zion Lask Abrahams refers to her "Jewish Protestantism"; the reviewer of her *Works* in *The Jewish Chronicle* (1 Sept. 1871) says "She did not write for Jews only. Her views were of a more catholic character."

5 Sarah Aguilar, "Memoir."

6 Sarah Aguilar, "Memoir."

During the time when Aguilar was composing *Vale of Cedars*, her mother Sarah underwent an operation for an ailment unspecified in the surviving documents. What we do know is that she required her daughter's bedside care for several years.[1] With both parents ill, the family began to suffer economically, and Aguilar increasingly saw it as her responsibility to care, not only for her parents, but also for her two substantially younger brothers.[2] She began to think seriously of trying to make a professional career as a writer. Beginning in 1834, she wrote regularly, trying her hand at all sorts of genres: short domestic sketches such as the surviving manuscript tale "The Friends," and poetry in the manner of Byron, Scott, and Hemans, including "Leila: Poem in Three Cantos with Notes."[3]

Another turning point arrived in 1835: her brothers were sent away to school and the family moved to Brighton, perhaps to be closer to the Jewish community in London. It was here that Aguilar found a publisher for her first book of poems, *The Magic Wreath of Hidden Flowers*, dedicated to the Right Honourable Countess of Munster. These slight poems resemble the riddle poems collected by Emma Woodhouse and Harriet Smith in Jane Austen's *Emma*, and fit well into the genre of magazine poetry for young women: each poem contained clues to the name of a particular flower. Perhaps it is not very surprising that the daughter of crypto-Jews would produce poems about the sort of beauty that can be found hidden just beneath an innocuous-seeming surface. On the other hand, what is surprising, given the juvenile quality of these poems, is that the book did well enough to deserve a second edition by a London publisher (Ackermann) in 1839.

Thus encouraged, and despite her serious bout with the measles, Aguilar now began the ceaseless stream of literary production that she would sustain until her death. In 1836 and 1837 she drafted the manuscript of her domestic novel *Home Influence: A Tale for Mothers and Daughters* (not published until 1847). In this novel, as in its sequel *A Mother's Recompense* (1851) and *Woman's Friendship* (1850), she offered her ideal models of the domestic woman: the woman

1 Sarah Aguilar, "Memoir."

2 "Grace Aguilar's Correspondence," Letter 5.

3 See the Grace Aguilar MSS.

who cared for husband and home, and, above all, the mother who inculcated religion and morality into the hearts of her children. Also in these years, she wrote the manuscript of "The Charmed Bell and Other Poems" (never published and now lost); and she sketched out a sermon, "Sabbath Thoughts," that later appeared in *Sabbath Thoughts and Sacred Communings*, a posthumous collection of her theological and liturgical writings.[1]

Her literary efforts were briefly interrupted when, at her father's request, she began a translation from French of Orobio de Castro's *Israel Defended*, which was printed for private circulation in Brighton in 1838.[2] Despite her youth and gender, Aguilar brought a self-confidence to her work that showed in her translator's preface. There, she confessed that she had broadly departed from the original text's castigation of Christians in order to address her Protestant audience, citing "the enlightened and liberal spirit with which [Jews] are regarded in this free and blessed island" and "the wide difference between the kindly charity of Protestants, and the bigoted cruelty of Catholicism."[3] In contemporaneous journal entries Aguilar expresses a similar belief in the toleration of Protestant England, especially associating this attitude with Queen Victoria, whom she idealizes as the model of the domestic woman.[4] But unlike the journal entries, the praise of England's tolerance in *Israel Defended* is mixed. Here, then, Aguilar was already striking the ambivalent tone—simultaneously trusting and suspicious, assimilationist and resistant—that would become the hallmark of many of her more mature works.

By 1840, Aguilar and her family had moved back to London, and she was writing letters from her new house at 5 Triangle, Hackney, from which she began to launch herself into the British and American literary worlds. She asked a young Benjamin Disraeli, whom she knew as a fellow member of the Sephardic community, to carry a letter from her to his father, Isaac D'Israeli. D'Israeli was a noted man of letters, the author of *Curiosities of Literature*, and she asked

---

1 Grace Aguilar MSS.

2 On the private circulation, see Sarah Aguilar, "Memoir".

3 Grace Aguilar, Translator's Preface to *Israel Defended* (Brighton: J. Wertheimer and Co., 1838). For more on Aguilar's differential treatment of Protestants and Catholics, see Ragussis, ch. 4 and Galchinsky, *Origin*, ch. 4.

4 "Notes on Excursion" in the Grace Aguilar MSS.

him to help her secure a publisher.[1] From 5 Triangle, she also made her first contact with Isaac Leeser, the leader of the Mikveh Israel synagogue in Philadelphia and the editor of the American Jewish periodical *The Occident*. D'Israeli declined to aid her, but Leeser agreed to publish Aguilar's theological meditation *The Spirit of Judaism* as the initial offering of his new series, The Jewish Publication Society of America. Unfortunately, Aguilar's manuscript was lost at sea on the way to Philadelphia.[2] With the promise of publication, however, she rewrote it from her notes, and it eventually found its way into print in 1842. When it did, Aguilar was angry to find that Leeser had attached an editorial preface and footnotes to her text in which he set forth "the chief points of difference between Miss Aguilar and myself."[3] Nonetheless, *Spirit* was well received by many Jews and Christians on both sides of the Atlantic. With this success behind her, Aguilar wrote to D'Israeli to ask again for his aid in finding a publisher for *Home Influence*.[4] This time he responded by introducing her to his publisher, Edward Moxon.[5] Perhaps it was Moxon who introduced Aguilar to an editor at R. Groombridge and Sons, the large and diverse publishing firm that had extensive lists in domestic fiction and historical romance and that produced most of Aguilar's work for the English market.

Her initial rebuff by D'Israeli did not keep Aguilar from seeking entrée into the British literary world. In 1841, she found her first success with occasional poems that began to appear in Anglo-Jewish periodicals such as the *Voice of Jacob* and the *Jewish Chronicle*.[6] From the first, however, she sought an audience outside the Jewish community, publishing short tales in such popular women's journals as *The Keepsake*, *Friendship's Offering*, and *La Belle Assemblée*.[7] No doubt

---

1 Aguilar's full correspondence with D'Israeli is housed with the Disraeli Papers, British National Trust, Dep. Hughenden 243/1, fols. 3-12. Grace Aguilar to Isaac D'Israeli, 29 July 1840.

2 For the history and an analysis of the publication of *Spirit of Judaism*, see Galchinsky, *Origin*, 73-75, 146.

3 Leeser, Editor's Preface, *Spirit of Judaism*; for Aguilar's anger at his editorial intrusions, see "Grace Aguilar's Correspondence," Letters 6 and 7 to Miriam Moses Cohen.

4 See Grace Aguilar to Isaac D'Israeli, 25 Aug. 1842.

5 Aguilar to Isaac D'Israeli, 16 Oct. 1842. "

6 See Aguilar, "A Poet's Dying Hymn," *Voice of Jacob* (18 February 1842): 87, printed below.

7 Aguilar explains that she writes for *La Belle Assemblée* in Letter 6 to Miriam Moses Cohen below. For an example, see her "Lucy: an Autumn Walk," *The Keepsake* (1844): 199-223.

it was through these contacts that Aguilar began to be acquainted with many writers of Romantic and early Victorian poetry, domestic fiction, and historical romance, including Anna Maria Hall, Mary Howitt, Camilla Toulmine, Jane Porter, and Caroline Bowles. Hall was particularly taken with Aguilar and, when Aguilar died, she wrote a long essay in memoriam entitled "Pilgrimage to the Grave of Grace Aguilar." The essay, excerpted in Appendix A, initially appeared in the journal *Art Union*, and was then reprinted by *The Occident*, *The Jewish Chronicle*, and the *Jewish Sabbath Journal* as well as in Hall's book *Pilgrimage to English Shrines* (1853).[1] Hall's book clearly placed Aguilar in the firmament of English writers.

The tales for women's journals brought Aguilar to the attention of Christian women; with *Spirit of Judaism*, she appealed to Jewish and Christian readers, both male and female. In *Spirit*, she was able to do several things at once. She meditated on the significance of the *Shema*, the central prayer in the Jewish worship service. She polemicized on behalf of both English tolerance and Jewish religious reform, calling for a vernacular translation of the Bible and changes in Jewish childhood education. And she offered a new vision of the spiritual needs of women in general and Jewish women in particular.

More practically, the book brought Aguilar into a steady association with Isaac Leeser. Despite her anger over his editorial intrusions, she continued to publish her work in his periodical, *The Occident*. Beginning in 1843 and continuing through the remainder of her life, Leeser published over thirty of her poems, the most important of which appear in this volume. These poems served as a steady and increasing source of income for her; it was not long before she was listed as the highest paid writer among the magazine's contributors.[2] This steady publishing relationship also gave her the opportunity to develop her own poetics, so that, while continuing to draw on the traditions of romantic nature poetry, Romantic era sensibility

1 Mrs. S.C. Hall, "Pilgrimage to the Grave of Grace Aguilar," *Art Journal* (May, 1851); *The Occident* 9 (Oct., 1851); *Jewish Sabbath Journal* (1855). Also published in Hall's book *Pilgrimages to English Shrines* (London: A. Hall, Virtue, 1853).

2 The Leeser Collection at the University of Pennsylvania Center for Judaic Studies includes a statement of accounts for the *Occident* between 1843 and 1847, which shows that Aguilar was the most frequent and most highly paid contributor, her wage increasing from £3.1.4 in June, 1843 to £11.7.10 in May, 1847. See Leeser Collection, Box 9, FF1.

and sentimentality, midrash, and prophecy, she began to be able to turn their conventions in innovative directions.[1]

The publication of *Spirit* and her occasional poems in *The Occident* also brought another lasting development to her life: a transatlantic friendship with Miriam and Solomon Cohen of Savannah, Georgia.[2] Miriam Cohen was the niece of Rebecca Gratz, the founder of the Jewish Sunday School movement in the United States.[3] Solomon Cohen was the first Jewish Senator from the state of Georgia. When Miriam Cohen wrote to Aguilar in praise of *Spirit of Judaism* in 1842, the two women began a correspondence that would continue up until Aguilar's death, after which Sarah Aguilar continued to correspond with the Cohens for many years, until 1853. From a literary perspective, this correspondence provides us with much of what we know about the financial details of Aguilar's writing career in the 1840s, the distribution of her works, her assessments of her own and others' literary efforts, and the intimate details of her family life. We find, for example, that despite her literary success, she and her mother could make ends meet only by opening a school for young boys (she complained bitterly that it took time away from her writing).[4] We find that her brother Emanuel became an accomplished musician in Frankfurt and that Henry, an irresponsible young man, went to sea and caused the family much anxiety.[5] We also hear of Aguilar's reaction to the death of her father in 1846.[6] From the perspective of nineteenth-century women's history, the letters contain Aguilar's reflections on domestic ideology, motherhood, and women's literary aspirations, and are mostly written in the

---

1 On Aguilar's poetics, see Scheinberg, 263-91; and Daniel Harris, "Hagar in Christian Britain: Grace Aguilar's "The Wanderers," *Victorian Literature and Culture* 27 (1999): 143-69.

2 Miriam Gratz Moses Papers, Manuscripts Department Library of the University of North Carolina at Chapel Hill, Southern Historical Collection #2639, Series 1, Folder 8. All letters to Miriam and Solomon Cohen are from this collection.

3 See Dianne Ashton, *Rebecca Gratz: Women and Judaism in Antebellum America* (Detroit: Wayne State UP, 1997).

4 See "Grace Aguilar's Correspondence," Aguilar to Miriam Moses Cohen, Letter 1. Aguilar's school served boys from four to ten years of age, with classes in Religion, English, Hebrew, Writing, Arithmetic, Geography and History.

5 Emanuel is discussed in "Grace Aguilar's Correspondence," Letter 5; Henry in Letters 2 and 5.

6 "Grace Aguilar's Correspondence," Letter 11.

sentimental mode she crafted for her domestic fiction. From the perspective of Jewish history, they contain Aguilar's reflections on theology and on the reform of English Jews' religious life, confirming her place as an active participant in the Victorian Jewish Enlightenment or *Haskalah*, the English Jews' movement into modernity. We find that despite continued pleas from the Cohens and from Rebecca Gratz herself, Aguilar refused to publish her liturgical works (a refusal that her mother ignored after her death).[1]

This correspondence also helps to explain several of the paradoxes of Aguilar's career. Critics have noted that this champion of women's domesticity and motherhood chose to remain unmarried and childless.[2] Yet the letters make clear that, what with writing to maintain her parents' household, looking after Henry, keeping up her school, and suffering her various illnesses, she had neither the health, energy, time, nor inclination for a family of her own. The letters also help explain why she was in many ways better known in the United States, particularly in the South, than she was in England. Solomon Cohen undertook to be her Southern distributor, and apparently did a thorough job of it: one can still find copies of Aguilar's books quite readily in Southern rare book shops.[3] Recently, the critic Paul Gilroy has demonstrated the existence of a "Black Atlantic," a transatlantic dialogue among blacks in the U.S., the Caribbean, Europe, and Africa.[4] Perhaps we have here evidence of the operation of a "Jewish Atlantic" as well, a transatlantic diasporic dialogue. Direct evidence for this goes beyond the correspondence: Rebecca Gratz was rumored to be the model for the character Rebecca in *Ivanhoe*, the character that had inspired Aguilar's earliest fictional efforts. And Gratz herself, besides using Aguilar's texts as teaching materials in her Sunday School, cited Aguilar as an inspiration in her determination to refuse marriage in order to continue with her work.[5]

As a writer of fiction, Aguilar began in the genre of historical

---

1 See "Grace Aguilar's Correspondence," Letters 7 and 9.

2 Galchinsky, *Origin*, 155; Linda Gordon Kuzmack, *Woman's Cause: The Jewish Woman's Movement in England and the United States, 1881-1933* (Columbus: Ohio State UP, 1990) 20.

3 See "Grace Aguilar's Correspondence," Letters 2, 4, 6, 8, and 10.

4 Paul Gilroy, *The Black Atlantic: Modernity and Double Consciousness* (Cambridge, MA: Harvard UP, 1993).

5 Kuzmack, *Woman's Cause*, 20.

romance, not only with *Vale of Cedars*, but with her popular Scottish romance *The Days of Bruce* (written at the same time as *Vale* and, like *Vale*, published posthumously). In fact, her Scottish romance proved more popular than most of her other work and eventually led her publisher to issue a series of short spin-offs collected as *Tales from British History*, including Macintosh the Highland Chief, Edmund the Exiled Prince, and other short Highland tales.[1] By the mid-1840s, she was still working in the vein of romance—culminating in "The Escape," and "The Edict," published together as *Records of Israel* in 1844. Increasingly, however, she began to turn toward domestic fiction. Aguilar found that historical romance distanced English readers from Jews. On the other hand, her earliest domestic fictions, such as *Home Influence* and "The Authoress," were studiously written about Christian characters, as though Aguilar felt it too dangerous to write about present-day Jews.[2] In her "Preface" to *Home Influence*, she reassured "Christian mothers" that the characters are "all Christian" and that "all *doctrinal* points have been most carefully avoided, the author seeking only to illustrate the spirit of true piety" (v).

Yet she increasingly wished for an opportunity to describe Jews as they actually were in the England of her own day. In her view, only this kind of contemporaneous reflection could serve the cause of Jews' emancipation, by showing Christian readers that their Jewish neighbors shared the same "spirit of true piety," differing only from Christians in their "forms" of worship. Aguilar found her opportunity when Charlotte Montefiore invited her to write a tale for a new series designed for the "humbler classes of Israelites," The Cheap Jewish Library. Montefiore was an aristocratic member of the Anglo-Jewish community. A writer herself, she was also interested in the intellectual and economic welfare of poor Jews. She felt that a tale from Aguilar about present-day middle class Jewish life might inspire members of the Jewish working poor and give them role models. The result was Aguilar's novella *The Perez Family*, the first detailed fictional account of contemporary nineteenth-century

---

1 For a consideration of Jewish-Scottish interrelations, see Ragussis, *Figures of Conversion*, ch. 2; and Galchinsky, "Otherness and Identity in the Victorian Novel" *Victorian Literary Cultures: A Critical Companion* eds. William Baker and Kenneth Womack (Westport, CT: Greenwood, 2002), 485-507.

2 See Aguilar, Preface to *Home Influence*.

Anglo-Jewish life ever published.[1] Although it met with wide acclaim among Jews, it did not find readers among Christians. This was due mainly to the circumstances of its publication, in a series distributed only to Jews. It remains, however, an important text for two reasons. First, Aguilar uses this sentimental and domestic tale to document English Jews' ambivalence toward their own modernization. Second, she uses it to articulate her individualistic and woman-centered approach to the Bible. When the family matriarch gathers her children around her on the Sabbath and asks them to interpret a biblical passage, she illustrates Aguilar's view that even women and children were capable of sophisticated biblical interpretation and did not need the extensive aid of rabbinical commentaries to understand and act on God's words. At a time when reforming Jews were arguing that the "Oral Law" (the commentaries contained in the Mishnah and Talmud) could be set aside in favor of the "Written Law" (the Bible), this seemingly innocuous text was taking sides in favor of reform.

Aguilar spent the last three years of her life writing intensively and gaining greater acclaim. In 1844, besides publishing *Records of Israel*, she produced *Women of Israel*, the series of biographical accounts of biblical, Talmudic, and modern Jewish women that critics immediately recognized as her masterpiece.[2] This text packed many of her passions into the space of three volumes. She was able to recenter Jewish history and midrash on women's experience, articulate her own versions of domestic ideology and theology, and appeal for Jews' emancipation and Christian social acceptance. Perhaps the success of both *Women* and *Records* was what enabled her to relocate with her family to 1 Clarence Place, Clapton Square in 1845, where she tended to her dying father. On the other hand, she was not yet financially secure, for even as she prepared *Women of Israel* for print she assured the Cohens, "I dare not publish at a loss."[3]

Although her illness was beginning to increase in severity, she continued to produce at a remarkable pace from her new home. She

---

1 Galchinsky, *Origin*, 171-85.

2 See, for example, Isaac Leeser's review in *The Occident* 2 (Dec. 1844); 3 (Jun. 1845); and the extended review by S. Solis, "Remarks on Miss Aguilar's 'Women of Israel'" *Occident* 4 (April-June 1846).

3 "Grace Aguilar's Correspondence," Letter 6.

wrote *The Jewish Faith*, a fictional series of letters from an old woman to a young woman on resisting Evangelical missionary efforts, published in 1846. Also in 1846, Anna Maria Hall introduced her to Robert Chambers, the radical Edinburgh publisher of *Chambers's Miscellany*, who solicited an essay from her entitled "The History of the Jews in England."[1] In keeping with the magazine's interests, this remarkable essay, published just months before her death, offered a more radical vision of Jewish/Christian relations than Aguilar had dared to put forward in any previous text. Here Aguilar substantially rejected assimilationism, while at the same time calling English Christians to more stringent account than she had ever done before.

By the spring of 1847 Aguilar's final illness had taken hold. Perhaps it was their knowledge that she was seriously ill that prompted a group of middle-class Anglo-Jewish women calling themselves the "Women of Israel" to present her with a public testimonial on June 14 (see Appendix A.1). Immediately afterward, she traveled to Frankfurt to visit her brother Emanuel and to try to recover her health. Until now, little has been known about this period. In September, 2002, however, Michael Dugdale, the great-great-grandson of Aguilar's brother Emanuel, provided me with a copy of Aguilar's Frankfurt Journal, her daily record of the period from June 15 to July 29, 1847, amounting to some 32,000 words. This journal provides a window into the profound physical, spiritual, and creative crisis Aguilar suffered at this time, as well as a tantalizing glimpse into potential future directions she might have taken as a writer had she survived. (An annotated transcription of selections from the journal can be found in Appendix E.)

As Aguilar's condition worsened, her doctor advised her to discontinue writing, and so the journal comes to an abrupt end—mid-sentence—on July 29, 1847. Soon afterward, Aguilar moved to Schwalbach to take the waters, but her condition deteriorated, and she returned to Frankfurt, where she died on September 16. She was buried in the Frankfurt Jewish Cemetery, the epitaph on her tombstone taken from Proverbs 31, the section of the biblical work on the

---

1 Aguilar to Robert Chambers, 30 June 1846 and 2 Aug. 1846, National Library of Scotland, Dep. 341/96, letter 95 and 341/94, letter 183.

"woman of valor": "Give her of the fruit of her hands; and let her own works praise her from the gates."[1] As the tributes in Appendix A of this volume illustrate, news of her death was called "a national calamity" on the front pages of Jewish newspapers in England and the United States. Jews from as far afield as France, Jamaica, and Germany wrote tributes and poems in commemoration of her life and work.

Had her publications ended with her death, she would have been known for the following works: *The Magic Wreath, Israel Defended, The Spirit of Judaism, Records of Israel, The Perez Family, Women of Israel, The Jewish Faith*, and "History of the Jews in England." *Home Influence: A Tale for Mothers and Daughters* was in press when she died, and it became far and away her most popular work, running through thirty-six editions. But in many ways Aguilar's publication history only began with her death. Her mother Sarah edited and published many of Aguilar's manuscripts posthumously. These included *The Vale of Cedars*, Aguilar's early historical romance (1850); *Woman's Friendship*, a domestic novel (1850); *A Mother's Recompense*, the sequel to *Home Influence* (1851); *Days of Bruce*, a Scottish historical romance (1852); *Home Scenes and Heart Studies*, an important collection of Aguilar's short fiction and midrashim (1852); *Essays and Miscellanies* (1853); and *Sabbath Thoughts and Sacred Communings*, a volume of Aguilar's meditations, prayers, and sermons (1853).

Of these, all but the last three existed in completed manuscript form when she died. Sarah Aguilar collected the stories in *Home Scenes* from her daughter's magazine publications. She also collected, culled, and edited the manuscripts that became *Essays and Miscellanies. Sabbath Thoughts and Sacred Communings* contains some of the liturgy that Grace Aguilar had refused to publish during her lifetime, on the grounds that it was for private use only and that, given that her theology in *Spirit of Judaism* had already been castigated as inauthentic, her liturgy would be thought all the more so. Sarah Aguilar gives an account of her difficult decision to ignore her daughter's wishes in several letters to Miriam and Solomon Cohen included in Appendix B.6.[2] She also explains that she held back those prayers

1 Sarah Aguilar, "Memoir."

2 See correspondence between Sarah Aguilar and Miriam and Solomon Cohen in Appendix B below.

and meditations that she felt were unfit. None of those she held back has been recovered.

Literary and Historical Contexts

Aguilar's writings, at once literary and political, become more fully comprehensible in the light of relevant contexts. Some of these include the history of nineteenth-century English economic expansion and political liberalism, the social and political history of the Anglo-Jewish diaspora, the history of the representation of Jews in English literature, Victorian women's literary practices, and the literary practices of other Victorian Jewish women.

Driven by the Industrial Revolution's vast production of wealth, by British colonial expansion, and by new technologies like the train, canal, and steamship, nineteenth-century England supported an increasingly mobile and urbanized population. Migrations, diasporas, and even, to some degree, the development of world trade networks were prominent features of the era of national consolidation and imperial expansion that followed the decisive British victories in the Napoleonic Wars in 1815. Such mobility inevitably compelled the Victorians to experience greater national, regional, religious, and racial diversity both in their travels abroad and on their own shores.

In the latter case, Victorians in the white, Protestant, English-speaking majority developed distinct and contradictory ways of apprehending those domestic groups whose collective identity was perceived to differ in fundamental ways from their own. On the one hand, majority writers often perceived a group's distinctiveness as an ineradicable barrier to its acceptance into the full rights and privileges of English citizenship. This perceptual barrier reinforced and was reinforced by immigration policies, economic and political restrictions, newspaper articles, social scientific reports, Darwinian racial rankings, and, not least, representations of foreigners and strangers in novels, poems, and plays. Such texts gave voice to the suspicion (growing, at various heated moments, into a widespread conviction) that foreign nationals, citizens of British regions other than England, colonized peoples, and racial and religious minorities were unalterably alien, unassailable, and inferior—Other. Victorians in the majority frequently posed questions about how England's

Others might be brought into relation with the apparently unified nation-state and empire. They debated the social and political status of Jews, of freed slaves, of immigrants from India, of migrants from Ireland and Scotland, and of non-conforming Christian groups.[1]

Yet if Victorians often treated culturally distinct minorities as Others, they sometimes also treated them with what they termed "toleration." In many respects, the nineteenth century witnessed the expansion of a tolerant liberalism in England, best seen in a number of key political events: the abolition of the slave trade in 1807 and of slavery itself in 1833, the Catholic Emancipation Act of 1829 that enabled Catholics to vote and occupy their seats in Parliament, and perhaps most of all the passage of the first Reform Bill in 1832 that laid the ground for slow extension of the electoral franchise that took place over the next century. The passage of The Catholic Emancipation Act inspired members of the Anglo-Jewish community, beginning in 1830, to argue for a Jewish equivalent that would remove all the civil disabilities from which they still suffered. These disabilities included being prevented from taking the Oath of Abjuration necessary for entering Parliament, since the Oath required new Members to swear "on the true faith of a Christian." (The Oath disclaimed allegiance to the Stuarts or their descendants.) Jews succeeded in having the offending words finally removed from the Oath only in 1858, after thirty years of struggle. During the same period, the Board of Deputies of British Jews also succeeded in lobbying Parliament to enable Jews to trade in the City and on the Exchange, to stand for Mayor of London, and to vote. Yet while tolerant liberalism enabled a gradual political emancipation, each step provoked public debates over the meaning of the Jewish Question for English national identity.[2]

Moreover, political emancipation was not the same as social emancipation. The removal of civil disabilities did not resolve the Jewish Question on a socio-cultural level. Whether Victorian Christians articulated their reaction to the Jewish Question in radical, lib-

---

1 On postcolonial theory, see for example, Edward Said, *Culture and Imperialism* (New York: Vintage, 1993); Gayatri Spivak, *In Other Worlds: Essays in Cultural Politics* (New York: Routledge, Kegan, and Paul, 1988); and Homi Bhabha, *The Location of Culture* (New York: Routledge, 1994).

2 See Feldman, and Salbstein.

eral or conservative terms, they continued throughout the century to use discourse about Jews and Jewishness as a means of contemplating their own national identity. When Victorian Christians wrote about Jews, they were also and necessarily writing about themselves. Debates about the meaning and acceptability of Jewishness typically arose during discussions of the shifting meanings of Englishness and reform, and thus served a crucial function in the production of the "imagined community" (Anderson) that was England. For example, opposed as they were on almost every issue, the conservative essayist Thomas Carlyle and the liberal historian and Member of Parliament Thomas Babington Macaulay agreed that Jews were a test case for how far liberal ideas of reform would be allowed to go.[1] For them, Jews and Jewishness became the locus for inquiring into the qualifications for citizenship.

Novelists and poets, too, used Jewishness for their own purposes. Even a brief acquaintance with literary representations—Walter Scott's Rebecca (*Ivanhoe*), Charles Dickens's Fagin (*Oliver Twist*) and later Judah Riah (*Our Mutual Friend*), Anthony Trollope's Augustus Melmotte (*The Way we Live Now*), George Eliot's Daniel Deronda and Mordecai Cohen (*Daniel Deronda*), Robert Browning's Rabbi Ben Ezra ("Rabbi Ben Ezra"), George Du Maurier's Svengali (*Trilby*)—illustrates that the meaning of Jews and Jewishness constantly shifted during the century according to the anxieties of the writer.[2] The writer could use Jews to express anxiety over the transition from the gold standard to a paper economy (as in Trollope's *The Way We Live Now*), or to figure the increasingly unsanitary and

1 See Macaulay, "Speech on Jewish Disabilities" in Appendix C in this volume; also, Carlyle, "The Jew Our Lawgiver" (London: Thomas Bosworth, 1853). For a consideration of Macaulay's role in both Jewish and Indian affairs, see Gauri Viswanathan, *Outside the Fold: Conversion, Modernity, and Belief* (Princeton: Princeton UP, 1998) 9-19.

2 Some analyses of English representations of Jews and Jewishness include Jonathan Freedman, *The Temple of Culture: Assimilation and Anti-Semitism in Literary Anglo-America* (Oxford: Oxford UP, 2000); James S. Shapiro, *Shakespeare and the Jews* (New York: Columbia UP, 1996); Ragussis, *Figures of Conversion*; Bryan Cheyette, *Constructions of "the Jew" in English Literature and Society: Racial Representations, 1875-1945* (Cambridge: Cambridge UP, 1993); Frank Felsenstein, *Anti-Semitic Stereotypes: A Paradigm of Otherness in English Popular Culture, 1660-1830* (Baltimore: Johns Hopkins UP, 1995); Edgar Rosenberg, *From Shylock to Svengali: Jewish Stereotypes in English Fiction* (Stanford: Stanford UP, 1960); Montagu Frank Modder, *The Jew in the Literature of England: To the End of the Nineteenth Century* (New York: Meridian, 1939).

criminal conditions of life in London (as in Dickens's *Oliver Twist*), or to meditate on progress (as in Browning's "Rabbi Ben Ezra").[1] A writer could associate whatever made him anxious with "Jewishness" in order to estrange it, in order to mark it as a foreign addition to the national identity, thus simultaneously recognizing it and denying that it was essential to Englishness. The writer could then, if only in the fiction of the text, kill off the anxiety by killing off the Jew (as in the cases of Fagin and Melmotte). Where the Jew was figured positively, the novelist might still ease tension over the prospect of introducing foreignness into the national identity by transporting a Jewish character elsewhere at the end of the text (as in the cases of Rebecca and Daniel Deronda).

Aguilar's writing, like that of other Victorian Jews, served to remind readers in the majority that Jews were not merely the subjects of Christian discourse or the projection of Christian anxieties. There existed an actual, and growing, community of Jews throughout England whose members had their own needs and desires. The existence of such a community still had to be asserted since its emergence was relatively recent. Jews were largely absent from England from the time they were officially expelled by Edward II in 1290 until the Readmission of Menasseh Ben Israel and a few other Jews from Amsterdam by Oliver Cromwell in 1656. Throughout the seventeenth and eighteenth centuries Jews began to make their way slowly into England, first wealthy Spanish and Portuguese Jews (Sephardim) and later poor German and Polish Jews (Ashkenazim). During the eighteenth century, except for a brief period, Jews were treated under the law as aliens. The Jewish Naturalization Bill ("Jew Bill") of 1753 was passed, theoretically enabling a few Jews who could pay for it to be naturalized. But after an ensuing pamphlet war, the Jew Bill was repealed the following year. Despite this setback, immigration continued into both the Sephardic and Ashkenazic communities. At first these communities functioned separately,

---

1 For some considerations of this phenomenon see Jonathan Freedman, *The Temple of Culture*, 87; Patrick Brantlinger, "Nations and Novels: Disraeli, George Eliot, and Orientalism," *Victorian Studies* 35 (1992): 255-75; Ragussis, *Figures of Conversion*, ch. 6; Julian Wolfreys, *Being English: Narratives, Idioms, and Performances of National Identity from Coleridge to Trollope* (Albany: State U of NY, 1994); Marc E. Wohlfarth, "*Daniel Deronda* and the Politics of Nationalism," *Nineteenth Century Literature* 53 (1998): 188-210.

each having its own synagogues, prayer rituals, languages, and dress: the wedding of a Sephardic woman to an Ashkenazic man was considered an intermarriage. But by 1815, the two communities had begun to merge into one, if only in order to represent themselves as a unified body to Parliament. For this purpose they formed the Board of Deputies of British Jews, and as the community continued to grow—from 20,000 in 1815 to 60,000 in 1850—it developed a broad array of self-governance structures, communal and charitable institutions, and cultural institutions (including 11 separate English-language periodicals).[1] Aguilar's writing helped make the concerns of this small but growing community audible.

She also helped defend Jews against anti-liberal efforts directed at them. Although English Jews met with an English citizenry that was liberalizing and secularizing, they also met with a well-supported missionary effort led by groups like the London Society for the Promotion of Christianity Amongst the Jews and the Philo-Judaeans. Conversionists often used seemingly tolerant efforts to attain their goal: they lobbied for repeal of Jewish disabilities in Parliament, and provided poor Jews with food and work in exchange for conversion classes, on the theory that their enlightened behavior would attract Jews to Christianity. Conversionist writers like Amelia Bristow also practiced a kind of philo-Semitism directed specifically at Jewish female characters. Such characters were depicted as uneducated and oppressed by their legalistic and materialistic fathers, and in conversionist novels they generally accept Christ as soon as they meet a charismatic Christian suitor. The conversionists promised full integration into English life at the mere cost of Jewishness.[2] In her romances, *Vale of Cedars* and *Records of Israel*, Aguilar often depicts women confronting the choice to convert in order to gain social integration—and each time she shows them rejecting this choice. In this way she wrote against the representations of Jewish women that

---

1 For a basic outline of early Anglo-Jewish history, see Aguilar's own "History of the Jews in England," below, and Cecil Roth, *History of the Jews in England*. On the "Jew Bill," see Endelman, *The Jews of Georgian England*, and Felsenstein.

2 On conversionism, see Todd Endelman, *Radical Assimilation*; Ragussis, *Figures of Conversion*, chs. 1-2; Galchinsky, *Origin*, ch. 1; Nadia Valman, "Speculating upon Human Feeling: Evangelical Writing and Anglo-Jewish Women's Autobiography," *The Uses of Autobiography* ed. Julia Swindells (London: Taylor & Francis, 1995) 98-109.

implied their malleability and lack of Jewish education.[1]

Aguilar's encounter with the Victorian literary world was not, however, only a negative or defensive one, since, as we have seen, she saw her own work positively within the context of Victorian women's writing. The 1995 volume, *Victorian Women Poets: An Anthology*, edited by Angela Leighton and Margaret Reynolds, has recently brought many of these writers back to our awareness (although they do not include Aguilar).[2] This anthology and other projects like it demonstrate that these writers were helping to construct the ideology of the separation of gender spheres, ascribing to women the natural characteristics of domesticity, maternalism, and religiosity. Yet it is important to recognize that gender ideology and gender practices during the nineteenth century were not always synchronized with one another. What women and men said they were doing or thought they ought to be doing was frequently at odds with what they were, in fact, thinking and doing. Ambitious and intellectual women often gained fame by publishing essays in which they insisted that women should not be ambitious, intellectual, or famous. Many women were able to write as though they were submitting to the separation of spheres while, through the very act of writing, they were transgressing the lines of separation. The work of the Romantic era women poets is soaked in this sort of tension—between paying obeisance to ostensibly traditional gender roles (that were in fact often being invented on the spot), and acting according to a Wollstonecraftian standard that Victorians might have called "liberal reform" or "emancipation."[3] These writers demonstrated a high capacity to hold such tensions between tradition and reform in relation to each other without attempting to resolve them. Felicia Hemans' poem "The Song of Miriam" and a section of Sarah Stick-

---

1 Galchinsky, *Origin*, 164-67.

2 Angela Leighton and Margaret Reynolds, eds., *Victorian Women Poets: An Anthology* (Cambridge, MA: Blackwell, 1995).

3 For an introduction to critical work on these writers, see Paula R. Feldman, ed., *Records of Woman: With Other Poems by Felicia Hemans* (Louisville: Kentucky UP, 1999); *Women's Poetry, Late Romantic to Late Victorian* ed. Armstrong and Blain; Dorothy Mermin, *Godiva's Ride: Women of Letters in England, 1830-1880* (Bloomington: Indiana UP, 1993); Norma Clarke, *Ambitious Heights: Writing, Friendship, Love—the Jewsbury Sisters, Felicia Hemans, and Jane Welsh Carlyle* (New York: Routledge, 1990); Susan Rabinow Gorsky, *Femininity to Feminism: Women and Literature in the Nineteenth Century* (New York: Twayne, 1992).

ney Ellis' *Women of England* are included in Appendix C for comparison with Aguilar's work.

Aguilar may have been drawn to these women in part because their dialectic between reform and tradition bears a striking resemblance to a dialectic experienced by Victorian Jews. In broad terms, both Jews and women gained legal, economic, and political rights during the nineteenth century, although the emancipatory process in both cases was uneven. Since the citizenship of both groups was being contested during the period, we should not be surprised that Jewishness and femininity were frequently conflated in nineteenth-century literary texts. In novels, women characters were represented as the "angels in the house," the spiritually pure guardians of domestic morality. They embodied quite well the "strictness of conscience" that Matthew Arnold defined as "Hebraism" in *Culture and Anarchy*.[1] Conversely, as was usual in dominant depictions of the Other, Jews were often represented collectively as "feminine," that is, as persuadable, weak and hysterical.[2] This cultural conflation of Jewishness and femininity must have meant that the dialectic between reform and tradition was especially evident to the dual minority, the Jew who was also female. Perhaps this cultural conflation accounts in part for why the most important Jewish writers to emerge in the early Victorian period were women: it was women who had a stake in responding to the public debate about Jews. Along with Grace Aguilar, the Victorian Jews' most important writers were Celia and Marion Moss, Emma Lyons, Maria Polack, Judith and Charlotte Montefiore, and Anna Maria Goldsmid.

Aguilar's writing cannot be fully understood outside of the context of the other Victorian Jews who produced novels, poems, midrashim, and polemics. She was by no means *sui generis* among early and mid-Victorian Jews, although in terms of popularity and lasting significance she was, and remains, pre-eminent. The other writers differed from her in many ways: they were more assimila-

---

1 Matthew Arnold, *Culture and Anarchy*, ed. Dover Wilson (New York: Cambridge UP, 1971) 132.

2 For some analyses of the feminization of the Other, see Said, *Orientalism* (New York: Vintage, 1978), 207; Sander Gilman, *The Jew's Body* (New York: Routledge, 1991); Livia Bitton-Jackson, *Madonna or Courtesan? The Jewish Woman in Christian Literature* (New York: Seabury, 1982); Galchinsky, *Origin*, 54-58.

tionist or more separatist; they were more reform-minded or more traditionalist; they were Ashkenazic rather than Sephardic; or they were upper rather than middle class. For example, the historical romances in Celia and Marion Moss' *Romance of Jewish History* (1840) rejected the kind of domesticity Aguilar required of Jewish women in favor of a more rebellious search for autonomy. Celia (Moss) Levetus' story "The Two Pictures" (1855), a tale of a young Anglo-Jewish girl's encounter with conversionism, presents a less idealized picture of Jewish domestic life than does Aguilar's *The Perez Family*. Charlotte Montefiore's satire *Caleb Asher* (1845) directly upbraids conversionists for their hypocrisy, and her *A Few Words to the Jews. By One of Themselves* (1855) is a series of fiery essays that directly address institutional and spiritual reform in the Jewish community. While Aguilar agreed with many of Montefiore's prescriptions, she preferred a more indirect route in both fiction and nonfiction. Judith Montefiore's *Private Journal of a Visit to Egypt and Palestine by Way of Italy and the Mediterranean* (1836) addresses itself to geographical, socio-economic, and spiritual vistas beyond Aguilar's reach. Thus Aguilar's works did not emerge in a vacuum. Victorian Jewish writers knew of each other, wrote for, to, against, and about each other, and in the process created an Anglo-Jewish subculture where none had previously existed.

The happiest outcome of this anthology would be to provide a window, not merely into Aguilar's life and writing, but into the vital, fascinating, and largely forgotten Victorian Jewish subculture.[1]

---

1 Marion and Celia Moss, *The Romance of Jewish History*, 2nd ed. (London: A.K. Newman, 1843) and *Tales of Jewish History* (London: Miller and Field, 1843); Celia Levetus, "The Two Pictures," *Jewish Sabbath Journal* 1.9 (Apr. 19, 1855) through 1:14 (June 28, 1855); Charlotte Montefiore, *Caleb Asher* (Philadelphia: Jewish Publication Society, 1845) and *A Few Words to the Jews. By One of Themselves* (London: John Chapman, 1855); Judith Montefiore, *Private Journal of a Visit to Egypt and Palestine by Way of Italy and the Mediterranean* (London: Printed by Joseph Rickerby, 1836). For literary analyses of these texts and others by early and mid-Victorian Jewish women, see Galchinsky, *Origin*; and Judith W. Page, "Jerusalem and Jewish Memory: Judith Montefiore's *Private Journal*," *Victorian Literature and Culture* (1999): 125-41.

Critical Reception

During her lifetime, Aguilar received critical attention from secular, Anglican, Evangelical, and Jewish readers. But there was no critical consensus on how to interpret her works. Rather, each interpretive community understood her according to its own lights. *The Athenaeum*, an important literary review, deplored her "prejudices" against Christianity in *Women of Israel* but found the work as a whole "a delightful contribution to the stock of our sacred literature."[1] William Howitt, in the evangelical *Howitt's Journal*, wrote in reference to *Home Influence* that "the works of Grace Aguilar prove of how little vital consequence are the differences of creed, where the heart is influenced by the spirit of true religion."[2] Conversionists, like one writer in the *Jewish Herald and Record of Christian Effort for Jews' Spiritual Progress*, tended to see in Aguilar proof that reform among Jews was leading toward mass conversion.[3]

Among Jewish critics the reaction was no more unified. Jewish men had difficulty making sense of the disparity between her manifest intelligence and their assumptions about women's intellectual capacities. Looking back at the literary production of the past generation, Abraham Benisch, editor of the *Jewish Chronicle*, wrote with amazement and pride of the "remarkable phenomenon on the horizon of Anglo-Jewish literature that it is women, not men, that shine there as the principal stars."[4] Yet he followed his review of women's accomplishments by calling for the creation of a popular Jewish literature, as though women like Aguilar had not already brought one into being. Similarly, when *Spirit of Judaism* was published, Jacob Franklin, the editor of *The Voice of Jacob*, saw it as the proof that "This is truly becoming a printing age among our people," yet he was disturbed that this movement should be fostered by a "young

1 *The Athenaeum*, 2 Aug. 1845.

2 *Howitt's Journal* 1.18 (1 May 1847): 251.

3 See J. K. S., rev. of *Spirit of Judaism*, *The Jewish Herald and Record of Christian Effort for the Spiritual Good of God's Ancient People* 2.13 (1847): 28-41; and review of *Jewish Faith*, *Howitt's Journal* 1 (6 Feb. 1847): 84.

4 Abraham Benisch, Review of *Imrei Lev* by Hester Rothschild, *Jewish Chronicle* (1 Aug. 1856) and "Our Women," *Jewish Chronicle* (8 Nov. 1861).

lady," and he asked, "where are our leaders?"[1] Isaac Leeser certainly encouraged and promoted Aguilar (as he did Marion and Celia Moss and other Jewish women), yet in his critical reactions he disputed her reform-minded approach to Jewish tradition.[2]

Jewish men were also split in their reaction to different genres. They dismissed as trivial Aguilar's efforts to produce what they called "light" literature—that is, fiction—although they praised the "tender womanly heart," "grace," "charm," "delicacy" and "beauties" expressed in her poetry and non-fiction.[3] While placing her theological works strictly within a female sphere, they took them more seriously than either poetry or fiction. Isaac Leeser devoted three long reviews to *Women of Israel* in *The Occident*, and advertised her *Spirit of Judaism*.[4] Yet while appreciating her efforts to provide women with spiritual models, Jewish men found fault with Aguilar's theology and prayer for transgressing on genres best left to men, who had the appropriate experience and training.[5]

Jewish women's public responses were somewhat more unified. In their testimonial just before Aguilar's final trip to Frankfurt, the group signing themselves the "Women of Israel" praised her as follows:

> Until you arose, it has, in modern times, never been the case that a woman in Israel should stand forth the public advocate of the faith of Israel.... You have taught us to know and to appreciate our own dignity, to feel and to prove that no female character can be more worthy than the Hebrew mother—none more pure than that of the Jewish maiden—none more pious than that of the women in Israel. You have vindicated our social and spiritual equality with our brethren in faith; you

1 Jacob Franklin, rev of *Spirit of Judaism, Voice of Jacob* (1 Apr. 1842).

2 Isaac Leeser, "Editor's Preface" to *Spirit of Judaism* (Philadelphia: Jewish Publication Society, 1842), 6, and in footnotes throughout the text.

3 See rev. of *Works, Jewish Chronicle* (1 Sept. 1871).

4 Leeser, rev. of *Women of Israel, Occident* 2 (Dec. 1844); 3 (Jun. 1845); and the extended review by S. Solis, "Remarks on Miss Aguilar's 'Women of Israel'" *Occident* 4 (Apr-June 1846).

5 Jacob Franklin, rev. of *Spirit of Judaism*; Isaac Leeser, "Editor's Preface" to *Spirit of Judaism*; Abraham Benisch, "Our Women."

have by your own excellent example triumphantly refuted the aspersion that the Jewish religion leaves unmoved the heart of the Jewish woman.[1]

This testimonial captures well the spirit of adulation that pervades many of the tributes women wrote upon Aguilar's death.

Her death caused contemporary critics to try to sum up her achievement, and in so doing they initiated three different strands of criticism, each of which has had a long afterlife. While uniformly referring to Aguilar's death as a "national" calamity, Jewish memorializers attempted to limit her achievement and its future impact. Jacob Franklin inaugurated a critical tradition about Aguilar by claiming that her work was *sui generis*.[2] This designation was then repeated for nearly a century and prevented Aguilar from being considered in the light of her most relevant historical contexts—other Jewish women writers, Victorian gender ideology, the Jewish Enlightenment, Victorian literary history, English national identity, and so on.[3]

Contemporary critics also inaugurated a myth of Aguilar's life that suggested that her early death was the result of her too strenuous literary efforts, rather than simply the result of disease. For example, in their tribute, the Ladies of the Society for the Religious Instruction of Jewish Youth in Charleston, South Carolina, wrote that "Her devotional offering was more costly than the oblation of the temple builder—a life consecrated to sacred culture; until ceaseless labour laid its fragile framework in ruins!"[4] This myth enabled critics to celebrate her achievements while warning other young women away from choosing to write in lieu of marrying and raising children.

Finally, the *Athenaeum* inaugurated the critical tradition that Aguilar's works were "yet more full of promise than performance," a tradition that was echoed by the earliest twentieth-century assess-

1 "Testimonial from the Misses Levison and Isaacs," *Jewish Chronicle* (9 July 1847).

2 Jacob Franklin, "A Memoir of the Late Grace Aguilar," *Voice of Jacob* (3 Dec. 1847).

3 See Galchinsky, *Origin*, 151–56.

4 Tribute, Ladies of the Society for the Religious Instruction of Jewish Youth, Charleston, SC, in Grace Aguilar MSS. See Appendix A.

ments of Aguilar by Rachel Lask Abrahams and Cecil Roth.[1] Since the 1970s, critics such as Phillip Weinberger, Linda Gertner Zatlin, Daniel Harris, Cynthia Scheinberg, Nadia Valman and I have offered a more positive evaluation. While agreeing with the earlier critics that Aguilar, writing hurriedly and under great strain, sometimes produced work that lacked polish, the more recent critics have nonetheless praised its cumulative power, and have seen in it much that recommends careful attention by students of Victorian literature, women's cultural history, and Jewish cultural history.

Despite these mixed assessments, Aguilar's reputation continued to grow for a generation after her death, due in large part to the extensive posthumous publication of many of her works by her mother, Sarah. The high point of her posthumous popularity came in 1869, with the publication of her collected *Works*. Paradoxically, however, it was only a matter of years after Aguilar's *Works* appeared that her writings began to undergo a long period of neglect that lasted for nearly a century. This eclipse was due to several historical changes that made her work seem outdated, including an increase in Jewish immigration to England, the rise of scientific racism, the emergence of the New Woman, and the establishment of literary realism.

Between 1870 and 1900, the Jewish population in England grew from 60,000 to 250,000, due to a wave of Eastern European immigration. These Eastern European Jews, many of whom arrived destitute, completely transformed the socio-economic profile, the organizational structure, the politics, and the religio-ethnic composition of the Anglo-Jewish community. The community to whom Aguilar had addressed herself was primarily middle class, featured Sephardim in leadership roles, was settled in the West End, and was liberal in political tendency. The new Anglo-Jewish community was largely comprised of working class and poor Ashkenazim settled in the East End, and it featured a bubbling stew of political factions unlike any Aguilar had known, including Zionists, socialists, and feminists. The best depiction of the late Victorian community is in Israel Zangwill's

---

1 Obituary, *Voice of Jacob*, Nov. 1847 in Grace Aguilar MSS; Obituary, *Athenaeum*, Nov. 1847 in Grace Aguilar MSS; Abrahams, "Grace Aguilar."

1892 novel *The Children of the Ghetto*, recently edited and reissued by Meri-Jane Rochelson.[1] Because of the wave of immigration, the Jewish community that Aguilar knew no longer existed, and to the extent her work was known it probably seemed irrelevant to British Jews.

During the same period, the British Empire expanded rapidly, increasing the Victorians' experience with members of ethnic, religious, racial, and regional groups other than their own. One of the Victorian responses to this encounter was social Darwinism, an attempt to rank "races" (defined biologically or nationally) along a scale of complexity, intelligence, superiority, and fitness to survive. New scientific disciplines that participated in establishing the supposed validity of these racial hierarchies included phrenology, chronometry, statistics, criminology, anthropology, and eugenics.[2] Scientific racism in turn had its impact upon the cultural representation of Jewish figures in literary texts. While in early and mid-Victorian texts, representations of Jews tended to figure them in "national" or religious terms, late Victorian texts figured them increasingly as members of an indelibly-marked, biologically-determined race. Even some late Victorian Anglo-Jewish novelists like Julia Frankau fell under the influence of racial science and engaged in race-based depictions of Jewishness.[3] But it was precisely in national and religious, not racial, terms that Aguilar had depicted Jews in her novels and poetry, and it was precisely in these terms that she had addressed her polemics on behalf of Jews' acculturation and citizenship. In this way as well, Aguilar's discourse was not aligned with late Victorian concerns.

Nor did it help her reputation that her gender politics differed radically from those widely expressed by women writers of the late

1 Israel Zangwill, *Children of the Ghetto: a Study of a Peculiar People*, ed. Meri-Jane Rochelson (Detroit: Wayne State UP, 1998).

2 Stephen Jay Gould, *The Mismeasure of Man* (New York: Norton, 1981); George Mosse, *Toward the Final Solution: A History of European Racism* (New York: Howard Fertig, 1997).

3 Galchinsky, "'Permanently Blacked': Julia Frankau's Jewish Race," *Victorian Literature and Culture* (1999): 171-84; Todd Endelman, "The Frankaus of London: A Study in Radical Assimilation," *Jewish History* 8 (1994): 117-54; Bryan Cheyette, "The Other Self: Anglo-Jewish Fiction and the Representation of Jews in English, 1875-1905," *The Making of Modern Anglo-Jewry* ed. David Cesarani (Oxford: Blackwell, 1990) 97-111.

Victorian period. The later part of the century had seen the development of a set of possibilities for women unlike any Aguilar had dared to imagine. These new possibilities collectively became attached to a literary figure, the New Woman, with whom Aguilar's heroines may be contrasted. The New Woman seeks feminist empowerment by stepping outside the domestic sphere into the masculine worlds of the university and the labor market or by working to secure women the vote. In novels and caricatures, she is frequently depicted rejecting the institution of marriage, either pursuing a celibate life or engaging in sexual relationships outside of marriage while attempting to evade the moral punishment usually meted out to "fallen woman."[1] The late Victorian Jewish writer who explored these themes most thoroughly was Amy Levy (1861-1889), in her novellas *The Romance of the Shop*, *Miss Meredith*, and *Reuben Sachs*, all recently edited and reissued by Melvyn New.[2] By contrast, while the heroines of Aguilar's romances and domestic fictions invariably work to secure a zone of women's empowerment, for them this zone is always based in the domestic sphere and sanctified through marriage, child-rearing, and women's friendship. Women characters in Aguilar's fiction who transgress this sphere suffer moral censure and punishment.

Finally, Aguilar's fictional technique probably seemed outdated due to the advent of literary realism. The realist subgenre of the novel required probability in its plot events; psychologized character development; a dispassionate, scientifically objective, and ironic nar-

---

1 See Sally Ledger, *The New Woman: Fiction and Feminism at the Fin de Siècle* (New York: St. Martin's, 1997) and Ann Heilmann, *New Woman Fiction: Women Writing First-wave Feminism* (New York: St. Martin's, 2000).

2 See Amy Levy, *The Complete Novels and Selected Writings of Amy Levy, 1861-1889*, ed. Melvyn New (Gainesville: UP of Florida, 1993). For recent critical and biographical considerations of Levy, see Linda Hunt Beckman, *Amy Levy: Her Life and Letters* (Athens, OH: Ohio UP, 2000); Cynthia Scheinberg, "Recasting 'Sympathy and Judgment': Amy Levy, Women Poets, and the Victorian Dramatic Monologue," *Victorian Poetry* 35 (1997): 173-92 and "Canonizing the Jew: Amy Levy's Challenge to Victorian Poetic Identity," *Victorian Studies* 39 (1996): 173-200; Bryan Cheyette, "From Apology to Revolt: Benjamin Farjeon, Amy Levy and the Post-Emancipation Anglo-Jewish Novel," *Transactions of the Jewish Historical Society of England* (Jan. 1985): 253-65; Emma Francis, "Amy Levy: Contradictions?—Feminism and Semitic Discourse," *Women's Poetry, Late Romantic to Victorian*; Armstrong and Blain, eds; Deborah Epstein Nord, "'Neither Pairs Nor Odd': Female Community in Late Nineteenth Century London," *Signs* 15 (1990): 733-54.

rative voice; and a contemporaneous setting.[1] Aguilar's historical romances and domestic fictions were written under the very conventions that realists rejected. In historical romance, for example, the conventions of the genre demand improbable coincidences, typological rather than psychological characterization, an impassioned and engaged narrative voice, and a setting that is distant both in location and in time.[2] As for domestic fiction, the other major genre in which Aguilar worked, while it satisfied the realist demand for contemporaneity, it typically provided an affective and idealized representation of life rather than a probable one. Its mothers and daughters were depicted as static types rather than as developing characters. And its narrator eschewed irony for a voice that was overtly didactic and implicitly political.[3]

For all these reasons Aguilar's work was not preserved by the later Victorians. But as the century turned, Aguilar was still remembered sporadically: a branch of the New York Public Library was named after her in 1899; *Young Champion*, a children's book by A. S. Isaacs, based on her life, appeared in 1913; Rachel Lask Abrahams, an amateur historian, gave a lecture about Aguilar for the Jewish Historical Society of England in 1952; Aguilar's *Women of Israel* was given as a Sunday School prize in some Protestant churches up through the 1950s.[4] The most important early historian of Anglo-Jewish life, Cecil Roth, noted many of her works in his *Magna Bibliotheca Anglo-Judaica*, and made a few dismissive remarks about her work in several essays.[5] For the most part, the work of this prolific and significant writer received little attention from historians, and none at all from literary critics. Until the 1990s there was no serious attempt to

1 For a classic definition of "formal realism," see Ian Watt, *The Rise of the Novel* (Berkeley: U of California P, 1957) 9-34.

2 See Gillian Beer, *The Romance* (London: Methuen, 1970).

3 See Nancy Armstrong, *Desire and Domestic Fiction: A Political History of the Novel* (New York: Oxford UP, 1987).

4 See Joseph C. Brooks, *New York Public Library, Aguilar Branch* (New York: Landmarks Preservation Commission, 1996); A. S. Isaacs, *Young Champion* (Philadelphia: Jewish Publication Society, 1913); Rachel Beth Zion Lask Abrahams, "Grace Aguilar: A Centenary Tribute," *Transactions of the Jewish Historical Society of England* 16 (1952): 137-48.

5 See Cecil Roth, ed., *Magna Bibliotheca Anglo-Judaica: A Bibliographical Guide to Anglo-Jewish History* (London: Jewish Historical Society of England, 1937), and his article "Evolution of Anglo-Jewish Literature" (London: Edward Goldston, 1937).

gauge the significance of Aguilar's contributions to Victorian literature, women's cultural history, Jewish cultural history, and English national identity.

Partly we must attribute the century of neglect to simple ignorance: out of print, out of mind. Yet there are other less simple reasons at work as well, for Aguilar's writing does not fit neatly into typical historical or critical models for approaching the Victorian period. Aguilar's extensive written appeals on behalf of British Jews conflict with typical Victorian Jewish historiography which has almost universally focused on the (relatively sparse) achievements of men, who were in general too occupied with agitating for emancipation to engage much in writing books.[1] Women's historians and critics have typically focused on English Christian women, sometimes particularizing them into various kinds of Protestants, Catholics, and secularizers, but rarely looking outside of the Christian frame.[2] Historians of racism and colonialism have not, for the most part, recognized the Jewish experience as part of their purview.[3] And literary critics for most of the century defined work by women and minorities (except in a few token cases) as non-canonical, and therefore of only marginal interest.

Aguilar's fortunes began to turn with the emergence of social history in the 1970s and the expansion of the literary canon in the 1980s. The first hint of renewed interest came in 1970 with the appearance of a Ph.D. dissertation in religious studies by Philip Weinberger, followed in 1981 by Linda Gertner Zatlin's brief account of Aguilar in her survey of *The Nineteenth-Century Anglo-Jewish Novel*.[4] These accounts brought Aguilar back to the awareness

---

1 The few exceptions include Rachel Beth Zion Lask Abrahams' article on Aguilar and her article "Amy Levy," *Transactions of the Jewish Historical Society of England* 11 (22 June 1926): 168-89; Lara Marks, "Carers and Servers of the Jewish Community: The Marginalized Heritage of Jewish Women in Britain," *The Jewish Heritage in British History* ed. Tony Kushner (London: Frank Cass, 1992) 106-27.

2 See for example Anita Levy, *Other Women: The Writing of Class, Race, and Gender, 1832-1898* (Princeton: Princeton UP, 1991); Anne McClintock, *Imperial Leather: Race, Gender, and Sexuality in the Colonial Contest* (New York: Routledge, 1995).

3 See McClintock; Said; Spivak; Melman; Bhabha.

4 See Phillip M. Weinberger, "The Social and Religious Thought of Grace Aguilar (1816-1847)," diss., New York U, 1970; and Linda Gertner Zatlin, *The Nineteenth-Century Anglo-Jewish Novel* (Boston: G. K. Hall, 1981).

of critics both in the United States and the United Kingdom, but more thorough investigations had to wait until the methodologies had been developed to recover the writings of neglected women and minorities and to understand the complexity of their encounters with majority aesthetics and culture.

By the mid-1990s these methodologies were widely available, and literary historians began to use them to examine Aguilar's oeuvre. Critics placed Aguilar's fiction in the context of the developing nineteenth-century genres of historical romance and domestic fiction.[1] Students of Victorian poetry began to read Aguilar's lyrics against the Christian poetic prophecies and hymns produced by Romantic women poets.[2] Women's historians began to parse the complex gender politics in which Aguilar engaged, to discuss her role in the feminization of Victorian religion and the development of the separation of spheres, to analyze her important letters recounting the intimate circumstances of middle class women's lives, and to construct her biography using feminist methodologies.[3] Her short stories and non-fiction have been anthologized in collections of writing by Victorians, Jews, and women.[4]

In many ways, the critical study of Aguilar's works is just beginning. There will be a role for her in diaspora studies and broader

1 Michael Ragussis, *Figures of Conversion*, ch. 4; Galchinsky, *Origin*, ch. 4 and "Modern Jewish Women's Dilemmas, Grace Aguilar's Bargains," *Literature and Theology* 11 (March 1997): 27-45; Cynthia Scheinberg, "Introduction: Re-Mapping Anglo-Jewish Literary History," *Victorian Literature and Culture* (1999): 115-24. For recent reviews of Anglo-Jewish literary criticism, see Scheinberg, "Introduction;" Nadia Valman, "Semitism and Criticism: Victorian Anglo-Jewish Literary History," *Victorian Literature and Culture* (1999): 235-48; Michael Ragussis, "The 'Secret' of English Anti-Semitism: Anglo-Jewish Studies and Victorian Studies," *Victorian Studies* (Winter 1997): 295-307; and Michael Galchinsky, "The New Anglo-Jewish Literary Criticism," *Prooftexts* 15 (Sept. 1995): 272-82.

2 See Daniel Harris, "Hagar in Christian Britain;" Scheinberg, "'Measure to Yourself a Prophet's Place;'" *Women's Poetry, Late Romantic to Late Victorian* ed. Armstrong and Blain, 263-91.

3 Cf. Galchinsky, *Origin*, ch. 4, and the articles "Engendering Liberal Jews: Jewish Women in Victorian England," in Baskin, 208-226 and "Grace Aguilar's Correspondence;" and Joss West-Burnham, "Travelling Towards Selfhood: Victorian Religion and the Process of Female Identity," *Women's Lives into Print: The Theory, Practice, and Writing of Feminist Auto/Biography* ed. Pauline Polkey (New York: St. Martin's, 1999) 80-95.

4 Aguilar's midrash on "The Exodus—Laws for the Mothers of Israel," originally a section of *The Women of Israel*, appears in *The Longman Anthology of Women's Literature*, ed. Mary K.

studies of marginalized writers. Historians will want to analyze her various roles in Anglo-Jewish history, as the Anglo-Jewish community's earliest historian, as perhaps its most formidable spokesperson for the religious reform and political emancipation movements, and as one of its most innovative midrashists and liturgists. There is still a great deal of work to be done in coming to understand Aguilar's complex relationship with traditional Jewish literature, including the Bible and the Talmud. If this blooming critical conversation is to come to full flower, however, critics and historians, teachers and students require greater access to Aguilar's texts.

DeShazer (New York: Longman, 2001) 690-95; her story "The Authoress," originally published in *Home Scenes and Heart Studies*, has been anthologized in *Victorian Love Stories: An Oxford Anthology*, ed. Kate Flint, (New York: Oxford UP, 1996) 1-17; and an excerpt from *The Spirit of Judaism* appears in *Four Centuries of Jewish Women's Spirituality*, eds. Ellen M. Umansky and Dianne Ashton (Boston: Beacon, 1992) 78-83.

Grace Aguilar: A Brief Chronology

1816 Born June 2 to Emmanuel Aguilar and Sarah Aguilar (née Dias Fernandez) in Hackney.

1819 Suffers childhood illness which permanently weakens her.

1823 Begins keeping a journal.

1824 Brother Emanuel born.

1825 Tours Oxford, Cheltenham, Gloucester, Worcester, Ross, and Bath.

1827 Brother Henry born.

1828 Father serves as *Parnas* (lay-leader) of the Bevis Marks, Spanish and Portuguese Synagogue in London until prevented by consumption from continuing; family moves to Devonshire for Emmanuel's health in September, where Aguilar writes her first drama, "Gustavus Vasa," never published and now lost.

1830 Father begins a "regular course of instruction" for Aguilar in history; she writes her first poem during a visit to Tavistock; studies piano.

1831 Begins writing manuscript of her romance *The Vale of Cedars; or, the Martyr*, published only posthumously in 1850; from this point forward, Aguilar's father acts as her amanuensis; begins to play the harp.

1832 Mother undergoes an operation and requires Aguilar's bedside care for several years.

1834 Finishes first manuscripts, including "The Friends: A Domestic Tale" and "Leila: A Poem in Three Cantos with Notes."

1835 Finishes manuscript of *The Vale of Cedars*; moves with family to Brighton; publishes first book of poetry, *The Magic Wreath of Hidden Flowers*, with W.H. Mason publishers in Brighton, dedicated to the Right Honourable Countess of Munster; suffers bout with measles from which Aguilar never fully recovers.

1836 Writes the first draft of the manuscript of *Home Influence: A Tale for Mothers and Daughters*, not published until 1847;

writes manuscript, never published, of "The Charmed Bell and Other Poems."

1837 Writes a sermon, "Sabbath Thoughts," based on a lecture on Psalm 32 by a Protestant divine, "the Rev. R.A."

1838 Publishes *Israel Defended*, her translation from French of Orobio de Castro's apologetic work; writes second manuscript tale, "Adah: A Simple Story."

1839 *The Magic Wreath* reprinted by London publisher Ackermann and Co.

1840 Asks Benjamin Disraeli to carry a letter to his father, the writer Isaac D'Israeli, in which she requests help finding a publisher for her writings (she continues to correspond with D'Israeli sporadically through 1844); is invited by Isaac Leeser, editor of the American Jewish periodical *The Occident*, to publish her theological work *Spirit of Judaism* as the initial offering of the Jewish Publication Society of America, but the manuscript is lost at sea and has to be rewritten; relocates with family to 5 Triangle, Hackney.

1841 Begins publishing poems in popular English periodicals such as *Keepsake*, *Friendship's Offering*, *Howitt's Journal*, and *La Belle Assemblée*; makes acquaintance with writers Mary Howitt, Anna Maria Hall, and Camilla Toulmine.

1842 Leeser edits and publishes rewritten *Spirit of Judaism*; the poem "A Poet's Dying Hymn" appears in the Anglo-Jewish periodical *Voice of Jacob*; Aguilar begins long-term correspondence with Miriam Cohen of Savannah, Georgia, niece of the educator Rebecca Gratz; Cohen's husband, Georgia's first Jewish Senator, Solomon Cohen, undertakes to distribute Aguilar's work in the United States; Aguilar's youngest brother Henry becomes a sailor, causing the family much anxiety.

1843 Corresponds with Edward Bulwer-Lytton; publishes *The Perez Family* with the Cheap Jewish Library, ed. Charlotte Montefiore; publishes the first of many poems, "Sabbath Thoughts," in *The Occident* (more than thirty will appear until October, 1847, the month after her death); writes manuscript "Notes on Excursion."

1844 Publishes *Records of Israel*, a collection of tales.

1845 Publishes her collection of biographical *midrashim*, *The Women of Israel*, in 3 vols.; relocates with family to 1 Clarence Place, Clapton Square, near London.

1846 Father dies of consumption on Jan. 18; Aguilar publishes *The Jewish Faith*, a series of letters between an older woman and a younger one on faith and conversion; brother Henry returns home and requires his sister's aid in finding employment.

1847 Publishes "The History of the Jews in England" in *Chambers' Miscellany*; suffers the onset of her final illness (a spinal ailment affecting the muscles and lungs); completes *Home Influence: A Tale for Mothers and Daughters*; receives a testimonial from a group of Anglo-Jewish "Women of Israel," June 14; travels to Frankfurt to visit musician brother Emanuel and to recover her health; takes the waters at Schwalbach for six weeks, but worsens, returns to Frankfurt, and dies on Sept. 16; is buried in the Frankfurt Jewish cemetery; *Home Influence* appears posthumously and becomes her most popular work; obituaries appear in *The Jewish Chronicle*, *The Athenaeum*, and *The Occident*; she receives multiple tributes, including Anna Maria Hall's "Pilgrimage to the Grave of Grace Aguilar," poems by Jewish writers Rebekah Hyneman and Marion Moss Hartog, and testimonials from Jewish readers in Charleston, Philadelphia, and Kingston, Jamaica.

1848 Sarah Aguilar continues her daughter's correspondence with Miriam and Solomon Cohen of Savannah, Georgia.

1850 Sarah Aguilar begins posthumous publication of her daughter's finished works, starting with the historical romance *The Vale of Cedars* and the domestic novel *Woman's Friendship*.

1851 Sarah Aguilar publishes *A Mother's Recompense*, her daughter's sequel to *Home Influence*.

1852 Sarah Aguilar publishes *Days of Bruce*, her daughter's Scottish historical romance written in tribute to Walter Scott; also publishes *Home Scenes and Heart Studies*, a collection of her daughter's short fiction, and "Memoir of Grace Aguilar," a brief biographical essay written as the preface to the 1852 edition of *Home Influence*.

1853 Sarah Aguilar publishes *Sabbath Thoughts and Sacred Communings*, a volume of her daughter's theological meditations, prayers, and sermons that Rebecca Gratz had repeatedly asked for during Grace's lifetime, but one that she had steadfastly refused to produce.

1869 Publication of Grace Aguilar's collected *Works*.

A Note on the Text

This anthology aims to meet the need of an easily available, annotated edition of selected texts in Aguilar's *oeuvre*. I have included only Aguilar's "Jewish" texts—i.e., those that bear directly on her understanding of Jewishness or Judaism, or reflect upon her status as a minority—since these texts are what make her contributions to Victorian letters, women's history, and Jewish history unique. For those interested in further reading, many of her "non-Jewish" texts, especially the short story "The Authoress" and her novels *The Days of Bruce* and *Home Influence*, will repay careful attention. I have included those texts that in my judgment have particular literary or historical merit, along with those that achieved commercial and critical success in Aguilar's day, those that had signal importance in the development of her career, and those that illuminate her thought. Wherever possible I have given the full text, or at least a complete section of the text. In the case of Aguilar's novels and her longer essays, space considerations rendered it necessary to provide excerpts. In some cases, rather than excerpt portions of the novels, I have chosen to include complete shorter fictions that in many ways replicate the plotting, characterization, style, and tone of the novels. Thus, although Aguilar's Jewish historical romance *The Vale of Cedars* is not included here, her short romance "The Escape" gives the reader a good sense of the kind of tale to be found in the longer work. Many of the concerns of her domestic novels, *Home Influence*, *A Mother's Recompense*, and *Woman's Friendship*, can be found in her novella *The Perez Family*.

Aguilar's manuscripts, published works, and correspondence are held in eight libraries throughout the United Kingdom and the United States. The most significant collection is the Grace Aguilar MSS, held at the Manuscripts Library of University College London on extended loan from the Jewish Museum in London. This was donated by the historian Rachel Beth Zion Lask Abrahams in the 1950s. My efforts to discover the provenance of the material prior to that have met with no success. The Southern Historical Collection of the Manuscripts Library at the University of North Carolina at Chapel Hill houses the correspondence between Grace and Sarah

Aguilar and Miriam and Solomon Cohen; copyright is held by the Jewish Museum in London. The Isaac Leeser Archive at the University of Pennsylvania Center for Judaic Studies contains *The Occident* and a number of important documents relating to Aguilar's American business connections. The remaining libraries have smaller holdings. A full list of all eight archives and their contents appears in the Select Bibliography below.

The texts are drawn both from Aguilar's published works and her manuscripts. In the case of published works, I have generally used the earliest published edition as the copy-text, since no manuscripts survive and there is no evidence that Aguilar revised any of her published works. Of the texts edited by Sarah Aguilar, no manuscript evidence, other than her own notes in her letters to Miriam Moses Cohen, has been found to indicate the extent of her hand in shaping the content or final form of the texts she published. In consequence, I have treated her editions as the bases for my copy-texts.

This volume is organized in sections by genre: fiction, poetry, and non-fiction prose. A headnote to each section gives a brief explanation of the section's contents. The footnotes give the sources of biblical allusions, identify historical references, explain unusual terms, and provide cross-references. The English translation of the Bible to which Aguilar referred was the King James Version. No Jewish translation of any part of the Bible existed in English until after 1844. There are, however, many times when Aguilar departs from the KJV and appears to be translating directly from Hebrew. At such times I offer the KJV along with her translation for comparison.

Five appendices are also provided to aid the reader in understanding Aguilar's work in its biographical and historical contexts, including selected Victorian tributes; Victorian criticism; reflections by Romantic and Victorian Christian writers on "The Jewish Question"; a few examples of Victorian Jewish writing; and selections from Aguilar's Frankfurt Journal.

SELECTED WRITINGS

I. FICTION

Aguilar's fictional productions consisted of historical romances, domestic novels, and *midrashim*. She wrote her earliest stories and novels as antidotes to what she perceived as the misrepresentations of Jewish women in historical romances by Christian writers. Early on, the writer to whose work she responded most was Walter Scott. Scott's *Ivanhoe* (1819) was a historical romance in which fictional characters appeared together with historical figures. In his novel, Scott depicted a spiritual and intelligent Jewish woman in conflict with her materialistic father over her love for a charismatic Christian suitor. In numerous novels that took inspiration from Scott, such as M.G. Lewis's *The Jewish Maiden* (1830) and Bulwer Lytton's *Leila; or, the Siege of Granada* (1837), nineteenth-century Christian writers resolved the conflict between father and daughter by having the daughter convert to Christianity, leave her father's house, and marry the Christian suitor.

Aguilar's earliest historical romance, *The Vale of Cedars; or, The Martyr* (written in 1834 though not published until 1852, five years after her death), likewise concerns a spiritual and intelligent Jewish woman who falls in love with a charismatic Christian suitor. But her heroine Maria decides not to leave her father's house to convert to Christianity. Aguilar assimilated the subject matter and genre from Scott's imitators, but significantly altered her plot so as to question the assumption that Jewish women were malleable and amenable to conversion. Like *Vale of Cedars*, many of Aguilar's romances—including "The Escape," reprinted here—are set in Spain or Portugal, from which her ancestors had fled to England, to escape the Inquisition. First published in *Records of Israel* (1844), "The Escape" attempts to use a historical depiction of eighteenth-century Jews living during the Portuguese Inquistion to meditate on the complicated position of the Jews in England in her own day. Although, in her "Preface" to *Records*, Aguilar insists that "The Escape" is not a romance, it does contain many of the features we associate with that genre.

Aguilar grew frustrated with writing Jewish historical romances when she realized that they would only reach a limited audience and that, by describing Jews only as they had been, the romances distanced readers from Jews as they actually were in her own time. In order to depict contemporary Jewish life, she turned to writing domestic fiction. To be sure, her first domestic fictions were entirely about Christian characters, including the novels *Home Influence: A Tale for Mothers and Daughters*, *A Woman's Recompense* (a sequel to *Home Influence*), and *Woman's Friendship*, and many of the stories collected in *Home Scenes and Heart Studies.* These were enormously popular: *Home Influence* sold out nearly thirty editions. By writing about Christian characters, Aguilar could avoid what, in the preface to *Home Influence*, she called "doctrinal matters." Yet, despite her success, she was frustrated that she could not represent Jewish life in these depictions of contemporary life. That changed when she was offered the chance, in 1843, to participate in a new literary series called the Cheap Jewish Library, edited by Charlotte Montefiore, a Jewish philanthropist, editor, satirist and essayist. Montefiore sought to bring inexpensive moral and domestic tales to the Jewish working class, and she asked Aguilar to write a moral and domestic tale about British Jews. Confident that the audience for her tale would comprise Jewish readers, Aguilar took the chance to write about Jews, not as they were in times past, but as they appeared to her in the present. The result was the novella *The Perez Family*, reprinted here, the first fictional representation ever written about British Jews by a Jew. The novella follows the conventions of domestic fiction as outlined in the Introduction above.

While Aguilar assimilated and altered contemporary literary forms such as the romance and the domestic novel, she also wrote using traditional Jewish forms, in particular the genre of *midrash aggadah. Midrash aggadah* had developed almost 2000 years before as a means by which Jewish writers could interpret the Bible. Confronting gaps or unanswered questions in a given biblical text, writers of *midrash* would retell the story, filling in the gaps with details taken from Jewish oral tradition or their own imaginations. In this way, although ostensibly retelling the text, they were in fact offering an interpretation of it. Aguilar's contemporary, Morris Raphall, was an Anglo-Jewish scholar and editor of *The Hebrew Review and Magazine of Rabbinical Literature* (1834-36). He frequently translated ancient *midrashim* into English and altered them to suit his tastes, publishing them in his periodical. Since fiction-writing was not an indigenous Jewish form, Raphall's *midrashim* were some of the first published Anglo-Jewish stories. In several cases, Aguilar responded to Raphall's tales by writing a *midrash* on his *midrash*. "The Sun and the Moon," reprinted in Appendix D.1 below, is Raphall's translation and interpretation of a *midrash* on Genesis 1:16 ("God made the two great lights, the greater to govern the day and the lesser to govern the night"). Aguilar's short story, "The Spirit of Night," is her *midrashic* response to Raphall. Taken from *Home Scenes and Heart Studies*, the original date of composition of this piece is unknown.

THE ESCAPE. A TALE OF 1755[1]

"Dark lowers our fate,
And terrible the storm that gathers o'er us;
But nothing, till that latest agony
Which severs thee from nature, shall unloose
This fixed and sacred hold. In thy dark prison-house;
In the terrific face of armed law;
Yea! on the scaffold, if it needs must be,
I never will forsake thee."

—Joanna Baillie[2]

About the middle of the eighteenth century, the little town of Montes, situated some forty or fifty miles from Lisbon, was thrown into most unusual excitement by the magnificence attending the nuptials of Alvar Rodriguez and Almah Diaz: an excitement which the extraordinary beauty of the bride, who, though the betrothed of Alvar from her childhood, had never been seen in Montes before, of course not a little increased. The little church of Montes looked gay and glittering for the large sums lavished by Alvar on the officiating priests, and in presents to their patron saints, had occasioned every picture, shrine, and image to blaze in uncovered gold and jewels, and the altar to be fed with the richest incense, and lighted with tapers of the finest wax, to do him honour.

The church was full; for, although thc bridal party did not exceed twenty, the village appeared to have emptied itself there; Alvar's

1 The year of a severe earthquake in Lisbon, Portugal. In 1755, Portugal was still in the midst of the Inquisition, which was a tribunal endorsed by the Pope to root out heretics from the Church. Begun in Spain under the infamous leadership of Torquemada in the fifteenth century, the Inquisition spread to Portugal, where it remained strong until the mid-nineteenth century. Those found guilty of heresy—frequently Jews and Muslims—often had their lands expropriated, were expelled from the country, had their businesses and places of worship shut down, were forcibly converted to Catholicism, were tortured, and were sometimes burned at the stake. To avoid such consequences, some Jews openly converted to Catholicism, only to continue to practice Judaism in secret. These secret Jews (called "crypto-Jews") were Aguilar's ancestors.

2 From Joanna Baillie, *De Monfort*, V.ii, a tragedy performed in the Theatre Royal in Drury Lane in 1807. Jane De Monfort is talking to her brother, who has just committed murder. Aguilar was probably familiar with Baillie's collected *Dramas*, 3 vols., (Longman, 1836). My thanks to Christine A. Colon for providing this information.

munificence to all classes, on all occasions, having rendered him the universal idol, and caused the fame of that day's rejoicing to extend many miles around.

There was nothing remarkable in the behaviour of either bride or bridegroom, except that both were decidedly more calm than such occasions usually warrant. Nay, in the manly countenance of Alvar ever and anon an expression seemed to flit, that in any but so true a son of the church would have been accounted scorn. In such a one, of course it was neither seen nor regarded, except by his bride; for at such times her eyes met his with an earnest and entreating glance, that the peculiar look was changed into a quiet, tender seriousness, which reassured her.

From the church they adjourned to the Lordly mansion of Rodriguez, which, in the midst of its flowering orange and citron trees, stood about two miles from the town.

The remainder of the day passed in festivity. The banquet, and dance, and song, both within and around the house, diversified the scene and increased hilarity in all. By sunset, all but the immediate friends and relatives of the newly wedded had departed. Some splendid and novel fireworks from the heights having attracted universal attention, Alvar, with his usual indulgence, gave his servants and retainers permission to join the festive crowds; liberty, to all who wished it, was given the next two hours.

In a very brief interval the house was cleared, with the exception of a young Moor,[1] the secretary or book-keeper of Alvar, and four or five middle-aged domestics of both sexes.

Gradually, and it appeared undesignedly, the bride and her female companions were left alone, and for the first time the beautiful face of Almah was shadowed by emotion.

"Shall I, oh, shall I indeed be his?" she said, half aloud. "There are moments when our dread secret is so terrible; it seems to forebode discovery at the very moment it would be most agonizing to bear."

"Hush, silly one!" was the reply of an older friend; "discovery is not so easily or readily accomplished. The persecuted and the nameless have purchased wisdom and caution at the price of blood—

---

1 A Moor is usually an African or Arab Muslim in the Iberian peninsula or Southern Europe, as in Shakespeare's *Tragedy of Othello: the Moor of Venice.*

learned to deceive, that they may triumph—to conceal, that they may flourish still. Almah, we are NOT to fall!"

"I know it, Inez. A superhuman agency upholds us; we had been cast off, rooted out, plucked from the very face of the earth long since else. But there are times when human nature will shrink and tremble—when the path of deception and concealment allotted for us to tread seems fraught with danger at every turn. I know it is all folly, yet there is a dim foreboding, shadowing our fair horizon of joy as a hovering thunder-cloud. There has been suspicion, torture, death. Oh, if my Alvar—"

"Nay, Almah; this is childish. It is only because you are too happy, and happiness in its extent is ever pain. In good time comes your venerable guardian, to chide and silence all such foolish fancies. How many weddings have there been, and will there still be, like this? Come, smile, love, while I rearrange your veil."

Almah obeyed, though the smile was faint, as if the soul yet trembled in its joy. On the entrance of Gonzalos, her guardian (she was an orphan and an heiress), [he saw] her veil was thrown around her, so as completely to envelope face and form. Taking his arm, and followed by all her female companions, she was hastily and silently led to a sort of ante-room or cabinet, opening, by a massive door concealed with tapestry, from the suite of rooms appropriated to the private use of the merchant and his family. There Alvar and his friends awaited her. A canopy, supported by four of the youngest males present, was held over the bride and bridegroom as they stood facing the east. A silver salver lay at their feet, and opposite stood an aged man, with a small, richly-bound volume in his hand.[1] It was open, and displayed letters and words of unusual form and sound. Another of Alvar's friends stood near, holding a goblet of sacred wine; and to a third was given a slight and thin Venetian glass. After a brief and solemn pause, the old man read or rather chanted from the book he held, joined in parts by those around; and then he tasted the sacred wine, and passed it to the bride and bridegroom. Almah's veil was upraised, for her to touch the goblet with her lips, now quivering with emotion, and not permitted to fall again. And Alvar,

---

1 A salver is a tray; the book is a Siddur, a Jewish prayer book, written in Hebrew and Aramaic.

where now was the expression of scorn and contempt that had been stamped on his bold brow and curling lip before? Gone—lost before the powerful emotion which scarcely permitted his lifting the goblet a second time to his lips. Then, taking the Venetian glass, he broke it on the salver at his feet, and the strange rites were concluded.[1]

Yet no words of congratulation came. Drawn together in a closer knot, while Alvar folded the now almost fainting Almah to his bosom, and said, in the deep, low tones of intense feeling, "Mine, mine for ever now—mine in the sight of our God, the God of the exile and the faithful; our fate, whatever it be, henceforth is one;" the old man lifted up his clasped hands, and prayed.

"God of the nameless and homeless," he said, and it was in the same strange yet solemn-sounding language as before, "have mercy on these Thy servants, joined together in Thy Holy name, to share the lot on earth Thy will assigns them, with one heart and mind. Strengthen Thou them to keep the secret of their faith and race—to teach it to their offspring as they received it from their fathers. Pardon Thou them and us the deceit we do to keep holy Thy law and Thine inheritance. In the land of the persecutor, the exterminator, be Thou their shield, and save them for Thy Holy name. But if discovery and its horrible consequences—imprisonment, torture, death—await them, strengthen Thou them for their endurance—to die as they would live for Thee. Father, hear us! homeless and nameless upon earth, we are Thine own!"

"Aye, strengthen me for him, my husband; turn my woman weakness into Thy strength for him, Almighty Father," the voiceless prayer with which Almah lifted up her pale face from her husband's bosom, where it had rested during the whole of that strange and terrible prayer and in the calmness stealing on her throbbing heart, she read her answer.

It was some few minutes ere the excited spirits of the devoted few then present, male or female, master or servant, could subside into their wonted control. But such scenes, such feelings were not of rare occurrence; and ere the domestics of Rodriguez returned, there was

---

1 The canopy, the breaking of the glass, and the other rituals described here are performed during the traditional Jewish wedding ceremony.

nothing either in the mansion or its inmates to denote that anything uncommon had taken place during their absence.

The Portuguese are not fond of society at any time, so that Alvar and his young bride should after one week of festivity, live in comparative retirement, elicited no surprise. The former attended his house of business at Montes as usual; and whoever chanced to visit him at his beautiful estate, returned delighted with his entertainment and his hosts; so that, far and near, the merchant Alvar became noted alike for his munificence and the strict orthodox Catholicism in which he conducted his establishment.

And was Alvar Rodriguez indeed what he seemed? If so, what were those strange mysterious rites with which in secret he celebrated his marriage? For what were those many contrivances in his mansion, secret receptacles even from his own sitting-rooms, into which all kinds of forbidden food were conveyed from his very table, that his soul might not be polluted by disobedience? How did it so happen that one day in every year Alvar gave a general holiday—leave of absence for four and twenty hours, under some well-arranged pretence, to all, save those who entreated permission to remain with him? And that on that day, Alvar, his wife, his Moorish secretary, and all those domestics who had witnessed his marriage, spent in holy fast and prayer—permitting no particle of food or drink to pass their lips from eve unto eve; or if by any chance, the holiday could not be given, their several meals to be laid and served, yet so contriving that, while the food looked as if it had been partaken of not a portion had they touched?[1] That the Saturday should be passed in seeming preparation for the Sunday, in cessation from work of any kind, and frequent prayer, was perhaps of trivial importance; but for the previous mysteries—mysteries known to Alvar, his wife, and five or six of his establishment, yet never by word or sign betrayed; how may we account for them? There may be some to whom the memory of such things, as common to their ancestors, may be yet familiar; but to by far the greater number of English readers, they are, in all probability, as incomprehensible as uncommon.

Alvar Rodriguez was a Jew. One of the many who, in Portugal

1 This fasting ritual is observed by Jews on the holy day of Yom Kippur, a day of introspection and atonement for sins.

and Spain, fulfilled the awful prophecy of their great lawgiver Moses, and bowed before the imaged saints and martyrs of the Catholic, to shrine the religion of their fathers yet closer in their hearts and homes. From father to son the secret of their faith and race descended, so early and mysteriously taught, that little children imbibed it—not alone the faith, but so effectually to conceal it, as to avert and mystify, all inquisitorial questioning, long before they knew the meaning or necessity of what they learned.

How this was accomplished, how the religion of God was thus preserved in the very midst of persecution and intolerance, must ever remain a mystery, as, happily for Israel, such fearful training is no longer needed. But that it did exist, that Jewish children in the very midst of monastic and convent tuition, yet adhered to the religion of their fathers, never by word or sign betrayed the secret with which they were intrusted; and, in their turn, became husbands and fathers, conveying their solemn and dangerous inheritance to their posterity—that such things were, there are those still amongst the Hebrews of England to affirm and recall, claiming among their own ancestry, but one generation removed, those who have thus concealed and thus adhered. It was the power of God, not the power of man. Human strength had been utterly inefficient. Torture and death would long before have annihilated every remnant of Israel's devoted race. But it might not be; for God had spoken. And, as a living miracle, a lasting record of His truth, His justice, aye and mercy, Israel was preserved in the midst of danger, in the very face of death, and will be preserved for ever.

It was no mere rejoicing ceremony, that of marriage, amongst the disguised and hidden Israelites of Portugal and Spain. They were binding themselves to preserve and propagate a persecuted faith. They were no longer its sole repositors. Did the strength of one waver all was at an end.[1] They were united in the sweet links of love—framing for themselves new ties, new hopes, new blessings in a rising family—all of which, at one blow, might be destroyed. They existed in an atmosphere of death, yet they lived and flourished. But so situated, it was not strange that human emotion, both in Alvar and his bride, should on their wedding-day, have gained ascendancy;

1 I.e., If the strength of one person were to waver, all would be at an end.

and the solemn hour which made them one in the sight of the God they worshipped, should have been fraught with a terror and a shuddering, of which Jewish lovers in free and happy England can have no knowledge.

Alvar Rodriguez was one of those high and noble spirits, on whom the chain of deceit and concealment weighed heavily; and there were times when it had been difficult to suppress and conceal his scorn of those outward observances which his apparent Catholicism compelled. When united to Almah, however, he had a stronger incentive than his own safety: and as time passed on, and he became a father, caution and circumspection, if possible, increased with the deep passionate feelings of tenderness towards the mother and child. As the boy grew and flourished, the first feelings of dread, which the very love he excited called forth at his birth subsided into a kind of tranquil calm, which even Almah's foreboding spirit trusted would last, as the happiness of others of her race.

Though Alvar's business was carried on both at Montes and at Lisbon, the bulk of both his own and his wife's property was, by a strange chance, invested at Badajoz, a frontier town of Spain, and whence he had often intended to remove but had always been prevented. It happened that early the month of June, some affairs calling him to Lisbon, he resolved to delay removing it no longer, smiling at his young wife's half solicitation to let it remain where it was, and playfully accusing her of superstition, a charge she cared not to deny. The night before his intended departure his young Moorish secretary, in other words, an Israelite of Barbary extraction, entered his private closet, with a countenance of entreaty and alarm, earnestly conjuring his master to give up his Lisbon expedition, and retire with his wife and son to Badajoz or Oporto, or some distant city, at least for a while. Anxiously Rodriguez inquired wherefore.

"You remember the Señor Leyva, your worship's guest a week or two ago?"

"Perfectly. What of him?"

"Master, I like him not. If danger befall us it will come through him. I watched him closely, and every hour of his stay shrunk from him the more. He was a stranger?"

"Yes; benighted, and had lost his way. It was impossible to refuse him hospitality. That he stayed longer than he had need, I grant; but there is no cause of alarm in that—he liked his quarters."

"Master," replied the Moor, earnestly, "I do not believe his tale. He was no casual traveller. I cannot trust him."

"You are not called upon to do so, man," said Alvar, laughing. "What do you believe him to be, that you would inoculate me with your own baseless alarm?"

Hassan Ben Ahmed's answer, whatever it might be, for it was whispered fearfully in his master's ear, had the effect of sending every drop of blood from Alvar's face to his very heart. But he shook off the stagnating dread. He combated the prejudices of his follower as unreasonable and unfounded. Hassan's alarm, however, could only be soothed by the fact, that so suddenly to change his plans would but excite suspicion. If Levya were what he feared, his visit must already have been followed by the usual terrific effects.

Alvar promised, however, to settle his affairs at Lisbon as speedily as he could, and return for Almah and his son, and convey them to some place of greater security until the imagined danger was passed.

In spite of his assumed indifference, however, Rodriguez could not bid his wife and child farewell without a pang of dread, which it was difficult to conceal. The step between life and death—security and destruction—was so small, it might be passed unconsciously, and then the strongest nerve might shudder at the dark abyss before him. Again and again he turned to go, and yet again returned; and it with a feeling literally of desperation he at length tore himself away.

A fearful trembling was on Almah's heart as she gazed after him, but she would not listen to its voice.

"It is folly," she said, self-upbraidingly. "My Alvar is ever chiding this too doubting heart. I will not disobey him, by fear and foreboding in his absence. The God of the nameless is with him and me," and she raised her eyes to the blue arch above her, with an expression that needed not voice to mark it prayer.

About a week after Alvar's departure, Almah was sitting by the cradle of her boy, watching his soft and rosy slumbers with a calm sweet thankfulness that such a treasure was her own. The season had been unusually hot and dry, but the apartment in which the young mother sat opened on a pleasant spot, thickly shaded with orange, lemon, and almond trees, and decked with a hundred other richly-hued and richly-scented plants; in the centre of which a fountain sent up its heavy showers, which fell back on the marble bed, with a splash and coolness peculiarly refreshing, and sparkled in the sun as glittering gems.

A fleet yet heavy step resounded from the garden, which seemed suddenly and forcibly restrained into a less agitated movement. A shadow fell between her and the sunshine, and, starting, Almah looked hastily up. Hassan Ben Ahmed stood before her, a paleness on his swarthy cheek, and a compression on his nether lip, betraying strong emotion painfully restrained.

"My husband! Hassan. What news bring you of him? Why are you alone?"

He laid his hand on her arm, and answered in a voice which so quivered that only ears eager as her own could have distinguished his meaning.

"Lady, dear, dear lady, you have a firm and faithful heart. Oh! for the love of Him who calls on you to suffer, awake its strength and firmness. My dear, my honoured lady, sink not, fail not! O God of mercy, support her now!" he added, flinging himself on his knees before her, as Almah one moment sprang up with a smothered shriek, and the next sank back on her seat rigid as marble.

Not another word she needed. Hassan thought to have prepared, gradually to have told, his dread intelligence; but he had said enough. Called upon to suffer, and for Him her God—her doom was revealed in those brief words. One minute of such agonized struggle, that her soul and body seemed about to part beneath it; and the wife and mother roused herself to do. Lip, cheek, and brow vied in their ashen whiteness with her robe; the blue veins rose distended as cords; and the voice—had not Hassan gazed upon her, he had not known it as her own.

She commanded him to tell her briefly all, and even while he spoke, seemed revolving in her own mind the decision which not four and twenty hours after Hassan's intelligence she put into execution.

It was as Ben Ahmed had feared. The known popularity and rumoured riches of Alvar Rodriguez had excited the jealousy of that secret and awful tribunal, the Inquisition, one of whose innumerable spies, under the feigned name of Leyva, had obtained entrance within Alvar's hospitable wall. One unguarded word or movement, the faintest semblance of secrecy or caution, were all sufficient; nay, without these, more than a common share of wealth or felicity was enough for the unconscious victims to be marked, tracked and seized, without preparation or suspicion of their fate. Alvar had chanced to mention his intended visit to Lisbon; and the better to conceal the agent of his arrest, as also to make it more secure, they waited till his arrival there, watched their opportunity, and seized and conveyed him to those cells whence few returned in life, propagating the charge of relapsed Judaism as the cause of his arrest. It was a charge too common for remark, and the power which interfered too mighty for resistance. The confusion of the arrest soon subsided; but it lasted long enough for the faithful Hassan to escape, and, by dint of very rapid travelling, reached Montes not four hours after his master's seizure. The day was in consequence before them, and he ceased not to conjure his lady to fly at once; the officers of the Inquisition could scarcely be there before nightfall.

"You must take advantage of it, Hassan, and all of you who love me. For my child, my boy," she had clasped to her bosom, and a convulsion contracted her beautiful features as she spoke, "you must take care of him; convey him to Holland or England. Take jewels and gold sufficient; and—and make him love his parents—he may never see either of them more. Hassan, Hassan, swear to protect my child!" she added, with a burst of such sudden and passionate agony it seemed as if life or reason must bend beneath it. Bewildered by her words, as terrified by her emotion, Ben Ahmed removed the trembling child from the fond arms that for the first time failed to support him, gave him hastily to the care of his nurse, who was also a Jewess, said a few words in Hebrew, detailing what had passed, beseeching her to prepare for flight, and then returned to his mistress. The effects of that prostrating agony remained, but she had so far conquered, as to seem outwardly calm; and in answer to his respectful and anxious looks, besought him not to fear for her, nor to dissuade her from her purpose, but to aid her in its accomplishment. She summoned her household around her, detailed what had befallen, and bade them seek their own safety in flight; and when in tears and grief they left her, and but those of her own faith remained, she solemnly committed her child to their care, and informed them of her own determination to proceed directly to Lisbon. In vain Hassan Ben Ahmed conjured her to give up the idea; it was little short of madness. How could she aid his master? Why not secure her own safety, that if indeed he should escape, the blessing of her love would be yet preserved him?

"Do not fear for your master, Hassan," was the calm reply; "ask not of my plans, for at this moment they seem but chaos, but of this be assured, we shall live or die together."

More she revealed not; but when the officers of the Inquisition arrived, near nightfall, they found nothing but deserted walls. The magnificent furniture and splendid paintings which alone remained, of course were seized by the Holy Office, by whom Alvar's property was also confiscated. Had his arrest been deferred three months longer, all would have gone—swept off by the same rapacious power, to whom great wealth was ever proof of great guilt—but as it was, the greater part, secured in Spain, remained untouched; a circumstance peculiarly fortunate, as Almah's plans needed the aid of gold.

We have no space to linger on the mother's feelings, as she parted from her boy; gazing on him, perhaps, for the last time. Yet she neither wept nor sighed. There was but one other feeling stronger in that gentle bosom—a wife's devotion—and to that alone she might listen now.

Great was old Gonzalos' terror and astonishment when Almah, attended only by Hassan Ben Ahmed, and both attired in the Moorish costume, entered his dwelling and implored his concealment and aid. The arrest of Alvar Rodriguez had, of course, thrown every secret Hebrew into the greatest alarm, though none dared be evinced. Gonzalos' only hope and consolation was that Almah and her child had escaped; and to see her in the very centre of danger, even to listen to her calmly proposed plans, seemed so like madness, that he used every effort to alarm her into their relinquishment. But this could not be; and with the darkest forebodings, the old man at length yielded to the stronger, more devoted spirit with whom he had to deal.

His mistress once safely under Gonzalos' roof, Ben Ahmed departed, under cover of night, in compliance with her earnest entreaties to rejoin her child, and to convey him and his nurse to England, that blessed land, where the veil of secrecy could be removed.

About a week after the incarceration of Alvar, a young Moor sought and obtained admission to the presence of Juan Pacheco, the secretary of the Inquisition, as informer against Alvar Rodriguez. He stated that he had taken service with him as clerk or secretary, on condition that he would give him baptism and instruction in the holy Catholic faith; that Alvar had not yet done so; that many things in his establishment proclaimed a looseness of orthodox principles, which the Holy Office would do well to notice. Meanwhile he humbly offered a purse containing seventy pieces of gold, to obtain masses for his salvation.

This last argument carried more weight than all the rest. The young Moor, who boldly gave his name as Hassan Ben Ahmed (which was confirmation strong of his previous statement, as in Leyva's information of Alvar and his household the Moorish secretary was particularly specified), was listened to with attention and finally received in Pacheco's own household as junior clerk and servant to the Holy Office.

Despite his extreme youthfulness and delicacy of figure, face, and voice, Hassan's activity and zeal to oblige every member of the Holy Office, superiors and inferiors, gradually gained him the favour and goodwill of all. There was no end to his resources for serving others; and thus he had more opportunities of seeing the prisoners in a few weeks, than others of the same rank as himself had had in years. But the prisoner he most longed to see was still unfound, and it was not till summoned before his judges, in the grand of inquisition and of torture, Hassan Ben Ahmed gazed once more upon his former master. He had attended Pacheco in his situation of junior clerk, but had seated himself so deeply in the shade that, though every movement in both the face and form of Alvar was distinguishable to him, Hassan himself was invisible.

The trial, if trial such iniquitous proceedings may be called, proceeded; but in nought did Alvar Rodriguez fail in his bearing or defence. Marvellous and superhuman must that power have been which, in such a scene and hour, prevented all betrayal of the true faith the victims bore. Once Judaism confessed, the doom was death; and again and again have the sons of Israel remained in the terrible dungeons of the Inquisition—endured every species of torture during a space of seven, ten, or twelve years, and then been released, because no proof could be brought of their being indeed that cursed thing—a Jew. And then it was that they fled from scenes of such fearful trial to lands of toleration and freedom, and there embraced openly and rejoicingly that blessed faith, for which in secret they had borne so much.

Alvar Rodriguez was one of these—prepared to suffer, but not reveal. They applied the torture, but neither word nor groan was extracted from him. Engrossed with the prisoner, for it was his task to write down whatever disjointed words might escape his lips, Pacheco neither noticed nor even remembered the presence of the young Moor. No unusual paleness could be visible on his embrowned check, but his whole frame felt to himself to have become rigid as stone; a deadly sickness had crept over him, and the terrible conviction of all which rested with him to do alone prevented his sinking senseless on the earth.

The terrible struggle was at length at an end. Alvar was released for the time being, and remanded to his dungeon. Availing himself of the liberty he enjoyed in the little notice now taken of his movements, Hassan reached the prison before either Alvar or his guards. A rapid glance told him its situation, overlooking a retired part of the court, cultivated as a garden. The height of the wall seemed about forty feet, and there were no windows of observation on either side. This was fortunate, the more so as Hassan had before made friends with the old gardener, and pretending excessive love of gardening, had worked just under the window, little dreaming its vicinity to him he sought.

A well-known Hebrew air, with its plaintive Hebrew words, sung tremblingly and softly under his window, first roused Alvar to the sense that a friend was near. He started, almost in superstitious terror, for the voice seemed an echo to that which was ever sounding in his heart. That loved one it could not be, nay, he dared not even wish it; but still the words were Hebrew, and, for the first time, memory flashed back a figure in Moorish garb who had flitted by him on his return to his prison, after his examination.

Hassan, the faithful Hassan! Alvar felt certain it could be none but he; though, in the moment of sudden excitement, the voice had seemed another's. He looked from the window; the Moor was bending over the flowers, but Alvar felt confirmed in his suspicions, and his heart throbbed with the sudden hope of liberty. He whistled, and a movement in the figure below convinced him he was heard.

One point was gained; the next was more fraught with danger, yet it was accomplished. In a bunch of flowers, drawn up by a thin string which Alvar chanced to possess, Ben Ahmed had concealed a file; and as he watched it ascend, and beheld the flowers scattered to the winds, in token that they had done their work, for Alvar dared not retain them in his prison, Hassan felt again the prostration of bodily power which had before assailed him for such a different cause, and it was an almost convulsive effort to retain his faculties; but a merciful Providence watched over him and Alvar making the feeblest and the weakest, instruments of his all-sustaining love.

We are not permitted space to linger on the various ingenious methods adopted by Hassan Ben Ahmed to forward and mature his plans. Suffice it that all seemed to smile upon him. The termination of the garden wall led, by a concealed door, to a subterranean passage running to the banks of the Tagus. This fact, as also the secret spring of the trap, the old gardener in a moment of unwise conviviality imparted to Ben Ahmed, little imagining the special blessing which such unexpected information secured.

An alcayde and about twenty guards did sometimes patrol the garden within sight of Alvar's window; but this did not occur often, such caution seeming unnecessary.[1]

It had been an evening of unwonted festivity among the soldiers and servants of the Holy Office, which had at length subsided into the heavy slumbers of general intoxication. Hassan had supped with the gardener, and plying him well with wine, soon produced the desired effect. Four months had the Moor spent within the dreaded walls, and the moment had now come when delay need be no more. At midnight all was hushed into profound silence, not a leaf stirred, and the night was so unusually still that the faintest sound would have been distinguished. Hassan stealthily crept round the outposts. Many of the guards were slumbering in various attitudes upon their posts, and others, dependent on his promised watchfulness, were literally deserted. He stood beneath the window. One moment he clasped his hands and bowed his head in one mighty, piercing,

1 Alcayde: a prison warden.

though silent prayer, and then dug hastily in the flower-bed at his feet, removing from thence a ladder of ropes, which had lain there some days concealed, and flung a pebble with correct aim against the bars of Alvar's window. The sound, though scarcely loud enough to disturb a bird, reverberated on the trembling heart which heard, as if a thousand cannons had been discharged.

A moment of agonized suspense and Alvar Rodriguez stood at the window, the bar he had removed in his hand. He let down the string, to which Hassan's now trembling hands secured the ladder and drew it to the wall. His descent could not have occupied two minutes, at the extent; but to that solitary watcher what eternity of suffering did they seem! Alvar was at his side, had clasped his hands, had called him "Hassan! brother!" in tones of intense feeling, but no word replied. He sought to fly, to point to the desired haven, but his feet seemed suddenly rooted to the earth. Alvar threw his arm around him, and drew him forwards. A sudden and unnatural strength returned. Noiselessly and fleetly as their feet could go, they sped beneath the shadow of the wall. A hundred yards alone divided them from the secret door. A sudden sound broke the oppressive stillness. It was the tramp of heavy feet and the clash of arms; the light of many torches flashed upon the darkness. They darted forward in the fearful excitement of despair; but the effort was void and vain. A wild shout of challenge—of alarm—and they were surrounded, captured, so suddenly, so rapidly, Alvar's very senses seemed to reel; but frightfully they were recalled. A shriek, so piercing, it seemed to rend the very heavens, burst through the still air. The figure of the Moor rushed from the detaining grasp of the soldiery, regardless of bared steel and pointed guns, and flung himself at the feet of Alvar.

"O God, my husband—I have murdered him!" were the strange appalling words which burst upon his ear, and the lights flashing upon his face, as he sank prostrate and lifeless on the earth, revealed to Alvar's tortured senses the features of his WIFE.

How long that dead faint continued Almah knew not, but when sense returned she found herself in a dark and dismal cell, her upper garment and turban removed, while the plentiful supply of water, which had partially restored life, had removed in a great degree the dye which had given her countenance its Moorish hue. Had she wished to continue concealment, one glance around her would have proved the effort vain. Her sex was already known, and the stern dark countenances near her breathed but ruthlessness and rage. Some brief questions were asked relative to her name, intent, and faith, which she answered calmly.

"In revealing my name," she said, "my intention must also be disclosed. The wife of Alvar Rodriguez had not sought these realms of torture and death, had not undergone all the miseries of disguise and servitude, but for one hope, one intent—the liberty of her husband."

"Thus proving his guilt," was the rejoinder. "Had you known him innocent, you would have waited the justice of the Holy Office to give him freedom."

"Justice," she repeated, bitterly. "Had the innocent never suffered, I might have trusted. But I know accusation was synonymous with death, and therefore came I here. For my faith, mine is my husband's."

"And know you the doom of all who attempt or abet escape? Death—death by burning! and this you have hurled upon him and yourself. It is not the Holy Office, but his wife who has condemned him;" and with gibing laugh they left her, securing with heavy bolt and bar the iron door. She darted forwards, beseeching them, as they hoped for mercy, to take her to her husband, to confine them underground a thousand fathoms deep, so that they might but be together; but only the hollow echo of her own voice replied, and the wretched girl sunk back upon the ground, relieved from present suffering by long hours of utter insensibility.

It was not till brought from their respective prisons to hear pronounced on them the sentence of death, that Alvar Rodriguez and his heroic wife once more gazed upon each other.

They had provided Almah, at her own entreaty, with female habiliments; for, in the bewildering agony of her spirit, she attributed the failure of her scheme for the rescue of her husband to her having disobeyed the positive command of God and adopted a male disguise, which in His eyes was abomination, but which in her wild desire to save Alvar she had completely overlooked, and she now in consequence shrunk from the fatal garb with agony and loathing. Yet despite the haggard look of intense mental and bodily suffering, the loss of her lovely hair, which she had cut close to her head, lest by the merest chance its length and luxuriance should discover her, so exquisite, so touching, was her delicate loveliness, that her very judges, stern, unbending as was their nature, looked on her with an admiration almost softening them to mercy.

And now, for the first time, Alvar's manly composure seemed about to desert him. He, too, had suffered almost as herself, save that her devotedness, her love, appeared to give strength, to endow him with courage, even to look upon her fate, blended as it now was with his own, with calm trust in the merciful God who called him thus early to Himself. Almah could not realise such thoughts. But one image was ever present, seeming to mock her very misery to madness. Her effort had failed; had she not so wildly sought her husband's escape—had she but waited—they might have released him; and now, what was she but his murderess?

Little passed between the prisoners and their judges. Their guilt was all sufficiently proved by their endeavours to escape, which in itself was a crime always visited by death; and for these manifold sins and misdemeanours they were sentenced to be burnt alive, on All Saints' day, in the grand square of the Inquisition, at nine o'clock in the morning, and proclamation commanded to be made throughout Lisbon, that all who sought to witness and assist at the ceremony should receive remission of sins, and be accounted worthy servants of Jesus Christ.[1] The lesser severity of strangling the victims before burning was denied them, as they neither repented nor had trusted to the justice and clemency of the Holy Office, but had attempted to avert a deserved fate by flight.

Not a muscle of Alvar's fine countenance moved during this awful sentence. He stood proudly and loftily erect, regarding those that spake with an eye, bright, stern, unflinching as their own; but a change passed over it as, breaking from the guard around, Almah flung herself on her knees at his feet.

"Alvar! Alvar! I have murdered—my husband, oh, my husband, say you forgive—forgive—"

"Hush, hush, beloved! mine own heroic Almah, fail not now!" he

---

1 All Saints' Day: a Catholic festival on the first of November, celebrating the saints. Often, churches are dedicated on this day.

answered, with a calm and tender seriousness, which to still that crushing agony, strengthened her to bear and raising her, he pressed her to his breast.

"We have but to die as we have lived, my own! true to that God whose chosen and whose first-born we are, have been, and shall be unto death, aye, and *beyond* it. He will protect our poor orphan, for He has promised the fatherless shall be His care. Look up, my beloved, and say you can face death with Alvar, calmly, faithfully, as you sought to live for him. God has chosen for us a better heritage than one of earth."

She raised her head from his bosom; the terror and the agony had passed from that sweet face—it was tranquil as his own.

"It was not my own death I feared," she said, unfalteringly, "it was but the weakness of human love; but it is over now. Love is mightier than death; there is only love in heaven."[1]

"Aye!" answered Alvar, and proudly and sternly he waved back the soldiers who had hurried forward to divide them. "Men of a mistaken and bloody creed, behold how the scorned and persecuted Israelites can love and die. While there was a hope that we could serve our God, the Holy and the only One, better in life than in death, it was our duty to preserve that life, and endure torture for His sake, rather than reveal the precious secret of our sainted faith and heavenly heritage. But now that hope is at an end, now that no human means can save us from the doom pronounced, know ye have judged rightly of our creed. We ARE those chosen children of God by you deemed blasphemous and heretic. Do what you will men of blood and guile, ye cannot rob us of our faith."

The impassioned tones of natural eloquence awed even the rude crowd around; but more was not permitted. Rudely severed, and committed to their own guards, the prisoners were borne to their respective dungeons. To Almah those earnest words had been as the voice of an angel, hushing every former pang to rest; and in the solitude and darkness of the intervening hours, even the thought of her child could not rob her soul of its calm or prayer of its strength.

The 1st of November, 1755, dawned cloudless and lovely as it had been the last forty days. Never had there been a season more gor-

1 Cf. Song of Songs 8.6: "Love is strong as death."

geous in its sunny splendour, more brilliant in the intense azure of its arching heaven than the present. Scarcely any rain had fallen for many months, and the heat had at first been intolerable, but within the last six weeks a freshness and coolness had infused the atmosphere and revived the earth.

As it was not a regular *auto da fe* (Alvar and his wife being the only victims), the awful ceremony of burning was to take place in the square, of which the buildings of the Inquisition formed one side.[1] Mass had been performed before daybreak in the chapel of the Inquisition, at which the victims were compelled to be present, and about half-past seven the dread procession left the Inquisition gates. The soldiers and minor servitors marched first, forming a hollow square, in the centre of which were the stakes and huge faggots piled around. Then came the sacred cross, covered with a black veil, and its bodyguard of priests. The victims, each surrounded by monks, appeared next, closely followed by the higher officers and inquisitors, and a band of fifty men, in rich dresses of black satin and silver, closed the procession.

We have no space to linger on the ceremonies always attendant on the burning of Inquisitorial prisoners. Although, from the more private nature of the rites, these ceremonies were greatly curtailed, it was rather more than half an hour after nine when the victims were bound to their respective stakes, and the executioners approached with their blazing brands.

There was no change in the countenance of either prisoner. Pale they were, yet calm and firm; all of human feeling had been merged in the martyr's courage and the martyr's faith.

One look had been exchanged between them—of love spiritualized to look beyond the grave—of encouragement to endure for their God, even to the end. The sky was still cloudless, the sun still looked down on that scene of horror; and then was a hush—a pause—for so it felt in nature, that stilled the very breathing of those around.

---

1 *Auto da fe*: test of faith. At first, those whom the Inquisition convicted of heresy were expelled from Spain and Portugal. Later, as the Inquisition took further hold, heretics were given the choice either to convert to Catholicism or be burned at the stake. The ritual burning was the "test of faith."

"Hear, O Israel, the Lord our God, the Lord is ONE[1]—the Sole and Holy One; there is no unity like His unity!" were the words which broke that awful pause, in a voice distinct, unfaltering, and musical as its wont; and it was echoed by the sweet tones from woman's lips, so thrilling in their melody, the rudest nature started. It was the signal of their fate. The executioners hastened forward, the brands were applied to the turf of the piles, the flames blazed up beneath their hand—when at that moment there came a shock as if the very earth were cloven asunder, the heavens rent in twain. A crash so loud, yea so fearful, so appalling, as if the whole of Lisbon had been shivered to its foundations, and a shriek, or rather thousands and thousands of human voices, blended in one wild piercing cry of agony and terror, seeming to burst from every quarter at the self-same instant, and fraught with universal woe. The buildings around shook, as impelled by a mighty whirl wind, though no sound of such was heard. The earth heaved, yawned, closed, and rocked again, as the billows of the ocean were lashed to fury. It was a moment of untold horror. The crowd assembled to witness the martyrs' death fled, wildly shrieking, on every side. Scattered to the heaving ground, the blazing piles lay powerless to injure; their bonds were shivered, their guards were fled. One bound brought Alvar to his wife, and he clasped her in his arms. "God, God of mercy, save us yet again! Be with us to the end!" he exclaimed, and faith winged the prayer. On, on he sped; up, up, in direction of the heights, where he knew comparative safety lay; but ere he reached them, the innumerable sights and sounds of horror that yawned upon his way! Every street, and square, and avenue was choked with shattered ruins, rent from top to bottom; houses, convents, and churches presented the most fearful aspect of ruin; while every second minute a new impetus seemed to be given to the convulsed earth, causing those that remained still perfect to rock and rend. Huge stones, falling from every crack, were crushing the miserable fugitives as they rushed on, seeking safety they knew not where. The rafters of

---

1 This is the first line of the *Shema*, the avowal of the Divine unity which was traditionally chanted by Jewish martyrs just before their deaths. The subsequent destruction of Lisbon alludes to the biblical stories of the Flood, Sodom and Gomorrah, and the Christian apocalypse in Revelation.

every roof, wrenched from their fastenings, stood upright a brief while, and then fell in hundreds together, with a crash perfectly appalling. The very ties of nature were severed in the wild search for safety. Individual life alone appeared worth preserving. None dared seek the fate of friends—none dared ask, "Who lives?" in that one scene of universal death.

On, on sped Alvar and his precious burden, on over the piles of ruins; on, unhurt amidst the showers of stones which, hurled in the air as easily as a ball cast from an infants hand, fell back again laden with a hundred deaths; on, amid the rocking and yawning earth, beholding thousands swallowed up, crushed and maimed, worse than death itself, for they were left to a lingering torture—to die a thousand deaths in anticipating one; on over the disfigured heaps of dead, and the unrecognised masses of what had once been magnificent and gorgeous buildings. His eye was well-nigh blinded with the shaking and tottering movement of all things animate and inanimate before him; and his path obscured by the sudden and awful darkness, which had changed that bright glowing hue of the sunny sky into a pall of dense and terrible blackness, becoming thicker and denser with every succeeding minute, till a darkness which might be felt, enveloped that devoted city as with the grim shadow of death. His ear was deafened by the appalling sounds of human agony and Nature's wrath; for now, sounds as of a hundred waterspouts, the dull continued roar of subterranean thunder, becoming at times loud as the discharge of a thousand cannons; at others, resembling the sharp grating sound of hundreds and hundreds of chariots driving full speed over the stones; and this, mingled with the piercing shrieks of women, the hoarser cries and shouts of men, the deep terrible groans of mental agony, and the shriller screams of instantaneous death, had usurped the place of the previous awful stillness, till every sense of those who yet survived seemed distorted and maddened. And Nature herself, convulsed and freed from restraining bonds, appeared about to return to that chaos whence she had leaped at the word of God.

Still, still Alvar rushed forwards, preserved amidst it all, as if the arm of a merciful Providence was indeed around him and his Almah, marking them for life in the very midst of death. Making his rapid way across the ruins of St. Paul's, which magnificent church had fallen in the first shock, crushing the vast congregation assembled within its walls, Alvar paused one moment, undecided whether to seek the banks of the river or still to make for the western heights. There was a moment's hush and pause in the convulsion of nature, but Alvar dared not hope for its continuance. Ever and anon the earth still heaved, and houses opened from base to roof and closed without further damage. With a brief fervid cry for continued guidance and protection, scarcely conscious which way in reality he took, and still folding Almah to his bosom—so supernaturally strengthened that the weakness of humanity seemed far from him—Rodriguez, hurried on, taking the most open path to the Estrella Hill. An open space was gained, half-way to the summit, commanding a view of the banks of the river and the ruins around. Panting, almost breathless, yet still struggling with his own exhaustion to encourage Almah, Alvar an instant rested, ere he plunged anew into the narrower streets. A shock, violent, destructive, convulsive as the first, flung them prostrate; while the renewed and increased sounds of wailing, the tremendous and repeated crashes on every side, the disappearance of the towers, steeples, and turrets which yet remained, revealed the further destructiveness which had befallen. A new and terrible cry added to the universal horror.

"The sea! the sea!" Alvar sprung to his feet and, clasped in each other's arms, he and Almah gazed beneath. Not a breath of wind stirred, yet the river (which being at that point four miles wide appeared like the element they had termed it) tossed and heaved as impelled by a mighty storm—and on it came, roaring, foaming, tumbling, as every bound were loosed; on, over the land to the very heart of the devoted city, sweeping off hundreds in its course, and retiring with such velocity, and so far beyond its natural banks, that vessels were left dry which had five minutes before ridden in water seven fathoms deep. Again and again this phenomenon took place; the vessels in the river, at the same instant, whirled round and round with frightful rapidity, and smaller boats dashed upwards, falling back to disappear beneath the booming waters. As if chained to the spot where they stood, fascinated by this very horror, Alvar and his wife yet gazed; their glance fixed on the new marble quay, where thousands and thousands of the fugitives had congregated, fixed, as if unconsciously foreboding what was to befall. Again the tide rushed in—on, on, over the massive ruins, heaving, raging, swelling, as a living thing; and at the same instant the quay and its vast burthen of humanity sunk within an abyss of boiling waters, into which the innumerable boats around were alike impelled, leaving not a trace, even when the angry waters returned to their channel, suddenly as they had left it, to mark what had been.

"'Twas the voice of God impelled me hither, rather than pausing beside those fated banks. Almah, my best beloved, bear up yet a brief while more—He will spare and save us as he hath done now. Merciful Providence! Behold another wrathful element threatens to swallow up all of life and property which yet remains. Great God, this is terrible!"

And terrible it was: from three several parts of the ruined city huge fires suddenly blazed up, hissing, crackling, ascending as clear columns of liquid flame; up against the pitchy darkness, infusing it with tenfold horror—spreading on every side—consuming all of wood and wall which the earth and water had left unscathed; wreathing its serpent-like folds in and out the ruins, forming strange and terribly beautiful shapes of glowing colouring; fascinating the eye with admiration, yet bidding the blood chill and the flesh creep. Fresh cries and shouts had marked its rise and progress; but, aghast and stupefied, those who yet survived made no effort to check its way, and on every side it spread, forming lanes and squares of glowing red, flinging its lurid glare so vividly around, that even those on the distant heights could see to read by it; and fearful was the scene that awful light revealed. Now, for the first time could Alvar trace the full extent of destruction which had befallen. That glorious city, which a few brief hours previous lay reposing in its gorgeous sunlight—mighty in its palaces and towers—in its churches, convents, theatres, magazines, and dwellings—rich in its numberless artizans and stores—lay perished and prostrate as the grim spectre of long ages past, save that the fearful groups yet passing to and fro, or huddled in kneeling and standing masses, some bathed in the red glare of the increasing fires, others black and shapeless—save when a sudden flame flashed on them, disclosing what they were—revealed a strange and horrible PRESENT, yet lingering amid what seemed the shadows of a fearful PAST. Nor was the convulsion of nature yet at an end;—the earth still rocked and heaved at intervals, often impelling the hissing flames more strongly and devouringly forward, and by tossing the masses of burning ruin to and fro, gave them the semblance of a sea of flame. The ocean itself too, yet rose and sunk, and rose again; vessels were torn from their cables, anchors wrenched from their soundings and hurled in the air—while the warring waters, the muttering thunders, the crackling flames, formed a combination of sounds which, even without their dread adjuncts of human agony and terror, were all-sufficient to freeze the very life-blood, and banish every sense and feeling, save that of stupefying dread.

But human love, and superhuman faith, saved from the stagnating horror. The conviction that the God of his fathers was present with him, and would save him and Almah to the end, never left him for an instant, but urged him to exertions which, had he not had this all-supporting faith, he would himself have deemed impossible. And his faith spake truth. The God of infinite mercy, who had stretched out His own right hand to save, and marked the impotence of the wrath and cruelty of man, was with him still, and, despite of the horrors yet lingering round them, despite of the varied trials, fatigues, and privations attendant on their rapid flight, led them to life and joy, and bade them stand forth the witnesses and proclaimers of His unfailing love, His everlasting providence!

With the great earthquake of Lisbon, the commencement of which our preceding pages have faintly endeavoured to portray, and its terrible effects on four millions of square miles, our tale has no further connection. The third day brought our poor fugitives to Badajoz, where Alvar's property had been secured. They tarried there only long enough to learn the blessed tidings of Hassan Ben Ahmed's safe arrival in England with their child; that his faithfulness, in conjunction with that of their agent in Spain, had already safely transmitted the bulk of their property to the English funds; and to obtain Ben Ahmed's address, forward tidings of their providential escape to him, and proceed on their journey.

An anxious but not a prolonged interval enabled them to accomplish it safely, and once more did the doubly-rescued press their precious boy to their yearning hearts and feel that conjugal and parental love burned, if it could be, the dearer, brighter, more unspeakably precious, from the dangers they had passed; and not human love alone. The veil of secrecy was removed, they were in a land whose merciful and liberal government granted to the exile and the wanderer a home of peace and rest, where they might worship the God of Israel according to the law he gave; and in hearts like those of Alvar and his Almah, prosperity could have no power to extinguish or deaden the religion of love and faith which adversity had engendered.

The appearance of old Gonzalos and his family in England, a short time after Alvah's arrival there, removed their last remaining anxiety, and gave them increased cause for thankfulness. Not a member of the merchant's family, and more wonderful still, not a portion of his property, had been lost amid the universal ruin; and to this very day, his descendants recall his providential preservation by giving, on every returning anniversary of that awful day, certain articles of clothing to a limited number of male and female poor.[1]

1844

1 A fact. [Aguilar's note.]

Figure 2. Line drawing of Rachel Perez carrying Ruth from the flaming house, frontispiece to *Home Scenes and Heart Studies* (London: Routledge, 1894). Photo: Michael Dunn.

THE PEREZ FAMILY

CHAPTER I.

LEADING out of one of those close, melancholy alleys in the environs of Liverpool was a small cottage, possessing little of comfort or beauty in outward appearance, but much in the interior in favour of its inhabitants; cleanliness and neatness were clearly visible, greatly in contradistinction to the neighbouring dwellings. There were no heaps of dirt and half-burnt ashes, no broken or even cracked panes in the brightly shining windows, not a grain of unseemly dust or stains either on door or ledge,—so that even poverty itself looked respectable. The cottage stood apart from the others, with a good piece of ground for a garden, which, stretching from the back, led through a narrow lane, to the banks of the Mersey, and thus permitted a fresher current of air. The garden was carefully and prettily laid out, and planted with the sweetest flowers; the small parlour and kitchen of the cottage opened into it, and so, greatly to the disappointment and vexation of the gossips of the alley, nothing could be gleaned of the sayings and doings of its inmates. Within the cottage the same refinement was visible; the furniture, though old and poor, was always clean and neatly arranged. The *Mezzuzot* (Deut. vi. 9, 20) were carefully secured to every doorpost and altogether there was an indescribable something pervading the dwelling, that in the very midst of present poverty seemed to tell of former and more prosperous days.[1]

Simeon and Rachel Perez had married with every prospect of getting on well in the world. Neither were very young; for though they had been many years truly devoted to each other, they were prudent, and had waited till mutual industry had removed many of the difficulties and obstacles to their union. All which might have

1 *Mezzuzot* are Jewish ritual objects hung on the doorposts of the house. The *mezzuzah* consists of a small rectangular case of wood, glass, metal, or stone inscribed on the outside with the Hebrew word for the Almighty (*Shaddai*), and containing parchment upon which Deut. 6.4-9 and 11.13-21 are written in Hebrew calligraphy. It serves as a visual reminder of one's commitment to Judaism. Jewish folk tradition saw the *mezzuzah* as an amulet, ascribing powers of divine protection to it.

been irksome was persevered in through the strength of this honest, unchanging affection; and when the goal was gained, and they were married, all the period of their mutual labour seemed but as a watch in the night, compared to the happiness they then enjoyed.

Simeon had been for several years foreman to a watchmaker, and was remarkably skilful in the business. Rachel had been principal assistant to a mantua-maker, and all her leisure hours were employed in plaiting straw and various fancy works, which greatly increased her little store. Never forgetting the end they had in view, their mutual savings had so accumulated, that on their marriage, Perez was enabled to set up a small shop, which, conducted with honesty and economy, soon flourished, and every year brought in something to lay aside, besides amply providing for their fast increasing family.

The precepts of their God were obeyed by this worthy couple, not only in word but in deed. They proved their love for their heavenly Father, not only in their social and domestic conduct, but in such acts of charity and kindness, that many wondered how they could do so much for others without wronging their own. Perez and his wife were, however, if possible, yet more industrious and economical after their marriage than before, and many a time preferred to sacrifice a personal indulgence for the purer pleasure of doing good to others; and never did they do so without feeling that God blessed them in the deed.

A painful event calling Perez to London was the first alloy to their happiness. A younger sister of his wife, less prudent because, perhaps, possessed of somewhat more personal attraction, had won the attentions of a young man who had come down to Liverpool, he said, for a week's pleasure. No one knew anything about Isaac Levison. As a companion, Perez himself owned he was very entertaining, but that was not quite sufficient to make him a good husband. Assurances that he was well able to support a wife and family, with Perez and Rachel (they were not then married), went for nothing; they wanted proofs, and these he either could not or would not bring; but in vain they remonstrated. Leah had never liked their authority or good example, and in this point determined to have her own way.

They were married, and left Liverpool to reside in London, and Leah's communications were too few and far between to betray much concerning their circumstances. At length came a letter, stating that Leah was a mother, but telling also that poverty and privation had stolen upon them. Their substance in a few troubled years had made itself wings, and flown away when most needed; and Leah now applied for assistance to those very friends whose kindness and virtue she had so often treated with contempt. The fact was, Levison had embarked all his little capital (collected no one knew how) in an establishment dashing in appearance but wanting the basis of honesty and religion. After seeming to flourish for a few years, it, of course, failed, at last exposing its proprietors to deserved odium and distrust, and their families to irretrievable distress.

For seven years Perez and his wife almost supported Leah and her child (secretly indeed, for no one in Liverpool imagined they had need to do so). Leah was still too dear, for the faults and follies of her husband, and perhaps her own imprudences, to form any subject of conversation with her relatives.

At length Leah wrote that she was ill, very ill. She thought the hand of death was on her; and she feared it for her child, her darling Sarah, whom she had striven to preserve pure amidst the scenes of misery and sin which she now confessed but too often neared her dwelling. What would become of her? Who would protect her? How dared she appeal to the God of the orphan, when her earthly father yet lived, seeming to forget there was a God? Perez and his wife perused that sad letter together; but ere it was completed, Rachel had sunk in bitter tears upon his bosom, seeking to speak the boon which was in her heart; but, though it found no words, Perez answered—

"You are right, dear wife; one more will make little difference in our household. Providence blessed us with four children, and has been pleased to deprive us of one. Sarah shall take her place: and in snatching her from the infection of vice and shame, may we not ask and hope a blessing? Do not weep then, my Rachel; Leah may not be so ill as she thinks. I will go and bring her and her child; and there may be happy days in store for them yet."

Perez departed that same night by the mail to London; but prompt as he was, poor Leah's sufferings were terminated before his arrival. Her death, though in itself a painful shock, was less a subject of misery and depression, to a mind almost rigid in its notions of integrity and honour as that of Perez, than the fearful state of wretchedness and shame into which Isaac Levison had fallen. Perez soon perceived that all hope of effecting a reformation was absolute folly. His poor child had been so repeatedly prevented attending school, by his intemperate or violent conduct, that she was at length excluded. Levison could give no good reason for depriving his little girl of these advantages, except that he hated the elders who were in office; that he did not see why some should be rich and some should be poor, and why the former should Lord it over the latter. He was as good as they were any day, and his daughter should not be browbeaten or governed by anyone, however she might call herself a lady. To reason with folly Perez felt was foolishness, and so he contented himself with entreating Levison to permit his taking the little Sarah, at least for a time, into his family. Levison imagined Perez was the same rank as himself, and, therefore, that his pride could not be injured by his consenting. Equal in *birth* perhaps they were, but as far removed in their present ranks as vice from virtue, dishonesty from truth.

Perez, however, glad and grateful for having gained his point, made no comment on the many muttered remarks of his brother-in-law, as to his *conferring*, not *receiving* an obligation, by giving his child to the care of her aunt, but hastened home, longing to offer the best comfort to his wife's sorrow by placing the rescued Sarah in her arms. And it was a comfort, for gradually Rachel traced a hand of love even in this affliction; the loss of her mother under such circumstances, proving perhaps, in the end, a blessing to the child, if her father would but leave her with them. She feared that he would not at first; but Perez smiled at the fear as foolishness, and it gradually dwindled away; for years passed, and the little Sarah grew from childhood into womanhood; still an inmate of her uncle's family, almost forgetting she had any father but himself.

But it is not to the unrighteous or the irreligious only that misfortunes come. Nay, *they* may flourish for a time, and give no evidence that there is a just and merciful God, who ruleth. But even those who have loved and served Him through long years of probity and justice, and who, according to frail human perceptions, would look for nothing but favour at His hand, are yet afflicted with many sorrows; and our feeble and insufficient wisdom would complain that such things are. If this world were all, then indeed we might murmur and rebel; but our God himself has assured us, "There will come a day when He will discern between the righteous and the wicked, between those who serve God and those who serve Him not."[1] And it is our part to wait patiently for that day, and that better world where that word will be fulfilled.

Perez had now five children. Reuben, his eldest son, was full five years older than the rest, a circumstance of rejoicing to Perez, as he hoped his son would supply his place to his family, should he be called away before the threescore and ten years allotted as the age of man.

To do all he could towards obtaining this end, Perez early associated his son with him in his own business of watchmaking; but too soon, unhappily, the parents discovered that a heavy grief awaited them, from him to whom they had most fondly looked for joy. They had indeed striven and prayed to train up their child in the way he should go, but it seemed as if his after years would not confirm the sage monarch's concluding words.[2] Wild, thoughtless, and headstrong, Reuben, after a very brief trial, determined that his father's business was not according to his taste, and he could not follow it. His father's authority indeed kept him steady for a few years, but it was continued rebellion and reproof; and often and often the father's hard-earned savings were sacrificed for the wild freaks and extravagance of the son. Perez trembled lest the other members of his family, equally dear, should suffer eventual loss; but there is something in the hearts of Jewish parents towards an eldest son, which calls imperatively for indulgence towards, and concealment of his failings. Again and again Perez expended sums much larger than he could conveniently afford, in endeavouring to fix his son in business according to his inclinations; but no sooner was he apparently settled and comfortable, and his really excellent abilities fairly drawn forth, than, by negligence or inattention, or some graver misdemeanour, he disgusted his employers, and, after a little longer trial, was returned on his father's hands.

Deeply and bitterly his parents grieved, using every affectionate

---

1 Mal. 3.18.

2 Prov. 22.6, traditionally ascribed to King Solomon, remarks, "Train up a child in the way he should go; and when he is old he will not depart from it."

argument to convince him of the evil of his ways, and bring him back again to the paths of joy. They did not desist, however their efforts and prayers seemed alike unanswered; they did not fail in faith, though often it was trembling and faint within them. One hope they had; Reuben was not hardened. Often he would repent in tears and agony of spirit, and deplore his own ill fate, that he was destined to bring misery to parents he so dearly loved. But he refused to believe that it only needed energy to rouse himself from his folly, for as yet it was scarcely more. He said he could not help himself, could not effect any change, and therefore made no effort to do so. But that which grieved his parents far more than all else, was his total indifference to the religion of his forefathers. His ears, even as his heart and mind, were closed to those divine truths his parents had so carefully inculcated. He knew his duty too well to betray infidelity and indifference in their presence, but they loved him too well to be blind to their existence.

"What is it to be a Jew," they heard him once say to a companion, "but to be cut off from every honourable and manly employment? To be bound, fettered to an obsolete belief, which does but cramp our energies, and bind us to detestable trade. No wonder we are looked upon with contempt, believed to be bowed, crushed to the very earth, as void of all spirit or energy, only because we have no opportunity of showing them."

Little did he know the bitter tears these words wrung from his poor mother, that no sleep visited his father's eyes that night. Was this an answer to their anxious prayer? Yet they trusted still.

Anxiety and grief did not prevent Perez attending to his business; but either from the many drains upon his little capital, or that trade was just at that time in a very low state, his prosperity had begun visibly to decrease. And not long afterwards a misfortune occurred productive of much more painful affliction than even the loss of property which it so seriously involved. A dreadful fire broke out in the neighbourhood, gaining such an alarming height ere it was discovered, that assistance was almost useless. Amongst the greatest sufferers were Perez and his family. Their happy home was entirely consumed, and all the little valuables it had contained completely destroyed. Perez gazed on ruin. For one brief moment he stood as thunderstricken, but then a terrible shriek aroused him. He looked around. He thought he had seen all whom he loved in safety, but at one glance he saw his little Ruth was not there. His wife had caught a glimpse of the child in a part of the building which the flames had not yet reached, and with that wild shriek had flown to save her. He saw her as she made her way through falling rafters and blazing walls; he made a rush forward to join and rescue, or die with her; but his children clung round him in speechless terror; his friends and neighbours seconded them, and before he could effectually break from them, a loud congratulatory shout proclaimed that the daring mother had reached her child. A dozen ladders were hurried forward, their bearers all eager to be the first to plant the means of effectual escape; and clasping her Ruth closely to her breast, regardless of her increasing weight (for terror had rendered the poor child utterly powerless), the mother's step was on the ladder, and a hush fell upon the assembled hundreds. There was no sound save the roar of the devouring element and the play of the engines. The flames were just nearing the beam on which the ladder leaned, but hope was strong that Rachel would reach the ground ere this frail support gave way; and numbers pressed round, regardless of the suffocating smoke and heat, in the vain hope of speeding her descent.

Perez had ceased his struggles the moment his wife appeared. With clasped hands, and cheeks and lips so blanched, as even in that lurid light to startle by their ghastliness, he remained, his eyes starting from their sockets in their intense and agonized gaze. He saw only his wife and child; but his children, with horror which froze their very blood, could look only on the fast-approaching flames. A wild cry of terror was bursting from young Joseph, Ruth's twin brother, but Sarah, with instinctive feeling, dreading lest that cry should reach his mother's ears, and awaken her to her danger, caught him in her arms, and soothed him into silence.

Carefully and slowly Rachel descended. She gave no look around her. No one knew if she was conscious of her danger, which was becoming more and more imminent. Then came a smothered groan from all, all save the husband and the father. The flame had reached the beam,—it cracked—caught—the top of the ladder was wreathed with smoke and fire. Was there faltering in her step, or did the frail support totter beneath her weight? The half was past, but one-third to the ground remained; fiercer and fiercer the flames roared and rose above her, but yet there was hope. It failed; the beam gave way, the ladder fell, and Rachel and her child were precipitated to the ground. A heavy groan mingled with the wild shriek of horror which burst around. Perez rushed like a maniac forward; but louder, shriller above it all a cry resounded, "Mother! mother! oh God, my mother! why was not I beside you, to save Ruth in your stead? Mother, speak; oh, speak to me again!" And the father and son, each unconscious of the other's presence, met beside what seemed the lifeless body of one to both so dear.

But Rachel was not dead, though fearfully injured; and it was in the long serious illness that followed, Reuben proved that, despite his many faults and follies, affection was not all extinguished; love for his mother remained in its full force, and in his devotion to her, his almost woman's tenderness, not only towards her but towards his little sister Ruth, whose eyes had been so injured by the heat and smoke as to occasion total blindness, he demonstrated qualities only too likely so to gain a woman's heart, as to shut her eyes to all other points of his character save them.

A subscription had indeed been made for the sufferers by the fire, but they were so numerous, that the portion of individuals was of course but small; and even this Perez's honest nature shrunk in suffering from accepting. Religious and energetic as he was, determined not to evince by word or sign how completely his spirit was crushed, and thus give the prejudiced of other faiths room to say, "the Jew has no resource, no comfort," he yet felt that he himself would never be enabled to hold up his head again; felt it at the very moment friends and neighbours were congratulating him on the equanimity, the cheerfulness with which he met and bore up against affliction.

Yet even now, when the skeptic and unbeliever would have said, surely the God he so faithfully served had deserted him, Perez felt he was not deserted,—that he had not laboured honestly and religiously so long in vain. The wild and wayward conduct of the son could not, in candid and liberal minds, tarnish the character of the father; and thus he was enabled easily and pleasantly to obtain advantageous situations for his two elder children.

The dwelling to which we originally introduced our reader was then to let; and from its miserably dilapidated condition (for when

Perez first saw it, it was not as we described), at a remarkably low rent. An influential friend made it habitable, and thither some three months after the fire, the family removed.

And where was Sarah Levison, in the midst of these changes and afflictions? In their heavy trial, did Rachel and Perez never regret they had made her as their own? nor permit the murmuring thought to enter, that, as the girl had a father, they had surely no need to support an additional burden? To such questions we think our readers will scarcely need an answer. As their own daughter Leah, they loved and cherished their niece, whose affection and gratitude towards them was yet stronger and more devoted than that of their own child, affectionate as she was. Leah had never known other than kind, untiring parents; never, even in dreams, imagined the misery in which her cousin's early years had passed. To Sarah, life had been a strange dark stream of grief and wrath, until she became an inmate of her uncle's house. Though only just seventeen when these heavy sorrows took place, her peculiarly quiet and reflective character and strong affections endowed her with the experience of more advanced age. She not only felt, but acted. Entering into the feelings alike of her uncle and aunt, she unconsciously soothed and strengthened both. She taught Leah's young, and, from its high and joyous temperament, somewhat rebellious spirit, submission and self-control. She strengthened in the young Simeon the ardent desire to work, and not only assist his father now, but to raise him again to his former station in life. She found time to impart to the little Joseph much instruction as she thought might aid in gaining him employment. Untiringly, caressingly, she nursed both her aunt and the poor little patient sufferer Ruth, telling such sweet tales of heaven, and its beautiful angels, and earth, and its pleasant places, and kind deeds, that the child would forget her sorrow as she listened, and fancy the sweet music of that gentle voice had never seemed so sweet before; and while it spoke, she could not forget to wish to look once more on the flowers, and trees, and sky. And Reuben, what was his cousin Sarah not to him in these months of remorseful agony, when he felt as if he could never more displease or grieve his parents; when again and again he cursed himself as the real cause of his father's ruin; for had not such large sums been wasted upon him, there might have been still capital enough to set him afloat again.

For several days and nights Sarah and Reuben had been joint watchers beside the beds of suffering; and the gentle voice of the former consoled, even while to the divine comfort and hope which she proffered, Reuben felt his heart was closed. He bade her speak on; he seemed, in those still, silent hours, to feel that, without her gentle influence, his very senses must have wandered; and that heart must have been colder and harsher than Sarah's, which could have done other than believe she was not indifferent to him. Sarah did not think of many little proofs of affection at the time; she was only conscious that, at the very period heavy affliction had entered her uncle's family, a new feeling, a new energy had awakened within her heart, and she was happy—oh, so happy!

It was to Sarah's exertions their new dwelling owed the comfort, cleanliness, and almost luxury of its interior arrangements; her example inspired Leah to throw aside the proud disdain with which she at first regarded their new home—to conquer the rebellious feeling which prompted her to entreat her father to apprentice her anywhere, so she need not live so differently at home; and not only to conquer that sinful pride, but use her every energy to rouse her natural spirits, and make her parents forget how their lot was changed: and the girl did so; for, in spite of youthful follies, there was good solid sense and warm feelings on which to work.

Sarah and Leah, then, worked in the interior, and Perez and Simeon improved the exterior of the house, so that when the little family assembled, there was comfort and peace around them, and thus their song of praise and thanksgiving mingled with and hallowed the customary prayer, with which the son of Israel ever sanctifies his newly-appointed dwelling.

Rachel could no longer work as she had done; her right arm had been so severely injured as to be nearly useless; but Sarah supplied her place so actively, so happily, that Rachel felt she had no right to murmur at her own uselessness: the poor motherless girl she had taken to her heart and home, returned tenfold all that had been bestowed. She could have entered into more than one lucrative situation, but she would not hear of leaving that home which she knew needed her presence and her services; and this was not the mere impulse of the moment: week after week, month after month, found her active, affectionate, persevering, as at first.

The most painful circumstance in their present dwelling was its low neighbourhood; and partially to remedy this evil, Sarah prevailed on her uncle to employ his leisure in cultivating the little garden behind the house, making their sitting-room and kitchen open into it, and contriving an entrance through them, so as scarcely to use the front, except for ingress and egress which necessity compelled. This arrangement was productive of a twofold good; it prevented all gossiping intercourse, which their neighbours had done all they could to introduce, and gave Perez an occupation which interested him although he might never have thought of it himself. Both local and national disadvantages often unite to debar the Jews from agriculture, and therefore it is a branch in which they are seldom, if ever, employed. Their scattered state among the nations, the occupations which misery and persecution compel them to adopt, are alone to blame for those peculiar characteristics which cause them to herd in the most miserable alleys of crowded cities, rather than the pure air and cheaper living of the country. Perez found pleasure and a degree of health in his new employment: the delight which it was to his poor little blind Ruth to sit by his side while he worked, and inhale the reviving scent of the newly-turned earth or budding flowers, would of itself have inspired him, but his wife too shared the enjoyment. It was a pleasure to her to take the twins by her side, and teach them their God was a God of love, alike through his inspired Word and through his works; and Joseph and Ruth learned to love their new house better than their last, because it had a garden and flowers, and they learned from that much more than they had ever learned before.

For nine months all was cheerfulness and joy in that lowly dwelling. The heavy sorrow and disquiet had partially subsided. Reuben was more often at home, and seemed more steadily and honourably employed. Twice in six months he had poured his earnings in his mother's lap; and while he lingered caressingly by her side, how might she doubt or fear for him? though when absent, his non-attendance at the synagogue, his too evident indifference to his faith, his visible impatience at all its enjoinments, caused many an anxious hour. Simeon and Leah gave satisfaction to their employers, and Sarah earned sufficient to make her aunt's compelled idleness of little consequence. Perez himself had been gladly received by his former master, as his principal journeyman, at excellent wages; and could he have felt less painfully the bitter change in his lot, all might have been well. Pride, however, was unhappily his heirloom, as well as that of Levison. With Perez it had always acted as a good spirit—with Levison as a bad; inciting the former to all honourable deeds and thoughts, and acting as religion's best agent in guarding him from wrong. Now, however, it was to enact a different part. In vain his solid good sense argued misfortune was no shame, and that he was as high, in a moral point of view, as he had ever been. Equally vain was the milder, more consoling voice of religion, in assuring him a Father's hand had sent the affliction, and therefore it was love; that he failed in submission if he could not bear up against it. In vain conscience told him, while she was at rest and glad, all outward things should be the same; that while his wife and children had been so mercifully preserved, thankfulness, not grief, should be his portion. Pride, that dark failing which will cling to Judaism, bore all other argument away, and crushed him. Had he complained, or given way to temper, his health perhaps would not have been injured; but he was silent on his own griefs, even to his wife, for he knew their encouragement was wrong. There was no outward change in his appearance or physical power, and had he not been attacked by a cold and fever, occasioned by a very inclement winter, the wreck of his constitution might never have been discovered. But trifling as his ailments at first appeared, it was but too soon evident that he had no strength to rally from them. Gradually, yet surely, he sunk, and with a grief which, demonstrating itself in each according to their different characters, was equally violent in all, his afflicted family felt they dared not hope; the husband and the father was passing to his home above, and they would soon indeed be desolate.

It was verging towards the early spring, when one evening Perez lay on his lowly pallet, surrounded by his family; his hand was clasped in that of his wife, whose eyes were fixed on him with a look of such deep love, it was scarcely possible to gaze on her without tears; the other rested lightly on the beautiful curls of his little Ruth, who, resting on a wooden stool close beside his bed, sometimes lifted up her sightless orbs, as if in listening to the dear, though now, alas! but too faint voice, she could see his beloved face once more. One alone was absent—one for whom the father yearned as the patriarch Jacob for his Joseph.[1] Reuben had been sent by his employer to Manchester, and though it was more than time for him to return, and tidings of his father's illness had been faithfully transmitted, he was still away. No one spoke of him, yet he was thought of by all; so little had his conduct alienated the affections of his family, that not one would utter aloud the wish for his presence, lest it should seem reproach; but the eyes of his mother, when they could turn from her husband, ever sought the door; and once, as an eager step seemed to approach, she had risen hastily and descended breathlessly, but it passed on, and she returned to her husband's pallet with large tears stealing down her cheeks.

"Rachel, my own dear wife, do not weep thus; he will come yet," whispered Perez, clasping her hands in both his, "and if he do not, oh, may God bless him still! Tell him there was no thought of anger or reproach within me. My firstborn, first beloved, beloved through all—for wayward, indifferent as he is, he is still my son—perhaps if he tarry till too late, remorse may work upon him for good, may awaken him to better thoughts and if our God in His mercy detain him for this, we must not grieve that he is absent."

For a moment he paused; then he added mournfully, "I had hoped he would have supplied my place—would have been to you, my Rachel, to his brothers and sisters all that a first born should; but it may not be God's will be done!"

"Oh, no, no; do not say it may not be, dear uncle! Think how young he is! Is there not hope still?" interposed Sarah, so earnestly that the colour rose to her cheeks. "He will be here, I know he will, or the letter has not reached him. You cannot doubt his love; and whilst there is love, is there not, must there not be hope?"

The dying man looked on her with a faint, sad smile: "I do not doubt his love, my child; but oh, if he love not his God, his love for a mortal will not keep him from the evil path. His youth is but a vain plea, my Sarah; if he see not his duty as a son and brother in Israel now, when may we hope he will? but you are right in bidding me not despond. He is my heaviest care in death; but my God can lighten even that."

---

1 In Gen. 37, Jacob's favorite son, Joseph, is left in a pit by his elder brothers. Midianites take him into slavery in Egypt. Jacob believes Joseph to be dead, and is heartsick.

"Death," sobbed Leah, suddenly flinging herself on her knees beside the bed, and covering her father's hand with tears and kisses, "death! Father, dear, dear father, do not say that dreadful word! You will live, you must live—God will not take you from us!"

"My child, call not death a dreadful word; it is only such to the evil-doers, to the proud and wicked men, of whom David tells us, 'They shall not stand in the judgment, nor enter the congregation of the righteous, but shall be as chaff, which the wind driveth away.'[1] For them death is fearful, for it is an end of all things; but not to me is it thus, my beloved ones. I have sought to love and serve my God in health and life, and His deep love and fathomless mercy is guiding me now, holding me up here through the dark shadows of death. His compassion is upon my soul, whispering my sins are all forgiven; that He has called me unto Him in love, and not in wrath. There was a time I feared and trembled at the bare dream of death; but now, oh, it seems but as the herald of joy, of bliss which will never, never change. My children, think that I go to God, and do not grieve for me."

"If not for you, my father, chide us not that we weep for ourselves," answered Simeon, struggling with the rising sob; "what have you not been to all of us? and how may we bear to feel that to us you are lost for ever; that the voice whose accents of love never failed to thrill our hearts with joy, and when in reproach ever brought the most obdurate in repentant sorrow to your feet, that dear, dear voice we may never—" he could not go on, for his own voice was choked.

"My boy, we shall all meet again; follow on in that path of good in which I have humbly sought to lead you; forget not your God, and the duties of your faith; obey those commands and behests which to Israel are enjoined; never forget that, as children of Israel, ye are the firstborn and beloved of the Lord; serve Him, trust in Him, wait for Him, and oh, believe the words of the dying! We shall meet again never more to part. I do but go before you, my beloved ones, and you will come to me; there are many homes in heaven where the loved of the Lord shall meet."

---

1 Cf. Ps. 1.4-5: "The ungodly are not so: but are like the chaff which the wind driveth away. Therefore the ungodly shall not stand in the judgment, nor sinners in the congregation of the righteous."

"And I and Ruth—father, dear father, how may we so love the Lord, as to be so loved by him?" tearfully inquired the young Joseph, drawing back the curtain at the head of the bed, which had before concealed him, for he did not like his father to see his tears. "Does He look upon us with the same love as upon you, who have served him so faithfully and well? Oh, what would I not do, that I may look upon death as you do, and feel that I may come to you in heaven, written amongst those He loves."

"And our God does love you, my little Joseph, child as you are, or you would not think and wish this; my works are not more in His sight than yours. Miserable indeed should I now be, if I had trusted in them alone for my salvation and comfort now. No, my sweet boy, you must not look to deeds alone; study the word of your God to know and love Him, and then will you obey His commandments and statutes with rejoicing, and glory that He has given you tests by which you may prove the love you bear Him: and in death, though the imperfection and insufficiency of your best deeds be then revealed, you will feel and know you have not loved your God in vain. His infinite mercy will purify and pardon."

His voice sunk from exhaustion; and Rachel, bending over him to wipe the moisture from his brow, tenderly entreated him not to speak any more then, despite the comfort of his simplest word.

"It will not hurt me, love," he answered, fondly, after a pause. "I bless God that He permits me thus to speak, before I pass from earth for ever. When we meet again, there will be no need for me to bid my children to know and love the Lord; for we shall all know Him, from the smallest to the greatest of us. But to you, my own faithful wife, oh, what shall I say to you in this sad moment? I can but give you to His care, the God of the widow and the fatherless, and feel and know He will not leave you nor forsake you, but bless you with exceeding blessing. And in that heavy care—which, alas! I must leave you to bear alone—care for our precious Reuben, oh, my beloved wife, remember those treasured words, which were our mutual strength and comfort, when we laboured in our youth. How well do I remember that blessed evening, when we first spoke our love, and in our momentary despondence that long years must pass ere we could hope for our union, we opened the hallowed word of God, and could only see this verse: 'Commit thy ways unto the Lord, trust also in him and he will bring it to pass.'[1] And did He not bring it to pass, dear wife? Did He not bless our efforts, and oh, will He not still? Yes, trust in Him; commit our Reuben unto Him, and all shall yet be well!"

"Yes yes, I know it will; but oh, my husband, pray for me, that I may realize this blessed trust when you are gone. You have been my support, my aid, till now, cheering my despondence, soothing my fears; and now—"

"Rachel, my own wife, I have not been to you more than you have to me; it is our God who has been to us more—oh, how much more!—than we have been to each other, and He is with you still. He will heal the wound His love inflicts. But for our erring, yet our much-loved boy, I need not bid you love him, forgive him to the end—and his brothers and sisters. Oh, listen to me, my children." He half raised himself in the energy of his supplication. "Promise me but this, throw him not off from your love, your kindness, however he may turn aside, however he may fall; even if that fearful indifference increase, and in faith he scarcely seems your brother, my children, my blessed children, oh, love him still. Seek by kindness and affection to bring him back to his deserted fold. Promise me to love him, to bear with him; forget not that he is your brother, even to the last. Many a wanderer would return if love welcomed him back, many a one who will not bear reproach. Do not cast him from your hearts, my children, for your dead father's sake."

"Father, father, can you doubt us?" burst at once from all, and rising from their varied postures, they joined hands around him. "Love him! yes. However he may forget and desert us, he is still our brother and your son. We will love him, bear with him. Oh, do not fear us, father. There needed not this promise, but we will give it. We will never cease to love him."

"Bless you, my children," murmured the exhausted man, as he sunk back. "Sarah, you have not spoken. Are you not our child?"

She flung down her work and darted to his side. She struggled to speak, but no words came, and throwing her arms round his neck, she fixed on his face one long, piercing look, and burst into passionate tears.

---

1 Ps. 37.5.

"It is enough, my child. I need not bid you love him," whispered Perez, so as to be heard only by her. "Would you were indeed our own; there would be less grief in store."

"And am I not your own?" she answered, disregarding his last words, which seemed, however, to have restored her to calmness. "Have you not been to me a true and tender father, and my aunt as kind a mother? Whose am I if I am not yours? Where shall I find another such home?"

"Yet you have a father, my gentle girl; one whom I have lately feared would claim you, because they told me he was once more a wealthy man. And if he should, if he would offer you the rest and comfort of competence, why should you labour throughout your young years for us? If he be rich, he surely will not forget he has a child, and therefore claim you."

"He has done so," replied Sarah, calmly, regardless of the various intonations of surprise in which her words were repeated. "My father did write for me to join him. He told me he was rich; would make me cease entirely from labour, and many similar kind offers."

"And you refused them! Sarah, my dear child, why have you done this?"

"Why," she repeated, pressing the trembling hand her aunt held out to her between both hers; "why, because now, only now, can I even in part return all you have done for me; because I cannot live apart from all whom I so love. I cannot exchange for short-lived riches all that makes life dear. Had my father sent for me in sickness or in woe, I should fly to him without an hour's pause. But it is he who is in affluence, in peace; and you, my best, kindest friends, in sorrow. No, no; my duty was to stay with you, to work for you, to love you; and I wrote to beseech his permission to remain, even if it were still to labour. I did not feel it labour when with you; and I have permission. I am still your child; he will not take me from you."

"God's blessing be upon him!" murmured Rachel, as she folded the weeping girl to her bosom.

A pause of deep emotion fell upon the group. Perez drew her faintly to him, and kissed her cheek; then saying he felt exhausted, and should wish to be left alone a brief while, Sarah led the twins away, and, followed by Leah, softly left the apartment. Simeon and his mother still remained beside his couch.

The night passed quietly. Sarah put the twins to bed, and persuaded Leah to follow their example, and, exhausted by sorrow, she was soon asleep, leaving Sarah to watch and pray alone; and the poor girl did pray, and think and weep, till it seemed strange the night could so soon pass, and morning smile again. She had not told that permission to remain with her aunt had been scornfully and painfully given; that her father had derided her, as mean-spirited and degraded; that as she had chosen to remain with her poor relations, she was no longer his daughter. Nor did she pray and weep for the dying, or for those around him. One alone was in that heart! Why was he not there at such a moment? and she shuddered as she pictured the violence of the self-accusing agony which would be upon him when he discovered he had lingered until too late. Hour after hour passed, and there was no footstep. She thought the chimes must have rung too near each other; for as one struck, she believed he must be at home ere it struck another, and yet he came not: she watched in vain.

Day dawned, and as light gleamed in upon the dying, there was a change upon his face. He had not suffered throughout the night, seeming to sleep at intervals, and then lay calmly without speaking; but as the day gradually brightened, he reopened his eyes and looked towards the richly glowing east.[1]

"Another sun!" he said, in a changed and hollow voice. "Blessed be the God who sets him in the heavens, strong and rejoicing as a young man to run a race: my race is over—my light will pass before his. I prayed one night's delay, but still he does not come; and now it will soon be over. Rachel, my true wife, call the children; let me bless them each once more."

They were called, and, awe-struck even to silence at the fearful change in that loved face, they one by one drew near, and bowed down their bright heads before him. Faintly, yet distinctly, he spoke a blessing upon each; then murmured, "The God of my Fathers bless you all, all as you love Him and each other. Never deny Him: acknowledge Him as One! Hear, O Israel! the Lord our God, the Lord is one!"[2]

---

1 Traditionally, Jews in diaspora pray toward the East, i.e., toward Jerusalem.

2 Deut. 6.4. These are the first words of the *Shema*, the central avowal of the Divine unity in the Jewish worship service, traditionally the last words said by Jewish martyrs or the dying.

The words were repeated in tears and sobs by all; he fell back, and they thought his spirit gone. Minutes rolled by, and then there was a rapid step without; it neared the door, one moment paused, and entered.

"My son, my son! O God, I thank thee! Reuben, my firstborn, in time, I bless, bless—" the words were lost in a fearful gurgling sound, but the father's arms were flung wildly, strongly round the son, who, with bitter tears, had thrown himself upon his neck—and there was silence.

"Father! oh, my father, speak—bless, forgive me!" at length Reuben wildly exclaimed, breaking from that convulsive hold to sink as a penitent upon the earth. He spoke in vain; the spirit had lingered to gaze once more upon the firstborn of his love, then fled from earth for ever.

CHAPTER II.

It is two years after the mournful event recorded in our last chapter that we recommence our simple narrative. When time and prayer had softened the first deep affliction, the widow and her family indeed proved the fulfilment of that blessed promise, "Leave thy fatherless children to me, and I will keep them alive, and let thy widows trust in me;"[1] for they prospered and were happy. Affliction, either of failing health in those compelled to labour, or in want of employment, was kept far from them. The widow, indeed, herself often suffered; but she thanked God, in the midst even of pain, as she compared the blessings of her lot with those of others. Little Ruth, too, from her affliction and very delicate health, was often an object of anxiety; but so tenderly was she beloved, that anxiety was scarcely pain in the delight her presence ever caused. Sweet-tempered, loving, and joyous, with a voice of song like a bird's, and a laugh of childlike glee, and yet such strong affections, such deep reverence for all things holy, that who might grieve for her afflictions when she was so happy, so gratified herself? She was the star of that lowly little dwelling, for sorrow, or discord, or care could not come near her.

Joseph, her twin brother, had attracted the notice of a respectable

1 Jer. 49.11.

jeweller, who, though he could not take the boy into his house as a regular apprentice till he was thirteen, not only employed him several hours in the day in cleaning jewels, etc., but allowed him small wages—an act of real benevolence, felt by the widow as an especial blessing, rendered perhaps the dearer from the thought, that it was the high character her husband had borne which gave his youngest son so responsible an office, intrusted as it was to none but the strictly honest.

Simeon, now nearly seventeen, was with the same watchmaker who had formerly brought forward his father. It was not a trade he liked; nay, the delicate machinery required was particularly annoying to him, but it was the only opening for him, and he conquered his disinclination. He had long since made a vow to use his every effort to restore his parents to the comfortable estate from which they had unfortunately fallen, and no thought of himself or his own wishes should interfere with its accomplishment. Persevering and resolute, he took a good heart with him to the business; and though his first attempts were awkward, and the laughter of his companions most discouraging, the praise of his master and his own conscience urged him on, and before the two years which we have passed over had elapsed, he had conquered every difficulty, and promised in time to be quite as good a workman as his father.

The extent of suffering which his father's death had been to him no one knew, but he had felt at first as if he could not rouse himself again. It was useless to struggle on; for the beloved parent, for whose sake he had made this solemn vow, was gone for ever. His mother indeed was spared him; but as much as he loved and reverenced her, his father had been, if possible, first in his affections. Perhaps it was that his own feelings, his own character, gave him a clue to all that his father had done and endured. He had all his honesty and honour, all his energy, and love for his ancient faith. One difference there was: Perez could bear with, nay, love all mankind—could find excuse for the erring, even for the apostate, much as he abhorred the deed; could believe in the sincerity and piety of others, though their faith differed from his own; but Simeon could not feel this. Often, even in his childhood, his father had to reprove him for prejudice; and as he grew older, his hatred against all those who left the faith, or united themselves in any way with other than Israelites, continued violent. Prejudice is almost the only feeling which reason cannot conquer—religion may, and Simeon was truly and sincerely religious; but he *loved his faith* better than he *loved his God.* He would have started and denied it, had any one told him so, and declared it was impossible—one feeling could not be distinct or divided from the other; yet so it was. An earnest and heartfelt love of God can never permit an emotion so violent as hatred to any of God's creatures. It is no test of our own sincerity to condemn or disbelieve in that of others; and those who do—who are prejudiced and violent against all who differ from them—may be, no doubt are, sincerely religious and well intentioned, but they love their faith better than they love their God.

These peculiar feelings occasioned a degree of coldness in Simeon's sentiments towards his brother Reuben, of whom we have little more to say than we know already.

The death of his father was indeed a fearful shock; yet from a few words which fell from him during some of his interviews with Sarah, she fancied that he almost rejoiced that he was bound by no promise to the dying. In the midst of repentant agony that he had arrived too late for his parent's blessing, he would break off with a half shudder, and mutter, "If he had spoken that, he might have spoken more, and I could not have disobeyed him on his death-bed. Whatever he bade me promise I must have promised; and then, then, after a few brief months, been perjured. Oh, my father, my father! why is it my fate to be the wretch I am?"

This grief was violent, but it did not produce the good effect which his parents had so fondly hoped. Even in the days of mourning, it was evident that the peculiar forms which his faith enjoined, as the son of the deceased, chafed and irritated him; and had it not been for the deep, silent suffering of his mother, which he could not bear to increase, he would have neglected them altogether. When he mixed with the world again, he followed his own course and his own will, scarcely ever mixing with those of his own race, but seeking and at last finding employment with the stranger. He had excellent abilities; and from his having received a better education than most youths of his race, obtained at length a lucrative situation in an establishment which, trading to many different parts of the British Isles, often required an active agent to travel for them. His peculiar creed had been at first against him; but when his abilities were put to the proof, and it was discovered he was in truth only *nominally* a Jew, that he cared not to sacrifice the Sabbath, and that no part of his religion was permitted to interfere with his employments, his services were accepted and well paid.

Had then Reuben Perez, the beloved and cherished son of such good and pious parents, indeed deserted the religion of his forefathers? Not in semblance, for there were times when he still visited the synagogue; and as he did so, he was by many still conceived a good Jew. The flagrant follies of his youth had subsided; he was no longer wild, wavering, and extravagant. Not a word could be spoken against his moral principles; his public, even his domestic conduct was unexceptional, and therefore he bore a high character in the estimation alike of the Jewish and Christian world. What cause had his mother, then, for the grief and pain which swelled her heart almost to bursting, when she thought upon her first-born? Alas! it was because she felt there was One who saw deeper than the world—One, between whom and himself Reuben had raised up a dark barrier of wrath—One who loved him, erring and sinful as he was, with an immeasurable love, but whose deep love was rejected and abused—even his God, that God who had been the Saviour of his forefathers through so many thousand ages. The mother would have preferred seeing him poor, dependent, obtaining but his daily bread, yet faithful to his faith and to his God, than prosperous, courted, and an alien.

The brothers seldom met, and therefore Simeon was ignorant how powerfully coldness was creeping over his affections for Reuben; how, in violently condemning his indifference and union with the stranger, he was rendering the observance of his promise to his dying father (to bear with and love his brother) a matter of difficulty and pain. Faithful and earnest himself, he could not understand a want of earnestness and fidelity in others. But, however the world might flatter and appear to honour his exemplary moral conduct, one truth it is our duty to record—Reuben was not happy. It was not the mere fancy of his mother and cousin, it was truth; they knew not wherefore—for if he neglected and contemned his religion, he could scarcely feel the want of it—but that he was unhappy, perhaps was the secret cause which held the love of his mother and Sarah so immovably enchained, bidding them hope sometimes in the very midst of gloom.

Of the female members of Perez' family we have little to remark. Leah's good conduct had not only made her the favourite of her mistress, but her liveliness and happy temper had actually triumphed over the sometimes harsh disposition she had had at first to encounter. There was no withstanding her good humour. She had the happy knack of making people good friends with themselves, as well as with each other, and was so happy herself, that, except when she thought of her dear father, and wished that he could but see her and hear her sing over her work, sorrow was unknown. Every Friday evening she went home to remain till the Sunday morning, and that was superlative enjoyment, not only to herself, for her mother looked to the visit of her merry, affectionate daughter as a source of pure feeling, delight, and recreation.

In Sarah there was no change. Still pensive, modest, and industrious, she continued quietly to retain the most devoted affections of her relatives, and the good-will and respect of her employers. Of her own individual feelings we must not now speak, save to say that few, even of her domestic circle imagined how strong and deep was the under-current of character which her quiet mien concealed.

It was the evening of the Sabbath, and the widow and her daughters were assembled in their pretty little parlour. Simeon and Joseph were not yet returned from synagogue. Reuben, alas! was seldom there on the Sabbath eve. The table was covered with a cloth, which, though not of the finest description, was white as the driven snow; and the Sabbath lamp was lighted, for in their greatest poverty this ceremony had never been omitted.[1] When they had no lamp, and could not have afforded oil, they burnt a wax candle, frequently depriving themselves of some week-day necessary to procure this indulgence. The first earnings of Sarah, Leah, and Simeon had been used to repurchase the ancient Sabbath lamp, the heirloom in their family for many generations. It was silver and very antique, and by a

1 Lighting the candles on Friday night, the eve of the Sabbath, is one of three commandments Jewish women are traditionally bound to keep. The "bread and salt" further on in the passage refer to the challah, the ritual bread baked for the Sabbath, which is dipped in salt as a reminder of the sacrifices the Israelites offered to God in the ancient Temple.

strange chance had escaped the fire, which rendered perhaps the sale of it the more painful to Perez. His gratification on beholding it again had amply repaid his affectionate children. Never being used but on Sabbaths, it seemed to partake of the sanctity of that holy day.

Bread and salt were also upon the table, and the large Bible and its attendant prayer-books there also, open, as if they had just been used. Ruth had plucked some sweet flowers just before Sabbath, and arranged them tastefully in a china cup, and Leah had playfully removed a sprig of rosebuds and wreathed it in the long glossy curls which hung round Ruth's sweet face and over her shoulders. The dresses of all were neat and clean, for they loved to make a distinction between the seventh day and the six days of labour.

"If we were about to pass a day in the presence of an earthly sovereign, my dear children," the widow had often been wont to say, "should we not deserve to be excluded if we appeared rudely and slovenly and dirtily attired? You think we could not possibly do so; it would not only be such marked disrespect, but we should not be admitted. How, then, dare we seek the presence of our heavenly sovereign in such rude and sinful disarray? The seventh day is His day. He calls upon us to throw aside all worldly thoughts and cares, and come to Him, and give our thoughts and hearts to His holy service. If an earthly king so called us, how anxious should we be to accept the invitation—shall we do less for God?"

"But, dear mother," Leah would answer, "will God regard that? Is He not too holy, too far removed from us, too pure to mark such little things?"

"Nothing is too small for Him to remark, if done in love and faith, my child. The heart anxious to mark the Sabbath by increase of cleanliness and neatness in personal attire, as well as household arrangements, must conceive it God's own day, and observing it as such will receive His blessing. It is not the *act* of dressing or the dress He observes. He only marks it as a proof his holy day is welcomed with love and rejoicing, as he commanded; and the smallest offering of OBEDIENCE is acceptable to Him."

"But I have heard you remark with regret, mother, that some of our neighbours are dressed so very smart on Sabbath. If it be to mark the holy difference between that day and the others, why should you regret it?"

"Because, love, there ought to be moderation in all things, and when I see very smart showy dresses, which, if not in material, in appearance are much too fine and smart for our station, I fear it is less a religious than a worldly feeling which dictates them. Have you not noticed that those who dress so gaily generally spend their Sabbath in walking about the streets and exchanging visits, conversing, of course, on the most frivolous topics? I do not think this the proper method of spending our Sabbath day, and therefore I regret to see them devote so much time and thought on mere outward decoration, which is so widely different from obedience to their God."

Leah thought of this little conversation many times. From thoughtlessness and dislike to trouble, she had hitherto been rather negligent than otherwise in her dress; then going to a contrary extreme, felt very much inclined to imitate some young companions in their finery. Her mother's word saved her from the one, and their subsequent misfortunes effectually from the other, as all her earnings were hoarded for one holy purpose, simply to assist her parents; and she would have thought it sacrilege to have spent any portion on herself except on things which she absolutely needed. But so neat and clean was she invariably in her dress, that her mistress always sent her to receive orders, and, trifling as appearance may seem, it repeatedly gained customers.

"They are coming—I hear their footsteps," said the little Ruth, springing up to open the parlour door. "Oh! I do so love the Sabbath eve, for it brings us all together again so happily."

"Is it only Simeon and Joseph, my child?" inquired the widow, mournfully; for there was one expectation on her heart and that of Sarah, which, alas! was seldom to be fulfilled.

Ruth listened attentively.

"Only they, mother!" she said, checking her voice of glee, and returning to her mother's side, for she knew the cause of that saddened tone, and she laid her little head caressingly on her mother's breast.

Simeon and Joseph at that moment entered, and each advancing, bent lowly before their mother, who, laying her hand upon each dear head, blessed them in a voice faltering from its emotion, and kissed them both. The kiss of love and peace went round, and gaily the brothers and sisters drew round the table, which Sarah's provident love speedily covered with the welcome evening meal. The happy laugh and affectionate interchange of the individual cares and pleasures, vexations and enjoyments of the past week, occupied them delightfully during tea. Sarah had to tell of a new kind of work which had diversified her usual employment, and been most successful; a kind of wadded slipper, which, after many trials, she had completed to her satisfaction, in the intervals of other work; and which not only sold well, but gave her dear aunt an occupation which she could accomplish without pain, in wadding and binding the silk. Leah told of a pretty dress and bonnet which her mistress had presented to her, in token of her approbation of her steadiness in refusing to accompany her companions to some place of amusement, which, from its respectability being doubted, she knew her mother would not approve; and, by staying at home, enabled Mrs. Magnus to finish an expensive order a day sooner than had been expected, and so gained her a new and wealthy customer.

"Dearest mother, you told me how to resist temptation even in trifles," continued the affectionate girl, with tears of feeling in her bright dark eyes. "You taught me from my earliest childhood there was purer and more lasting pleasure in conquering my own wishes than any doubtful recreation could bestow; and that in that inward pleasure our heavenly Father's approval was made manifest. And so, you see, though you were not near me and I could not, as I wished, ask your advice and permission, it was you who enabled me to conquer myself, and resist this temptation. I did want to go, and felt very, very lonely when all went; but when Mrs. Magnus thanked me for enabling her to give so much satisfaction, and said I gained her a new customer, oh, no *circus* or *play* could have given me such happiness as that; and it was all through you, mother, and so I told her."

The happy mother smiled on her animated girl; but her heart did not glorify itself, it thanked God that her early efforts had been so blessed. "And Ruth!" some of our readers may exclaim, "poor blind Ruth, what can she have to say?" And we answer, happy little Ruth had much of industry and enjoyment to dilate on. The straw she had plaited, the hymns she had learnt through Sarah's kindly teaching, the dead leaves she had plucked from the shrubs and flowers, for so delicate had her sense of touch become, she could follow this occupation in perfect security to the plants, distinguishing the dead and dying from the perfect leaves at a touch. Then she told of a poor little orphan beggar girl, whom Sarah had one day brought in cold and crying, because she had been begging all day and had received nothing, and she knew she should be beat when she went home; and how she had said she hated begging, but she could do nothing else; and little Ruth had asked her if she would like to sell flowers; and poor Mary had told her she should like it very very much, but she could not get any. She knew no one who would let her take them from the garden. How she (Ruth) had promised to make her some little nosegays, and Sarah and her mother said they would make her some little nick-nacks, pin-cushions, and housewives to put with her flowers.[1]

"Ah, we made her so happy!" continued the child, clasping her little hands in delight. "Mother gave her some of my old things, which were quite good to her, and it is quite a pleasure to me to make her nosegays, and feel they give her a few pence better than begging; and Sarah is going to try if I can make her some little fancy things when winter comes. You know I am quite rich to her, for God has given me a home and such a kind mother, and dear brothers and sisters, and she has neither home nor mother, nor any one to love her. Poor, poor Mary! and then, too, some say the Christians do not like the Jews, and I know she will and does like us, and she may make others of her people like us too."

"Ruth," said her brother Simeon, in a very strange husky voice, "Ruth, darling, come here and kiss me. I wish you would make me as good as you."

"As good!" exclaimed the child, springing on his knee, and throwing her arms round his neck; "dear naughty Simeon, to say such a thing. How much more you can do than I. Do you not work so very much, that dear mother sometimes fears for your health? and it is all for us, to help to support us, mother and me, because we cannot work for ourselves. Ah, I am blind, and can only do little things, and try to make every one happy, that they may love me; but I am only a little girl; I cannot be as good as you."

"Ruth, darling, I could not do as you have done. I cannot love and serve those who hate and persecute us as Israelites."

---

1 Housewives: carrying cases for needles, pins, and thread.

"They do not persecute us now, brother. Sarah told me sad tales of what we suffered once; but God was angry with us then, and he made the nations punish us. But now, if they still dislike us, we ought not to dislike them, but do all we can to make them love us."

Simeon bent his head upon his sister's; her artless words had rebuked and shamed him. But prejudice might not even then be overcome. He knew she was right and he was wrong, so he would not answer, glad to hear Leah gaily demand a history of his weekly proceedings, as he had not yet spoken. He had little to relate, except that he was now beginning really to understand his business. His master had said that he would soon be obliged to raise his salary; and, what was a real source of happiness, from the care and quickness with which he now accomplished his tasks, he found time for his favourite amusement of modelling, which circumstances had compelled him so long to neglect. Joseph had to tell similar kindness on the part of his master, and industry on his own. He told, too, with great glee, that Mr. Bennet had promised to give him some lessons in the evenings, in the language which of all others he wished most particularly to understand. He knew many were satisfied merely to read their prayers in Hebrew, whether they understood them or not, but he wished to understand it thoroughly; and all the time he was cleaning jewels—for he was now quite expert—he thought over what his master had so kindly taught him; perhaps one day he might be able to know Hebrew thoroughly himself, and a delight that would be!

By the time Joseph had finished his tale, the table had been cleared; and then the widow opened the large Bible, and after fervently blessing God for His mercy in permitting them all to see the close of another week in health and peace, read aloud a chapter and psalm. Varied as were the characters and wishes of all present, every heart united in reverence and love towards this weekly service—in, if possible, increased devotion towards that beloved parent, who so faithfully endeavoured to support not alone her own duties towards her offspring, but those of their departed father. She had not lost those hours and days, aye, and sometimes long weeks of suffering, with which it had pleased God to afflict her. When confined to her bed, the Bible had been her sole companion, and she so communed with it and her own heart, that many passages, which had before been veiled, were now made clear and light, and her constant prayer for wisdom and religion to lead her offspring in its paths of pleasantness and peace granted to the full. Yet Rachel was no great scholar. Let it not be imagined amongst those who read this little tale, that she was unusually gifted. She was indeed so far gifted that she had a *trusting spirit and a most humble and childlike mind,* and of worldly ways was most entirely ignorant; and it was these feelings which kept her so persevering in the path of duty, and, leading her to the footstool of her God, gave her the strength of wisdom that she needed: and to every mother in Israel these powers are given.

"Well, my dear children, to whom must I look for the text which is to occupy us this evening?" said the widow glancing affectionately round as she ceased to read.

"To me and Ruth, mother; for you know we always think together," answered Joseph, eagerly. "And you don't know how we have both been longing for this evening, for the verse we have chosen has made us think so much, and with all our thinking, we cannot quite satisfy ourselves."

"But what is it, my boy!"

"It is the one our dear father repeated on his death-bed, mother. I have often thought of it since, but feared it would make you sorrowful, if we spoke of it for the first year or two; but as I found Ruth had thought of it and wished it explained also, we said we would ask you to talk about it tonight. You repeat it, Ruth; you pronounce the Hebrew so prettily!"

And timidly, but sweetly, Ruth said, first in Hebrew and then in English, "'Commit your ways unto the Lord; trust also in him, and he will bring it to pass.' *Ways,*" continued the child, "was the word which first puzzled us, but Sarah has explained it to me so plainly, I understand it better now."

"Tell us then, Sarah dear," said her aunt.

"It seems to me," she said, "that the word *ways* has many meanings. In the verse, 'Show me thy ways, O Lord,'[1] I think it means actions. In another verse, 'The Lord made known his *ways* unto Moses, his acts unto the children of Israel,'[2] I think ways mean *thoughts.*"

1 Ps. 25.4.
2 Ps. 103.7.

"And there are several in Proverbs," interposed Simeon, "which would make us regard *ways* as the path we are to tread; as for instance. 'Who leaveth the *path* of righteousness, to walk in the *ways* of darkness.'"[1]

"But Ruth and I want to know in which of these ways we are to regard it in our verse," persisted Joseph.

"As meaning both *outward actions and inward thoughts*, my dear children," replied his mother. "I have thought long on this verse, and I am glad you have chosen it for discussion. Perhaps you do not know, my little Joseph, that we *must think to act*; that it is very seldom any good or bad action is performed without previous thought; and, consequently, if we would be pure in act, we must commit our thoughts unto the Lord."

"But how are we to do this, mother?" asked Leah.

"By constant prayer, my love; by endeavouring, wherever we are, or whatever we may be doing, to remember God knows our every thought before it has words, and long before it becomes action. We are apt, perhaps, to indulge in the wildest thoughts, simply because we imagine ourselves secure from all observation. From *human* observation we are secure, but not from our Father who is in heaven; and therefore we should endeavour so to train our thoughts as to banish all which we dare not commit unto our God."

"But are there not some things, dear aunt, too trivial, too much mingled with earthly feelings, to bring before a Being of such ineffable holiness and purity?" inquired Sarah in a voice which, notwithstanding all her efforts, audibly faltered.

"Ah, that is what I want so much to know," added Joseph.

"You must not forget, my dear Sarah," resumed Mrs. Perez, "that our God is a God of love and compassion, as infinite as His holiness; that every throb of pain or joy in the creature His love has formed, is felt as well as *ordained* by Him. No nation has a God so near to them as Israel; and we, of all others, ought to derive and realize comfort from the belief that He knows our nature in its strivings after righteousness, as well as in its sin. He knows all our temptations, all our struggles, far better than our dearest earthly friends, and His loving mercy towards us is infinitely stronger. Therefore we can better

---

1 Prov. 2.13.

commit our secret thoughts and feelings unto His keeping, than to that of our nearest friends on earth."

"And may children do this, mother?"

"Yes, dear boy; our Father has children in His tender care and guiding, even as those of more experienced age. Accustom yourselves, while engaged in thought, to ask, 'Can I ask my Father's blessing on these thoughts, and on the actions they lead to?' and rest assured conscience will give you a true answer. If it say, 'No,' dismiss the trifling or sinful meditations on the instant; send up a brief prayer to God for help, and He will hear you. If, on the contrary, conscience approve your thought, encourage it, as leading you nearer, closer, and more lovingly to God."

"But is not this close communion more necessary for women than for men, mother?" inquired Simeon.

"Women may need it more, my dear boy; but believe me it is equally, if not more necessary for man. Think of the many temptations to evil which men have in their intercourse with the world; the daily, almost hourly call for the conquest of inclination and passion, which, without some very strong incentive, can never be subdued. One unguarded moment, and the labour of years after righteousness may be annihilated. Man may not need the *comfort* of this close communion so much as woman, but he yet more requires its *strength*. Nothing is so likely to keep him from sin as committing his thoughts even as his actions unto the Lord."

"Thank you, my dear mother; that first bit is clear," said Joseph. "Now, I want the second: the third is the most puzzling of all, but we shall come to that by and bye."

"You surely know what it means by to 'trust in Him,' Joseph?" said Leah.

"I think I do, sister mine, for it was mother's humble trust in the Lord that supported her in her sorrows; that I saw, I felt, though I was a child; but—" he hesitated.

"Well, my boy?"

"To *trust*, I think, means to have faith. Now, Henry Stevens said the other day, Jews have no faith—and how can we trust then?"

"My dearest Joseph, do not let your companions so mislead you," answered his mother, earnestly. "I know that is a charge often brought against us; but it is always from those who do not know our religion, and who judge us only from those who, by their words and actions, condemn it themselves. The Jew must have faith, not only in the existence of God, but in the sacred history our God inspired, or he is no Jew. He must feel faith—believe God hears and will answer, or his prayers, however fervent, are of no avail. Without faith, his very existence must be an enigma, and his whole life misery. Oh, believe me, my dear children, as no nation has God so near them, so no nation has so much need of faith, and no nation has so experienced the strength, and peace, and fulness which it brings."

"But how does our verse mean that we are to trust in the Lord, mother?" asked Ruth.

"It belongs both to the first and last division of the verse, my love. If we commit our ways unto the Lord, and *trust also in Him* (remember one is of no avail without the other), then He will bring it to pass."

"Ah! that is it. I am so glad we have come to that," eagerly exclaimed Joseph. "Mother, does it mean, can it mean that our Father will grant our prayers, will give us what we most wish?"

"If it be for our good, my boy; if our wishes be acceptable in His sight; if they will tend to our eternal as well as our temporal welfare; and we bring them before Him in unfailing confidence, believing firmly that he will answer in His own good time—we may rest assured that he will answer us, that He will grant our prayers."

"But that which is for our good may not be what we most wish for," resumed Joseph, despondingly.

"But, my boy, if what we wish for is *not* for our good, is it not more merciful and kind to deny than to grant it? Remember, God knows us better than we know ourselves; and we may ask what would lead us to evil temporally and eternally. If, for a wise and merciful purpose, even our good desires are not granted, be assured that peace, strength, and healing will be given in their stead."

The little circle looked very thoughtful as the impressive voice of the widow ceased.

Sarah seemed more than usually moved; for, as she bent over her little Bible, which she had opened at the verse, tears one by one fell silently upon the page. Whether Ruth heard them drop, or from her seat close by her cousin, felt that the hand she caressingly held trembled, we know not, but the child rose, and threw her little arms around her neck.

"Do you remember who it was wrote the verse we are considering?" said the widow, after a pause.

"King David," answered Joseph and Simeon together.

"Then you see it was no prosperous monarch, no peaceful lawgiver, but one whose life had passed in trials, compared to which our severest misfortunes must seem trifling. Hunted from place to place, in daily danger of his life, compelled even to feign madness, separated from all whom he loved, from all of happiness or peace, even debarred from the public exercise of his faith, his very prayers at times seemingly unheeded—yet it is this faithful servant of God who exclaims, 'Commit your ways unto the Lord; trust also in him, and he will bring it to pass.' We know not the exact time he wrote these words; but we know he wrote from experience; for did not God indeed bring happiness to pass for him? If we think of the *life* of him who wrote these blessed words, as well as the words themselves, we must derive strength and comfort from the reflection."[1]

"Yes, yes; I see and feel it all now," exclaimed Joseph, eagerly as before. "Oh, mother, I can think about it now without any puzzling at all. I am so glad. Cannot you, Ruth?"

"Hush!" answered the child, as she suddenly started up in an attitude of attentive listening. "Hush! I am sure that is Reuben's step: he is coming, he is coming. Oh, what joy for me!"

"You are wrong, dear; and it only disappoints mother," said Leah, gently.

"No, no! I know I am not. There—listen; do you not hear steps now?"

"Yes: but how can you be sure they are his?" answered Simeon. "It is so very unlikely, I should have thought of everybody else first."

Ruth made no answer; but she bounded from the room, and had opened the street-door, regardless of Leah's entreaties to wait at least till the steps came nearer. A very few minutes more, and all doubts were solved by the entrance of Ruth, not walking, but clinging round her brother Reuben's neck, and almost stifling him with kiss-

---

1 David's eventful story can be found in the Bible, 1 Sam. 6 – I Kings 2.

es, only interrupting herself to say, "Who was right, Miss Leah and Master Simeon? Ah, you did not have Reuben for long weeks to attend and nurse, as I had, or you would have known his step too."

"You can love me still, then?" murmured her brother, as only to be heard by her; then added aloud, "my mother should have had the first kiss, dearest; let me ask her blessing, Ruth."

She released him, though she still held his hand; and hastening to his mother, he bent his head before her.

"Is it too late to ask my mother's Sabbath blessing?" he said, and his voice was strangely choked. "Bless me, dearest mother, as you used to do."

The widow rose, and, laying her hands upon his head repeated the customary Hebrew blessing, and then folded him to her heart.

"It is never, never too late for a mother's blessing—a mother's love, my Reuben," she said, her voice quivering with the efforts she made to restrain her emotion. "I could have wished it oftener and earlier asked on the Sabbath eve; but it is yours, my boy, each night and morning, though you hear it not."

"And will it always be? Mother! mother! will you never withdraw it from me? No, no, you will not. You love me only too, too well," and abruptly breaking from her, after kissing her passionately, he turned to greet his brothers and sisters.

All met him cordially and affectionately, except perhaps that there was a stern look of inquiry in Simeon's eyes, which Reuben, from some unexpressed feeling, could not meet; and, looking from him, exclaimed—

"Sarah! where is my kind cousin Sarah? will she not give me welcome?"

"She was here this moment," said Leah ; "where can she have vanished?"

"Not very far, dear cousin: I am here. Reuben, can you believe one moment that I do not rejoice to see you once again at home?" said Sarah, advancing from the farther side of the room, and placing her hand frankly in her cousin's, looking up in his face with her clear pensive eyes, but cheeks as pale as marble.

Reuben pressed her hand within his own, tried to meet smilingly her glance, and speak as usual; but both efforts failed, and again he turned away.

"And he has come to stay with us—he will not leave us in a hurry again," said the affectionate little Ruth, keeping her seat on is knee, and nestling her head in his bosom. "I wanted but you to make this evening quite, quite happy."

Reuben kissed her, to conceal a sigh, and controlling himself, he entered cheerfully and caressingly into all Ruth and Joseph had to tell, called for all interesting information from the other members of his family, and imparted many particulars of himself. He was rising high in the world, had been the fortunate means of preventing a great loss to the firm of which he was a servant, and so raised his salary, and himself in the estimation of his employers. Fortune smiled on him, he said, in many ways, and he had had the happiness of securing a trifling fund for his mother, which, though small, was sure, and would provide her yearly with a moderate sum. He had something else to propose, but there would be time enough for that. His mother blessed and thanked him; but her heart was not at rest. Cheerful as the conversation was, happy as the last hour ought to have been, there was a dim foreboding on her spirit which she could not conquer. Something was yet to be told: Reuben was not at peace; and when indeed he did speak that something, it was with a confused more than a joyous tone.

"I do not know why I should delay telling you of my intention, mother," he said at length: "I have had too many proofs of your affection to doubt of your rejoicing in anything that will make my happiness—I am going to be married."

There was a general start and exclamation from all but two in the group—his mother and cousin.

"If it will make your happiness, my son, I do indeed rejoice," the former said very calmly. "Whom do you give me for another daughter?"

"You do not know her yet, mother; but I am sure you will learn to love her dearly: it is Jeanie Wilson, the only child of my fellow-clerk."

"Jeanie Wilson—a Christian! Reuben, Reuben, how have you fallen!" burst angrily, almost fiercely, from Simeon; "but it is folly to be surprised—I knew it would be so."

"Indeed! wonderfully clear-sighted as you were then, if you consider such a union humiliation, it would have been more brotherly, perhaps, to have warned me of the precipice on which I stood," answered Reuben, sarcastically.

"Yes! you gave me so fair an opportunity to act a brother's part; never seeking me, or permitting me to seek you, for weeks together; herding with strangers alone—following them alike in the store and in the mart—loving what they love, doing as they do—and, like them, scorning, despising, and persecuting that holy people who once called you son—forgetting your birthright, your sainted heritage—throwing dishonour on the dead as on the living, to link yourself with those who assuredly will, if they do not now, despise you. Shame, foul shame upon you!"

"Have you done?" calmly inquired Reuben, though the red spot was on his cheek. "It is something for the elder to be bearded thus by the younger. Yet be it so. I have done nothing for which to feel shame—nothing to dishonour those with whom I am related. If they feel themselves dishonoured, let them leave me; I can meet the world alone."

"Aye, so far alone, that you will rejoice that others have cast aside the chains of nature, and given you freedom to follow your own apostate path unquestioned and unrebuked."

"Peace, I command you!" exclaimed the widow, with a tone and gesture of authority which awed Simeon into silence, and checked the wrathful reply on Reuben's lips. "My sons, profane not the Sabbath of your God with this wild and wicked contention. Simeon, however you may lament what Reuben has disclosed, it is not your part to forget he is your brother—yes, and an elder brother—still."

"I will own no apostate for my brother!" muttered the still irritated young man. "Others may regard him as they list; if he have given up his faith, I will not call him brother."

"I have neither the will nor occasion to forswear my faith," replied Reuben, calmly. "Mr. Wilson has made no condition in giving me his daughter, except that she may follow her own faith, which I were indeed prejudiced and foolish to deny. He believes as I do; to believe in God is enough—all religions are the same before Him."

"That is to say, he is, like yourself, of no religion at all," rejoined Simeon, bitterly. "Better he had been prejudiced, rigid, even despising us as others do; then this misfortune would not have befallen us."

"Is it a misfortune to you, mother? Leah—Ruth—Joseph, will you all refuse to love my wife? You will not, cannot, when you see and know her."

"As your wife, Reuben, we cannot feel indifference towards her," replied Leah, tears standing in her eyes; "yet if you had brought us one of our own people, oh, how much happier it would have made us!"

"And why should it, my dear sister? Mother, why should it be such a source of grief? *I* do not turn from the faith of my fathers: I may neglect, disregard those forms and ordinances which I do not feel at all incumbent on me to obey, but I must be a Jew—I cannot believe with the Christian, and I cannot feel how my marriage with a gentle, loving, and most amiable girl can make me other than I am. We are in no way commanded to marry only amongst ourselves."

"You are mistaken; we *are* so commanded, my dear son. In very many parts of our Holy Law we are positively forbidden to intermarry with the stranger; and, as a proof that so to wed was considered criminal, one of the first and most important points on which Ezra and Nehemiah insisted, was the putting away of strange wives."[1]

"But they were idolaters, mother. Jeanie and I worship the same God."

"But you do not believe in the same creed, and therefore is the belief in one God more dangerous. We ought to keep ourselves yet more distinct, now that we are mingled up amongst those who know God and serve Him, though not as we do. You do not think thus, my dear son; and therefore all we may do is but to pray that the happiness you expect may be realized."

"And in praying for it, of course you doubt it, though I still cannot imagine why. Sarah, you have not spoken: do you believe me so terrible a reprobate that there is no chance for my happiness, temporally and eternally?"

He spoke bitterly, perhaps harshly, for he had longed for her to speak and her silence strangely, painfully reproached him. He did not choose to know why, and so he vented in bitter words to her the anger he felt towards himself.

1 Ezra 10:10-18, and Neh. 13:27. Ezra and Nehemiah were the leaders who brought the Israelites back to the Promised Land at the end of their first exile in Babylonia (c. 536 B.C.E.). Babylonia is often treated in subsequent Jewish literature as the type of all exile.

"My opinion can be of little value after my aunt's," she answered, meekly; "but this believe, dear cousin, if you and Jeanie are only as blessed and happy together as I wish you, you will be one of the happiest couples on earth."

"I do believe it!" he said, passionately springing towards her, and. seizing both her hands. "Sarah, dear Sarah, forgive me. I was harsh and bitter to you, who were always my better angel; say *you forgive me*!" He repeated the word, with a strong emphasis upon it.

"I did not know that you had given me any thing to forgive, Reuben," she replied, struggling to smile; "but if you think you have, I do forgive you from my very heart."

"Bless you for the word!" he said, still gazing fixedly in her face, which calmly met his look.

"Thank God, one misery is spared me," he muttered to himself; then added, "and you think I may be happy?"

"I trust you will; and if it please God to bless you with prosperity, I think you may."

"How do you mean?"

"That while all things go smoothly, you will not feel the division, the barrier which your opposing creeds must silently erect between you. But if affliction, if death should happen, Reuben, dearest Reuben, may you never repent this engagement then."

The young man actually trembled at the startling earnestness of her words.

"And will you—surely you will not marry in church, brother?" timidly inquired Joseph.

"He must; he cannot help himself!" hoarsely interposed Simeon, who had remained sitting in moody silence for some time; "and yet he would say he is no apostate, no deserter from our faith."

"You said you had something to ask mother, Reuben," said Ruth, pressing close to his side, for she feared the painful altercation between her brothers might recommence.

"I had," he answered, "but I fear it is useless now. Mother, Jeanie and I hoped to have offered you a home—to have entreated you to live with us, and return to the comforts which were yours; we should seek but to give you joy. But what has passed this evening, I fear we have hoped in vain."

"I wonder you dared hope it," muttered Simeon. "Would our

mother live with any one who lives not as a Jew, whose dearest pride is to seem in all points like the stranger with whom he lives?"

"Thank you for the kind will, my dear son," replied the widow affectionately, though sorrowfully; "but you are right in thinking it cannot be. I am too old and too ailing to mingle now with strangers. I cannot leave my own lowly dwelling; I cannot give up these forms and ordinances which I have learned to love, and believe obligatory upon me. Bring your wife to me, if indeed she does not scorn your poor Jewish mother; she will meet but love from me and mine."

Reuben flung himself impetuously on her neck, and she felt his whole frame tremble as with choking sobs. His sister, Sarah, and Joseph reiterated their mother's words; Simeon alone was silent. Another half-hour passed—an interval painful to all parties, despite the exertions of Sarah and the widow to make it cheerful, and then Reuben rose to depart. His affectionate embrace, his warm "Good night, God bless you," was welcomed and returned as warmly by all, and then he looked for Simeon. The youth was standing at the farther end of the apartment, in the deepest shadow, his arms folded on his breast, his lip compressed, and eyes fixed sternly on the ground.

"Simeon!" exclaimed Reuben, as he approached him with frankly extended hand, "Simeon we are brothers; let us part friends."

"Give up this intended marriage, come back to the faith you have deserted, and we *are* brothers," answered Simeon, sternly. "If not, we are severed, and for ever."

"Be it as you will, then," answered Reuben, controlling anger with a violent effort. "Should you need a brother or a friend, you will find them both in me; the God of our fathers demands not violence like this."

"He does not—He does not. Simeon, I beseech, COMMAND you, do not part thus with your brother; on your love, your duty to me, as your only remaining parent, I command this," his mother said, mildly, but imperatively; but for once she spoke in vain. Leah, Sarah, Joseph, all according to their different characters, sought to soften him; but the dark cloud only thickened on his brow. At that moment a light form pressed through them all, and clasping his knees, looked up in that agitated face, as if those sightless orbs had more than common power—and Ruth it was that spoke.

"Brother," she said, in her clear, sweet voice, "brother, our father bade us love our brother, even if he turned aside from all we hold most sacred and most dear. We stood around his death-bed, and we promised this—to love him to the end. Brother, you will not break this vow? No, no, our father looks upon us, hears us still!"

There was a strong and terrible struggle on the part of Simeon, and a heavy groan of repentant anguish broke from the very heart of Reuben.

"My father, my poor father! did he so love me? And will you still hate me, Simeon?" he gasped forth.

Another moment, and the brothers were clasped in each other's arms.

CHAPTER III.

It had been with the most simple and heartfelt faith, that the widow Perez had sought to instil the beautiful spirit breathing in the verse forming the subject of their Sabbath conversation in the hearts of her children. Yet ere the evening closed, how sadly and painfully had her faith been tried, and how bitterly did she feel that to her prayers there seemed indeed no answer. It was her firstborn whom she had daily, almost hourly "committed to the Lord;"[1] for him she sought with her whole heart, "to trust" that He would, in His deep mercy, awaken her boy to the error of his ways; but did it appear as if indeed the gracious promise would be fulfilled, and the Lord would indeed "bring it to pass?" Alas! farther and farther did it now seem removed from fulfilment. By his marriage with a Gentile what must ensue?—a yet more complete estrangement from his father's faith.

The mother's heart indeed felt breaking; but quiet and ever gentle, who but her loving children might trace this bitter grief? And there were not wanting very many to give the mother all the blame of the son's course of acting. "What else could she expect by her weak indulgence?" was almost universally said. "Why did she not threaten to cast him off; if he persisted in this sinful connection, instead of encouraging such things in her other children, which of

---

1 Alludes both to the verse "Commit thy ways to the Lord," quoted above, and also to the story of Hannah, who commits her son, the prophet Samuel, to the Lord's service in 1 Sam. 1.28.

course she did, by receiving Reuben as usual? Why had she not commanded him, on peril of a parent's curse, to break off the intended match? Then she would have done her duty; as it was, it would be something very extraordinary if all her other children did not follow their elder brother's example."

The widow might have heard their unkind remarks, but she heeded them little; for she had long learned that the spirit guiding the blessed religion which she and her husband had felt and practised, was too often misunderstood and undervalued by many of her co-religionists; the idea of love bringing back a wanderer was, by the many, thought too perfectly ridiculous ever to be counted upon. But her conscience was at rest. None but her own heart and her God knew how she had striven to bring up her firstborn as he should go, or how agonizing she had ever felt this failure of her struggles and prayers in the conduct of her son, and this last act more agonizing than all. She knew, aye, felt secure, that neither of her other children needed severity towards Reuben to prevent their following his example. In them she saw the fruits of her efforts in their education, and she knew that they felt their brother's wanderings from their beloved faith too sorrowfully ever to walk in his ways. They saw enough of their poor mother's silent, uncomplaining grief, to suppose for a moment that her absence of all harshness towards Reuben proceeded from her *approval* of his marriage; and each and all lifted up the fervent cry for strength always to resist such fearful temptation, and to adhere to the faith of their fathers, even until death.

We are quite aware that, by far the greater number of our readers, widow Perez will be either violently condemned or contemptuously scorned as a weak, mean-spirited, foolish woman. We can only say that if so, we are sorry so few have the power of understanding her, and that the loving piety, the spiritual religion of her character should find so faint an echo in the Jewish heart. The *consequences* of her forbearance will be too clearly traced in our simple tale, to demand any further notice on our own part. We would only ask, with all humility, our readers of every class and grade, to recall any one single instance in which parental violence and severity, even coupled with malediction, have ever succeeded in bringing back a wanderer to his fold; if so, we will grant that our idea of love and forbearance effecting more than hate and violence is both dangerous and false. But to return to our tale:

There was another in that little household bowed like the mother in grief. Sarah had believed that it was her care for Reuben's spiritual welfare which had engrossed her so much—that it was as distinct from him temporally as from herself. A rude shock awakened her from this dream, and oh, so fearfully! The wild tumult of thought pressing on her heart and brain needs no description. From the first year of her residence with her aunt, Reuben had been dear to her; affection so strengthening, increasing with her growth, so mingled with her being, that she was unconscious of its power. And now that consciousness had come—the prayers, the wishes of a lifetime were dashed down unheard and unregarded—could she believe in the soothing comfort of that inspired promise? Had she not committed her ways? had she not trusted? and had it not proved in vain? Sarah was young, had all the inexperience, the elasticity, and consequent impatience of early life; and so it was, that while the mother trusted and believed, despite of all, aye, trusted her boy would yet be saved, to Sarah life was one cheerless blank; her heart so chilled and stagnant, it seemed, as it were, the power of prayer was gone—there could be no darker woes in store. Perhaps her very determination to conceal these feelings from every eye increased the difficulties of self-conquest.

Day after day passed, and her aunt and cousins saw nothing different from her usually quiet, cheerful ways. It might be that they suspected nothing—that even the widow knew not Sarah's trials were yet greater than her own. But at night it was that the effects of the day's control were felt; and weeks passed, and time seemed to bring no respite.

"You can trust, if you cannot pray," the clear, still voice of conscience one night breathed in the ear of the poor sufferer, so strangely distinct, it seemed as if some spiritual voice had spoken. "Come back to the Father, the God, who has love and tenderness for all—who loves, despite of indifference and neglect—who has balm for every wound, even such as thine. Doth He not say, 'Cast your burden on him, and he will sustain you; trust in his word, and sin no more?'"[1] It was strange, almost awful in the dead stillness of night,

1 Cf. Ps. 55.22-23: "Cast thy burden upon the Lord, and he shall sustain thee: he shall never suffer the righteous to be moved. But thou, O God, shalt bring them down into the pit of

that low piercing whisper; but it had effect, for the hot tears streamed down like rain upon the deathlike cheek; the words of prayer, faint, broken, yet still trustful, burst from that sorrowing heart, and brought their balm: from that hour the stagnant misery was at an end. Sarah awoke to duty, alike to her God as to herself; and then it was she felt to the full how unutterably precious was the close commune with the Father in heaven, which her aunt's counsels had infused. Where could she have turned for comfort, had she been taught to regard Him as too far removed from earth and earthly things to love and be approached?

Time passed. Reuben's marriage took place at the time appointed, and still with him all seemed prosperity. It was impossible to see and not to love his gentle wife. Still in seeming a mere child, so delicate in appearance, one could scarcely believe her healthful, as she said she was. It was, however, only with his mother and sisters that Reuben permitted her to associate.

He called himself, at least to his mother, a son of Israel but all real feeling of nationality was dead within him—yet he was not a Christian, nor was his wife, except in name. They believed there was a God, at least they said they did; but life smiled on them. He was not needed, and so they lived without Him.

Simeon, true to his prejudices, would not meet his brother's wife, nor did his mother demand such from him. It was enough that with Reuben himself, when they chanced to meet, he was on kindly terms. Ruth's appeal had touched his heart, for the remembrance of his father was as omnipotent as his wishes had been during his lifetime. The interests of the brothers, alike temporal as eternal, were, however too widely severed to permit confidence between them, and so they passed on their separate ways; loving perhaps in their inward hearts, but each year apparently more and more divided.

About six months after Reuben's wedding, Sarah received a letter which caused her great uneasiness. Our readers may remember, at the conclusion of our first chapter, we mentioned Isaac Levison having written to his daughter, stating he was again well to do in the world, and offering her affluence and a cessation from all labour, if she liked to join him. We know also that Sarah refused those offers,

---

destruction: bloody and deceitful men shall not live out half their days; but I will trust in thee."

feeling that both inclination and duty bade her remain with the benefactors of her youth, when they were in affliction and needed her; and that, irritated at her reply, her father had cast her off; and from that time to the present, nearly three years, she had never heard anything of him. The letter she now received told her that Levison was in the greatest distress, and seriously ill. His suspiciously-amassed riches had been, like his former, partly squandered away in unnecessary luxuries for house and palate, and partly sunk in large speculations which had all failed; that he was now too ill to do anything, or even to write to her himself, but that he desired his daughter to come to him at once. She had been ready enough to labour for others, and therefore she could not hesitate for him, who was the only one who had any real claim upon her.

"The only one who can claim my labour," thought the poor girl, as she read the harsh epistle, again and again. "What should I have been without the beloved friends whom he thus commands me to leave? Yet he is my father; he sent for me in prosperity—I could, I did refuse him then, but not now. No, no; I must go to him now, and leave all, all I so dearly love," and letting the paper fall, she covered her face with her hands and wept bitterly.

"Yet perhaps it is better," she thought, after a brief interval of bitter sorrow; "I can never conquer this one consuming grief while I am here, and so constantly liable to see its cause. My heavenly Father may have ordained this in love; and even if it bring new trials I can look up to Him, trust in Him still. I do not leave Him behind me—He will not leave me, nor forsake me, whatever I may be called upon to bear," and inexpressibly strengthened by this thought, she was enabled, without much emotion, to seek her much-loved aunt, to show her letter and its mandate. The widow saw at a glance the duty of her adopted child, and though to part with her was a real source of grief, she loved her too well to increase the difficulty of her trial by endeavouring to dissuade her from it.

"You must go, my beloved girl," she said, folding her to her heart; "but I trust it will be but for a short time. My *home* is yours, remember—always your *home*, wherever else be, as only a passing sojourn. Your duty is indeed trying, but fear not, you will be strengthened to perform it."

Yet however determined were the widow and her family to control all weakening sorrow and regret, there was not one who did not feel the unexpected departure of Sarah as an individual misfortune. Each was in some way or other so connected with her, that separation caused a blank in their affections; and what then must have been her own feelings? They parted with but one dear friend; she from them all, to go amongst those with whom she had not one thought or feeling in common.

But she who had worked so perseveringly for them, who had felt herself a child in blood as well in heart of the widow's, that she had never thought of making a distinct provision for herself, this unselfish one was not to leave them portionless; and with so much attention to her feelings did her aunt and cousins proffer their gifts, it was impossible, pained as she was, to refuse. They said, it would be long perhaps before she could find employment in her new home, and she might need it; besides, it was not a gift, it was her due; her earnings had all gone for them, and they offered but her rightful share. Reuben and his wife were not at Liverpool when Sarah was compelled to leave it; and she rejoiced that it was so.

We will not linger either on the day of parting or the poor girl's sad and solitary journey. Simeon went with her as far as Birmingham, and when he left her, the scene of loneliness, of foreboding sorrow, pressed so heavily upon her that her tears fell unrestrainedly; but though her heart did feel desolate, she knew she was not forsaken. Her God was with her still, and He would in his own good time bring peace. She was obeying his call, by discharging her duty, and He would lead her through her dreary path.

"Fear not, Abraham, I am thy shield and exceeding great reward," were the words in her little Bible, on which her eyes had that morning glanced, dim with tears—they could see but those; again and yet again she read them, till they seemed to fix themselves upon her heart, as peculiarly and strangely appropriate to herself. Like Abraham, she was leaving home and friends, to dwell in what was to her a strange land, and the same God who had been with him, the God of Abraham and Israel, was her God also.[1] "His arm was not shortened, nor his ear heavy, that he could not save."[2] And oh, what

---

1 See Gen. 26.24.

2 Cf. Isa. 59.1: "Behold, the Lord's hand is not shortened, that it cannot save; neither his ear heavy, that it cannot hear."

unspeakable comfort came in such thoughts. Century on century had passed; but the descendants of Abraham were still the favoured of the Lord, having, in the simple fact of their existence, evidence of the Bible truth, Sarah had often gloried in being a daughter of Israel, but never felt so truly, so gratefully thankful for that holy privilege as she did when thinking over the history of Abraham, and the promise made to him and his descendants, in her lonely journey, and feeling to the full the comfort of the conviction that Abraham's God was hers.

It was a dull and dreary evening when Sarah entered the great city of London. The stage put her down about half an hour's walk from her destination, and she proceeded on foot, followed by a boy conveying her little luggage. She struggled hard to subdue the despondency again creeping over her, as she traversed the crowded streets, in which there was not one to extend the hand of kindly greeting. She felt almost ashamed, though she could not define why, that the boy should see the low dark alleys which she was obliged to tread before she could discover where her father now lived, and when she did reach it, she stood and hesitated before the door as if the house she sought could scarcely be there, it was such a wretched-looking place.

Her timid knock was unheard, and the impatient porter volunteered a tap, loud enough to bring many a curious head to the other doors in the alley, and hastily to open the one wanted. A long curious stare greeted Sarah, from an old woman, repulsive in feature and slovenly and dirty in dress, who to Sarah's faltering question if Mr. Levison lived there, somewhat harshly replied—

"Yes, to be sure he does; and who may you be that wants him? He is not at home, whatever your business is."

"Did he not expect me, then? I wrote to say I should be with him to-night," answered Sarah, trying to conquer the painful choking in her throat. "I thought he was too ill to go out."

"Why, sure now, you cannot be his daughter!" was the reply, in a softened tone, and the woman looked at her with something very like pity. "Come in with you, then, if you really are Sarah Levison; send the boy away and come in."

Trembling from a variety of feelings, Sarah mechanically obeyed, giving the boy the customary fee ere she discharged him; a proceeding which caused the woman to look at her with increased astonishment, and to exclaim, when Sarah was fairly in the dirty miserable room called a parlour, "She can do that too, and yet she comes here. Sarah Levison, are you not a great fool?"

The poor girl started, fairly bewildered by the question, and looked at her companion very much as if she thought she had lost her wits. "A fool!" she repeated.

"My good girl, yes. What have you left a comfortable house and kind friends and perhaps a good business for?"

"To obey my father," replied Sarah, simply. "Did he not send to tell me he was ill, and wanted me; that he was no longer the wealthy prosperous man that he was, and I must labour for him now? or have I been deceived, and is it all false," she added, in accents of terror, as she grasped old Esther's arm, "and has some one only decoyed me here?"

"No, child, no; folks about here are bad enough, but not as bad as that. Levison is poor enough, both in health and pocket, and wrote as you say; but for all that, I say you are a fool for coming."

"Was it not my duty?" asked Sarah. "Oh, it was sad enough to leave all I love!"

"I dare say it was, dear, I dare say it was," and the old woman's face actually lost its repulsiveness, in such a strong expression of pity, that the desolate girl drew closer to her, and clasped her hand. "And more's the pity you should have left them at all. Duty—it is a fine sounding word; but I don't know what duty Levison can claim—he has never acted like a father, never done anything for you; how can he expect you should for him?"

"Still he is my father," repeated Sarah. "He sent for me when he was prosperous; and though I did not come, his kind wish was the same, and proved he did not forget me. Besides, even if he had, God's plain command is, to honour our father and mother. We can scarcely imagine any case when this command is not to be obeyed; and surely not when a parent is in distress."

"You have learned fine feelings, my poor child. I hope you will be able to keep them; but I don't know, I tried to do my duty, God knows, when I was young and hearty, but now poverty and old age have come upon me, and I have left off caring for anybody or anything. It is better to take life as we find it, and hard enough it is."

"Not if we believe and feel that God is with us, and will lead us in the end to joy and peace," rejoined Sarah, timidly.

"Why, you cannot be so silly, child, as to believe that God," her voice deepened into awe, "cares for such miserable worms as we are, and would lead us as you say?"

"We are taught so, and I do believe and feel it," replied Sarah, earnestly.

"Taught so; where, child, where?" reiterated old Esther, eagerly.

"In God's own book, the Bible," answered Sarah. The old woman's countenance fell.

"The Bible, child! now that must be your own fancy. I never found it there, and I think I must have read it more than you have."

"Have you looked for it?" inquired Sarah, timidly, she feared to be thought presumptuous.

"Looked for it—I don't know what you mean. I read it every Saturday, the parts they tell us to read; and I do not find much comfort in them, for they seem to tell me God is too far off to care for such as us."

"Oh, do not, do not say so," replied Sarah, with unaffected earnestness. "Every word of that blessed book brings our God near us as a tender and loving father—tells us we are His children. He loves us, cares for us, bears all our sorrows, feels for us more deeply than any earthly friend. I am not very old, but I have learned this from his holy book and so, I am sure, will you. Forgive me," she added, meekly, taking the old woman's withered hand, "I am too young perhaps to speak so to one old and experienced as you are."

"Forgive you—you are a sweet angel!" hastily replied Esther, suddenly rising, and pressing Sarah in her arms. "Too good, too good, to come to such a house as this. God forbid you should have such trials as to make you doubt what you now so steadfastly believe; the more you talk, the more I wish you had not come."

"But why do you regret it? What is it I must expect? Pray tell me; be my friend. I have none on earth near me to love me now."

"I wish I could be a friend to you, poor child, but I am of little service now, and you can better tutor me than I can you. It is a hard thing to say to a child of her own father, but you are too good for such as he."

"Oh, no, no; pray do not say so. Tell me, only tell me I may love my father!" entreated Sarah.

"You cannot, child; you have been used to kindness and love, you will find harshness and anger; you have only associated with religion and virtue, you have come to misery and vice. As the niece of the worthy widow Perez, you have been respected, and always found employment; as the daughter of Isaac Levison, you will be shunned, and may be left to starve. It is hard enough to find employment for children of respectable parents amongst us poor Jews; and so how can we expect it for others? Don't cry, dear: it is sad enough, but it is only too true; and so I grieve you have given up even your character to come here."

"But what can I do—what can I do?" repeated Sarah, lifting up her streaming eyes with an expression which almost brought tears to those of Esther. "Could I desert my own father, and I heard he needed me? Is he not in poverty and distress? And is his own child to forsake him because others do?"

"Poor he is, child, and so are most of us. But how can you help him?"

"Can I not work for him as I did for my aunt?"

"Yes; if you can get employment, which will not be very easy. You are known in Liverpool, and you are not in London; and the few trades in which we poor Jews can work are overstocked. Take old Esther's advice—return as you came; your father will never know you have been here, and you may be sure I will not betray you. Go back to your happy home and kind friends: it cannot be your duty to give up happiness for misery; and as he forsook you, your conscience can be quite at rest in your leaving him. Do not hesitate, my good child; go at once: he has no claim upon you."

There are some who doubt the necessity of daily prayer; that we need not pray against temptation, there being so few times in which any great temptation is likely to assail us. Great temptations to sin perhaps we seldom have, but small—oh, of what hour can we be secure? Little did poor Sarah imagine, when she entered that lowly roof, the almost overpowering temptation which was to assail her. The home of peace, cleanliness, and comfort which she had deserted; the beloved friends of her youth; the happy hours that were gone; all rose so vividly before her, conjuring her to return to them, not to devote herself to misery—which, after all, was but a doubtful duty—that her first impulse was indeed to fly from a scene where everything around her confirmed old Esther's ominous words. But Sarah was no weak, wavering child of impulse; her principles were steady, her faith was fixed, and the inward petition arose, with a *fervour* and *faith* which gave it power to penetrate the skies—

"Save me from myself, O God! Do not forsake me now. Teach me my duty, the one straight path, and whatever may befall, let me abide by it."

The brief orison was heard, for the God of Israel has love and mercy for the lowest of his creatures, and strength was given.

"No, Esther, no," she answered mildly, yet firmly; "I will not turn aside, whatever may await me. God sees my heart, knows that I am here to do my duty, even if I be mistaken in the means. He will strengthen me for its performance. Do not try to frighten me away," she added, trying to smile. "I dare say all you tell me may be very true, and it will be difficult to bear; but a good heart and a firm faith may make it lighter, you know. I want a friend sadly, and I feel as if you would be a kind one; your experience may smooth my way."

"Blessings on your sweet face for such words, my darling!" murmured the old woman; "it is long since old Esther has heard anything but abuse and unkindness. I wish I could do for you all my heart tells me; but, deary me, that is a vain wish; for I would take away all sorrow from you, and how can a poor creature like me do that?"

Esther would have run on much more in the same strain, and Sarah felt much too grateful for the kind feeling, however rudely expressed, to check her, had not the old woman suddenly recollected the poor traveller might like some tea, which she hastened to prepare. It was, indeed, a different meal, both in quality and comfort, to that which, even in her uncle's poorest days, she had been accustomed to; but Sarah was too much engrossed in anxiety for her father to heed it, and only made the effort to partake of it, in gratitude to her companion. She had time to conclude her meal, and hear much concerning her father, before he appeared. Esther said he had been ill, but never seriously so; that he could often have procured employment in various humble ways; but for some of them he was too proud, and in others behaved so as to disgust those who would have befriended him, and that he now literally had not a friend in the world, either amongst his superiors or his equals. It was a sad, sad tale; and Sarah's feelings, as she listened, may easily be imagined. But how could he live? Old Esther really did not know. She lodged in the same house with him, but she knew little of his private concerns; she only knew he had a wretched temper, which, of course, daily grew worse and worse. He went to the synagogue regularly; that he did, but it did not seem to benefit him much. How could it, when his actions denied his prayers?

It was late before Levison returned. He was still a good-looking man, but miserably attired, and pale from recent illness. He greeted his daughter with affection; for in the lowest and most debased amongst Israel, that redeeming virtue is seldom found wanting; and Sarah felt, as she looked on him, all the daughter glowing in her heart: that she could love, work for, do anything for him. Little sleep had she that night; not because her bed was hard, its covering coarse and unseemly, but from the many thoughts pressing on her mind. Her path was all dark; nothing but the unexpected warmth of her father's welcome and old Esther's kindness to make it light. She could but trust and pray, not only for strength to meet her trials, but that she might so be blessed as to erase from her heart the pang which lingered in it still.

Weary days passed; often and often did Sarah's spirit so sink within her, that she felt as if it could never rise again. Her father's moroseness returned; affection, in a character like his, could not obtain effective power over the evil habits of long years. Sarah could not realize that he loved her, and had it not been for her firm confidence in the love which was unending, pitying, strengthening, as the gracious Lord from whom it comes, her every energy must have failed. She exerted herself to effect a reformation in their dwelling and in her father's slender wardrobe. To look on him, any one would have believed him a very mendicant; yet there were some few articles of clothing easily to be repaired, and so made decent; and this Sarah did. Struck by her method, her perseverance, and the quiet, easy way in which she did everything, Esther Cardoza, old, and often ailing as she was, did not disdain to profit by her example; she became more tidy, more careful, and was surprised to find that it was just as easy to be clean and neat, however poor her apparel, as the contrary, and for comfort, the one could not be mentioned with the other. One sweet source of pleasure Sarah indeed had. She had excited an ardent desire in the old woman's mind to become thoroughly acquainted with God's holy volume; and many an evening did they sit together, and Esther listened to the sweet pleading voice of her young companion, till she felt with her whole heart that God must be with Sarah; she could not be the good, gentle, yet strong-minded creature she was, without His help; and then came the thought and belief, that if she sought Him, He would be found too of her, unworthy and lowly as she was. Such a rich treasury of promises did Sarah open to her longing heart and eyes, that she often wondered how she could have been blind so long; and she would thank and bless her with such strong feeling, that Sarah would feel with thankfulness, and chastened joy, in the midst of her own sorrows, that she had not left her own dear home in vain.

"I begin to think, dearie," Esther one day said, "that I must have been cross and harsh myself, which made folks abuse me as they did; since you have been here, I feel an altered creature, and now meet with kindness instead of wrong."

"Perhaps you are more inclined to think it kindness," said Sarah, smiling.

"Perhaps so, dear; but that is all your doing. Since you have read to me, and proved to me that God, even Abraham's God, cares for and loves me, I am as happy again, and I think if *He* can love me, why, surely some of my fellow-creatures can too. They cannot be as unjust and harsh as I once thought them. What would have become of me if you had taken my advice, and gone home again?"

"Then you see, Esther, I was not sent here for nothing, humble as I am, I have made one fellow-creature happy."

"You must make every one happy who talks with you, darling; but I want you to be happy yourself; and you have not come here to be that, I'm thinking."

"It is better for me that I should not be happy yet, Esther, or our Father would make me so. You know He could, with a word, and He will in His own good time. I did not think I should find one friend, but His love provided you." Her voice quivered, and she threw her arms round old Esther's neck, to hide and subdue her emotion, which kindness alone had power to excite.

But though for Esther she had been permitted to do so much, her father seemed neither to understand nor appreciate her; and to change the opinions to which he so often gave vent, and which, from their strangeness and laxity, often actually appalled her, seemed to her utterly impossible. The sacred name of God was with him a common interjection, introduced in every phrase; it mattered not whether called for by anger or vexation, or any other feeling. Sarah shuddered with agony as she heard it—that awful name, which she never dared pronounce save with reverence and love, which should be kept far from all moods and tempers of sin—that name, the holiness of which was enjoined as strictly, as solemnly, as "thou shalt not kill," and "thou shalt not steal."[1] She could not conquer the feeling which its constant and sinful use excited, and once so horror-struck was her countenance, that her father marked it and demanded its cause. Tremblingly she told him, and a rude laugh was his reply, coupled with an injunction not to preach to him—words which ever checked her when, in his moments of irritation against the whole world and his own fate, she sought to comfort him by the religion of her own pure mind; she gave up the effort at length, but she did not give up prayer. She would not listen to the agonized supposition that for such as he even the long-suffering of an infinitely compassionate God would be of no avail. She prayed and wept for those who prayed not for themselves, and there was comfort in her prayer.

But to pass her life in idleness was impossible. From the first week of her residence in London, she had sought for employment. Her father would not hear of her living out, and so she endeavoured to find daily occupation, or to work at home. In both of these wishes, as old Esther had foreboded, she failed.

In the low neighbourhood where her father dwelt there was no one to employ her, and she had no friend to speak for her in the higher classes. In vain she had at first urged she must seek for a situation in a private family, as upper housemaid, lady's maid, or nurse. Levison so raged and stormed at the first mention of the plan, that

---

1 The Ten Commandments appear in Exod. 20.1-14 and Deut. 5.6-18.

Sarah felt as if she never dared resume it. Yet as weeks passed, and the little fund she had brought from Liverpool would very soon be exhausted, something must be done. Our readers, perhaps, think that her idea of the duty she owed her father went so far as even in this to obey him; they are wrong if they do. Sarah's mind was not of that weak cast which could not discern right from wrong. She knew it was a false and sinful pride which actuated Levison's refusal. "Jews were Jews," he declared, "and one class should not serve the other; his daughter was as good as any in the land, and she should not call any one mistress." Mildly, yet firmly, Sarah resisted his arguments. We have not space to repeat all she said, but her father at length yielded, with an ill grace indeed, and vowing she should go nowhere unless they would let her come to him when he wanted her. But still he yielded, and Sarah thankfully pursued her plan. But, alas! she encountered only disappointment; there were no Jewesses established as milliners, dressmakers, or similar trades in London, and therefore no possibility of her getting occupation with them as she wished. She would not heed old Esther's assurances that no one would take Jewish servants. Unsophisticated and guileless herself, she could not believe that her nation would refuse their aid and patronage to those of their own faith; and she strained every energy, she conquered her own shrinking diffidence, but all without effect. Again and again the fact of her being a Jewess completed the conference at once. One said, Jewish servants were more plague than enough, they should never enter her house. Another, that their pride and ignorance were beyond all bounds, and as for a proper deference towards their superiors, a willingness to be taught or guided, it was not in their nature. Another, that a Jewish cook might be all very well, but for anything else it was quite out of the question; they knew the low habits, the laziness and insolence that characterized such kind of people, and they certainly would not expose themselves to it with their eyes open. In vain Sarah pleaded for a trial—that she was willing, most willing to be taught her duty; that she was not wholly ignorant, and humbly yet earnestly trusted she was not proud. Her duty to her God had, she hoped, taught her proper deference towards her superiors on earth. Some there were who, only her superiors in point of fortune, stared at her with stupid surprise, and utterly unable to understand such pure and truthful feelings, sharply terminated their conference at once. Others would not even hear her. Some there were really superior in something more than fortune, and anxiously desirous to alleviate distress and aid their poorer brethren, but they shrank from being the *first* to engage a Jewess as lady's maid or nurse. Some, touched by her respectful and gentle manner, would have waived this, but when the question who was her father, was asked and answered, the most kindly intentioned shrank back—it could not be. In vain she told them she had never been under his care, and offered references to many respectable families in Liverpool. A daughter of Levison was no fit servant for any respectable family; they were sorry, but they could do nothing for her.

Day after day, week after week thus passed, till even months had elapsed, and, despite her unwavering faith, Sarah's weary spirit flagged.

"But why should it be?" she asked one day, as she sat by the rude bed to which poor old Esther was confined, and in answer to her observation, it was only what she had feared; "But why should it be?" there must be some reason for our being shunned. Those of the stranger faith, of course, could not employ us; but our own?—how much better and happier we might be if they would take us into their families, and unite us by kindness on the one hand, and obedience and faithfulness on the other."

"It certainly would make us happier, but we must be better fitted for it, Sarah, dear, before it can be accomplished," replied the old woman. "You don't know anything of the majority of us here; how many of us hate the very idea of going into service. What a dreadful deal of pride is amongst us, and such false pride; we very often throw away those that would be our friends, and repay sometimes with abuse any kindness. Then, again, we want to be taught our proper duties. It is not enough to read our Bibles and prayer-books, because a great many are blinded to what they tell us. We want some one to explain them, and tell us plainly what we ought to do, and may do, without breaking our religion. Because you see, dear, when we were in Jerusalem, some things must have been different to what they can be now; and, as servants, we might be called upon to do some things which we think we ought not. Then, it is all very true about being lazy and sometimes insolent. We must set about doing all we can to be *kinder to ourselves,* before we can expect anybody to be kinder to us. I see that now quite clearly, though I did not once; but for you, darling, you are good enough for anybody to find a treasure in you. I wish I could help you; there is one good, kind, charitable lady that I would send you to, but a sister of mine behaved so ungratefully to her, that I do not like intruding on her again. She nearly clothed my sister's little girl, and, would you believe it, Becky went to her house and abused her. What right, forsooth, had she to know that her child wanted clothes."

Sarah uttered an exclamation of surprise.

"Indeed, and yes, dear; and so you see, though I had nothing to do with it, I don't much like to go to Miss Leon again; but you might, though. I am sure she would do what she could for you."

Sarah eagerly inquired who this Miss Leon was.

"None of your very rich carriage people, dear; indeed I don't know how she contrives to do all the good she does, for she is not half as rich as many who think themselves poor. She finds out those who want help; she employs all she possibly can; she gets us work from others; makes our interests hers; teaches our girls all sorts of useful knowledge; gives many a very poor family the meal on which they break their fast, and all such good acts; comes amongst us, and, somehow or other, always does us good. I don't know how many people she cured of rheumatism last winter, by supplying them with some doctor's stuff and warm clothing. Then, as for the girls' schools, I don't know what would become of them without her; she gets them work, cuts out all they want, and teaches them often herself. She is a good creature, God bless her! I lost a kind friend by Becky's behaving as she did, for I never had the face to go to her again, and I would not have her come to this low place; but that she would not mind, as she does not care for the world in doing good."

Sarah listened eagerly; had she indeed found a friend? yet she checked her rising hopes. Miss Leon might do her service, but might not have the power. Before she could make up her mind to seek her, she received, as was her custom, every month at least, a long letter from the dear home she had left; she had stated her many disappointments to her aunt, and that beloved relative entreated her to return.

"Tell your father," she wrote, "two-thirds you earn shall be honestly sent to him; and you can better, much better, support him here than in London. Entreat him to let you return to us—all our happiness is damped when we think of your heavy trials. Come to us, my love; it can scarcely be your duty to remain any longer where you are."

Sarah read this letter to her father, hoping more than she dared acknowledge to herself, that he would see how much better it would be for her to return. But for this he was far too selfish. Sarah had so riveted all the affection which he was capable of feeling, that he would not let her leave him. He was jealous and angry that she should so love her absent friends, and swore that they should not take any more of her heart from him; he would rather remain as he was, than she should work for him at Liverpool; he did not want her labour, he wanted her love, and that she would not give him. Sarah submitted with a strange feeling of consolation amidst her sorrow—did he indeed want her love? Oh, if she could but believe it, she might have some influence over him yet.

Not long after this, as she was sitting reading one morning to poor old Esther that holy book, which was now as great a comfort to Esther as to herself, a lady unexpectedly entered, and before even she heard her name, Sarah guessed who she was. There was the decided manner and kind speech of which Esther had spoken; the plain attire with which, to avert notice, she ever went her rounds of charity; and even had there been none of these peculiarities, the very fact of her coming to that poor place at all proclaimed Miss Leon. She gently upbraided the poor old woman for not letting her know she was ill and needed kindness; would not accept her plea that after her sister's ungrateful conduct she could have no right to appeal to her, and by a very few judicious words set Esther's heart to rest. She inquired what her ailing was, seemed to understand it at once, and promised soon to get her about again.

"God bless you, lady dear!" exclaimed the grateful creature, fervently; "only the other day was I talking about you and all you did; not that I wanted you—for you see my threescore and ten years are almost run out, and it signifies little now if I suffer more or less—but for this poor girl, bless you, lady, you could do so much for her. I ought not to call her poor though, for in one sense God has made her rich enough, and she has been a good angel to me.

With a vivid blush of true modest feeling, that attracted Miss

Leon's penetrative eye at once, Sarah tried to check the old woman's garrulity, but in vain. She would pour out all that Sarah had done for her, and wanted and suffered for herself, and who she was, and how brought up, and where she came from. Miss Leon meanwhile had quietly taken a seat, and, without the smallest symptom of impatience or failing interest, listened to the tale. When it was concluded, she put some questions to Sarah, the answers to which appeared much to please and satisfy her. She promised to do what she could, making, however, no professions that could excite delusive hopes, yet somehow, leaving such comfort behind her, that on her departure Sarah sought her own room to pour forth her swelling thanksgiving to God.

Miss Leon never made professions, but she always acted. When it was known amongst her friends where she had been, and whose daughter she intended, if possible, to befriend, a complete storm of advice and warning and censure had to be encountered, but Adelaide Leon was not to be daunted; for advice she was grateful, but timidity and selfish consideration never entered her code of charity. She felt no fear of consequences whatever; even had she to come in contact with Levison himself, she saw nothing very dreadful in it, and as for the censure, she smiled very quietly at the idea; but when her conscience told her she was right, it mattered little what other people said. In a word, she did as most strong-minded, right people do—finally carried her point. She went to see Esther three times that week, and before a month had passed the old woman was able to sit up, doing a little knitting, which Miss Leon herself had taught her; and Sarah went sometimes four days in the week to work at the Square.

A very brief period of intercourse convinced Miss Leon that Sarah certainly was a superior person, and her benevolent intentions did not terminate in merely getting her daily work. She had not enough in her own family to occupy her sufficiently, and many in her circle were too prejudiced to follow her good example.

Now it so happened Miss Leon had a widowed sister, a Mrs. Corea, who had four little girls, and was in want of a young woman to attend on and work for them, and take care of them when they were not with her or their governess. Genteel and modest in her manners, without a portion of pride or insolence, truly and unostentatiously pious, and withal better informed on many subjects than very many who profess a great deal, Sarah was just the very person whom Miss Leon could desire to be with her nieces; but the difficulties she had to contend with, before she accomplished the end, we have no space to dilate on. Mrs. Corea was about as weak-minded, prejudiced, and foolish as Miss Leon was the contrary. First, she had a horror of all low-born people, however they might be brought up; and no one could say but that, if Sarah was Levison's child, she was the very lowest of the low. Secondly, she could not have a Jewess; she would give the children all sorts of superstitious, ignorant ideas, and was as helpless and exacting as any fine lady. And thirdly, and most convincing of all, in her own ideas, she did not like the plan, and would not have her; what would people say too—doing what nobody else did?

Fortunately for our poor Sarah, Miss Leon never desponded when determined to do good; the more difficulties she had to contend with, the more determined was she to carry her point, and, to the surprise of everybody, even in this she succeeded. Mrs. Corea yielded to perseverance. It was too much trouble to say "no" any longer. She had seen no one that would do, and Adelaide had promised she would take all the blame, and answer everybody who meddled and found fault; and if Sarah did not suit, why Adelaide would take the blame for that too, and never torment her to take a Jewess again.

Sarah did not know all that Miss Leon had encountered in her cause, but she knew it was to her she owed the comfortable situation in which she was at length installed; and the grateful girl not only prayed God to bless her benefactress, but to bless her own efforts, that she might do her duty to her young charge, and, in serving them, prove her gratitude to their aunt.

With her father she had had at first a difficult part to play. He, of course, could not be allowed to come to the house to see her, and he had sworn she should go nowhere, where he not be admitted. A voiceless prayer that his heart might be changed rose from Sarah's heart, as she attempted to tell him of her plans; and the prayer was heard, for, to her own astonishment, her gentle arguments and meek persuasions were successful. His anger subsided at first into sullenness, then he seemed endeavouring to conceal some strong emotion, and at last, as she drew closer to him, trembling and fearful, conjuring his reply, he caught her in his arms, kissed her again and again, bade God bless her and spare her till he was a better man, when she would love him more. He knew she could not as he was; but for her sake there was nothing she could not persuade him to do; she did not know how much he loved her, and, as Sarah sobbed from many varied feelings on his bosom, she thanked God that He had called her to her father, and permitted her even in the midst of sorrow and sin to cling to him still.

CHAPTER IV.

Our readers must imagine a period of eighteen months since we bade them farewell. But few changes had taken place. Leah, Simeon, and Joseph continued in their respective situations, every year increasing their wages, and riveting the esteem and good-will of their employers.

The widow might have had another home in a gayer part of the town, but she refused to leave the lowly dwelling she had so dearly loved, until Leah or one of her sons had a home, to keep which she was needed. One change in the widow's household had indeed taken place, for Ruth was in London. Sarah's excellent conduct had interested Miss Leon not only in herself, but in her family. As they were all comfortably providing for themselves, Miss Leon could find no object for her active benevolence but the little Ruth. The poor child had not indeed so many resources as many similarly afflicted, for though all were desirous, none knew how to teach her. It so happened Miss Leon was peculiarly interested in Ruth, because she had once had a sister who was blind; one whom she had so dearly loved, that she had learned the whole method of tuition for the blind simply for that sister's sake. She died just when she was of an age to know all that affection had done for her; and Miss Leon now offered to impart all she knew to Ruth, to give her board and lodging at her house till she was enabled to earn something for herself, when she would herself send her to her mother.

It was a hard struggle before the widow could consent to part with her darling; but the representations of Leah and Simeon, and Ruth's own yearnings to be able to do something for herself, overcame all selfish considerations. She could not feel Miss Leon a stranger, for her kindness to Sarah had made her name never spoken without a blessing, and Sarah would always be near Ruth to watch over and write of her; and so with tears of thankfulness the widow consented. Leah was often permitted to take her work to the widow's cottage and pursue it there; and the little Christian girl, to whom Ruth and Sarah had been so kind, was delighted to come and do any cleaning or scouring in the house, or sit with the widow and work and read for her, to prove how grateful she was.

And where was Reuben Perez all this while? Were his mother's prayers for him still unanswered? Alas! farther and farther did they seem from fulfilment. He had left Liverpool to accept, in conjunction with his father-in-law, the management of a bank, in one of the smaller towns of Yorkshire, and, of course, even his casual visits were discontinued. Not that they were of much avail, going as he did; but still his mother had hoped against her better reason, that while near her he would never entirely take himself away. Now that hope was at an end. He was thrown entirely amongst Gentiles, and Sabbaths and holidays seemed wholly given up. He did not often write home, but when he did, always affectionately; and his mother's allowance was regularly paid. She yearned to see and bless him once again, but months, above a year passed, and his foot had never passed her threshold.

With regard to Sarah, a very few months' association with her, though only in the relative position of mistress and servant, had completely conquered Mrs. Corea's prejudices; and the very indolence and foolishness, which had originally been so difficult to overcome, were now as likely to ruin as they formerly had been to oppose. But fortunately Sarah was not one for indulgence and confidence to spoil; indeed she often regretted her mistress's indolence, from the responsibility it devolved on her. Mrs. Corea had repeatedly allowed herself to be cheated and deceived, because it was too much trouble to find fault. She often permitted the most serious annoyances in her establishment—keys and even money repeatedly lying about, her children neglected, their clothes often thrown aside long before they were worn out. In a very few months Sarah's ready mind discovered this state of things. One only she had the power of herself to remedy—the neglect of her charge; and so admirably did she do her duty by them, that Miss Leon felt herself amply rewarded. Finding it was of no use to entreat Mrs. Corea to have more regard to her own interest, and not allow herself so repeatedly to be deceived, Sarah in distress appealed to Miss Leon, who quietly smiled, and assured her she would soon settle matters entirely to Mrs. Corea's satisfaction. She did so, by giving to Sarah's care almost the entire charge of the housekeeping, with strict injunctions to take care of her mistress's keys and purse, whenever she saw them lying about. Sarah at first painfully shrunk from the responsibility, knowing well it would expose her yet more to the dislike of her fellow servants, who, as a Jewess, already regarded her with prejudice. Mrs. Corea was charmed that such a vast amount of trouble was spared her; telling everybody Sarah was a treasure, and she only wondered there were not more Jewish servants.

But our readers must not imagine that Sarah's situation was all delightful. She had many painful prejudices to bear with, many slights and unkindness in her fellow-servants to forgive and forget, many jests at her peculiar religion, and ridicule at its forms—much that, to a character less gently firm and forbearing, would have led to such domestic bickering and misery, that she would have been compelled to leave her place, or perhaps have been induced weakly to hide, if it did not shake her reverence for, the observance of her ancient faith. But Sarah had not read her Bible in vain. She had not now to learn that such prejudice and scorn were of God, not of man. That He permitted these things, in His wisdom, to teach His people, though they were still His own, still His beloved, their sins had demanded chastisement, and thus received it. That the very prejudice in which by the ignorant they were held, was proof of the Bible's truth—proof that they were His chosen and His firstborn; and more consolatory still, that as the *threatenings* were thus fulfilled, so, in His own good time, would be His *promises*. Sarah never wavered in the line of duty which she had marked out for herself—to make manifest that her faith was of God by *actions*, not by *words*; and she so far succeeded, that after a while peace was established between her and her fellow-servants. They began to think, even if she were a heathen, she was a very harmless and often a very kind one, and there was not so much difference between them as at first they had fancied.

These are but trifling things to mention; but we most particularly wish our readers to understand that though good conduct will inevitably find reward even on earth, it is not to be expected that it will have no trials. Virtue and religion will *not* exempt us from suffering, but they teach us so to bear them, that we can derive consolation and unfailing hope even in the darkest hours; and, instead of raising a barrier between us and our God, they draw us nearer and nearer to Him, till we can realize His immeasurable love towards us; and, tracing every suffering from His hand sent for our good, love Him more and more, and in that very love find comfort. Do not then let us practise religion and virtue because we think they have power to shield us from all trial and sorrow, but simply for the love of Him who bids us practise them, and who has promised, if we seek Him, He will heal our sorrows and heighten our joys.

One unspeakable source of comfort Sarah had: it was that her influence with her father rather increased than lessened with him. Once every month she spent the Sabbath evening with him, and she felt that indeed he loved her. Old Esther told her, even that when she was absent he was an altered man. He sought employment, and after some difficulty found it, though it was of a kind so humble, that before Sarah came to town he would have spurned it as so derogatory to his pride, he would rather starve than have it; but now it was welcome, because he would not be a burden on his Sarah.

His Sarah!—virtue seemed to spring into life with those dear precious words. The very interjections of that sacred name of God, which had been once ever on his lips, were now constantly checked. "She does not like it, my angel Sarah, and I *will* not say it," Esther heard him mutter when the accustomed phrase broke from him, and many other evil habits that thought—"my angel Sarah"—had equal power to remove. The bad man seemed fast breaking from his sins, and it was from the influence of his gentle pious child. The father was at work within him, and God blessed him through that feeling, and through his daughter's unceasing prayers. Every time Sarah visited him she saw more to hope, more for which with grateful tears to bless her God; and each time to love him more, and feel she was yet more beloved.

On Sarah's returning home one afternoon, after a brief visit to old Esther, who was not quite well, she was informed a young man had called to see her, and stayed some time; but as she did not come as soon as they expected, he had gone away, promising to return in the course of the evening. He had not left his name, they added; but he seemed a gentleman, quite a gentleman, though one of her own nation, and was in the deepest mourning. Sarah was not one given to speculation or curiosity, though she did wonder who this gentleman could be, but quietly continued her usual employments. She had just finished dressing her young ladies to go with their mother to the theatre, and ran down to see them safely in the carriage, when the footman called out—

"Sarah, the gentleman has come again, he is waiting for you in the housekeeper's room."

She went accordingly; but her self-possession almost deserted her when, on looking up in the face of the stranger as she entered, she recognised at once her cousin Reuben—pale, thin, and worn indeed, but still himself, and it required a powerful effort, even in that strong and simple mind, to evince no feeling but surprise and welcome.

Few words, however, at the first moment passed between them. Reuben sprang forward as she entered, and clasped both her hands in his, which were cold and trembling; and she saw his lips quiver painfully, and, to her grief and almost terror, as she spoke to him he gradually let go her hands, and, sinking on the nearest chair, covered his face with his handkerchief, and wept like a child.

"I terrify you, dear cousin, do forgive me," he said at length, as he heard the gentle voice which sought to soothe him falter in spite of herself. "Sarah, dear Sarah, I do not know why your kind voice should affect me thus. I cannot tell you why I have come to grieve you with my grief, except that when I least desired it, you were always kind and good feeling, and gave me comfort when I could not console myself; and my heart has so yearned to you now—now, when your own word has come to pass, to tell you you were right. In prosperity I might be happy, though God knows it was but a strange unnatural happiness; but in affliction—Sarah, do you remember your own words?"

She did remember them; but she had no voice to repeat them then, and her quivering lip alone gave answer. Her cousin continued, almost choked with many emotions—

"'If affliction, if death—may ye never repent your engagement then.' These were the words you said; and oh, how often, the last few months, have they returned to me. Affliction has come, my own cousin; affliction, oh, such affliction that God alone could send—death, even death!" The word was almost inaudible.

"Death!" repeated Sarah, startled at once into perfect consciousness. She looked at his dress—the deepest mourning—and the words more fell from her than were spoken. "Not Jeanie, your own Jeanie—tell me, it is not she?" Then, as she read his answer in the tighter pressure of his hand, the convulsive movement of his lips, she threw her arms round him, and faintly exclaiming, "Reuben, my poor Reuben, may God grant you His comfort!" burst into tears.

Nothing is so true a balm to the afflicted as unaffected sympathy; and Reuben roused himself from his own sorrow, to bless his cousin for her tears, yet bid her not weep for him.

"It is better thus, my gentle cousin. The God of my parents has revealed Himself to their sinful offspring, even in His chastening. I cannot tell you all now, dear Sarah; how, even when life seemed all prosperous around me, there was still a void within—I was not happy. I had returned to virtue, turned aside from all irregular and sinful pursuits, kept steady to business, and in doing kind acts towards men; more still, I had a gentle being who so loved me, that she forced me into loving her more than when I first sought her; for then, then—Sarah, do not hate me—I did but seek her, because I thought a union with a Christian would put a barrier between me and the race I had taught myself to hate—would mark me no more a Jew; and so for this, this dreadful sin, I banished feelings which had once been mine. Sarah, do not ask me what they were. Yet still, still, even when I did love my fair and gentle wife, when she lavished on me such affection it ought to have brought but joy, I was not happy. I was away from all who knew my birth and race; the once hated name, a Jew, no longer hurt my ears; courted, flattered, admired, Sarah, Sarah, was it not strange there was still that gnawing void?"

She looked up with streaming eyes. "It was a void no man could fill, dear cousin. You thought its cause was of earth, and sought with earth to fill it; but now, oh, let us thank God, His image fills it now."

"You have guessed aright, my Sarah, as you always do; but, oh, you know not all I endured before it was so filled. I tried to believe with my Jeanie and her father, but I could not. I attended their church at times, I listened to their doctrines, I read their books; but no, no, God's finger was upon me. I could not believe in any Saviour, any Redeemer, but Himself; and then that holy name, that sacred subject, which should be the dearest link between those that love, never found voice. We dared not read each other's thoughts. When we married, you know Jeanie thought little of those things; but she became acquainted with a good and holy man, a pious minister of her own faith, and he made her think more seriously: and what followed? She loved me, more and more, but she knew I did not believe in that Saviour whose recognition she deemed necessary for my salvation, and so she drooped and drooped at the very time when nature demanded greater sustenance and support. In a few months I was a father. O God, the agony of that hour which should have been all bliss! Then I felt in all its fulness, there was a God, and I had neglected Him. My innocent babe might be snatched from me, as David's was, for its father's sin;[1] and how was I to avert this misery—how devote it to its God, as its mother believed? I shuddered. From that hour my Jeanie sunk, even though they said she had recovered all effects of her confinement. Month after month I watched over her. I heard her clinging to a faith, a Saviour, which to me was mockery. I heard her call aloud for help and mercy from Jesus, not from God. Sarah, it is vain, I cannot tell you what those hours were. You can tell their anguish, for you warned me such might be." He paused, every limb trembling with his emotion; and Sarah, almost as much affected, entreated him not to harrow his feelings by such recollections any more.

"Bear with me, dear cousin; I shall be better, happier when all is told. I saw her look on our infant (thank God, it was a girl) with the big tear stealing down her pale face, and I knew of what she thought; yet I could not, I dared not give her the only promise that might be her comfort, and her love for me was so strong, so intense, she had no voice to ask it. At length, one evening, after Mr. Vaughan, the clergyman, had been urging on her the necessity of her child

1 Reuben alludes to the death of David's and Bathsheba's first son as punishment for the sin David committed by murdering Uriah the Hittite in order to take Bathsheba as his wife. See 2 Sam. 11-12.

receiving baptism, she called me to her, and, laying her head on my bosom, conjured me to grant her last request, the only one she said, she had ever feared to ask me. Her voice was faint from weakness, yet it thrilled so on my heart, that it was a struggle to reply, and conjure her not to say more. I knew what she would ask, but she interrupted me by sinking on her knees before me, and wildly reiterating her prayer, 'My child, my child! let her be made pure—let me feel I shall look upon her again. Reuben, my husband, have mercy on us all!' Sarah, had that moment been all my punishment, it would have been enough. Why could I not feel then, as I had so often declared before, that all faiths were the same in the sight of God? Why could I not make this promise to the dying and beloved? I know not, I know not now, save that I felt myself a father, and the immortal spirit of my child was of more value than my own had ever been. I raised her: I solemnly vowed that I would study both faiths—I would read with and listen to Mr. Vaughan, and *if I could believe,* my "child should be reared a Christian, and be baptized with myself. She raised her sweet face to mine with such a smile. 'Bless you, bless you, my own husband! we shall all meet again, then. Oh, you have made me so happy! Jesus will save—will bring us all to—' Her sweet voice sunk, and her head drooped down on my bosom; and thinking she was exhausted, I clasped her closer to me, and kissed her again. Nearly half an hour passed, and I felt no movement, heard no breath. It was quite dark, and with sudden terror I called aloud for lights. They were brought: I lifted the bright curls from her dear face, and raised her head. It was vain, vain."

He ceased abruptly, and there was silence, for Sarah could not speak. Reuben hastily paced the room; then, reseating himself by his cousin, continued more calmly; but, limited as we are for space, we are forbidden to continue the conversation, though it deepened in interest, even as it subsided in emotion. Reuben told how he had faithfully kept his promise—how, for two months, he had remained with his father-in law, studying the word of God, and listening to all the instructions of Mr. Vaughan, whose very kindness and true piety in spirit made his arguments more difficult to resist, than had they been harshly and determinately enforced. A year was the period Reuben had promised to devote to the fulfilment of his vow; and if, at the end of that time, he could believe in Jesus, he and his child would, of course, be made Christians; but if his studies had a contrary effect, no more, either by Mr. Wilson or the clergyman, would be said to him on the subject.

"Sarah, my dear cousin, do not fear for me. My God did not forsake me, even when I forsook Him. He will not then forsake me now that I seek Him, and night and day implore Him to reveal that path, that faith, which is most acceptable to Him. I have already read and felt enough to glory in the faith I once despised—to feel it is a privilege, aye, and a proud one, to be a Jew: for the rest, let us trust in Him."

"And your child, dear Reuben—where is she?"

"With Mrs. Vaughan, at present. At the conclusion of the year, God willing, and my mother is spared, she shall be cared for by the same tender love which her erring father only now knows how to value and return."

"And does my aunt know this?"

"No, Sarah, no. I cannot tell her. I feel as if I had no right to go to her again, until I have indeed returned with heart and soul to the faith in which all her gentle counsels had not power to retain me. No, no, no; I cannot, cannot claim the solace of her love till I am worthy to be called her son in faith as well as love."

The cousins were long together, and much, much was spoken between them, which we would fain repeat, as likely to be useful to our readers, but we are warned to desist: enough to know that Sarah prevailed on Reuben to write to his mother and tell her all, even if the story of his inward life were otherwise kept secret.

Reuben said he had given up his place in the bank, and intended, for the remainder of the year, to endeavour to obtain a situation in some Jewish counting-house as clerk, for some hours in the day; and thus allow him evenings, Sabbaths, and holidays for his sacred purpose. It was with this intention he had come up to London, as though he might have procured employment in Liverpool or Manchester, he shrunk from all remark, even kindness, from his own nation, until he had in truth returned to them. He had brought with him letters of high recommendation, which had obtained a capital situation in a thriving house of his own nation; a branch of which resided in Birmingham, to which place it was likely he should go.

"It is not that I fear the temptations of this large city, dearest

Sarah, that I would rather live elsewhere. No, I shrink from all scenes of pleasure now with sensation of loathing; but I feel as if it would be better for me to be alone, even away from those I most love, till this one year is passed. Sarah, will you think of me, pray for me?" he took both her hands, and looked pleadingly in her face. "It would be a comfort, such a comfort to come to you for sympathy, for counsel; for you it was, when we watched together by my sick mother's bed, who first made me feel that were all like you, the name 'a Jew' would cease to be reproached; but no, no, it is better for me—perhaps, too, for your character, dear girl—that we should not meet yet awhile. I threw away happiness once when it might perchance have been mine; and now—but it is better thus."

He had spoken incoherently, and he broke off abruptly. Sarah only answered by the simple assurance that she never ceased to pray for his happiness, nor would she now; and soon after they separated affectionately, confidingly, as in long past years, perchance yet more so; for then a barrier was between them, now there was none; their rock of refuge, the shield of their salvation, was the same.

To define Sarah's feelings, as she prostrated herself before her God in prayer that night, is indeed impossible; nor is there need—surely the coldest, the most callous, can imagine them, and give her sympathy. Not indeed that hope was dawning for her long-tried, long-hidden affection; for Reuben never dreamed he was so loved. It was simply thanksgiving, the purest, most heartfelt, that her prayers were heard—the beloved one of her heart brought back to his God.

Yet many were the secret tears she shed, as she pictured her cousin's anguish. She gave not one single thought to those words, which a less guileless heart might have believed related to herself. She never thought of the consequences which Reuben's return to his faith might bring to her individually. It was enough of happiness to feel he had sought her in his sorrow, had felt her as his friend.

But sorrow was at hand, as unexpected as terrible. About four or five months after her interview with Reuben, old Esther came to her one day in such extremity of grief and horror, that even her little share of discretion vanished before it, and she imparted her tidings to Sarah so suddenly, that the poor girl stood stunned and paralysed, preserved only by a strong though almost unconscious effort from fainting. Levison had been taken up and carried to Newgate as an accomplice in act of burglary and robbery, which, attended by circumstances of unusual notoriety, had been lately committed in the neighbourhood of Epping. Levison had loudly and fiercely asserted his innocence; but of course his asseverations had been disregarded.

"But he has said it—he has said it! He has declared he is innocent, and he is—he is!" reiterated poor Sarah, with a violent burst of tears, which restored sense and energy. Esther however, seemed to derive no comfort from the assertion.

"Yes, dear, yes; I do believe he is not guilty—bad as some of us are, we do not do such things. Who ever heard of a Jew being a housebreaker or a thief? But who will believe him? Who will take his word, his oath? Oh, what will become of us?" and the old woman rocked herself to and fro, in the misery of the thought. Sarah was in no state to offer the usual comfort; but stunned, bewildered as she was, her thought formed itself into unconscious prayer for help and strength. Her plan of action was decided on the instant; she would, she must go to him. In vain Esther bade her think of the consequences; what would her mistress say, if she knew that Sarah was any way related to Levison, the reputed housebreaker, much less that she was his daughter?

"Would you then advise me, if this misery come to her knowledge, deny my father, now that he may need me more than ever? Oh, Esther, I cannot do this," replied Sarah mournfully, though firmly. "My mistress need not know my errand now perhaps, and this terrible trial may be permitted to pass away before it comes to the worst. But should it indeed reach her ears, I cannot deny him; he has only me, and if it cause me the loss of my situation, of my character in the opinion of my fellow-creatures, my God will love me, care for me still. I cannot desert my father."

And while she seeks him, we must inform our readers, briefly as may be, how the matter really stood. Levison had been seen and recognised talking to a party of men the evening previous to the night's robbery. No one could swear to his person as accessory to the act by having seen him in the house, but in such earnest conversation with those who were taken in the fact, that he was, in consequence, committed as one of the gang, for the apprehension of whom a large reward had been offered. It was true, none of the stolen property had been found on his person, or in his dwelling; but these facts were little heeded in his favour.

He was a Jew—a man who had been noted for his dishonest practices in business, and consequently there was no one to come forward with such report of his former character as could be taken in his favour.

He persisted that he was innocent; that though he had been talking to the men as was alleged, he knew nothing of their real character or intentions; that he had been acquainted with them formerly, but only in the way of business; that they knew he had separated from them, at seven o'clock that evening, to proceed several miles in a contrary direction, to the burial-ground of his people, where he had been engaged to watch beside the grave of one that day interred; the person who had been engaged to do so having been suddenly taken ill and asked him, Levison, to watch in his stead. How could he prove this? he was asked.

The unhappy man groaned aloud for answer—he had no proof. Some one, a gentleman, had indeed visited the grave at break of day, had demanded who he was, and why he was there instead of the person engaged; and he answered, giving his full name. The gentleman had thrown him money, and hastily departed; but who or what he was, except a Jew, as himself; Levison did not know.

Of course, such a tale, and from such a person, was not to be believed, and he was committed to Newgate, with his supposed accomplices, to take his trial.

It was with great difficulty Sarah gained admittance to his cell; but it was not till in his presence, till the door was closed upon her for a specified time, that the energy which supported her throughout gave way.

She could but throw herself on her knees before him, but fling her arms round him, and sob forth, "Father!" the convulsions of agony and fear which shook her every limb depriving her at once of power and of voice.

The effect of her presence on Levison was terrible. He gave vent to a wild, shrill cry, then catching her to his bosom, gasped forth, "My daughter! oh, my daughter! the God of wrath and justice will withdraw his hand, if you are near," and then sunk back in a strong convulsive fit. Perhaps it was as well that the poor girl was thus compelled to exertion. Terrified as she was, she knew to call for help was useless, for who could hear her? But by unloosening his collar, and the application of cold water, which happened to be in the room, after a few minutes of intense terror, she saw the convulsive struggles gradually give way, and he lay sensible, but exhausted. It was then she saw the ravages either illness or imprisonment had made; it seemed as if even death itself was upon him. He had never quite recovered the illness which had originally called her to London, and the last few days seemed to have brought it back with increase of suffering and complete prostration of physical power. His black hair had whitened, and his form was bent, as if a burden of many years had descended upon him; his features were contracted, and wan as death.

"Sarah, Sarah, I thought God had forsaken me; but I see you, and I know he has not. Miserable and *guilty* as I am—guilty of many sins, as I know, I feel now—but not of this: no, no, no; my child, my child, I am innocent of this. I turned away from vice and sin for your sake. I made a vow to try and become worthy of such an angel child; and see, see what has come upon me! I have been deceiving and dishonest in former days, but even then I never, never turned aside to steal—to join a gang of thieves. Sarah, Sarah, I thought to make you happy at last; and I shall be but your curse, your misery. Perhaps you too will not believe me; but I am innocent of this crime; my child, my child, I am indeed!"

It was long ere Sarah's gentle soothings and earnest assurances of her firm belief in his perfect innocence could calm the fearful agitation of her unhappy father. Still her presence, the pressure of her hand was such comfort, that a light appeared to have gleamed on the darkness of his despair, and he poured forth his agonizing thoughts, his terrors, alike of life and death and eternity, as if his child were indeed the ministering angel of hope and faith and comfort which his deep love believed her.

"Had I not you, my daughter, oh, there would be no hope, no mercy for one like me. I have disobeyed and profaned my God, and taken His holy name in vain, and called down on me His wrath, His vengeance; and how can I, how dare I hope for mercy? I cannot repent—I cannot seek righteousness now; it is too late, too late! Yet God has given me you; and is He then all wrath, all punishment? Tell me, tell me, there is mercy for the sinner, even now."

"Father, dear father, there is! Has He not said it? Yes, and reiterated it in His holy book, till the most doubting of us must believe. 'He hath no pleasure in the death of the wicked, but rather that he should turn from his wickedness and live;'[1] bidding us repent and believe, and that in the day we did so our guilt should not be remembered—should not appear against us; telling us but to confess our sin, to throw ourselves on His mercy, that mercy all perfect to purify, redeem, and save—that He is merciful and gracious, long-suffering, abundant in mercy and love—showing mercy unto thousands![2] My father, oh, my father, there is no sin so infinite as His mercy—no sin for which repentance and love and faith in Him will not in His sight atone."

"But I can make no atonement, my child. I can do nothing to prove repentance—that I would serve and love Him now—nothing to make reparation for past sin: too late, too late!" and he groaned aloud.

"He does not ask works, my father, when He knows they cannot be performed. Have you not sought Him this last year, in penitence and prayer, and amendment of your ways? and does He not record this, though man may not? and now, oh, do but believe in Him, in His will and power to forgive and save—do but call upon Him with the faith and repentance of a sorrowing child. Oh, my father, God asks no more than we can do. His sacrifices are a broken heart and a contrite spirit, which we all have power to bestow.[3] He has told us this blessed truth, through the lips of one who had the power to do and give much more in atonement for his sin, that we, who can do nothing but believe and repent, may be comforted. Father, my own dear father, if indeed you repent and love, and believe, oh, God is near you, will save you still!"

Much, much more did Sarah say, as she sat on the straw pallet where her unhappy father half reclined, her dark, truthful eyes, often swelling in large tears, fixed on his face as she spoke. It was impossible for one whom her influence the last twelvemonth had already, through God's mercy, changed in heart, to listen to her healing

---

1 Ezek. 33.11.

2 Exod. 34.6–7.

3 Cf. Ps. 34.18: "The Lord is nigh unto them that are of a broken heart; and saveth such as be of a contrite spirit."

words, and look on her sweet pleading face, and yet retain the doubts and terrors of despair. It seemed to Levison that if such a being could love and pity him, and cling to him thus even in a prison cell, he could not be cut off from all of heavenly hope—the all pitying love and consoling promises of God appeared to him through her as if by a voice from heaven. They could not deceive, and even in the depth of repentant agony—for it was true repentance—there was comfort. Sarah was summoned away only too soon, but she promised to visit him often again. The piece of gold which she had slid into the turnkey's hand, she knew, would be her passport; but to do this unknown to her mistress was an act of injustice towards her, which her pure mind rejected.

Yet how to tell her? The determination was made, but on the manner of fulfilling it poor Sarah thought some time. Perhaps it was fortunate she was roused to exertion. On entering the kitchen for something she wanted, she saw her fellow-servants congregated in a knot together, the footman reading aloud the account of the robbery, and the committal of the gang, from the newspapers. He stopped as she entered, and every eye turned on her. Her cheek grew white as ashes, and her lip quivered, so as to be remarked by all. The footman seemed about to speak, but the housemaid laid her hand on his arm, with an imploring look to forbear. It was enough. Sarah felt she could better leave her mistress than encounter the questions or suspicions of her fellow-servants, and that instant she sought the parlour. Miss Leon was with her sister. The ghastly paleness and agonized expression of the poor girl's face struck her at once, and with accents of earnest kindness she inquired what was the matter. Bursting into tears, Sarah almost inarticulately related the heavy trial which had befallen her, and her intention to give up her situation. Confidential, happy as it was to devote herself to her unfortunate father, feeling that the child of one suspected as he was could bring but disreputableness to a respectable family, Sarah felt her story was incoherent; but that it was understood was visible in its effects. Mrs. Corea, selfish and weak as her wont, thought only of the trouble and annoyance Sarah's resignation of her situation would bring her; and overwhelmed her with reproaches, as ungrateful and capricious. Miss Leon spoke calmly and reasonably. There was no need for any decisive parting. Sarah might leave for a time, if she were desirous of doing so, though she did not think it wise; that if Mrs. Corea valued her so much, she could have no objection to her returning. "What! the daughter of a pickpocket, a housebreaker! No, no, if Sarah were fool enough to say she was the daughter of such a person, she would have nothing more to do with her; but there was no need for her to do so. What was to prevent her disclaiming all relationship; and what good could she do to him or herself by going to him? It was all folly. There were plenty of Levisons in the world. Nobody need know this Levison was Sarah's father, if the girl herself were not such a fool as to betray it."

"And can you advise this, Miss Leon?" implored Sarah, turning towards her. "Oh, do not, do not say so. I would not displease one so kind and good as you are. I would do anything, everything to show you I am grateful; but I cannot, oh, I cannot deny my father! I should never know a happy day again."

Miss Leon was not at all a person to evince useless emotion, but there was certainly something rising in her throat which made her voice husky ere she replied. Reasonable and feeling, however, as her arguments were, that, without actually denying or deserting her father, she need not ruin her own reputation for ever, by proclaiming it was to visit him in prison, she left her place. Sarah could at that moment only *feel*; her future was bound up in her father's.

We have not, however, space to dilate on all Miss Leon urged or Sarah felt. Suffice it, that the next morning Sarah turned away from the house which for nearly two years had been a happy home. She knew not if she should ever be welcome there again. Miss Leon was indeed still her friend; but how could even she aid her now? She returned to that dilapidated dwelling where old Esther still lived, feeling that heavy as she had thought her trial when she had first entered those doors, it was light, it was joy to that which was hers now.

Day after day, in the brief period intervening before Levison's final trial, did his devoted daughter visit his cell, and not in vain. The terror, the anguish which had possessed him were passing from his soul. He did believe in the saving power of his God. He did approach His throne with a broken and contrite heart; and it was the prayers, the faith, the forbearing devotion of his child, which brought him there. Sarah had told all his story to Miss Leon, who had listened attentively, though she herself feared that to remedy this and prove him innocent was, even to her energetic benevolence, impossible.

The morning of the trial came, the court was crowded; for the extensive robberies traced home to this gang occasioned unusual excitement. The trembling heart of the daughter felt that to wait to hear of its termination, and her father's sentence, was impossible, the very effort would drive her mad. In vain old Esther remonstrated; offered, infirm as she was, to go herself if Sarah would but remain quietly at home. Sarah insisted on accompanying her, muffled up so as not to be recognised. They mingled with the thronging crowds, jostled, pushed, and otherwise annoyed, yet Sarah knew it not—seemed conscious of nothing till her eyes rested on her misguided father. What was it she hoped? She knew not, except a strange undefined belief that even now, in the eleventh hour, his innocence would be made evident. Alas, poor girl! the summary proceedings of a court of justice on a gang of noted criminals allowed no saving clause. He was sworn to as having been seen with them, and that was sufficient. All he said was unheeded, perhaps unheard; and sentence of transportation for life was pronounced on every man by name, Isaac Levison included.

Sarah did not scream; she thought she did not faint, for the words rung in her ears as repeated by a hundred echoes, one louder than the other; but except this power of hearing, every other sense seemed suddenly stilled. She did not know whose arm led her from that terrible scene—who was conducting her hastily yet tenderly towards home. She walked on quick, quicker still, as if the rapidity of movement should hush that mocking sound. It would not, it could not; and when she was at home, she sunk down powerless, conscious only of misery that even faith might not remove.

"Sarah, my own Sarah! look up, speak to me, this silence is terrible!" exclaimed a voice which roused her as with an electric shock. Reuben Perez was beside her, his arm around her; the ice of misery, the restraint of long-hidden feelings, were broken by the power of that voice, and laying her head on his shoulder, she sobbed in uncontrollable agony. He told her how he had seen the name of Levison in the papers, and his defence, and how he had trembled lest it should be her father: how anxiously he had wished to come up at once to London, but was unavoidably prevented leaving Birmingham till the previous night. How he had proceeded to the court; at once recognised Levison, and at the same moment, guided by some strange instinct, looked for and found Sarah, muffled as she was.

He had gradually and with difficulty made his way through the crowd towards her, and reached her just as the sentence was pronounced. Old Esther had begged him to take care of Sarah home, as she could follow more slowly. He tried to speak comfort respecting her father; but in this he failed. Shudderingly, she reiterated the sentence. "Transportation, and for life—to be sent away to work, to die, untended, unloved," and then, as with sudden thought, she started up—

"No, no, no!" she exclaimed, a hectic glow tinging her pallid cheek. "Why cannot I go too? not with him, they will not let me do that; but there are ships enough taking out emigrants, and I can meet him there—be with him again. They shall not separate the father from his child; and he is innocent! My father, my poor father, your Sarah will not forsake you even now!" and she wept again, but less painfully than before. Startled as he was, Reuben could yet feel this was scarcely a resolution to be kept, and with argument and persuasion sought to turn her from her purpose. Her father could not need such sacrifice; how could she aid him in his far distant dwelling?

"He has but me—he has but me!" she reiterated; "who is there that has claim enough to keep me from him? I have thought a formal trial heavy to be borne; but had it not been for that, my poor father might have died in sin, for perhaps I could not have come to him as I did when free. No, no, I was destined to be the instrument, in the hands of mercy, in bringing him back to the God he had offended, and I may do so still. Reuben, Reuben, who is there has such claim upon me, as my poor, poor father? Others love me, and oh, God only knows how I love them! but they are happy and prosperous, they do not need me."

"Sarah," answered Reuben, his voice choked with emotion, "Sarah, you spoke of a former heavy trial, one hard to bear. Oh, answer me, speak to me! Was not I its cause? I deceived myself when I thought I had not injured your peace when I wrecked my own."

"It matters little now," replied Sarah, turning from his look, while her cheek again blanched to marble; "my path is marked out for me.

I may not leave it, even to think of what has been or might be; it cannot, must not matter now."

"It must—it shall!" exclaimed Reuben, with more than wonted impetuosity. "Sarah, Sarah, you ask me who needs you as your father does—to whom you can be as you are to him? I answer, there is one, one to whom, as to your father, you have been a guardian angel, winning him back even by your memory, when far separated, to the God he had forsaken. I trampled on the love I bore you—my own feelings as well as yours—to unite myself with a stranger race, to bid all who knew me cease to regard me as a Jew. I sought to believe I had nothing to reproach myself with, as I had not caused you grief, and yet—conscience, conscience! Oh, Sarah, my poor Jeanie's very love was constant agony, for I could not return it. I never loved her as I loved you, even though she wound herself about my very heart, and her death seemed misery. I looked to the end of this twelvemonth to feel myself worthy to tell you all my sin, my misery, and, if you could forgive me, to conjure you to become mine. Oh, do not sentence me to increase of trial! I looked to you to train up my motherless Jeanie, as indeed a child of God, according to your own pure belief; and to bind me to Him by links I could never, even in the strongest temptation, turn aside. And now, now, when my heart tells me I was deceived and I had injured you—for you did love me, you do love me—oh will you leave me—for a doubtful duty, part from me for ever? I care not how long I serve to win you. Sarah, Sarah, only tell me you can still love me, you will be mine."

"Too late, too late, oh, it is all too late!" replied Sarah, firmly, though her voice was choked with tears.

"Reuben, dear Reuben, why have you spoken thus, and at this moment? It was a weak and idle folly to deny that to be your wife would be the dearest happiness which could be mine; that I have loved you, long before I knew what love could mean; and prayed for you, wept for you—but I must not think of these things now. Months ago, such words from you would have been all joy; but now—do not speak them, dearest Reuben—they increase my trial, but cannot change my purpose. My poor father is innocent, condemned unjustly. Were he guilty, I might decide otherwise; for perhaps it were then less a positive duty to tend him to the last."

And in vain did Reuben combat this determination. In vain, rendered more eloquent from his conviction that he was beloved, did he speak and urge, and speak again. He desisted at length; not from lack of argument, but because he saw it only increased the anguish of her feelings.

"If it must be so, dearest—yet indeed, indeed, it is a mistaken duty; do not look on me so beseechingly, I will urge no more. For myself I know I did not merit the joy I had dared to picture; yet still, still to resign it thus, to know you love me spite of all—Sarah, how may I struggle on, with very hope and promise blighted?"

"Do not say so, Reuben." Our Father will not leave you lonely. Seek Him, love Him, and He will fill up all the void which my absence may create; and do not think we part for ever. Oh, Reuben, the love borne in my heart so long can know no cloud or change, and though years may pass on—my first duty be accomplished—yet when it is, and my poor father's weary course is ended, if you be still free, may I not return to you, all, all your own?"

She lifted up her pale face to his with such a look of confidence and love, that Reuben's only answer was to fold her to his heart and bid God bless her for such words.

Days passed on, and though all who heard her resolution were against it, though she had to encounter even Miss Leon's arguments and entreaties that she would forego a purpose as uncalled for as misguided, Sarah never for one moment wavered. Vainly Miss Leon sketched the miseries that would wait her in a savage land; the little chance there was of her even being permitted to be near her father; the little she could do for him, even if they were together. She reasoned well and strongly and even feelingly, but there are times and duties when the heart hears only its own impulses, its own feelings, and must follow them. Had she wavered before she again met her father after his condemnation, which, however, she did not, her first interview would have strengthened her yet more. There was a wild and haggard look about him, a hollow tone and wandering words, that made her at the first moment tremble for his reason.

"Sarah, my daughter! they have banished me from my God! they have sentenced me to return to sin. Better, better had they said I was to die, for then I should have gone direct from you to judgement, and your prayers, your angel words, had turned me from my sin: but they will send me from you, and I shall sin again. I shall fall away from all the good you taught me. With you, with you only I am safe—my daughter, oh, my daughter!"

"And I will not leave you, father—I go with you, not in the same ship, but I will meet you in a strange land. We shall be together there as here. I will not leave you while you need me. Do not look so, father, I have sworn it to my God."

She threw herself upon his neck, and the sinful but repentant man wept as an infant on her shoulder; and from that hour her dread that his reason was departing never tormented her again.

The evening before Levison's removal with his fellow-convicts to Portsmouth—the ship awaiting them there—the influence of a larger bribe than usual from Reuben to the turnkey had secured to Sarah a few uninterrupted hours with her father in a separate cell. There was something strange in Levison's countenance which rather alarmed him when he joined them; it was flushed and excited, and as he walked across the cell his limbs seemed to totter beneath him.

They had not much longer to be together, when an unusual number of footsteps crowded along the passage; and, soon after, the turnkey, a sheriff, and a gentleman whom neither Sarah nor Reuben knew, though he was evidently of their own nation, entered the cell. There was still quite daylight sufficient to distinguish persons and features, and the very instant Levison's eye caught the stranger, he started with a shrill cry to his feet, endeavoured to spring forward, but failed, and would have fallen had not Reuben caught him in his arm; where he remained in a fit of trembling, which almost seemed convulsion. "Now, be quiet, my good fellow, you will do well enough," whispered the turnkey, as he stepped forward to assist in supporting Levison upon his feet. "Here is this here gentleman come to swear to your person, as having seen you in the burial-ground, just as how you said, that there night; proving an alibi d'ye see. They'll let you go even now—who'd ha' thought it?"

"You said, sir, that you saw and spoke to a man named Isaac Levison, of the Jewish nation, in the burial-ground of your people, on the morning of Wednesday, the 14th of May, exactly as the clock of Mile End Church chimed three," deliberately began the pompous sheriff, on whose blunted sensibilities the various attitudes of agonized suspense, hope, and terror delineated in the group before him excited no emotion whatever. "I have troubled you to come here to see this man, who calls himself by that name, and tells the same tale, seeing, that if you can swear to his person, he must be detained from accompanying the rest of the gang, and undergo a second trial, that your assertion in the court may publicly prove it."

"I do not see much use in that," interrupted the gentleman, who, no lawyer, did not quite comprehend technicalities; "I should think my oath as to his person enough to free him. I did not appear on his trial, simply because I was abroad, and only heard of it through a friend sending me a newspaper and the particulars of the case—a friend of his wishing the man's innocence to be proved. He wrote to me, knowing that either I or some one belonging to me had employed a watcher that night, and vague as the tale was, I might help to clear it; this, however, is nothing to the purpose. If the robbery you speak of was committed at Epping on the 14th of May, just about three o'clock in the morning, that man, Isaac Levison, is as innocent as I am; for I can take my oath as to seeing and speaking with him that very morning, at that very hour, in the burial-ground of our people at Mile End. I particularly remarked him, as he was not the person I had engaged. There is no justice in England if you do not let him go—he is innocent."

"Innocent—innocent—innocent! My child, you are right; there is a God, and a God of love! Blessed—blessed—forgiven !" He bounded from the detaining arms of Reuben and the turnkey, clasped Sarah to his heart with strange unnatural strength, and fell back a corpse!

CHAPTER V.

A SMALL but most comfortably-furnished parlour of a new, respectable-looking dwelling, in one of the best streets of Liverpool, is the scene to which we must conduct our readers about two years after the conclusion of our last chapter. The furniture all looked new, except a kind of antique silver lamp, which stood on an oaken bracket opposite the window. It was a room thrown out from the usual back of the house, opening by a large French window, and one or two steps into a small but beautifully laid-out flower garden, divided by a passage and another parlour from the handsome shop which opened on the street. It was a silversmith and watchmaker's, with the words "Perez Brothers," in large but not showy characters, over the door. The shop seemed much frequented, there was a constant ingress and egress of respectable people but there was no bustle, nothing going wrong, all seemed quietness and regularity; orders received and questions answered and often articles of particularly skilful workmanship displayed with that gentle courtesy and good feeling which can spring but from the heart.

But we are forgetting—it is the parlour and not the shop with which we have to do. The room and its furniture may be strangers to us—perhaps one of its inmates—but not the other. The still infirm and aged, but the thrice-blessed thrice-happy mother was still spared to bless God for the prosperity, the well-doing, and the unchanging faith and piety of her beloved children. Simeon's wish was fulfilled—his mother was restored to her former station, nay, raised higher in the scale of society than she had ever been; but meek in prosperity as faithful in adversity, there was no change in that widowed heart, save, if possible, yet deeper love and gratitude to God. And a beautiful picture might that gentle face have made, bending down with such a smile of caressing love on the lovely infant of nearly three years, who had clambered on her knee, and was folding its little round arms about her neck. It was a touching contrast of age and infancy, for Rachel looked much older than she really was, but there was nothing sad in it. The unusual loveliness of the child cannot be passed unnoticed; the snowy skin, the rich golden curls, just touched with that chestnut which takes away all insipidity from fairness, might have proclaimed her not a child of Israel; but then there was the large, lustrous, black eye and its long fringe, the subdued, soul-speaking beauty of the other features—that was Israel's and Israel's alone! Full of life and joyousness, her infant prattle amused her grandmother, till at the closing, about six in the evening, her son Simeon joined her. We should perhaps have said that an elderly Jewess, remarkably clean and tidy in her person, had very often entered the parlour to see, she said, if the dear widow were comfortable or wanted anything, or little Jeanie were troublesome, etc. It was old Esther, who fulfilling all sorts of offices in the family, acting companion and nurse to the widow and Jeanie, cleaning silver—in which she was very expert—seeing to the cooking of the dinner, and taking care of the lads' clothes, delighted herself; and more than satisfied those with whom she lived.

To satisfy our readers' curiosity as to how this great change in the widow's condition had been brought about, we will briefly narrate its origin. When Reuben's year of probation was over, and he felt he was a Jew in heart and soul and reason, as well as name, he returned to Liverpool, to delight his mother with the change. He was met with love and with rejoicing, no reference was made to the past, and between himself and Simeon not a shadow of estrangement remained. The latter had at first hung back, feeling self-reproached that he had wronged his brother; but Reuben's truly noble nature conquered these feelings, and soon after bound him to him with the ties of gratitude as well as love. Simeon's talent for modelling in silver was now as marked as his dislike to that trade, which, despite of disinclination, he had perseveringly followed. Reuben, on the contrary, retained all his father's instructions in watch-making, and had determined, when he returned to Liverpool, to set up that business, which, from the excellent capital he had amassed and laid by, was not difficult to accomplish. He had determined on this plan, feeling as if he thus tacitly acknowledged and followed his lamented father's wishes, and atoned to him, even in death, for former disregard. He, of course, wished to associate Simeon in the business; but as the young man's desires and talents seemed pointed otherwise, he placed him for a year with a first-rate silversmith in London. Morris, Simeon's late master, had given up business, and this in itself was a capital opening for Reuben. He made use of it, and flourished. In less than eighteen months after his return to Liverpool, "Perez Brothers" opened their new shop as silversmiths and watchmakers, and from the careful, economical, and strictly honourable way in which the business was carried on—the name, too, with its associations of the honest hardworking man of whom these were the sons, adding golden weight—a very few months' trial proved that industry, economy, and honesty must carry their own reward.

But why was the widow alone? Was not Reuben married, and should not Sarah have been with her? Gentle reader, Reuben is not yet married; he has now gone to fetch his Sarah, for the term of probation for both is over. The morrow is the thirteenth birthday of the twins; and the widow is expecting the return of Reuben and Sarah and Ruth, as she sits with her darling Jeanie in her little parlour, the evening we meet her again.

Levison's innocence and his sudden death had, of course, been made public, not only in an official way, but through the eagerness of Reuben that not a shadow of shame should ever approach his Sarah. When the first month of mourning had expired, Sarah returned to her situation; her mistress quite forgetting former anger, and ready to declare Sarah had only done just as she ought towards her poor innocent father; that she was a pattern of Jewish daughters, and poured forth a volume of praises, all in the joy of getting her back.

Reuben had been anxious for their marriage as soon as he had completed two years from poor Jeanie Wilson's early death. Sarah fully sympathised in his feelings towards Jeanie, and they would often talk of her as a being dear to and cherished by them both. When the two years were completed, the marriage was still delayed, Mrs. Corea entreating Sarah to remain with her till she went on the Continent with her daughters, which she intended to do in about six or eight months. She had been too indulgent a mistress, and Miss Leon too sincere a friend, for Sarah to hesitate a moment in postponing her own happiness. Besides, the delay, though Reuben did not like it, might be beneficial to him, in allowing him time to get settled in his business. Before the period elapsed, Sarah and Reuben too were rejoiced that she was still in London, for Ruth needed her; the wherefore we shall find presently.

"Are they not late, mother?" inquired Simeon, as he joined his mother in her own parlour. "Troublesome loiterers! I wish they would arrive—I want my tea."

"And is that all you want, Simeon?" said the widow, smiling; "because that may easily be satisfied."

"No, no; not quite so voracious as that comes to. I want the loiterers themselves, though I have seen them later than you have, you know. You won't find Sarah a whit altered; she is just the gentle yet energetic creature she always was, only more animated, more happy, I think. Then Ruth, darling Ruth—oh, how much I owe to her! I never shall forget her reminding me of my promise to my poor father—her compelling me, as it were, to love my brother; and now, what is not that brother to me? Mother, is it not strange how completely prejudice has gone?"

"No, no; my dear son; your heart was too truly and faithfully pious, too desirous really to love its God, for prejudice long to obtain the ascendant. It comes sometimes in very early youth, when we are apt to think we alone are quite right, but, unless encouraged, cannot long stand the light of strengthening reason and real spiritual love."

"But does it not seem strange, mother, that I alone of my family should have been the one selected to receive such extreme kindness from a Christian—one of those whom, in former days, I was more prejudiced against than I dared acknowledge? I was very ill on my way home from London, and, as you know, Mr. Morton had me conveyed to his house, instead of leaving me to the care of heartless strangers at the public inn—had a physician to attend me, nursed me as his own son—would read and talk to me, even after he knew I was a Jew, on the *spirit* of religion, which we both felt. Never shall I forget the impressive tone and manner with which he said, when parting with me, 'Young man, never forget this important truth—*that heart alone in sincerity loves God, who can see, in every pious man, a brother, despite of difference of creed. That difference lies between man and his God: to do good and love one another is man's duty unto man,* and can, under no circumstances and in no places, be evaded. Learn this lesson, and all the kindness I have shown you is amply rewarded.' Is it not strange this should have occurred to me?"

"I do not think it strange, my dear son," replied Mrs. Perez, affectionately, though seriously. "I believe so firmly that God's eye is ever on us, that He so loves us, that He guides every event of our lives as will be most for our eternal good. He saw you sought to love and serve him—that the very prejudice borne towards others had its origin in the ardent love you bore your faith, and His infinite mercy permitted you to receive kindness from a Gentile and a stranger, that this one dark cloud should be removed, and your love for Him be increased in the love you bear your fellow-creatures."

"May I believe this, mother? It would be such a comfort, such a redoubled excitement to love and worship," answered Simeon, fixing his large dark eyes beseechingly on his mother's face. "But can I do so without profaneness, without robbing our gracious God of the sanctity which is so imperatively His due?"

"Surely you may, my dear boy. We have the whole word of God to prove and tell us that we are each individually and peculiarly His care—that He demands the *heart*; for dearer even than a mother's love for her infant child is His love towards us. How may we give Him our heart, if we never think of Him but as a Being too inexpressibly awful to approach? How feel the thanksgiving and gratitude He loves to receive, if we do not perceive His guiding hand, even in the simplest events of our individual lives? How seek Him in morrow, if we do not think He has power and will to hear and to relieve?—in daily prayer, if we were not each of us especially His own? My boy, if the hairs of our head are numbered, can we doubt the events of our life are guided as will be but for our eternal good, and draw us closer to our God? Think but of one dear to us both did it not seem, to our imperfect wisdom that Reuben's marriage must for ever have divided him from his nation? Yet that very circumstance brought him back. Our Father in mercy permitted him to follow his own will, to be prosperous, to lose even the hated badge of Israel, that his own heart might be his judge. Affliction also, sent from that same gracious hand, deepened the peculiar feelings which becoming a parent had already excited. Then the year of research put the final seal on his return to us. His mind could never have believed without calm, unimpassioned, steady examination. He has examined not alone his own faith. Mr. Vaughan, from being the explainer, was forced to become the defender of his own creed. He drew back, avowing, with a candour and charity which proved how truly of God was the *spirit* of religion within him, spite of the mistaken faith, that Reuben never could become a convert. And we know what true friends they are, notwithstanding Mr. Vaughan's disappointment. They have strengthened themselves in their own peculiar doctrines, without in the least shaking each other's."

"Yes, yes; you are quite right, mother dear, as you always are, replied Simeon, putting his arm round her, and affectionately kissing her. "What a blessing it has been for me to have such a mother.

Why, how now, master Joseph, what has happened? have you lost your wits?"

"If I have, it is for very joy!" exclaimed the boy, springing into the parlour, flinging his cap up to the ceiling, and so stifling his mother with kisses, as obliged her to call for mercy. "Mother, mother, how can I tell you the good news? I must scamper about before I can give them vent."

"Not another jump, not another step, till you have told us," exclaimed Simeon, laughing heartily at the boy's grotesque movements, and catching him midway in a jump that would not have disgraced a harlequin. Now, what is it, you overgrown baby? Are you not ashamed not to meet joy like a man?"

"No baby ever felt such joy, Simeon; and though I am a man to-morrow, I am not ashamed to act the madcap to-night. Mother, have I not told you the notice Mr. Morales has always taken of me, and the books he has lent me? Well, my master must have said such kind things of me; for what, what do you think he has offered?—that is, if you will consent; and I know, oh, I know you love me too well to refuse. He will call on you himself to-morrow about it."

"About what?" reiterated Simeon. "My good fellow, it is of no use his calling. You are gone distracted, mad, fit for nothing!"

"What does he offer, my love?" anxiously rejoined the widow.

"To take me home with him, as companion and friend to his own son, a boy just about my age—and such a fellow! He has often come to talk with me about the books we have both read. And Mr. Morales said I shall learn all that Conrad does. That I shall go abroad with them, and receive such an education, that years to come, if I still wish it, I may be fitted to be, what of all others I long to be, the *Hazan* of our people.[1] Hebrew, the Bible and the Talmud, and Latin, and Greek, and every thing that can help me for such an office; besides the lighter literature and studies, which will make me an enlightened friend for his son. Oh, mother! Simeon! is it not enough to make me lose my wits? But I must not though, for I shall want them more than ever. You do not speak, my own dear mother; but you will not, oh, I know you will not refuse."

---

1 *Hazan*: a singer trained to lead the special prayers and readings that constitute the Jewish worship services throughout the year.

"Refuse!" repeated the grateful widow, whose voice returned. "No, no! I would deserve to lose all the friends and blessings my God has given me, could I be so selfish to refuse, because for a few years, my beloved child, I must part with you. I do not fear for you; you will never forget to love your mother, or to remember and obey her precepts!"

"Give you joy, brother mine! though, by my honour, I had better not wish you any more joy, for this has well-nigh done for you," laughingly rejoined Simeon; for he saw that both Joseph and his mother's eyes were wet with grateful tears, and he did not wish emotion to become pain.

"Yes, one more joy, but one: it is almost sinful to wish more, when so much has been granted me," replied Joseph, almost sorrowfully. "Would that Ruth, my own Ruth, could but look on me once more; could but have sight restored, that I might think of her as happy, independent, not needing me to supply her sight. Oh, I should not have one wish remaining; but sometimes I think, afflicted as she is, and bound so closely as we are, I ought not to leave her."

"Then don't think any more silliness, my boy. Reuben and your humble servant are much obliged to you for imagining, because we do not happen to be her twin brothers, we cannot be to her what you are—out on your conceit! Make haste, and be a *Hazan,* and give her a home, and then you shall have her all to yourself; till then we will take care of her!"

Joseph's laughing reply was checked by the entrance of Leah, attended by a young man of very prepossessing appearance. It was Maurice Carvalho, the son and heir of a thriving bookseller and fancy stationer, of Liverpool, noted for a very devoted attendance on the pretty young milliner.

"Not arrived yet! why, I feared they would have been here before me, and thought me so unkind," said Leah, after affectionately greeting her mother. "Are we not late?"

"Dreadfully!" replied Simeon, mischievously. "Mrs. Valentine said you were at liberty after five; what have you been doing with yourselves!"

"Taking a walk, and went further than we thought," said Maurice, with affected carelessness, while Leah turned away with a blush.

"A walk! whew," and Simeon gave a prolonged whistle; "were you not cold?"

"Cold, you stupid fellow! why it is scarce autumn yet—the evenings are delightful."

"Particularly when the subject of conversation is of a remarkably summer warmth; with doves billing and cooing in the trees, and nightingales singing to the rose—there, am I not poetical! Leah, my girl, you used to like poetry; you ought to like it better now."

"Better—why?"

"Oh, because—because poetry and love are twin brothers, you know!"

"Simeon!" remonstrated Leah; but the pleased expression of young Carvalho's face and the satisfaction beaming on the widow's betrayed at once that the bachelor was quite at liberty to talk and amuse himself at their expense; their love was acknowledged to each other, and hallowed by a parent's blessing and consent.

Joseph had scarcely had time to tell his joyful tale to his sister, before a loud shout from Simeon, who had gone to the front to watch, proclaimed the anxiously-desired arrival. Joseph and Maurice darted out, and in less than a minute Reuben and Sarah entered the parlour.

"Mother, dearest mother, she is here—never, never, with God's blessing, to leave us again!" exclaimed Reuben, as Sarah threw herself alternately in the arms of the widow and Leah, and then again sought the embrace of the former, to hide the gushing tears of joy and feeling on her bosom, without the power of uttering a single word.

"My child, my own darling child! oh, what a blessing it is to look on your dear face again! Still my own Sarah, spite of all the cares and trials you have borne since we parted!" exclaimed the widow, fondly putting back the braids of beautiful hair to look intently on that sweet gentle face.

"And your blessing, mother, dearest mother; oh, say as you have so often told me, you could wish and ask no dearer, better wife for your Reuben; and such blessing may give my Sarah voice!" He threw his arm round her as he spoke, and both bent reverently before the widow, whose voice trembled audibly as she gave the desired blessing, and told how she had prayed and yearned that this might be, and

Sarah's voice returned, with a tone so glad, so bird-like in its joy, it needed but few words.

"My Ruth, where is my Ruth? and where are Joseph and Simeon gone?" asked the widow, when one joy was sufficiently relieved to permit her thinking of another.

"She will be here almost directly, mother. She was rather tired with the journey, and so I persuaded her to rest quiet at the inn close by, till I sent Simeon and Joseph with a coach for her and our luggage; they will not be long before they return. But tell me, where is my Jeanie? not in bed I hope, though we are late?"

"No; Esther took her away about half an hour ago, to amuse and keep her awake—not very difficult to do, as she is as lively as ever." Reuben was off in a moment.

"And Esther, dear Reuben, bid her come and see me," rejoined Sarah; and then clasping her aunt's hand, "oh, my dear aunt, what have I not felt, since we last met, that I owe you! I thought I was grateful, felt it to the full before; but not till I was tried, not till I learned the value of strong principles, steady conduct, and firm control, did I know all you had done for me. My God, indeed, was with me throughout; but this would not have been, had not your care and your affection taught me how to seek and love Him. Oh, will a life of devotion to our Reuben, and to you, and to his offspring, in part repay your kindness, dearest aunt!"

The widow's answer we leave our readers to imagine, fearing they should accuse us of again becoming sentimental. Old Esther speedily made her appearance, and her greeting was second only in affection to the widow's own.

"Father, dear father, come home, come home!" was the next sweet lisping voice that met the delighted ears of Sarah, and in another moment Reuben appeared with the child in his arms, her little rosy fingers twisted in his hair, and her round soft cheek resting against his.

"This is my poor motherless babe, for whom I have bespoken your love, your protection, your guiding hand, my Sarah," he whispered, in a low, earnest voice. "Will you love her for my sake?"

"And for her own and for her mother's; do not doubt me, Reuben. If she is yours, is she not, then, mine?" she answered, in the same voice. The child looked at her as if half inclined to spring into the caressing, extended arms, but then, with sudden shyness, hid her face on her father's shoulder.

"Jeanie, darling, what was the word I taught you to say? Look at her and say it, and kiss her as you do me."

The child still hesitated; but then, as if emboldened by Sarah's sweet voice calling her name, she looked full in her face and lisped out, "Mother," held up her little face to kiss her, and was quite contented to be transferred from Reuben's arms to those of Sarah.

"Ruth, Ruth—I think I hear her coming!" joyfully exclaimed Leah, a few minutes afterwards.

"Go to her then, dear—detain her one minute," hastily whispered Reuben, in a tone and manner that made his sister start. "Do not ask me why now—you will know the moment you see her—only go. I must prepare my mother. I did not think she would have been here so soon."

Leah obeyed him, her heart beating, she did not know why, and Reuben turned to his mother. Sarah had given little Jeanie to Esther's care, and was kneeling by her as if to intercept her starting up.

"What is it—what is it? Why do you keep my child from me? why send her brothers and sisters to her, instead of letting her come to me? Reuben, Sarah! what new affliction has befallen my angel child?"

"Affliction? None, none!" repeated Sarah and Reuben together. "It is joy, dearest aunt, all joy. Oh, bear but joy as you have borne sorrow, and all will be well."

"Joy!" she repeated, almost wildly; "what greater joy can there be than to have my children all once again around me? I have heard my Ruth has been ill, but that she was quite well, quite strong again, and have blessed God for that great mercy."

"But there may be more, my mother, yet more for which to bless Him. Oh, are not all things possible with Him? He who in His wisdom once deprived of sight, can He not restore it?"

"Reuben, Sarah! what can you mean? My child, my Ruth!" but voice and almost power failed, for such a trembling seized her limbs that Reuben was compelled to support her as she sat. It was but for a moment, for the next a light figure had bounded into the room, followed by Simeon and Joseph, Maurice and Leah.

"Mother! mother! mother! They need not tell me where you are. You need not come to your poor blind Ruth. I can SEE your dear face—see it once again."

The widow had sprung up from her chair; but ere she had made one step forward her child was in her arms—was fixing those long-closed eyes upon her face as if they would take in every feature with one delighted gaze. One look was sufficient. A deadly faintness, from over-excited feelings, passed over the widow's heart; but as she felt Ruth's passionate kisses on her lips and cheeks, life returned in a wild burst of thanksgiving, and the widow folded her child closer and yet closer to her heart, and, overpowered by joy as she had never been by sorrow, "she lifted up her voice and wept."[1]

Reader, our task is done—for need we say it was the benevolent exertion of Miss Leon, under a merciful Providence, which procured the last most unlooked-for blessing to the widow and her family? She had remarked there was a slight change in the appearance of the child's eyes, had taken her without delay to the most eminent oculist of the day, and received his opinion that sight might be restored. The rest, to a character such as hers, was easy; and thus twice was she the means of materially brightening the happiness of the Perez family; for, though we had not space in our last chapter to dilate on it, it had been actually through her means the innocence of Levison had been discovered, though she herself was at the time scarcely conscious how. She had mentioned it to everybody she thought likely to be useful in discovering it, had been laughed at for her folly in believing such a tale, warned against taking up the guilt or innocence of such a person's character; and, in short, almost every one dissuaded her from mentioning the subject; it really would do her harm. But she had persevered against even her own hope of effecting good, and was, as we have seen, successful.

Before we quite say farewell, we would ask our readers if we have indeed been happy enough in this simple narration to make one solemn and most important truth clear as our own heart would wish—that, however dark may be our horizon, however our prayers and trust may for a while seem unheeded, our eager wishes denied us, our dearest feelings the mere means of woe, yet there is an

1 Ruth 1.9.

answering and pitying God above us still, who, when He bids us "commit our ways unto Him, and trust also in Him," has not alone the power, but the will, the loving-kindness, the infinite mercy, to "bring it to pass." My friends, that God is still our God; and though the events of our simple tale may have no origin in real life, is there one amongst us who can look back upon his life and prayers, and thoughts, and yet say that overruling Providence is but fiction, for we feel it, know it not? Oh, if so, it is his own heart, not the love and word of his God, at fault. All may not be blessed so visibly as the widow and her family, but all who wait on and trust in the Lord will have their reward, if not on earth, yet dearer, more gloriously in heaven.

1843

THE SPIRIT OF NIGHT

FOUNDED ON A HEBREW APOLOGUE[1]

"LET there be light!" the Omnific Word had spoken, and light was.[2] Over the newly-created world the pure element rushed from the spiritual courts of the High Empyrean, where it had reigned from everlasting in its subtle essence, its ethereal exhalations, fit only for the atmosphere of those angelic spirits, who, at the word of the Highest, took their appointed stations in the new-formed world. Radiance too glorious, too resplendent for mortal view, filled the illimitable space, uniting earth with heaven as by a cloud of glory. Where had been Chaos, circled with shapeless darkness, now revolved, in its vast flood of Irradiating lustre, the new work of the Eternal. Thousands of radiant spirits floated to and fro on the refulgent flood. The dazzling iris of their wings, the music of their movements, filling space with beauty and with sound; while up, up from the lowest Heaven to the High Empyrean—from the young seraph to the mighty spirits nighest the Invisible Throne, whose resplendent presence dazzled even the purified orbs of their angelic brethren—up, through every heaven and every rank, sounded the glad hallelujahs of love and praise.

At every word of the Highest, creation sprung. Darkness, borne back by the mighty torrent of effulgent light, would have passed annihilated from the face of the new-born world, but, shielded by angelic ministers, it lingered, in its new-appointed sphere, to do its destined bidding. A firmament of sapphire, stretched between the waters and the waters, veiling the glory of the spiritual heavens from the grosser earth. Land rose from the liquid deep. The rolling waters rushed impetuously to their destined boundaries, held there by the Omnific will. And over the land the creating Word went forth; and, at once, the mountains raised their stupendous forms, crowned with

1 An apologue is a *midrash* or fable. The *midrash* upon which this tale is founded is Morris Raphall's "The Sun and the Moon," reprinted in Appendix D of this volume. The biblical prooftext is Gen. 1.16.

2 Omnific: all powerful. High Empyrean: the realm of the angels. The tale refers to the account of creation in Gen. 1.

imperishable verdure; the valleys, and woods, and glens rose and sunk in their appointed rests; and flowers, and trees, and streams, and thousand other charms of sight, and sound, and sense, burst forth into perfected being. Myriads of angels hovered round, visible *then* in their beauty; but *now* heard only in the sweet breath of the gentle flowers in the varied sounds of the forest trees as the wind floats by; in the summer breeze, or the wintry storm; in the musical gush of the silvery rill; aye, and in the deep hush and calm of the evening hour, when nature herself, as conscious of their ministering presence, sinks into deep and spiritual repose.

But not for the abode of angelic spirits was this lovely world. A new creation was to raise the voice of love and adoration! and for such, the spiritual light enveloping the infant globe was too ethereal, too resplendent. Nought but the purified orbs of the angelic and archangelic hosts could gaze on its refined effulgence; and, therefore, from the council of the Eternal went forth the decree:—

"Let there be two great lights to rule the earth, the one by day, and the one by night, and they shall rule times and seasons." And as He spake it was. Instantaneously the minute particles of the ethereal essence formed into an orb of splendour, fraught with such power and glory, that the lustrous flood rushed back into the Heavenly Fount—earth needing it no more;—circled by a diadem of many-coloured light, extending in resplendent rays over the new-born world, infusing its golden glory over the azure heavens; clouds, dyed with the brilliant tints of amethyst, and rose, and ruby, formed before him and faded into glory as He passed. Earth, through her ministering spirits of mount, and wood, and stream, and flower, sent up her thrilling song of thanksgiving, echoed and re-echoed by the myriads and myriads of angels peopling the spiritual courts. Heaven and Earth rejoiced. Increased and dazzling beauty enveloped the new creation. Luscious fragrance issued from the flowers; their petals, adorned by their guardian seraphs, expanded to the glorious orb, and shone in his rays like gems. The Spirit of Day, selected from the highest and purest order of angels, to renew and tend the beauteous work, ascended his throne in the burning centre, whence the effulgent rays emanate on earth, but on which no mortal eye can look; and proudly and rejoicingly as a bridegroom coming forth from his chamber, as a youthful hero from his victorious career, he guided the glorious luminary on its resplendent course, joining his voice to the hallelujahs pealing around.

And in varied but equal beauty rose the second light; but its guardian spirit, selected from the same pure and exalted ranks, looked on the effulgence of the Orb of Day, and beheld his brother spirit circled by glory more dazzling than his own. His invisible throne was within the silver radiance of his orb. Light, ethereal and pure as the heavenly essence of which both sun and moon had been formed, enriched him less glittering, but equally resplendent. But a deep shadow stole over the exquisite colouring of the spirit's wings. His voice of music refused to join the pealing hallelujahs.

"Wherefore?" he exclaimed; and the troubled accents sounded through space, strangely and darkly falling on the full tide of song. "Wherefore do two monarchs occupy one throne? Wherefore to me is given less than to my brother? I have loved, I have served as faithfully as he. Why, then, should I be second, and he the first? Earth rejoices when he comes. Heaven greets him with songs of love. What need is there for me, unless to me the same is given?"

The hallelujahs ceased. A sudden silence, awful in its profoundness, sunk on the rejoicing myriads. The pure founts of ever-living light became obscured. Thunder rolled over the illimitable expanse. The superb radiance of the effulgent moon vanished, and, spreading far into the Empyrean, became the glorious host of stars, each with its attendant spirit as it formed. Darkness clothed the complaining angel; the beautiful luminary given to his charge, seemed quivering and fading into space; while, still strong and rejoicing, the Orb of Day held on his victorious career.

Prostrate and convulsed with remorseful anguish, the spirit sunk before the celestial hosts. He who had been of that favoured class to whom the ways as well as the works of the Highest were revealed, had fallen lower in intellect and love than the youthful seraph, whose task was only to worship and adore. Where could he hide himself from their searching orbs? Where fly from the flashing light that, as the thunder rolled, played round him, marking him disgraced and criminal? But Him whom he had offended, he loved as only angels love. And so he welcomed that remorseful agony, and prayed, "Have mercy, Father of all Beings! My Father, have mercy on me!" And out of that awful stillness issued a thrilling strain of gushing music—low, soft, spiritual—the murmured prayer, from countless myriads, for pardon for an erring brother. The dimness fled from the founts of light. The thunder ceased; the scorching lightnings blazed no longer. A mild effulgence circled the sorrowing spirit as he lay, burying his refulgent brow in the darkened iris of his wings.

From the invisible throne of the Highest, the mightiest, the best beloved, most favoured messenger of the Eternal, the SPIRIT OF LOVE, winged his downward flight, and on the instant, space became irradiated. New lustre spread over the vast courts of Heaven; the richest harmonies attended every movement of his wings. Angels and archangels, seraphs and ministers, pressed forward as he passed, to bask in the wondrous beauty of his lustrous face, and raise anew the irrepressible burst of song.

"Spirit of Night, arise!" he said, and the repentant angel lifted up his brow once more in returning hope, so thrillingly that voice of liquid music fell; "arise, and list the irrevocable decree of the Eternal! Because thou has envied the resplendence of the Spirit of Day, the radiance of thine orb will henceforth be borrowed from His lustre; and when yonder earth passes thee thou wilt stand, as now thou dost, deprived of thy glory, and eclipsed, either wholly or in part. Thou hast dared arraign the wisdom and the goodness of the Highest and though He pardons, yet must He chastise, lest others sin yet more. Yet weep not, repentant brother, thy repining is forgiven, and thou too shalt reign a monarch in thy radiance! Queen of the lovely night will thine orb be hailed; the tears of thy repentance shall be a reviving balm to all that languish; imparting consolation to the mourner, rest to the weary, soothing to the careworn, strength to the exhausted. Peace shall be thy whisper, and in thy kingdom of stillness and repose, breathe thrillingly the promise of Heaven, and its rest. Go forth, then, on thy mild and vivifying career. The Orb of Day will do his work, and be hailed with rejoicing mirth; but many a one shall turn to thee from him, and in the radiance of thy tears find consolation."

He spake: and behold the pale but lovely lustre in which the Orb of Night still shines flowed round her. The Spirit of Night resumed his silvery throne, and in the profound submissiveness of most perfect love entered upon his silent and beautiful career, circled by the glittering radiance of the attendant stars. Soon was revealed the benignant mercy of His sentence. Even ere sin darkened the lovely earth, His beauteous orb was hailed by all creation with rejoicing; and when man fell, when labour and weariness, sickness and woe, obtained dominion, how soothing the consolation whispered by the Spirit of Night! Weeping oft at the remembrance of his own fault, the Spirit commiserates the tears of others, floating over the earth, invisible, save through the exquisite beauty of his orb, and the thrilling thoughts of Heaven and immortality awakening in the soul, which, formed of kindred essence, becomes thus conscious of his presence, the Spirit sends his soft rays, formed from the liquid lustre of his tears, on all who need his pity and repose. By the couch of the sufferer—the side of the sorrowing—by the kneeling penitent—by the wakeful mourner—by the careworn and the weary—to the hut of the beggar as the palace of the king—he sends pity, and peace, and consolation. Nor does he sympathise with sorrow alone: the joy which, in the sunshine and midst the turmoil of the world, has agitated the soul even to pain, he softens into such deep calm, as to whisper of that Heaven whence alone the full bliss comes. Love, shrinking from the garish day, finds in his presence eloquence and voice. The poet, oppressed and suffering in the rich blaze of day, at night pours out his full soul in stirring words; for, conscious of a spirit's presence, the pressure of infinity is then less painful to be borne. The artist, does he dream of giving life to the vacant canvas, the senseless marble, or voice and sound to the rich harmonies for ever breathing in his ear—labours in toil, often in despondency, during the day, for Earth only is present then; but when alone with his own soul and the holy night; when the Spirit visible either through his silvery tears, or in the rich beauty of his starry zone, penetrates his whole being with his heavenly presence, then life is strong once more! The dream of Immortality on Earth, even as in Heaven, dashes down all earthly fears. The spark of the Deity in every soul is rekindled by the touch of its kindred essence, and Hope, and Truth, and Beauty start into enduring glory beneath the vivifying flash.

Beautiful Spirit! such has been, and is, and will still be thy task. Over the earth thou floatest, and man, be he in gloom or gladness, aspiring or desponding, hails thee with rejoicing; and even as the pale flowers drooping beneath the noontide heat, and the parched and languishing earth, so does he turn to thee for coolness and repose. Beautiful Spirit! thou hast sinned and been forgiven—therefore we rest on thee.

1852

II. POETRY

Aguilar's first major successes were as a poet. Along with Celia and Marion Moss, she was the first Anglo-Jewish woman to publish poetry. She published in several Jewish periodicals, including *The Occident*, the major American Jewish magazine edited by Isaac Leeser in Philadelphia; *The Jewish Chronicle*, the most important Anglo-Jewish weekly newspaper, edited by Abraham Benisch; and *The Voice of Jacob*, a monthly Anglo-Jewish periodical edited by Jacob Franklin. She also published occasional pieces in Christian women's magazines such as *The Keepsake* and *La Belle Assemblée.*

The majority of the poems included here were first printed in *The Occident*, where they were especially well received.[1] Poems like "The Address to the Ocean," from her song cycle, "Communings with Nature," reflect the influence of Romantic nature poetry, but turn the Romantics' natural supernaturalism on its head. Some, like "An Hour of Peace" and "Sabbath Thoughts III" (the latter from her song cycle, "Sabbath Thoughts"), are liturgical in nature. These might be profitably compared to the tradition of *tekhinot*, or liturgical poems and meditations originating among Jewish women in Eastern Europe. Unlike male liturgy, which was canonized in the official prayer book and usually written in Hebrew, *tekhinot* were usually written in Yiddish, the Eastern European Jewish vernacular, and addressed spiritual issues specific to women. For example, many *tekhinot* were written on the subjects of virginity, miscarriage, childbirth, or the death of children.

In other poems, Aguilar writes in and against the traditions of Romantic women's poetry, including the sentimental focus on mothers and children and the invocation of Biblical women as progenitor's of English women's poetry. In poems such as "Song of the Spanish Jews," "The Hebrew's Appeal," "The Dialogue Stanzas," "The Wanderers," and "A Vision of Jerusalem," she deals imaginatively with political, spiritual, aesthetic issues raised by Jews' experience of diaspora. For example, in "The Song of Spanish Jews," she

1 A statement of accounts for *The Occident* between 1843 and 1847 shows that Aguilar was one of its most highly paid writers, and her income increased each year from £3.1.4 in 1843 to £11.7.10 in 1847. Box 9, FF1, Isaac Leeser Collection, Center for Judaic Studies, U of Pennsylvania.

imagines the gratitude Jews must have felt toward Spain in the eleventh and twelfth centuries, when the country allowed Jews to settle, flourish, and produce the great Hebrew poetry of writers like Yehudah Halevy. Aguilar implicitly contrasts the Spanish Golden Age with the expulsion of the Jews in 1492 and the Inquisition (from which her own parents fled). She hopes that Jews' residence in England will inaugurate a new Jewish Golden Age. "A Poet's Dying Hymn" meditates on the problem of originating a Jewish poetry in England, while "A Vision of Jerusalem" and "Rocks of Elim" lament Jews' lost homeland in Jerusalem. In the former case, Aguilar's ecstatic vision of Jerusalem ironically comes to her while she sits in a Protestant church listening to the organ.

Perhaps her most successful poem is "The Wanderers," a retelling of the story of Abraham, Sarah, Hagar and Ishmael from the point of view of Hagar. Hagar, Abraham's Egyptian servant, whose name in Hebrew means "the stranger," has been cast out from her home due to Sarah's jealousy. Ironically, for Aguilar, Hagar is a figure for Jews in diaspora who have been forcibly exiled from their homes.[1] Here, Sarah is the oppressive figure. It is worth comparing the delineation of Sarah here and in the excerpt below from *The Women of Israel*, where she is idealized as a wife and mother. In "The Wanderers," it is Hagar who is identified with the sanctified maternal voice, and it is her voice to which God responds.

1 See Daniel Harris, "Hagar in Christian Britain: Grace Aguilar's 'The Wanderers,' *Victorian Literature and Culture* 27 (1999): 143-69.

SABBATH THOUGHTS III.

"I will never leave thee, nor forsake thee."[1]

AND is there peace and rest in heaven,
And wilt *Thou* never leave me, Lord?
Tho' this fair earth has never given,
To yearning hearts, one answering word?

And is't with Thee our souls shall find 5
The craving void of suffering filled—
The throbbing pulse, the care-worn mind,
The anguish'd heart, be hush'd and still'd?

Oh breathe thy promise, Lord of Peace,[2]
My spirit yearns and craves for Thee, 10
I pray not sorrow's pang to cease,
Let me but feel Thou art with me!

Let me but clasp again the Love
Thou did'st vouchsafe, erewhile to me,
When first my soul look'd up above, 15
And pined and thirsted, Lord, for Thee!

Oh leave me not, forsake me not!
Unto my own rebellious will,[3]
Whate'er of trial cloud my lot,
Let me but love Thee, trust Thee still! 20

Keep me but constant in my trust,
Father! oh grant it fail not now,
Lest sinking prostrate in the dust,
Despair and doubt should cloud my brow.

---

1 See Deut. 31.6, 8.

2 Cf. Isa. 66.12, "For thus saith the Lord, Behold, I will extend peace to her like a river."

3 A reference to the Yetzer haRa, or "evil inclination," a rabbinic concept.

25 Again, again the waves of Life
Are o'er me rushing in their might,
Whose troubled currents' storm and strife,
Hurl my weak spirit back to night.

I deem'd the gleam of heav'n, that stole,
30 When prostrate on my couch I lay,
Had left sweet peace upon my soul,
To strengthen't for a darker day.

But it hath pass'd, and left no sign,
The struggle, duty to fulfil,
35 Has robbed me of the bliss divine,
Which smiled, when weariness chained me still.

Oh, if no comfort be mine own,
Father, still fix my hope on Thee!
Till I may feel thy love alone,
40 And break my chains and set me free.[1]

'Tis but to try my faltering faith,
Thou dost awhile thy presence veil,
Yet tho' thy worm[2] be tried to death,
My trust, my hope, shall never fail.

45 Back, back unto the waves of Life,
My shrinking soul, still firmly on!
What if the path, with storm be rife?
The crown of faith[3] may yet be won!

In his own time, my yearning cry,
50 Shall pierce his radiant courts of love,

---

1 Perhaps a reference to Isa. 58.6, "Is not this the fast that I have chosen? to loose the bands of wickedness, to undo the heavy burdens, and to let the oppressed go free, and that ye break every yoke?"

2 Cf. Job 25.6, "How much less man, that is a worm? and the son of man, which is a worm?"

3 Cf. Is. 28.5, "In that day shall the Lord of hosts be for a crown of glory, and for a diadem of beauty, unto the residue of his people."

And faith shall change to pray'r each sigh,
That wings its quivering flight above.

1844

AN HOUR OF PEACE

Oh, wake me not from this sweet dream
  Now o'er my spirit stealing,
Of heaven's deep calm, a shadowy gleam,
  This care-worn heart is feeling.

This is not suff'ring, though my frame, 5
  Be weak and pain-struck lying;
While life's sad cares no thought can claim,
  There is no need for sighing.

This—this is peace! disturb it not,
  To heav'n that dream has won me, 10
Oh let me lie, the world forgot—
  God's eye alone upon me!

'Tis thoughts of heav'n, of God, of death
  That now are round me clinging,
That o'er my soul one balmy breath 15
  Of purest joys are flinging.

Oh break them not, too few, too fleet,
  Like gleams of light departing,
Sent with such perfect calm replete,
  To soothe earth's restless smarting. 20

And oh! when death is near at hand,
  May such bless'd thoughts be given;
My throbbing heart be softly fann'd,
  By breezes sent from heaven!

No need e'en then of sigh or groan, 25
  If those I love surround me,

My mother's kiss to soothe my moan,
  My father's arm around me!

And one loved friend my hand to hold,
30 And whisper tales of heaven,
And one in mem'ry long enfold,
  When life's last link is riven.

And oh, if music may descend,
  To hail the soul that's flying,
35 Let it with love's soft accents blend,
  To soothe me e'en in dying.

No need for tears, an hour like this
  Forbids all sounds of wailing,
It whispereth of immortal bliss,
40 Whose joy is never failing.

These are the visions sweet, that twine
  Their lustrous rays around me,
When pain and weakness oft are mine,
  And to my couch have bound me.

45 Oh, think not then, this tearful eye
  Thus heavy is with sorrow,
Nor seek to soothe me as I lie,
  And promise health to-morrow.

Nor wake me from these blessed dreams—
50 The cares of life oppress me,
I would lie still in heaven's own gleams,
  And feel—my God doth bless me!

1843

A POET'S DYING HYMN

And must I hence depart?
  Without one flow'r of fame,
That spring from one loving heart,
  Might sweetly wreathe my name?
And all those glowing dreams, 5
  Within my soul enshrined,
Passing—like Summer's—fitful gleams,
  'Neath Autumn's nipping wind.

Oh! am I called away,
  Ere all my harp is strung?[1] 10
With none to wake the magic lay,
  That joy o'er *me*, hath flung.
Softly its numbers flow,
  Yet rich, and full, and deep,
Can ye not hear its music low 15
  Lulling my soul to sleep?

I go—I go—Oh Earth!
  Thy glist'ning dreams are o'er;
The voice of Love—the song of mirth,
  Shall never bless me more. 20
The yellow leaves that fall
  Around me in decay,
Have spirit tones, that gently call
  My yearning soul away.

But tears will have their way, 25
  Thus—thus unknown to fade,
Oh why—why am I called away,
  Ere one bright wreath I've made?

---

1 The harp, the psaltery, the cymbal, and the timbrel were instruments used by the Levites during prayer in the ancient Temple, as recorded in numerous Psalms, e.g., Ps. 98.5, "Sing unto the Lord with the harp; with the harp, and the voice of a psalm." Subsequently the harp became a symbol for Jewish poetry, as well as a ubiquitous symbol for women's poetry in English Romantic poetry.

Sweet flowers, that sleep in earth
Will burst dark winter's chain,
And deck the world with love and mirth,
When spring doth smile again.

And must I with'ring lie,
On earth's cold mould'ring breast?
No! no! my soul shall wake on high,
Where flow'rs immortal rest.
Thou—thou a seraph's song
My harp's full notes shall wake,
And soon, oh soon, an angel throng,
Their deep response shall make.

Then, Autumn's plaintive moan,
Shall breathe of death no theme,
But flow'rs and leaves now seared and strewn,
Shall bloom in fadeless spring.
And man is but a flow'r,
Cut down a little while,
To wake again in Eden's bower,
'Neath Spring's eternal smile.

1842

SONG OF THE SPANISH JEWS, DURING THEIR "GOLDEN AGE"

"It was in Spain that the golden age of the Jews shone with the brightest and most enduring splendour.

"In emulation of their Moslemite brethren, they began to cultivate their long disused and neglected poetry; the harp of Judah was heard to sound again, though with something of a foreign tone."

—*Milman's History of the Jews.*

Oh, dark is the spirit that loves not the land
Whose breezes his brow have in infancy fann'd,
That feels not his bosom responsively thrill
To the voice of her forest, the gush of her rill.

Who hails not the flowers that bloom on his way, 5
As blessings there scattered his love to repay;
Who loves not to wander o'er mountain and vale,
Where echoes the voice of the loud rushing gale.

Who treads not with awe where his ancestors lie,
As their spirits around him are hovering nigh, 10
Who seeks not to cherish the flowers that bloom,
Amid the fresh herbs that o'ershadow their tomb.

Oh, cold is such spirit: and yet colder still
The heart that for Spain does not gratefully thrill,
The land, which the foot of the weary has pressed, 15
Where exile and wand'rer found blessing and rest.

On the face of the earth our doom was to roam,
To meet not a brother, to find not a home,
But Spain has the exile and homeless received,
And we feel not of country so darkly bereaved. 20

Home of the exiles! oh ne'er will we leave thee,
As mother to orphan, fair land we now greet thee,

Sweet peace and rejoicing may dwell in thy bowers,
For even as Judah, fair land! thou art ours.

25 Oh, dearest and brightest! the homeless do bless thee,
From ages to ages they yearn to possess thee,
In life and in death they cling to thy breast,
And seek not and wish not a lovelier rest.

1843

A VISION OF JERUSALEM,

While Listening to a Beautiful Organ in One of the Gentile Shrines

I SAW thee, oh, my fatherland, my beautiful, my own!
As if thy God had raised thee from the dust where thou art strewn,[1]
His glory cast around thee, and thy children bound to Him,
In links so brightly woven, no sin their light could dim.

5 Methought the cymbal's sacred sound came softly on my ear,
The timbrel, and the psaltery, and the harp's full notes were near;
And thousand voices chaunted, his glory to upraise,
More heavenly and thrillingly, than e'en in David's days.

Methought the sons of Levi were in holy garments there,
10 Th' anointed one upon his throne in holiness so fair,
That all who gazed on him might feel the promise he fulfill'd,
And sin, and all her baleful train, now he had come, were still'd.[2]

And thousands of my people thronged the pure and holy fane,
The curse removed from ev'ry brow, ne'er more to come again;
Th' Almighty hand from each, from all, had ta'en the scorching
15 brand,
And Israel, forgiven, knelt within our own bright land!

---

1 An allusion to Ezekiel's vision of the ressurection of the House of Israel, Ezek. 37.1-4. Subsequent lines draw on Jewish mystical visions of the Divine court derived from Ezek. 1.

2 Milton personifies Sin as female in *Paradise Lost*, Bk. 2, 650 ff.

My country! oh, my country! was my soul enrapt in thee
One passing moment, that mine eyes might all thy glory see?
What magic power upheld me there?—alas, alas! it past,
And darkness o'er my aspiring soul the heavy present cast. 20

I stood ALONE 'mid thronging crowds who filled that stranger
shrine,
For there were none who kept the faith I hold so dearly mine:
An exile felt I, in that house, from Israel's native sod,—
An exile yearning for my *home*,—yet loved still by my God.

No exile from his love! No, no; tho' captive I may be, 25
And I must weep, whene'er I think, my fatherland, on thee!
Jerusalem! my beautiful! my own! I feel thee still,
Though for our sins thy sainted sod the Moslem strangers fill.

Oh! that thy children all would feel what our sins have done,
And by our ev'ry action prove such guilt the exiles shun, 30
Until they seek their God in prayer, oh! will He turn to them,
And raise thee once again in life, my own Jerusalem![1]

"If they their own iniquity in humbleness confess,
And all their fathers' trespasses,—nor seek to make them less;
If they my judgments say are right, and penitently own 35
They reap the chastisement of sin, whose seeds long years have
sown:

"Then will I all my vows recall, and from them take my hand,
My covenant remember, and have mercy on their land."[2]
So spake the Lord in boundless love to Israel his son;[3]
But can we, dare we say these things we *do*, or we *have* done? 40

---

1 These themes—of exile as a punishment for sin, and of return to the land as a reward for repentance—are common in the Prophets, especially in Deuteronomy and Jeremiah.

2 Cf. Lev. 26.40-45.

3 Cf. Exod. 4.22: "Thus saith the Lord, Israel is my son, even my first-born."

Alas, my country! thou must yet deserted rest and lone,
Thy glory, loveliness, and life, a Father's gifts, are flown!
Oh! that my prayers could raise thee radiant from the sod,
And turn from Judah's exiled sons their God's avenging rod!

45 And like an oak thou standest, of leaves and branches shorn;[1]
And we are like the withered leaves by autumn tempests torn
From parent stems, and scattered wide o'er hill, and vale, and sea,[2]
And known as Judah's ingrate race wherever we may be.

Oh! blessed was that visioned light that flash'd before mine eye;
50 But, oh, the quick awakening check'd my soul's ecstatic sigh!
Yet still, still wilt thou rise again, my beautiful, my home,
Our God will bring thy children back, ne'er, ne'er again to roam!

1844

THE ADDRESS TO THE OCEAN

SOUND on, thou mighty Deep, sound on, thou Sea,[3]
Lash thy blue waves to snowy crested foam,
Wake into music, glorious and free,
Proclaim thee bulwark of our island home.

5 Sound on! thou hast a voice of freedom, Sound!
My soul hath thrilling echoes to thy voice,
And throbs and bounds, as if on thee were found,
A home where life all chainless, might rejoice!

Thou beautiful! thou glorious! all unstained
10 With earth's sad curse, thou rollest on thy way;
Might! majesty! music! all retained,
Thro' whelming ages, tinged not by decay.

---

1 Cf. Isa. 1.29-30 and 6.13.

2 Deut. 28.64.

3 Cf. Byron, *Childe Harold's Pilgrimage*, IV.1603: "Roll on, thou deep and dark blue ocean—roll!" Much of Aguilar's poem echoes and replies to stanzas 178-179 in Byron's poem, from which this line comes.

Thou hast no dream of shadow or of change,
No murm'ring voice of wailing or of woe;
Free on thy glorious path, uncheck'd to range 15
And do His will, who rules thy billowy flow.

I dream not of thy gem'd and treasured caves,
The slumbering riches, on thy breast that lie,
Or treacherous smiles, that beam from sunny waves,
When death-fraught storms are darkly hov'ring nigh. 20

Thou speakest not of these, I do but gaze
In childish marvel on thy billowy sea,
And list the breeze, with thy bright waves that plays,
And feel thee still, the beautiful! the free!

Then, oh sound on! my soul drinks in each tone, 25
Of gushing waters, as a voice of love,
Whose melody in infancy was known,
Lifting my spirit on those depths above.

Yes, 'tis of God thou speakest, ay, of Him
Who held thy rolling billows in His hand, 30
Before whose voice thy wildest war sounds dim,
And 'neath whose eye, thy whelming depths are span'd.

Fit altar for His praise, thou mighty deep,
Oh, my full soul doth faint and quiv'ring lie,
Whelm'd 'neath the thoughts, which o'er it rushing sweep, 35
Ere they burst forth in words of ecstacy!

Hail! hail! once more I come to thee, thine own,
Thine own true, loving child, with bounding heart,
And fancy free—and memory's deep tone,
And hope's sweet dream, that hath in care no part. 40

I deem'd them flown; but, oh they did but sleep
Neath the full grasp of inward care and pain;

Thy voice, the spell hath broken, and they sweep
O'er my full soul, rejoicingly again!

45 Let thy rich voice sound on! roll on thy waves
'Mid storm and sunshine, still the blue, the free!
Life is upspringing from my soul's deep caves,
To hail, to bless thee, oh, thou glorious sea!

1847

THE HEBREW'S APPEAL, On Occasion of the Late Fearful *Ukase* Promulgated by the Emperor of Russia[1]

Awake! arise! ye friends of Israel's race,
The wail of thousands lingers on the air,
By heavy pinions borne, thro' realms of space,
'Till Israel shudd'ring, Israel's woe must bear;
5 The voice of suff'ring echoes to the skies,
And oh, not yet! one pitying heart replies.

List to the groan from manly bosoms rent,
The wilder sob from weaker spirits wrung,
The deep woe that hath in voice no vent,
10 Yet round the heart her deathly robe has flung,
And childish tears flow thick and fast like rain,
From eyes that never wept, and ne'er shall weep again.

---

1 Beginning with Catherine the Great in the 1790s, successive Russian Emperors issued *ukases*, or decrees, restricting Jewish settlement, commercial activity, and communal associations to a certain area of residence on the border of Russia and Poland known as the Pale of Settlement. Aguilar refers to a decree issued by Nicholas I in 1844 that dissolved all Jewish communal organizations and forcibly resettled Jews into the Pale. Aguilar notes: "The above poem was written nearly six months ago, when the Russian *ukase* was first made public, and sent to the only paper in England devoted to Jewish interests—the *Voice of Jacob*,—the writer wishing to prove that at least one female Jewish heart and voice were raised in an appeal for her afflicted brethren. The Editor of the V. of J. did not insert it, on the plea of having so much press of matter as to prevent giving it the required space. The *Christian Lady's Magazine* not only accepted and inserted it, but in bold and spirited prose appealed to her countrymen on the same subject. Still a Jewish paper is the natural channel for the public appearance of the poem, and therefore the writer sends it to the *Occident*, believing that though somewhat late, it will not there be disregarded."

Vain, vain, the mother's piteous shriek of woe,
Her dying infants clinging to her breast;
And age infirm, and youth, whose high hearts glow; 15
Vain, vain their cry for mercy on the oppress'd.
The *Ukase* has gone forth—a word, a breath,
And thousands are cast out, to exile and to death.

Ay, death! for such is exile—fearful doom,
From homes expell'd—yet still to Poland chain'd; 20
'Till want and famine mind and life consume,
And sorrow's poison'd chalice, all is drain'd.
Oh God, that this should be! that one frail man
Hath power to crush a nation 'neath his ban.

Will none arise! with outstretch'd hand to save! 25
No prayer for pity, and for aid awake?
Will SHE who gave to Liberty the slave,
For God's own people not one effort make?
Will SHE not rise once more, in mercy clad,
And heal the bleeding heart, and Sorrow's sons make glad?[1] 30

Will England sleep, when Justice bids her wake,
And send her voice all thrillingly afar?
Will England sleep, when her rebuke might shake
With shame and terror, e'en the tyrant Czar,
And 'neath the magic of her mild appeal, 35
Move Russia's frozen soul for Israel to feel?

Oh England! thou hast call'd us to thy breast,
And done to orphans all a mother's part,
And given them peace, and liberty, and rest,
And healing pour'd into the homeless heart; 40
Then, oh once more, let Israel mercy claim,
And suff'ring thousands bless our England's honour'd name.

---

1 "She" is England. England abolished the slave trade in 1807, and put an end to all slavery in the British Empire in 1837.

And let *one* prayer from Hebrew hearths ascend
To Israel's God, that HE may deign reply,
45 And yet again His chosen race defend,
And "have respect" once more "unto their cry,"[1]
And e'en from depths of darkness and despair,
Give freedom to His own, and "all their burden bear."[2]

For shall we sink, tho' dark our way and drear,
50 And Hope hath found in misery a tomb?
Though man be silent, Mercy hath no tear,
And Love and Joy are wither'd 'neath the gloom?
No! GOD is near to hear us while we crave,
And HE will "bare His holy arm, to shield us and to save."[3]

1844

DIALOGUE STANZAS.

Composed for, and Repeated by, Two Dear Little Animated Girls, at a Family Celebration of the Festival of Purim.[4]

"Come forth, sweet sister! leave your book, we have no task to-day,
The flowers, and birds, and sunny sky, invite us forth to play;
Oh! think what joys, what happy hours, this long'd-for day we share,
And let us hunt for spring's sweet flowers, to wreathe our mother's
hair.
5 Come, we have days enough to read, sweet sister, come with me,
Away with such grave looks and thoughts! to-day is but for glee."

---

1 Cf. Ps. 34.15, "The eyes of the Lord are upon the righteous, and his ears are open unto their cry."

2 Cf. Ps. 55.22, "Cast thy burden upon the Lord, and he shall sustain thee: he shall never suffer the righteous to be moved."

3 This line combines allusions to Isa. 52.10 ("The Lord hath made bare his holy arm in the eyes of all the nations; and all the ends of the earth shall see the salvation of our God.") and Ps. 18.35 ("Thou hast also given me the shield of thy salvation: and thy right hand hath holden me up, and thy gentleness hath made me great.").

4 Purim, a festival celebrated each spring, commemorates the story in the biblical Book of Esther of the Jews' escape from massacre at the hands of Haman, King Ahasuerus's evil minister. The festival is celebrated with raucous mirth.

"A little while and I will come,—I only want to know
What pass'd upon this very day—a long time ago;
Our mother told us a sad tale—that thousands were to die,
E'en little children, sister dear—as young as you or I. 10
And all because a cruel foe swore vengeance on our race,
That from the noble MORDECAI no homage could he trace."[1]

"But we were saved, sweet sister; death was averted then,
Our mother told us ESTHER came, and there was joy again;
She was so lovely, and so good, the king could naught deny, 15
And so she sent fleet messengers, that Israel should not die.
There! I have told you all the tale,—you need not read it now,
Come, dearest! to our birds and flowers—and clear that thoughtful
brow."

"Sweet sister! let me think a while, and then I'll merry be.
Should we not think a grateful thought e'en in our sunny glee? 20
It was not *only* Esther's words—but Israel's God was there,
The king of Persia's heart to turn—His chosen ones to spare.
And we should bless Him, sister dear, that He protects us still,
And such kind friends bestows on us, to guard us from all ill."

"Yes, yes, sweet sister, you are right, not only is to-day 25
For idle mirth, and noisy games, and merry thoughtless play.
We'll love our mother more and more, and all our dear kind friends,
And grateful be that hours of dread, no more our Father sends;
That we may sport amid the flowers as happy as a bee,
And cruel foes can never come, to mar our childish glee." 30

"See, see! I'm ready, sister dear—I've put the book away;
Come while the sun so brightly shines, we'll weave our garland gay.
What joy!—what joy! this happy day shall see us all together,

---

1 In the Book of Esther, Haman demands that the Jew, Mordecai, bow to him whenever he passes. Mordecai's refusal is the motive for Haman's plan to destroy the Jews. But Mordecai's niece, unbeknownst to Haman, is Esther, who defeats Haman by winning the favor of Ahasuerus and becoming Queen. She tells the King that he must kill her if he kills the Jews. Haman and his sons are hung on the scaffold that had been prepared for Mordecai.

E'en those dear friends, whom time and space so long from us did sever;
35 Oh! many, many happy years, still spare us to each other.
Sweet sister, come! I'm ready now—the garland for our mother."

1845

THE WANDERERS

GENESIS, xxi. 14-20.

WITH sadden'd heart and tearful eye the mother went her way,
The Patriarch's mandate had gone forth, and Hagar must not stay.[1]
Oh! who can tell the emotions deep that pressed on Abra'am's heart—
As thus, obedient to his God, from Ismael called to part!

5 But God had spoken, and he knew His word was changeless truth,
He could not doubt His blessing would protect the friendless youth;
He bade him go, nor would he heed the anguish of his soul;
He turned aside,—a father's woe in silence to control.

Now hand in hand they wend their way, o'er hills and vale and wild;
10 The mother's heart was full of grief, but smiled in glee her child:
Fearless and free, he felt restraint would never gall him now—
And hail'd with joy the fresh'ning breeze that fann'd his fair young brow.

His mother's heart was desolate, and tears swell'd in her eye;
Scarce to his artless words of love her quiv'ring lips reply.
15 *She* only saw the *future* as a lone and dreary wild:
The *present* stood before the lad in joyance undefil'd.

---

1 The Patriarch is Abraham, who has had a son, Ishmael, with his concubine, Hagar. Subsequently, when Abraham's wife Sarah bears a son (Isaac), she insists that Abraham cast Ishmael and Hagar out of the house so that Ishmael will not share Isaac's inheritance. Hagar and Ishmael wander in the midst of a wilderness and have run out of water when Hagar cries out to God for help. God hears her prayer and promises to make Ishmael into a great nation.

She knew, alas! his boyish strength too soon would droop and fade;
And who was, in that lonely scene, to give them food and aid?
With trembling gaze she oft would mark the flushing of his cheek,
And list in terror, lest he should 'gin falteringly to speak! 20

Fatigue she felt not for herself, nor heeded care nor pain—
But nearer, nearer to her breast her boy at times she'd strain;
Beersheba's wilderness they see before them dark and wide;
Oh, who across its scorching sand their wandering steps will guide?

The flush departed from the cheek which she so oft has kiss'd; 25
To his glad tones of childish glee no longer may she list;
A pallor as of death is spread o'er those sweet features now—
She sees him droop before the blast that fann'd his aching brow.

"Oh, mother lay me down," he cried, "I know not what I feel,
But something cold and rushing seems thro' all my limbs to steal— 30
Oh kiss me, mother dear, and then ah, lay me down to sleep—
Nay, do not look upon me thus—kiss me and do not weep!"

Scarce could her feeble arms support her child, and lay him where
Some clustering shrubs might shield him from the heavy scorching
air;
His drooping eyelids closed; his breath came painfully and slow— 35
She bent her head on his a while in wild yet speechless woe.

Then from his side she hurried, as impelled she knew not why,
Save that she could not linger there—she could not see him die—
She lifted up her voice and wept—and o'er the lonely wild
"Let me not see his death!" was borne, "my Ismael, my child!" 40

And silence came upon her then, her stricken soul to calm;
And suddenly and strange there fell a soft and soothing balm—
And then a voice came stealing, on the still and fragrant air—
A still small voice that would be heard, tho' solitude was there.

"What aileth thee, oh Hagar?" thus it spoke: "fear not, for God hath
45 heard
The lad's voice where he is,—and thou, trust in thy Maker's word!
Awake! arise! lift up the lad and hold him in thine hand—
I will of him a nation make, before Me, he shall stand."

It ceased, that voice; and silence now, as strangely soft and still,
50 The boundless desert once again with eloquence would fill—
And strength returned to Hagar's frame, for God hath oped her
eyes—
And lo! amid the arid sands a well of water lies!

Quick to her boy, with beating heart, the anxious mother flies,
And to his lips, and hands, and brow, the cooling draught applies—
55 He wakes! he breathes! the flush of life is mantling on his cheek—
He smiles! he speaks! oh those quick tears his mother's joy shall
speak!

She held him to her throbbing breast, she gazed upon his face—
The beaming features, one by one, in silent love to trace.
She bade him kneel to bless the Hand that saved him in the wild—
60 But oh! few words her lips could speak, save these—"My child, my
child!"

1845

THE ROCKS OF ELIM[1]

Suggested by a perusal of Lord Lyndsey's Letters on the Holy Land, &c. Vol. 1, pages 260–1.

The sun was sinking slowly in the west,
Yet filling that fair scene with golden light,
Which, soft and mellow'd, heat intense suppress'd,
Yet gilded rock and wave with radiance bright;
5 And o'er the lovely azure of the sky,
Clouds, gold and crimson, gorgeously swept by,

1 In the Hebrew Bible, Elim is a lush oasis in the desert where the Israelites twice set up camp during their forty years of wandering. Elim is described as having "twelve wells of water" and "three-score and ten palm trees" (Exod. 15.27 and Num. 33.9).

But all breathed peace and stillness; not a sound
Broke the full silence lingering around,
Save the low murmur of the rippling wave,
As pensively it came, the shores to lave; 10
No sea-bird clave the soft yet breezy air;
No note of life, from the huge mountains there;
In smooth repose, the fair and glist'ning plain
Stretched forth from mount to sea; bearing no stain
Of man's disturbing step,—but rock and sea 15
And mount and wood, in deep repose lay free,
Burden'd with mighty memories—that came
E'en in the thrilling stillness, to proclaim
The God of might and love—and breathe the theme
Of His great deeds—till a bright sunny gleam 20
Of truth inspir'd, would sudden light impart,
E'en to that thing unknown—an atheist heart!
A voice was cradled in that soft blue sky,
Whisp'ring that the same God of love was nigh,
Who in that heaven had set his shadowy cloud, 25
And fiery pillar, his beloved to shroud;—[1]
Darkness to Mitzraim's host—but radiant light
To them He saved from slavery's starless night.
A voice had those blue waters, now so still—
Whose rippling, waveless, heart and ear could fill 30
With melodies of heav'n. That glorious sea!
In its full swelling tide—the glad, the free!
Rushing in thunder to the quiv'ring shore,
Or stilled, and hushed to peace, its wild rage o'er,
Unchained—unsilenced—scorning man's vain call, 35
Obeying but his will, who measured all

---

1 These lines and those that follow allude to Exod. 13.17 – 15.27. After the Israelites escape from slavery in Egypt, God protects them by night as a pillar of fire, and by day as a pillar of cloud. In rabbinic tradition the fire and cloud represent the divine attributes of justice and mercy, respectively. "Mitzraim's host" is Pharoah's Egyptian army, which pursues the freed Israelite slaves from Egypt to the Red Sea. The sea parts for the Israelites to pass through but the sea walls close again on Pharoah's army, drowning them. Once the Israelites are free, Moses and Miriam lead them in a victory song. Moses then leads them immediately to Marah, a place of bitter waters, but once the people take an oath to abide by God's statutes, Moses leads them to the oasis at Elim.

The waters in the hollow of his hand,[1]
And numbered ev'ry grain of the far spreading sand
He spake! at once their wat'ry depths upheaving,
40 As walls on either side—and dry land leaving
Till all had pass'd—the first son of the Lord,
And witness of his truth—again that word—
Back rush'd the mighty waters with a roar,
Which spake their strange restraining yoke was o'er,
45 And wave on wave came thundering down the steep,
Raised by their upheaved floods, and madly sweep
Th' Egyptian hosts before them—man and horse
Whelm'd 'neath the torrent's wildly rushing course!
Oh! was it but the phantom of the past,
50 Or did once more the silver clarion's blast
Sound in mine ears, and mount and rock and plain,
'Neath those full notes, are quiv'ring again?[2]
The Jewish hosts are marshalling the ground
From mount to sea—their lines encamping round,
55 And priests, and warriors, women, children, all—
And stalwart youths, in ranks respective fall,
Their tall spears gleaming in the sunset light,
Till rock and ridge, with sudden radiance bright,
Fling back the song of praise, of glory loud,
60 That wakes in chorus from the holy crowd.
From north to south it bursts—from east to west
Alternate pealing, echoing e'er suppress'd.[3]
The rushing waves their mighty paean lend,

1 Cf. Isa. 40.12, "Who hath measured the waters in the hollow of his hand, and meted out heaven with the span, and comprehended the dust of the earth in a measure, and weighed the mountains in scales, and the hills in a balance?" The poem's next line reverses a typical biblical metaphor, in which Israelites are said to be as numberless as the sand. As is Jer. 33.22, "As the host of heaven cannot be numbered, neither the sand of the sea measured: so will I multiply the seed of David my servant, and the Levites that minister unto me."

2 The "silver clarion" may be a reference to the ram's horn, or shofar, which is blown on Rosh HaShanah and Yom Kippur, the holiest days of the Jewish calendar, in order to awaken Jews to their ethical and ritual responsibilities.

3 An allusion to the Israelites' victory songs at the Red Sea, Exod. 15. Aguilar quotes first Moses' song, then Miriam's in the lines that follow. Mitzraim: the Hebrew word for Egyptians (from the root for "narrow place").

And deeper tones the tow'ring mountains send—
"Sing, sing ye to the Lord of Hosts, for He 65
On Mitzraim's hosts hath triumphed gloriously,
The horse and rider in the seas o'erthrown,
The depths have cover'd them, they sank as stone!
Sing, sing ye to the Lord!" Then soft again
From gentler voices woke th' inspired strain, 70
And harp and timbrel swell'd the ling'ring chord
Of the rich anthem—"Sing ye to the Lord!"
The very breeze upon his wild flight stay'd
And whispering responses softly made,
And on his pinions bore the strain along, 75
Till earth and ocean quiver'd 'neath the song,
And shook before the deep thanksgiving poured,
When the full chorus peal'd, "Sing, sing ye to the Lord!"

The vision past! Hush'd was the glorious sound,
The rocks in stillness, solemnly profound, 80
Hung deepening shadows, on the sandy plain,
And all was hush'd and desolate again.
Spirit of truth! Thou didst my soul enfold,
And wrapt it in thy robe—till scenes of old
Embodied came, to thrill my yearning heart, 85
And deeper love and thanksgiving impart!
Oh! let the scorner and the sceptic seek
Where nature's self-inspired love can speak,
Where rock and ocean, mount and moaning blast,
Proclaim aloud the story of the past. 90
Hither, oh hither, let the doubting come,
And e'en thy meanest works, oh God, shall strike the scoffer
dumb!

1840

III. NON-FICTION PROSE

Although Aguilar's fiction and poetry were quite popular, her contemporaries treated most seriously her non-fiction prose writings, including her essays in theology and *midrash*, her apologetics, her prayers and meditations, and her history of British Jews. Both Jews and Christians particularly prized the theological and *midrashic* essays included in *The Spirit of Judaism* (1842) and *The Women of Israel* (1845). In the guise of an extended meditation on the *Shema*, the avowal of the divine unity chanted in every Jewish prayer service, *Spirit* was in fact one of the first major statements by an English Jew of the theological position that later came to be called Reform or Liberal Judaism. Like contemporary Jewish reformers in Germany, Aguilar understood the Jews' "Oral Law"—consisting of the Talmud and the centuries of rabbinical commentary that followed it—as the production of fallible human beings, not as sacred scripture. She believed Talmudic tradition had sometimes been contaminated by the surrounding Eastern cultures in which it had originally been formulated, particularly where its ideas of women were concerned. She insisted that Jewish women had the capacity to produce valid interpretations of the Bible for themselves without referring to the accumulated rabbinical tradition, from which, in any case, they were denied access due to the prohibition on women learning Talmud. In her view, as long as women adhered to the dictates of reason and to the "still, small voice" of conscience—which was the mark of the divine within every human, female as well as male—they need not fear misinterpreting the Biblical text or violating divine precepts. This stance was disputed by a number of Aguilar's contemporaries, including her editor, Isaac Leeser, who inserted comments within her text attempting to refute her reformist leanings. Space limitations prevent the inclusion here of all of Leeser's extensive editorial comments, but several are included in the notes to give the reader the flavor of his responses.

The wide-ranging discussions in *Spirit* include considerations on the pedagogical value of fiction, the distinction between the form and spirit of Jewish ritual, the mother's role in instructing Jewish youth, the continuing significance of the Hebrew language for Jews in diaspora, Jewish women's resistance to conversion efforts, and the need for a Jewish translation of the Bible in English. Despite Isaac Leeser's editorial refutations, the book became very popular, especially among Jewish women in the United States. Rebecca Gratz, founder of the Jewish Sunday School movement in the U.S., used it as a classroom text.

The Women of Israel was a collection of *midrashic* biographies of Biblical, Talmudic and historical Jewish women from Eve up through Aguilar's own day. In these *midrashim*, Aguilar sought to do several things at once: to retell Jewish history from a female-centered perspective, to counter Christian contentions that Judaism oppressed women, to provide Jewish women with a voice and history they lacked, and to argue for increased female education in the Anglo-Jewish community. Along the way she attempted to demonstrate that a woman could understand and engage with Hebrew and the Jewish interpretive tradition, incorporating discussions of Rashi and other Jewish biblical commentators to support her ideas. She admitted with some exasperation that for the Talmudic sections she had to rely on a male friend and *The Hebrew Review and Magazine of Rabbinical Literature* (an English-language periodical). These sources, she remarks, have "enabled us to form an opinion: but the Talmud itself should be its foundation; and from that, we, as a female, are unhappily debarred" (2:290).

Aguilar presents her biblical heroines as positive or negative models of proper Victorian femininity. The matriarch, Sarah, exemplifies Aguilar's ideal of the Jewish "angel in the house." (For a stunning contrast, compare the Sarah depicted here to Aguilar's earlier rendering of the matriarch in the poem "The Wanderers.") Similarly, although in recent years Jewish feminists have depicted Miriam as a prophet nearly co-equal with Moses, Aguilar's Miriam more nearly resembles the Victorian stereotype of the "old maid," jealous of both her brother's wife and his power. Aguilar's Miriam is also worth contrasting with the same figure in Felicia Hemans' poem "The Song of Miriam," included in Appendix C. Finally, the biblical figure of Deborah tests the limits of Aguilar's domestic ideology. As a prophet, warrior, poet, and judge, Deborah transgresses the Victorian gender roles for which Aguilar sought to find a foundation in the Bible; yet the Bible celebrates Deborah's accomplishments rather than punishing her. Aguilar has to find a way to validate the Bible's treatment of this unVictorian heroine while cautioning Victorian women against imitating Deborah's behavior.

The year following the publication of *The Women of Israel*, Aguilar published *The Jewish Faith*, a series of letters from an older woman to a younger one counseling her on matters of faith in the doctrine of immortality, and urging reasons for resisting the efforts of Evangelical conversionists who targeted young women. Aguilar may well have taken as her model Elizabeth Hamilton's *Letters, addressed to the Daughter of a Nobleman, on the Formation of Religious and Moral Principle* (1814, 3rd ed.).

While writing emancipationist apologetics for public consumption, Aguilar was also writing liturgy for her own private use, composing prayers, meditations, and sermons to fill what she saw as a gap in Jewish vernacular devotional materials, especially for women. These liturgical compositions draw stylistically on the Psalms and on the *Siddur*, the Jewish prayer book. Her meditation on Isaiah was written in the form of a biblical exegesis. Because exegesis was considered a male form, Aguilar's was one of the first to be written by a Jewish woman. She refused her friends' repeated attempts to persuade her to publish her liturgy. After her death, her mother and editor Sarah Aguilar agreed to publish some of them under the title *Sabbath Thoughts and Sacred Communings* (1853), several pieces of which are included here.

Aguilar's final published work was her "History of the Jews in England." It should be seen as the founding text of Anglo-Jewish historiography. Ranging from the Saxon period, to the "social arrangements of English Jews" in Aguilar's own time, to the present condition of Jews throughout Europe and the Ottoman Empire, the history is fascinating in its scope as well as for its atypically critical tone towards British Protestants. Aguilar argues that "the characteristics so often assigned to [Jews] in tales [by Christians] professing to introduce a Jew or a Jewish family, are almost all incorrect," that "[l]ike the rest of the human race, [Jews] are, as individuals, neither wholly good nor wholly bad; as a people, their virtues very greatly predominate." She argues that the degradation of many Jews during her day did not mean that Jews were innately degraded, as was often argued, but that they had been subjected to centuries of persecution. She repeatedly counters stereotypes of Jews' cowardice or venality by offering evidence that, even in diaspora, they have demonstrated time and again the capacity for virtue, courage, and heroism. The essay was commissioned by the Scottish publisher Robert Chambers for his radical journal *Chambers' Miscellany*, and appeared just before Aguilar's death in 1847.

From THE SPIRIT OF JUDAISM

[Our Hearts Must Breathe from Our Lips][1]

IT is right to learn this prayer [the *Shema*] in our earliest childhood;[2] it would be wrong to wait till we could understand its importance to attain the words; but if their sense has been neglected, let us seek it ourselves, we must not remain Hebrews, only because our fathers were. The faith we receive merely as an inheritance, will not enable us to defend it from insidious attack or open warfare, will not satisfy the cravings of our nature, will not give us a rock whereon to cling in hope and such deep love, that we could be strengthened even to die for it, if it were needed; nor can it be pleasing unto Him, who declaring himself a God of Truth and Love, will so be worshipped. Our hearts must breathe from our lips in this avowal of our faith—we need not utter it aloud, God alone may hear us;[3]—yet should we so dwell on this important subject, that if called upon, we might proclaim aloud our faith in the presence of angry thousands, fearlessly acknowledge our belief in the unity of God—ay, dare even scorn, and proudly and steadily tread the sainted paths which our fathers trod.

[The Bible as Foundation and Defense]

That in former times the Christian should have been regarded with loathing, and hate, and terror, can astonish none acquainted with the history of persecution; but now that in all civilized lands we are protected, cherished, nay, often honoured and beloved, why should this feeling continue to rankle in the Israelitish bosom? Treated with charity and kindness, why should we not encourage the same sooth-

---

1 The titles to the sections of *The Spirit of Judaism* are, for the most part, not Aguilar's, but were created for this edition. Where Aguilar's own chapter titles appear, they are indicated in the text with an asterisk (*).

2 The *Shema* consists of Deut. 6.4, "Hear O Israel, the Lord our God, the Lord is One," followed by three paragraphs taken respectively from Deut. 6.5-9, Deut. 11.13-21, and Num. 15:37-41.

3 Cf. 1 Sam. 1.13: "Now Hannah, she spake in her heart; only her lips moved, but her voice was not heard." This description of Hannah is often cited by Jewish authorities as the model of silent, heartfelt prayer.

ing emotions? It is alleged that it is dangerous to associate intimately with those of other creeds, that it is as dangerous to our faith as the open warfare of old. They are mistaken who thus think; were the Jewish religion studied as it ought to be by its professors of every age and sex; were the BIBLE, *not tradition,*[1] its foundation and defence; were its spirit felt, pervading the inmost heart, giving strength and hope, and faith and comfort: we should stand forth firm as the ocean rock, which neither tempest nor the slow, still, constant dripping of the waters can bend or shake. We should do more; thus prepared, thus convinced of truth, we should find that every argument they might employ, every book we might be persuaded to peruse, would but strengthen conviction in the faith of Israel; charity to them indeed would increase, for the more we studied of their belief, the more we should feel the veil cast upon them is indeed of God. Never has the Hebrew, glorying in, and openly professing the belief of his fathers, not merely attending to form but proving the spirit which guides and aids him, failed to gather round him the respect and admiration of every Christian whose respect is something worth. It is those, who by mean and petty manoeuvres, seek to hide their faith, who are ashamed of it themselves, who draw down the contempt and pity of all they would deceive, and this not on themselves alone, but unfortunately on the whole nation.

---

1 Isaac Leeser's note: "Again, I fear, that Miss Aguilar has imbibed too strong a prejudice against tradition. It is mainly our general acquiescence in the received mode of interpretation which forms the characteristic distinction between us and others; for how else can we at all maintain any opposition against the views advanced by the other believers in the Bible? It is useless to say, that the Scriptures speak for themselves; they assuredly do so to the person who has received instruction; but it requires no argument to prove that difference of education makes people take different views of the sacred Text; or else all readers of the Bible would entertain the same doctrines and pursue one course of conduct. Is this the case? Certainly the Scriptures should constitute the daily exercise of every Israelite; but the interpretations, dogmas, and opinions of our ancients should not be neglected; ay, tradition is the firm support of the Unity of God. Say if you will, that Rabbins [Rabbis] have occasionally promulgated things of no value; yet would this constitute no argument against the good they have left us. They teach nothing opposed to the most elevated piety; faith, hope and charity are doctrines of theirs no less than of the Nazarene code, and it remains to be proved, that a strict conformity to form, ceremony or outward religion in general is in the least injurious to moral perfectibility.... No one would pull down his house, because a few stones were discoloured, when a slight labour might remedy the defect. So let us be cautious how we reject tradition, because of the few incongruities it may occasionally present" (21).

[The Hebrew's Neglect of the Bible]

The Bible is the foundation of religion. In it we find the history of the past, the present, and the future; laws to guide us; threatenings, awfully fulfilled; promises to soothe, console, and bless us. Those who deny its divine truths are neither Jew nor Christian; for the acknowledgment of its divinity is equally binding to the one as to the other. But the great evil under which the Hebrew nation is still suffering, is not so much the *denial* as the *neglect* of this precious word. We are in general perfectly satisfied with reading the Parasas and Haftorahs marked out as our Sabbath portions. The other parts of the Bible rest utterly unknown.[1] Brought out on the Sabbath for the brief space of half an hour, the portions are read, and hastily dismissed, as a completed task, bringing with it no pleasure and little profit. Even this is but too often neglected, and we adhere to the forms and ceremonies of our ancestors, scarcely knowing wherefore; and we permit our Bibles to rest undisturbed on their shelves not even seeking them, to know the meaning of what we do. Others again, earnest in the cause, yet mistaken in the means, search and believe the writings of the Rabbis, take as divine truths all they have suggested, and neglect the Bible as not to be compared with such learned dissertations.[2]

And why should this be? Why should the Bible be so shunned by that people, to whom it was so peculiarly intrusted? Surely they cannot bring forward the too often quoted and unfounded assertion, that the English translation is imperfect, and not fitted to be placed in the hands of Hebrew youth, that it would confuse and rather lead them to embrace the Nazarene, than strengthen their adherence to the Jewish creed. The evidence of learned men of either faith, con-

---

1 A *parasa* (or *parashah*) is a portion of the Torah, which is divided into fifty-two separate sections to be read weekly at the synagogue. In this way, each Jewish congregation reads through the entirety of the Torah each year. The *haftarah* is a selection from one of the prophets that is chanted aloud immediately following the chanting of each week's *parashah*. The *haftarah* is usually thematically related to the *parashah*. Isaac Leeser notes at this point: "The above remarks are rather too sweeping, at least for the Israelites of America; still there is a great deal of truth and force in them [...]" (52).

2 Isaac Leeser's note: "Again I must remark that Miss A. has relied too much upon the calumniators of the Jewish character as authority. If there are any who place the Rabbis above the Bible, they are unknown to me [...]" (52).

vince us of the fallacy of this reasoning. It is not the actual words of the Bible, but the view in which they are taken, which gives weapons to our opponents. There is scarcely a word mistranslated, and the Hebrew of obscure passages, is generally placed in the margins, underlined by a literal translation. The heads of the chapters are the only portions likely to mislead; but they are perfectly harmless to those unto whom the Jewish religion has been *taught*, and whose youth has not been suffered to imbibe religion as they could.[1]

Mournfully they err, who thus preserve the English Bible from the hands and hearts of their children. It is this great error, which prevents the spirit of piety from taking possession of the heart, and binds us to cold and lifeless forms; it is this which is the real cause of so many Israelites having embraced Christianity.[2] If, as it only too often happens, young minds are first led to think on religion at all by the example of pious Christian friends, and are engaged to read or rather study the Bible, for the first time, under their direction, and come to them for enlightenment on passages or chapters that may seem obscure: must it not follow as a natural consequence, that the ideas they thus imbibe must favour the Christian and not the Hebrew creed? How can they produce arguments against arguments, if they have never been taught to read the Bible according to the belief of their fathers? Why do we only too often hear even amongst professing Hebrews, that the morality of the New Testament infinitely surpasses in beauty and charity that of the Old? Why? because they see the effects of the one on the lives and characters of its believers, and they see it not in the other; because they adopt as the doctrines of Christianity the beautiful moral sentences and proverbs they chance to hear, wholly unconscious, that these very sentences which so much attract their admiration, have all, without exception, their original foundation in the pages of the Old

1 In general, Christian titles are thematic; Jewish titles are derived from the first word of the book, chapter, or *parashah*. Jewish and Christian chapter titles vary. For example, the Christian title of the first book of the Bible is Genesis, a broadly thematic title. The Jewish title is *B'reshit*, Hebrew for "In the beginning," which is the first word in the text.

2 Isaac Leeser's note: "...[I]t would be rendering a service to the cause of truth and religion, if a revised translation, edited by a society of learned and pious Israelites, without any of the headings Miss A. alludes to, could be issued; for then no one even in England could hesitate to make it a household book for his children." Leeser went on to publish his own English translation of the Bible.

Testament either in the law, the Psalms, or the prophets; nay, that the whole system of morality preached by the founder of Christianity is that, in which WE were instructed by God Himself, either in direct communion with Moses, or through His chosen servants the prophets! Its only change is from the lofty language of inspiration which the chosen of the Lord alone could be supposed to understand, to the brief and simple phrases better suited to the comprehension of the heathen to whom it was addressed. The Christian divines themselves acknowledge this; and shall we, descended as we are from a race whom God so peculiarly blessed—shall we, by our whole lives deny it? and declare the Christian Ethics are the best, when we know nothing, seek to know nothing of our own?

[A Minority's Faith and Observance]

In some respects the power of proving the beauty and comfort of a religious life is to the Hebrew painfully contracted. It is not now as in those joyous times when "the field, the vineyard, and the altar" alone occupied the sons and daughters of Israel, when their every thought was connected with their universal Father; for it was His law they obeyed.[1] The first fruits of the vineyard and the field were laid aside, not as tributes to an earthly king, but as an accepted offering even to the King of kings. If we were asked why we were so careful "to leave the gleanings of the harvest, and the olive, and the grass, for the poor and the stranger;" or wherefore "we rose up before the hoary head, and honoured the face of the old man;" or why "so watchful to prevent unrighteousness in judgment, weight, or measure;" the Hebrews would reply, because our Father in heaven so commanded; and thus the simplest action of courtesy was blessed and hallowed by its connexion with the Lord, its obedience to His will.[2] Such intimate communion was forfeited by the sins of our fathers; nor is it even now as it was in the dark ages of persecution, when the Hebrew clung with yet greater firmness, more endearing fondness, to the faith for which he suffered. The determination, in

1 Aguilar refers to the periods when the first and second Temples stood (between about 950 B.C.E. and 70 C.E.).

2 Cf. Lev. 19:9-10, 35.

secret to adhere unchangeably to the law of Moses, incited many to live a holier life, and ponder frequently on Him, in whose service their very lives were risked. When occupying posts of high trust and favour in the Spanish court, their lineage unknown, their race unsuspected, though they could scarcely keep the forms, the SPIRIT glowed more warmly within. In those times, when torture and death were ever hovering round them, was a son of Israel ever tempted to become a Christian? Did we then hear of conversions, of abandonment of that belief which we received from the Eternal? Nay, was it not then, many turned from abodes of luxury and ease, deserting the cherished hoards of years, exposing themselves to every imaginable misery by becoming wanderers on the face of the earth, rather than accede to the conditions of their persecutors, and desert their faith? Was it not then the sons of Israel in deed and thought obeyed the command of their Lord, and in very truth loved Him with all their heart, and soul, and might? Would we do this now?[1]

Through the infinite mercy of an infinitely merciful God, the inexpressible horrors of persecution are over: not alone are we granted toleration, and permitted to dwell in safety, and undisturbed to continue the practice of our religion, but by the truly sincere and pious Christian the consistent Hebrew is ever esteemed, honoured, even loved; and how do we repay our Father in heaven? Has that faith so beloved in adversity become less beautiful, less glorious, less loveable in prosperity, that we turn from it to embrace another? "Is the hand of our Father become shortened that it cannot save?" that we live as if we needed His blessing, His saving mercies no more? "Is His ear heavy that it cannot hear," that we cease to call upon Him, save with careless lips and wandering hearts?[2] Reposing in security, we hear not or heed not the imperious call breathing in His law; or, engaged in the heartless repetition of the *antiquated* form, forget the *antiquated* spirit, without which it is a void. We neglect to instruct our children in the religion of their fathers, to enforce the necessity

1 Aguilar modulates the discussion from Biblical times to the period of the Spanish Inquisition (ca. 1500–1900), when many Jews converted to Catholicism in public only to maintain their Jewish identity in private rituals.

2 Aguilar conflates Is. 50:2 and 59:1.

and the comfort of constant communion with their God; it is enough if they fail not to do as we do; and is it strange then that those whose hearts thirst and hunger after divine love, divine instruction, should at length fly to that fold where they believe there are shepherds to guide and to console? Or that some ambitious spirits, imagining the spiritless forms, to which *alone* their attention has been directed, are so many chains which confine them to one spot, one employ, and permit no enlarging of the mind, no ascendancy in worldly honours, that they, too, should become either forswearers of religion altogether, or embrace the first creed which promises distinction or increase of worldly gain? If the love and duty they owe their Father in heaven has never been impressed upon their infant minds; if their childish reverence and adoration have never been excited by the love He bears to them: is it marvel worldly interest and earthly ambition should fill their hearts to the exclusion of those better and holier thoughts which, as the chosen people, should be peculiarly their own?

It is this melancholy state of things which renders the Hebrew's powers of exalting his religion, in the minds of men, so painfully contracted. Yet his influence should be exercised not only to exalt his faith in the views of his more worldly-minded brethren alone, but in the sight of the whole Christian world. He is peculiarly situated; comparatively speaking, he stands alone amidst a vast multitude; on his conduct, his constancy, depends whether scorn or admiration shall be excited towards the religion which stands forth embodied in himself. According as his life is actuated by its principles, so will it be deemed divine or otherwise; and at the present time, when to prove the superiority of the Christian religion is the avowed or secret determination of all its earnest members, endeavouring *thus* to obtain converts: has not the Hebrew a double incentive to make manifest the spiritual beauty, the unfailing comfort of his own? This would be a far weightier proof of the divinity and sacred nature of our faith than the most convincing argument with regard to actual points of doctrine. This would be evincing our love to our universal Father, and our desire to exalt His glory, much more to the improving of our own hearts, and to the enlarging of charity towards our fellows, than the endeavour, too often made in scorn and haste, to found the truth of our own belief on the falsity and degradation of the Christian [...].[1]

[Hints on the Religious Instruction of the Hebrew Youth*]

The seventh verse of the sixth chapter of Deuteronomy, and the fourth of the שמע [*Shema*], contains so much important matter in a few words that each member of the sentence demands to be considered separately. In the preceding verses we have desired to reflect on and lay up the words of the Lord in our own hearts, in this to teach them to our children. "And thou shalt teach them diligently unto thy children," i. e. the love of God and all that is therein comprised.

To instruct young children in the dull routine of daily lessons, to force the wandering mind to attention, the unwilling spirit to subjection, to bear with natural disinclination to irksome tasks, all this, as a modern writer very justly observes, is far more attractive in theory than in practice. It is a drudgery for which even some mothers themselves have not sufficient patience; but very different is the instruction commanded in the verse we are regarding. To speak of God, to teach the child His will, to instil His love into the infant heart, should never be looked on as a daily task, nor associated with all the dreaded paraphernalia of books and lessons. The Bible alone should be the guide to, and assistance in, this precious employment. There are moments when children are peculiarly alive to emotions of devotion. The Hebrew mother who desires her offspring to say their prayers morning and evening, to abstain from writing, working, or cutting on the Sabbath, to adhere to particular forms and observe particular days, as she does, has yet not wholly fulfilled her solemn duty. This will not be enough to make the Hebrew child love his God or his religion; not enough to restrain him in manhood from becoming a Christian if it favour his interest or ambition so to do.

Far more depends on Hebrew parents than on Christian; the latter have their places of public worship wherever they may dwell,

---

1 Isaac Leeser's note: "Miss Aguilar has in the above failed to convey her thoughts as clearly as they might have been. She surely does not mean that all the Jews do not enforce a holiness of life, and that they base the truth of their belief upon the falsity of the Christian. I should regret, greatly regret, if this were the prevailing error among our English friends...."

their ministers whose whole lives are devoted to the service of their God, to the moral and religious welfare of their fellow-creatures. In their earliest years Christian children attend once-a-week the house of God. They join in prayers which, if not wholly understood, are yet sufficient to impress some feelings different to the impressions of the six days of labour. They hear the Bible explained, they see it regarded as indeed the book of life; and though they may not understand why some portions attract their ear which, in after years, are recalled with peculiar pleasure. The intervening days may weaken the impression, perhaps it is entirely forgotten; but their next Sabbath they go again, and the feeling is renewed and rendered stronger. They see a large concourse around them engaged in the same solemn service, praying in a language familiar to them, and this would be of itself enough to chain a child's attention. They feel it as a privilege thus to seek their God; and this feeling follows the child to youth, to manhood, and almost involuntarily religion is imbibed. Even those deprived of religious parents have yet advantages peculiar to themselves, in the fact that the faith they profess is the faith of their country and of all around them.

The Hebrew child has not these advantages. Debarred from the public exercise of devotion on his Sabbath day; never hearing public prayers in a language he can understand;—having no public minister on whom he can call for that instruction he may not have received at home;—never hearing the law expounded, or the Bible in any way explained: to his mother alone the Hebrew child must look, on his mother alone depend for the spirit of religion, the inculcation of that faith which must follow him through life.

[...] Our Father knows every difficulty and every circumstance that combine to render the Hebrew mother's task more arduous, more responsible than the Christian. He expects not more than weak humanity can perform; but He will not accept the plea of disadvantages, of difficulties, as acquitting us of a parent's duty.

Were love and gratitude to Him banished from every other human heart, surely they would swell in a young mother's breast, as she gazes upon the little creature undeniably His gift, and feels the gushing tide of rapture ever attendant on maternal love. Surely in such a moment there must be whisperings of devotion, leading the soul in gratitude to the beneficent Giver of her babe, or swelling it with prayer to guide that precious charge aright. It may be that doubts of her own capability of executing a task, as solemnly important as inexpressibly sweet, may naturally arise; but these doubts, instead of leading her to give up the task in despair, should lead her to the footstool of her God in prayer; and her petition, even as that of Hannah was, will be granted.[1]

That truly pious Jewess not only devoted her child to God, but so devoted him, that but once in the year she could behold him; and at first he was her only child—the little being for whom morning and evening she had implored the Lord, implored Him in tears, in fasting, in bitterness of soul. Her prayer was heard; and how fervent must have been her gratitude, how great the love *she* bore her God, how implicit her reliance on His love for her, that she stilled the yearnings of a mother's tenderness, and as soon as the boy was weaned, brought him up to the high priest and left him there. And was not her pious faithfulness rewarded? Three other sons and two daughters did she bear, and her eldest, the joy, the hope of her heart, became the favoured prophet of the Lord.

To part thus from her child is not now demanded of the Hebrew mother; nor can there now be such a blessed consummation of such a self-conquering struggle. Yet the example of Hannah should be treasured up by all the daughters of her race, whom the same beneficent God has blessed with children. It must be remembered that in the present state of Israel the word of God cannot and must not be taken literally as it regards the immediate answers to prayers, or punishment of sin. The lapse of years, the difference of position, must not be forgotten. All the pious actions there described, cannot now be performed, nor dare we expect the same direct manifestation of our Father in reward: yet this is no cause of, nor excuse for, the neglect of the Bible. Vouchsafed in love and mercy as an unfailing guide, it at least teaches what is pleasing in the sight of our God [...].

We cannot devote our sons to the service of the Lord as Hannah, nor even if we could, would we all be required to do so; but we may teach them to know and to fear Him, and to guide their every action by their love for Him. We may teach them, by their conduct to display His glory, the honour of Jerusalem, the comfort of the

1 Cf. 1 Sam. 1-2.

Hebrew faith. Even scattered as we are amongst the stranger, we can do this; and this is devoting them unto their God. The same reward may not be ours, as was bestowed on Hannah; yet we shall be blessed. The Lord will forsake us not; and as we behold our children grow around us in true piety, and consequently in the exercise of every virtue: will not every Hebrew mother feel that the word of the Lord is true and she is blessed indeed?

To do this, to obtain this desirable end, religion must not be learnt from a book, nor be regarded as a severe restraint. A mother, whose heart is in her work will find many opportunities, which properly improved, will lead her little charge to God. Our prayers are long, and not applicable to childish wants and feelings; but a mother may find a sweet employment, in throwing together some well selected passages, either from our ritual or the Book of Life, to form short but impressive prayers for both morning and evening. A mother's lips should teach them to her child, and not leave the first impressions of religion to be received from a Christian nurse. Were the associations of a mother connected with the act of praying, associations of such long continuance that the child knew not when they were implanted: the piety of maturer years would not be so likely to waver.

There is a peculiar sweetness in the remembrance of a mother. When a young man has raised himself by his own virtues and talents in the world, when he feels himself esteemed and beloved by his fellow-men: he will still think of his mother, if it have been from her lips, the first lessons of virtue were imbibed; and if religion were as zealously and carefully implanted, would not her memory have equal influence in guarding him from temptation, strengthening him to walk on in the paths she loved? It may be that continued occupation, perhaps arduous labour, or severe thought and study have withdrawn his attention awhile from his God; or that the paths of pleasure, encircling him with their delusive rays, conceal from his eyes the light of eternity. Some sudden association recalls his mother to his mind; the days of his early infancy, his happy boyhood, rise before him, and with it the remembrance of duties he has neglected, the hours of prayer that have passed by unheeded. He hears again the sweet and gentle voice which first spoke to him of God; he sees again those happy hours when, seated at her feet, he rested his little hands upon her lap, and repeated with her the words of prayer, or listened with tearful eyes, and swelling heart, to the tales of sacred love, her gentle accents told. Few hearts could remain cold and unmoved in the midst of such recollections; he is more likely to prostrate himself before the God *that* mother worshipped, and pray again even as in childhood. And will the Hebrew mother neglect this solemn yet blessed duty? Will she refrain from thus associating herself in the heart of her child, when, far more than the Nazarene, the sons of Israel require it? Will she not teach the *religion* of the heart unto her children, instead of merely inculcating peculiar forms, and desiring them to observe peculiar rites? Will she not teach them to fly to the footstool of their God for guidance, instruction, strength, and grace, to resist temptation—blessing on all they undertake—comfort in affliction—moderation in prosperity:—will she not teach them this, instead of so banishing religion from the early education that her sons in manhood stand and act as if all depended on themselves, on good and evil fortune—acknowledging indeed a God, yet living as if of Him they had no need? her daughters, either wholly occupied with the affairs of this world, living as if there were no eternity, and consequently trembling at the very name of death?—or needing comfort, strength, hope, and finding them not in the religion of their fathers: are tempted to seek it, where they fancy, no spiritless form restrains the soul, and consolation is more easily attained? [...].

To the mothers of every faith and every class these hints may be equally applicable; but to Jewish mothers more particularly. We have but to study the Book of Life, and every history of our nation: and we shall not fail to perceive that the religion Moses taught was intended to unite the thought of God with our every action. If a Christian writer finds sufficient foundation for the assertion that "there can be no half measures in devotion, religion must be *all* or nothing:" how much more powerfully should *we* feel it, we—who are a peculiar people, the firstborn of the Lord, thus called by the Eternal Himself, and therefore absolutely *set apart*, to exalt by our conduct His glory amidst the nations. It is urged perhaps, our situation is not now what it was, that it does not depend on us alone, "to magnify the Lord,"[1] that we are but as a handful amidst the nations that now worship Him; yet this fact in no way decreases our responsibility. It is rather increased; for it was easy to divide the worship of the one true God from idolatry,—many civil as well as religious customs did this; but now mingling intimately with the nations that worship God, though not as we do, living under the same civil jurisdiction, acknowledging the same sovereign: unless the adherence to the laws of Moses be even more exact, it is more than likely our nationality would be entirely lost, as well as all pride, all glory in the Hebrew faith.

To prevent this great evil should be the Hebrew mother's aim. The youngest child may be taught that he is a member of a distinct and peculiar nation. The great mercies and unchanging love of the Lord will, if well related, find very early an answering chord in the youthful heart. The wonderful providence, the stupendous miracles, the innumerable instances of our Father's long suffering and loving kindness, which our eventful history records, might be related as interesting tales in those many leisure hours that the child looks up so clingingly and fondly to his mother for amusement. Vividly and interestingly might these narratives be opened to the young and eager mind, till almost insensibly he feels it a privilege, even at this long lapse of years, to belong to a nation so peculiarly blessed, so singularly the object of God's gracious providence; and that false shame, now alas, but too familiar to the Hebrew, would never flush the cheek, or lead the tongue to falsehood [...].

By laying this foundation in childhood, carefully guarding against the very smallest approach to bitterness or scorn towards any other creed: we instill their religion with their growth; conversion cannot take place when released from the parental yoke; for the very weapons which the Nazarene would use against them, have become in their hands weapons of defence. Proofs of the truth of Christianity are to the young Hebrew, proofs of the truth of Judaism. Conversion cannot take place on either side; but mutual esteem and charity will take the place of such desire; for if both religions appear to have the same foundation, it is evident God alone in His own good time can remove the veil which each believes flung over the other [...].

---

1 Aguilar refers both to Ps. 34:3 and Luke 1:46.

Even if the religious instruction hinted above should sometimes fail to bring forth such blessed fruit: the Hebrew mother will yet have done her duty; and not on her head will fall the carelessness, disobedience, or apostacy, of her children. She will stand absolved in the sight of her God; for He will have seen her struggles to lead her offspring in the right way; and if earth brings no reward, she will find it at His right hand for evermore. Oh! let but the Hebrew mother persevere, and far more likely is it that she will find a sweet foretaste of heaven upon earth in the conduct of her children, than that her efforts will all be blighted [...].

[The Significance of the Hebrew Language]

Ere we proceed to the remainder of this verse [of the *Shema*], may we be permitted to hint on the importance of making the Hebrew language familiar to every Hebrew child. It cannot be considered a dead language, for the nation to which it originally belonged continues to exist, and will exist for ever. It is not indeed spoken as it would have been, had we remained in our own land; yet it might still continue the link uniting the sons of Israel wherever they may be. The sojourners in England, France, Austria, Spain, might be enabled to converse or to commune with each other in their own native tongue, though of the language of their respective homes each might be ignorant.

But this end cannot be attained if the Hebrew child is merely taught to read and translate his prayers, as was formerly the case, and his aptitude in the language judged according to his proficiency in following the service of the Synagogues. Why should Hebrew be the only language which is never learnt grammatically? Why should it not be taught the infant [...] even as the language of the land in which he is a sojourner? Hebrew is scarcely more difficult or complicated than English; but the latter is attained so gradually, we are so prepared for its grammar when we arrive at it, that we are never aware of the difficulties its acquirement presents to a foreigner; and in the same manner the difficulties of Hebrew would vanish were the child equally prepared to encounter them; and the gradual acquirement of familiar words and sentences in this ancient language would do this far better than charging the memory with portions of prayer which only succeed in divesting the sacred words from all holiness, and cause the prayer-book to be regarded as a hated task instead of being welcomed as the blessed means of communion between man and his Maker. Never may we hope for the perfect attainment of this ancient and glorious language till the present system has given place to one more calculated to engage a child's fancy, till the prayer-book is not the first which we place in an infant's hands, till other than words so sacred as prayer are the first we teach our children to repeat. Our aim indeed should be to enable them to address their Creator in the language of their ancestors, to read His word pure and unaltered, even as it came from heaven; but by placing it too early before them, we frustrate our own desires.

We would think it strange if, as soon as a child had acquired his letters in French or Italian, the Henriade or Dante should be placed before him, and he should be desired to learn passages by rote with merely the assistance of a subjoined translation. We would not hesitate to dismiss a master who thus taught; for we should know the impossibility of his pupils obtaining either a familiar or grammatical idea of the language. How then can we expect to succeed in imparting Hebrew, if this same plan be followed? For the poetry of Dante and Voltaire is not more difficult than the sublime strains of the Hebrew poets. What are the Psalms which form our prayers but poetry, the most inspired, most difficult poetry? and we might as well expect that charging the memory with them will teach our children Hebrew, as the making them repeat Milton, as soon as they had learnt their English letters, would teach them their native tongue. Gradually and pleasantly we should pave the way, that difficulties may be encountered and overcome *singly*; that, when they do approach the sacred volumes, it may be to *understand* and to enjoy them, to find new pleasures, new truths in every page; and not to fling them aside with distaste and loathing, as soon as the chains of the school-room are broken, and the young aspirants are set free.

Liable as we are to religious arguments with the Nazarene, it is absolutely necessary that Hebrew should be part of the education we bestow on our children. The English Bibles are translated by the Christian divines, and though the text is generally correct, the heads of the chapters are very likely to mislead. There are also some passages which mysteriously written in English may appear capable of a double meaning;[1] and it is more than likely, the young Israelites would refer to the head of the chapter for the explanation of the text, and thus become confused, and either waver, or throw aside the sacred volume, as tending rather to destroy than to give peace. A perfect knowledge of Hebrew would banish this evil without interfering with the solid comfort found in the perusal of English Bibles. It would confirm them in their faith; for it is a known fact that, when an Israelite is thoroughly acquainted with Hebrew, he understands it much more fully and perfectly than an English divine. He will understand the peculiar structure of the language, not only to discover its real meaning, but also to trace how the Nazarene has been enabled to turn the same passages to favour his own belief. He will be enabled to produce argument for argument, and guard against those errors in the translation of the Bible which have been permitted to remain as favouring the Christian creed. Many words in English allow of a double meaning, and very many also in Hebrew; therefore we cannot wonder the Christian translators should adopt those renderings bearing most upon the revelation in which they believe.

Instead of condemning them for this, and being positive they are wrong and we are right, simply because for many generations we have been so taught: how much better would it be to refer to the Hebrew Bible, to find our belief and comfort there, and be prepared to answer every argument founded on some particular transaction, by a reference to the passage in its original language, and explain the sense as we regard it.

Then indeed might the chosen children of God be enabled to cope with those English divines, who have made the word of God the study of a life. How few amongst us now can do so! How many shrink from all argument, and tacitly allow the truth of the mistaken doctrines pressed upon them; because they feel they can bring forward nothing to support their faith; and others even depart from the strict line of truth, because there are so few amongst the Jewish nation to whom they can refer.

Yet it is sometimes thought, that religious knowledge should be

---

1 In her sermon on "The Prophecies of Isaiah" below, Aguilar discusses the translation of a word in Is. Christian texts translate it as "virgin," seeing the text as a prefiguration of the Virgin Mary. Jewish translators record the text as "young woman."

the business of priests or ministers, not of the laymen of a nation. The observation is just, regarding other nations; but not to the first-born of the Lord—that one people so peculiarly set apart that it was to be a "nation of priests;" even the king himself was to "write a copy of the Law in a book, to be with him that he might read therein all the days of his life, and learn to fear the Lord his God, to keep *all the* words of this law and these statutes to do them." (Deut. xvii. 18, 19.)

If these were the commands of the Lord in our own land, and when His spirit still dwelt amongst us: how much more requisite must it be now to attend to the preservation of our law in its original purity; how requisite that every child of Israel, male or female, should perfectly understand the language of our ancestors, that in which the awful yet invisible Voice delivered His dictates to Moses, that we may indeed feel, Hebrew is bound to Hebrew by a link neither oceans of water nor spreading wastes of land can sever. It matters not, that it is the opposite ends of the world in which they are domesticated. The sacred language is the silver link which, uniting them to each other, separates them from other nations, and makes them feel that they are indeed the witnesses of the Lord. And while they read in rejoicing faith the Book of Life in the language in which it was given, or in humble adoration prostrate themselves before God's throne: must not a glowing of the whole soul attend the addressing of the Eternal, in the same language in which His awful voice addressed His favoured servants?

Thousands of years have past away—yet that language and that nation still exist; can they, oh can they then, doubt its truth? Surely they must feel their religion comes indeed from their God; that they *are* members of a people, to whom such extraordinary mercies have been vouchsafed, and that they are the First-Born, the chosen of the Lord!

[The Value of Profane History and Fiction]

There is scarcely any profane history which, if read attentively, will not afford matter for instruction, thought, and subsequent conversation on the wonderful providence of the Lord. Here events can be traced from their very embryo to their final completion, either in success or overthrow. The airy trifles, so often the hinges on which great events turn, the almost invisible seeds of mighty revolutions stand revealed on the pages of history, and if properly considered often serve as keys to the continual incongruities passing around us. "The history of human affairs," an intelligent author observes, "is but the history of Divine Providence;"[1] and the remark is perfectly correct. Did the spirit of piety pervade, as was intended, the intellect, those very works read for profane instruction would assist to promote obedience to the command we are regarding.

Nor is it only history that may do this. There are tales, simple, domestic, highly moral tales, which, though as a whole fictitious, are in the main point but narrations of what, could we but lift up the veil of the world, is continually passing around us. "Truth is strange, stranger than fiction;" and were this fact more considered, the very tales read for recreation and enjoyment might be made of service in the promotion of piety. There are many who deem the perusal of such works but mere waste of time and intellect, creating evils even worse, in filling the mind with romance and folly. Nay, so far is this mistaken prejudice extended, that all books but those of instruction either in history, geography, arts, or sciences, are excluded from the child's library. The infant mind is crammed, its intellect exhausted, while the moral training and the guidance of the *feelings* are left to their own discretion, instead of permitting them to expand, in admiration of the good and detestation of the bad, whose actions and feelings are recorded in tales relative to children of their own age.[2]

It is the same with youth. Formerly indeed light works were not fitted either to attract the eye or engage the heart; and there are very many now, too many alas! far more likely to produce evil than good. Yet while England may boast the names of Edgeworth, Hemans, Hall, Mitford, Ellis, Sinclair, Ferrier, Opie, and Howitt, amongst her female literati, and Scott, and James, and Fay, to swell the brilliant list,

---

1 John Bigland, *Letters on the Study and Use of Ancient and Modern History*, 2nd ed. (London, 1808).

2 Isaac Leeser's note: "Miss Aguilar is right in the main regarding the usefulness of tales properly told. But in permitting such works to be placed in the hands of children, especially in our novel, romance, and story writing age, great care must absolutely be exercised in the selection, so that no distorted or extravagant view of life be early implanted in the youthful mind" (194).

the young can never be in want of recreation at once as improving to the heart, as delightful to the fancy; and if the mind has been properly trained, the spirit of piety indelibly infused, even the perusal of such works will strengthen and improve it.[1]

Few will believe this: a fanciful hypothesis it will in all probability be deemed; yet it is nevertheless true, as a reference to those whose minds have not been *cultivated* alone, but *regulated*, and are ever under the guiding influence of a spirit not of earth, would prove. To them it is not the romance and sentiment which are alone devoured and treasured up and thought upon, to the forgetfulness of all the rest. The same tale perused by pupils of diverse schools, would be productive of completely opposite effects. They who have been taught to drown all feeling, to conceal every emotion, to contemn as romance and folly every exalted sentiment, will be the very minds to which such food will bring evil instead of good; for they will seek in the pages of fiction the indulgence of all those whisperings of romance and high-flown sentiment which has become the stronger, from its ever being kept restrained and concealed. They condemn as vapid and dry, or as saintly sermons, all that would speak of morality and piety; they seek for no moral, laugh at the notion of good being derived from such works; and as a necessary consequence derive none; and their mind, being palled from such a continued succession of sweets and excitement, at length rejects all other food.

Very different is the effect of such pleasant recreation on minds which, educated in the school of piety, and of feelings, regulated not *contemned*, are ever accustomed to seek for the good, to cull flowers where others may see but weeds. They deem it no sin to trace the operations of an ever acting Providence, even in the events recorded as fictitious tales. They know that the cause of seeming incongruity and mystery in human affairs only originates in our being unable to trace them from their commencement to their completion, from the number of years they take in their fulfilment; while those more striking events, which chiefly form the basis of tales, generally pass

---

1 Aguilar's list of praiseworthy women writers of her day includes novelists Maria Edgeworth, Susan Ferrier, Anna Maria Hall, and Amelia Opie, poets Felicia Hemans and Mary Howitt, and writers of conduct manuals Sarah Stickney Ellis and Mary Russell Mitford. Among men, she refers to the historical romance writers Walter Scott, Theodore S. Fay, and George Payne Rainsford James.

unnoticed in real life, from the multiplicity and confusion ever attendant on human affairs. In a well narrated tale, these obstructions to the tracing of providence are removed. Sorrows, proceeding from ill regulated or irreligious minds, are traced to their source. Virtue and vice stand more strongly drawn before us, than they ever can in life. Our own faults or weaknesses frequently strike the mind, by their reflection on the pages which we read. Humility is frequently strengthened by the contrast, the well-guided heart discovers between itself, and those whose actions excite our admiration and love; for it does not drown the still small voice by the common excuse for evil, that perfection is only found in books; it knows that often, unsuspected and unseen, yet more exalted virtue dwells on earth than ever fiction can portray; and when it dwells on faults and passion falling before temptation, led astray by pleasure and success: it is often led to look within itself, and silently and voicelessly send up the prayer for grace and strength, not to stumble through the like means.

And thus, can it be considered impious and profane to render even recreative reading subservient to the cause of piety? to the immortal interests of the soul? will it not rather lead the youthful student to look yet more diligently within his own heart, and prepare his mind to recognise in a measure the ever acting Providence which guides and governs the actions alike of individuals, and those of the whole universe around him?

[The Spirit and the Forms of Judaism Considered Separately and Together*]

The concluding verses of the Shemang [*Shema*] bring us to a subject on which, in the preceding chapters, we may have often been accused of touching too lightly;—the peculiar forms and ceremonies of our religion.[1] The frontlets and bracelets alluded to in these verses were ornaments peculiar to the Eastern dress, and the

1 The concluding verses of the first paragraph of the *Shema* (known as the *V'Ahavta* after the first word "And thou shalt love") are taken from Deut. 6.8-9: "And thou shalt bind them [My commandments] for a sign upon thine hand, and they shall be for frontlets between thine eyes. And thou shalt write them upon the doorposts of thy house, and upon thy gates." To fulfill these prescriptions, male Jews traditionally wear *tefillin*, or phylacteries,

very fact of the children of Israel being commanded to associate the word of God with their very ornaments, to bind them upon their hands and between their eyes, and to go a little further, to make a fringe and place on it a thread of blue, "that they might remember the commandments of the Lord, and do them; that man might not seek those things which his heart and eyes incline after, and in the pursuit of which he might be led astray:"[1] all these directions, trifling as they may seem, are but unanswerable proofs of the close and intimate communion which man was to hold with his Maker; proofs, how entirely and completely religion, the *spirit* of religion, the whisperings of the Eternal, was to be associated with the actions of man—to follow him through life, to be bound upon his heart—not to be kept at that immense distance which is by some deemed the only way to retain holiness, for the alleged reason that such frequent communings only lessen the trembling awe in which we should approach our God. It is not as a Judge we are to behold and approach Him; but as an ever-watchful, ever-loving Father, an ever-faithful, ever-sympathizing Friend, to whom we may pour forth every sorrow, every joy, our cares, our hopes, our wishes; for He alone can know the extent of their influence upon our hearts,—He alone can comfort or can aid. To think continually on all the precepts contained in the preceding verses of the Shemang, was in all probability the origin of this command, to bind them on our hands and eyes, and place them on the doorposts and gates of our dwellings. Gradually and beautifully each verse links into the other. The binding the word of the Lord on our hands and eyes is connected with the precept, "these words which I command thee this day, shall be upon *thy heart*," referring to ourselves individually; the other [i.e. the *mezzuzah*], when obeyed, aids us imperceptibly in thinking or speaking of the Lord at all times; for surely His word cannot be seen upon our gates in walking out, or coming in, without a thought of Him who, "unless *He* build the house, they labour in vain that

during prayer wrapped around their arm and placed on their foreheads ("between thine eyes"). Observant Jews also affix a *mezzuzah* (small boxes containing parchment with the first two paragraphs of the *Shema* written on them) to each door of their house.

1 From Num. 15.37-41 (v. 39), this passage constitutes the third and final paragraph of the *Shema*. It commands male Jews to wear a *tallit*, or prayer shawl, whose white and blue fringes are supposed to remind them of their commitment to the divine law.

build it, unless *He* keep the city, the watchman waketh but in vain."[1]

It is not the mere obedience to the letter of the law, the mere adoption of the ancient dress in the hour of prayer, which will render our prayers acceptable. Their purpose is to aid the mind in withdrawing itself from its mere worldly occupations, to tempt the Hebrew youth to seek and know more of the law, a portion of which he bears upon his brow and hand; to employ his mind, or intellect, of which the brow may be a significant figure, in the study of that precious word; his hands—in those things acceptable to his Father in heaven. "A clean hand and a pure heart," the frequent repetition of those words in the Holy Scripture is sufficiently convincing of the peculiar meaning attached to this rite; and by studying the will of the Eternal, the Israelite learns how to obey it so as to have a beneficial effect on his spirit.[2]

Such must ever be the intent of religious ceremonies. They are given to *aid* and *strengthen* the spirit of piety, resting within this spirit, yet NOT to take its place. The Eternal saw the heart of man and knew that, when Adam sinned, the inclination and desires of his children would be for the evil, not for the good; and, therefore, that if religion were left to the promptings of natural man, she would speedily fly from this fallen world, and resume her native seat above. THAT MAN therefore who, despite the wickedness and heathenism darkly reigning round him, lifted up his affections and his intellects to his God; devoted his whole soul unto His bidding; believing, without question, the word of the Eternal, even to the resigning his only and his darling child,—that man was peculiarly the object of God's love and care; for it was human righteousness shining forth clear and unmoved, as a bright star amidst surrounding darkness, dispersing 'neath its rays the clouds of natural sin and corruption which in Abraham's heart, even as in his fellows, had originally birth; and it was his own pure, simple, trusting righteousness which excited the attention, and called down the blessing of the Lord. And for *this* faithful servant's sake, His love and mercy resolved on giving his descendants a law of light, and life, and joy, to aid them in knowing and serving Him, in governing the evil of their own hearts, so that

---

1 Ps. 127.1

2 Ps. 24.4.

the better principle, being the stronger, might bring forth good [...].

The spirit of piety, that yearning desire after holy things, and clinging love to God, are still, even as in the time of Abraham, direct gifts from the Father of all; His grace[1] acts still imperceptibly upon natural man, though unperceived by our outward senses,—but the dictates of the law, the acts of obedience therein commanded, the revelation of the Lord and of His glorious attributes, the numerous aids to becoming worthy servants in His sight, and conquering evil propensities by the clear explanation of right and wrong which, through Moses, He has so mercifully set down:—all these are now common to us all; and therefore man's natural depravity and unenlightened ignorance can *never* be brought forward as excuses for sin and disobedience. The principle of good within us was naturally as powerful as that of evil, the example of our first father occasioned the fearful prevalence of the latter; but the principle of good is not even now extinguished; and, aided by the *strength* and *grace* of God which we have called down by *prayer*, it is yet enabled to conquer the evil, and walk on in the way of the Lord. It will *not* indeed obtain for us salvation; but it will be pleasing unto our Father, and incline His heart mercifully and favourably towards us.

This is one of the great distinctions between the Hebrew and Christian creeds. The God of the Christians does need a saviour and mediator; but the God of the Hebrew needs it not. They look on our beautiful law as one of fire and blood; that even when God gave it He knew it was impossible for man to keep it; that man's depravity would entirely prevent his obedience; that all under the law are subject to misery and curses, are chained down to a heavy, lifeless weight, to redeem them from which our Father, at the same time the law was framed and given, resolved on the holocaust (sacrifice) of one who knew not sin, to take away the sins of men, to remove the curse of the law, and institute a law of love instead of the law of fire, and the awful dispensation revealed in the Old Testament.

According to this belief, the law was framed to be destroyed; given to be removed; sent as a curse instead of a blessing; and the

1 Aguilar's note: "'Whoever comes to purify himself will be aided from heaven.'—*Talmud*." This note is apparently an attempt to preempt criticism that the concept of "grace" has only a Christian derivation.

descendants of Abraham, instead of being peculiarly blessed above all nations, according to the solemn word of the Lord, must have been marked out from the very first as the objects of His wrath. But the God of the Hebrew is a God of TRUTH, whose words fail not, nor change, in whom there is not a shadow of turning; and therefore is it that we reject this doctrine. When so repeatedly we read words to this import, "My covenant will I not break, nor alter the thing that is gone out of my lips," we dare not depart from that covenant; for we know that it is to last to eternity.[1] We cannot recognise our God in the Being who would impose a law upon His people, simply and solely to destroy them; who would mock us by unmeaning ordinances; who would desire obedience when He knew the nature of man could NOT bestow it; who would fetter instead of freeing; fetter with infinitely more oppression and cruel bondage than the chains of Egypt from which He freed us; who with such deep solemnity, such majestic power, yet with such beneficence and tender love, would frame a law, and proclaim it eternal, yet at the same moment fix the period of its continuance and look to its annihilation. We cannot recognise the God of truth and love in one that would act thus. There is *not one* portion of that law which, when it was given, man could *not* obey; not one command, one ordinance, to which man could not implicitly adhere;—and that man fell from it was not the fault of the law or the ordinance of the Eternal. The law, as we have before said, was given to teach man his duties, to assist him in conquering natural depravity, and permitting the principle of good, also placed within him, to obtain ascendancy. He had thus the free will to choose his own path, to seek the favour of his God, or to reject it; and that he chose the latter *was not* because he had not the *power* to choose the former, or that he *could not* obey the law; but because, like Cain, he loved the evil more than the good, and resisted the still small voice which the love of our God has placed within every breast, resisted its entreaty to fly from temptation, and implore the infused strength of the Lord, till its soft, yet piercing whisper was drowned in the roar of transgression and debauch [...].

If we thus acknowledge the beneficent purpose of the law, how completely appropriate is it to our need! how evidently is it the

1 Ps. 89.34.

work of an all-wise, all-merciful Father, who had but the good and everlasting welfare of His children in view, when He ordained it, and selected Moses to make it known. We cannot but feel an earnest desire to obey its very dictate, to adhere to it, as strictly, as closely as ever our scattered and fallen state will permit; and not strictly and closely alone, but freely, unconditionally, lovingly, giving the heart, not the servile obedience of slaves. And this is still in our power to do, though to very many of our rites and ceremonies we cannot adhere in our dispersed and captive state.

When men are drawn together to attend to peculiar rites, and keep holy particular days: their thoughts naturally revert from their individual concerns, to the combination of interest which draws them thus together. They are forced for the time to leave their temporal affairs, even though the thought should still cling more earnestly to these than to their spiritual welfare; they feel conscious of some obligation binding them to a Higher Power, and by degrees they attain some portion of holiness. To others, again, public observance of forms gives the opportunity to ponder on their God, which they might otherwise seek for in vain. And to other and yet more exalted minds it strengthens and supports the inward piety, it gives them that which they so earnestly desire, opportunities of proving their *love* by a willing and perfect obedience. Religious ceremonies also attract the attention of children, and sometimes lead them to ask and search for that which, through neglect or irreligion on the part of parents, they might never know. Many condemn form entirely; but if the rites and ceremonies of religion were not intended to bring forth good, the God of goodness would not have ordained them. *Subordinate* to the spirit they were to be indeed; to *assist* the worship of the heart, but not to take its place. Ordained to preserve us wholly distinct from other nations, many of the minor laws, relating only to the customs of the nations under God's wrath, cannot of course now be observed; but they are not to be pronounced trifling and unimportant on that account; nor, because we cannot attend to *them*, are we to disregard others; for these are the words of the Eternal: "Ye shall not walk in the manners of the nations which I cast out before you; for they committed all these things, and therefore I abhorred them: but I have said unto you, ye shall inherit their land, that floweth with milk and honey; I am the Lord your God which separates you from other people: and ye shall be holy unto me for I the Lord am holy, and have severed you from all other people, that you should be MINE."[1]

We need go no farther than these beautiful verses, to perceive the origin and necessity of our peculiar ceremonies. We were to abstain from some to sever us from wickedness, and adhere to others to mark us as the holy of the Lord. Instead then of seeking to find excuses for their non-performance: should we not rather glory in the minutest reservation which would stamp us as so peculiarly the Lord's own, and deem it a glorious privilege to be thus marked out not only in feature and in faith, but in our civil and religious code, as the chosen of God? Had we been thus selected by an earthly sovereign, who would not have gloried in the distinction; and shall the Hebrew think less of the favour of his God?

True, the heathen nations, against whose evil example we were warned, no longer surround us; but we live in the midst of others with whom we are still more likely to become assimilated if we relax, in the very smallest degree, from our adherence to the law of Moses. With regard to this blessed law, the Bible is the only unerring guide; nor should the *end* and *intent* of its statutes ever be forgotten. The spirit of love, so beautifully breathing through the preceding verses of the Shemang, must hallow the observance of the two last [verses], or obedience will be of little avail. If, when the Hebrew arrays himself in the Tephilin, he thinks on all that is comprised in the brief passages he has bound on his brow and hand, and earnestly and faithfully he seeks for strength to obey their dictates throughout the day, and he asks for grace that his hands work not evil, his feet turn not astray, his thoughts cleave not to transgression: the command of Moses is indeed obeyed, not only in form, but in *spirit.* If the scroll of the law, fastened to the door-post of his house, remind the son of Israel of a preceding command, "to speak and think of his God when he sitteth in his house or walketh by the way;" if it evince to the strangers around that he is not one of them, however intimately he may mingle in social intercourse; that he glories in standing thus apart as the chosen of God: the form has done its duty, it springs from, and yet assists the spirit resting within.

Thus should every Hebrew rite be considered, and reason, not

1 A somewhat truncated version of Lev. 20:23-26.

superstition, be traced as its foundation. The *Mind*, from whom every law in the Pentateuch originated, far exceeds in wisdom those which that celestial Mind has framed;—and therefore, in love, He threw a veil over that overpowering light of wisdom; and, choosing from among the seed of Abraham the best and meekest of His favourite servants: He delivered through his means laws which, though proceeding from the most profound wisdom, were yet couched in words suited to the weak comprehension of His creatures.

Not one of these laws has a mysterious, or admits of a double meaning. All who seek to know the Jewish ethics, will find them in the word of God; for it is to the ordinances of Scripture *alone* we refer. There may be some observances which superstition and bigotry have introduced, some which tarnish and choke up the law of love which came direct from Heaven; but to them we allude not. The Bible and reason are the only guides to which the child of Israel can look in security. The laws for which we can find no foundation in the one, and which will not stand the test of the other, need no farther proof; they are not the dictates of the law, they are wanderings from the true and only law, the inventions of man, and not the words of God. The Bible gives us a cause, a reason for every statute it enjoins. It would have been sufficient had man been desired to obey simply because God willed it; but the Eternal would not thus blind His children; He would not the obedience of ignorance and fear; and therefore He condescended to inform us *wherefore* each law was given, that we might obey more willingly, and give the homage of the intellect as well as the sacrifice of the will.

It is therefore evident that those observances which not only confine the soaring spirit, but frequently occasion ordinances of far more weight to be neglected, and for which no reason can be assigned save the ideas of our ancient fathers, cannot be compared in weight and consequence to the piety of the heart, which but too often they supersede. To explain the words of Moses and adapt them to the comprehension of all classes amongst their brethren was, in all probability, the sole intent of the Hebrew elders, an intent equally judicious as praiseworthy; but they would have shrunk back in sorrow and alarm could they have known that in future ages *their* words would take the place of the word of God; that they would be made the means of superstition creeping in amongst us, of bigotry raising her dark and lowering standard, till together they had well nigh expelled the pure spirit originally pervading the religion of Moses; that the very rites and ceremonies instituted to keep up a lively remembrance of the Lord should be the very means of bidding us forget Him, as if religion consisted only in outward form.

When we think on the many inconsistencies discoverable in the mere formalist; the contradictions which his strict yet lifeless adherence to mere ceremonial things and neglect of the spirit generally comprise; when we know that they who depart from the faith of their fathers are ever those reared in the severest obedience to mere forms: we have quite sufficient evidence that such are not the consequences of obedience to the *law of Moses*, that they proceed not from the spirit of religion, which the forms were given to aid and strengthen, that they come of weak, capricious, changeful man, not from the immutable and eternal God. And their universal obedience generally proceeds from the Hebrew following in the steps of his fathers, without knowing the why and the wherefore. Nor is it extraordinary that, when the *spirit* is not inculcated, succeeding generations should either become yet more severely bigoted and darkly superstitious, or, disgusted with a religion which brings no comfort, no support, throw it off entirely, embrace another, or live as if they had no God. And is not this an awful consideration? Can it be one moment imagined, the God of love will accept the religion of petty ceremonies in lieu of the *heart* which He so continually demands? Will He, who hath desired the love of the heart, and soul, and might, be content with the mere offering of outward form? What are the words of his righteous servant David, when monarch of Israel, and it was in his power to attend to all and every rite enjoined by Moses? "Thou desirest not sacrifice, else would I give it; thou delightest not in burnt-offering; the sacrifices of God are a broken spirit, a broken and a contrite heart, oh God! thou wilt not despise […]."[1]

Yet while we feel and acknowledge the insufficiency of form alone: the sons of Israel must beware the contrary extreme, and, deeming that all consists of spirit worship, fail in that most important article of their faith, a willing and perfect *obedience*. If they adhere

1 Ps. 51.16-17.

not to the rites of their forefathers, they cannot take unto themselves the gracious promises made to the children of Israel; for their religion degenerates into that, which is termed, natural theology; in a word, they are Deists not Hebrews, and they deprive themselves alike of faith, hope, and comfort [...].[1]

In the observance of these minute forms publicity should be most carefully avoided. It is enough, if to the world he demonstrate the peculiar holiness of his religion by the superiority of his moral conduct. The son of Israel, who has been in early years awakened to the *spirit* of Judaism, will gladly observe the minutest form, which will assist his devotions, and chain his wandering thoughts; and though the act of attaching the scroll of the law to the door posts of his house may not be in any way connected with the strengthening of the spirit: he will yet gladly avail himself of this command, to prove, he fears not the scorn of the world's attacking perhaps this public manifestation of his religion; he rather overcomes it as a *trial* and proof of willing obedience, and glories in thus keeping himself distinct from the nations, and holy unto his God [...].

Obedience depends neither on country, time, nor situation; it is required whether we are free citizens of Jerusalem, or wanderers and captives in the stranger's land; whether all things are smiling around us, or dark clouds obscure us beneath their shades; whether coeval with Moses, the present time, or a thousand years hence. And would we be still the first-born of the Lord: we must adhere without hesitation or inquiry to the law of Moses—the pure, the beautiful, and consistent law, of which the whole Bible is the glorious record.

Obedience extends over every rank and station. We cannot now bring burnt-offerings, and sacrifices unto the Lord; but verses similar to this should be engraved on every youthful heart: "Hath the Lord as great delight in burnt-offerings and sacrifices, as in *obeying* the voice of the Lord? Behold to *obey* is better than sacrifice, to *hearken* than the fat of rams—for rebellion (or disobedience) is as the sin of witchcraft, and stubbornness is as iniquity and idolatry."[2]

---

1 Deism: Late eighteenth-century belief in a God who created the universe according to unchanging and mechanistic natural laws, and then stepped back to let it work. Deists rejected the belief in Providence, the concept of a personal God who intervenes in human history.

2 1 Sam. 15.22.

It is impossible to peruse the holy Scriptures without the conviction striking home to every Hebrew mind, that we may worship and love the Lord our God, as fervently, as steadily, as acceptably to Him in our captive state, as in Jerusalem. And should we not sometimes ponder on these things, and endeavour by individual conduct to uphold the glory of the nation, and assist by example our wavering brethren? [...].

Every Hebrew should look upon his faith as a temple extending over every land, to prove the immutability, the eternity of God, the unity of His purposes, the truth of the past, the present, and the future; and regard himself as one of the pillars which support it from falling to the ground, and adds, however insignificant in itself, to the strength, the durability, and the beauty of the whole.

That we do not think enough of these things proceeds from that spirit of independence, which would prompt every man to worship after his own fancy. Religion has no more powerful foe than independence. It is contrary to every law of nature. Who is it dare proclaim himself a being independent alike of God and man? Who dare say we are not dependent beings? Yet it is of little use acknowledging a God, One who frames, upholds, and guides: if man turn aside from His everlasting statutes to walk in his own ways, his, who himself is but the being of a day [...].

In these brief remarks on the great importance of steadily adhering to *form*, (for in the adhering or non-adhering we expose ourselves to the blessing or the curse so emphatically promised by Moses) our review of the two last verses of the Shemang is concluded; and we have now but to notice the beautiful union, observable in the six verses, forming this daily prayer. Each is distinct, and forms a complete study of itself; yet each is so connected with the other, that the whole forms a more complete and summary rule of life, than can be found in any other part of the Bible.

It is scarcely possible for the reflecting mind to remain insensible to the precise and beautiful arrangement of every sentence, almost of every word.

Proclaiming the unity of our God, we are daily reminded of our nationality, and all the weighty reflections and responsibilities which that nationality includes. Then desired to love the Lord with heart, and soul, and might. It is morally impossible to obey this command, unless the spirit of religion pervade our every action. Affections, intellect, springing from the pure fount of light, and love, must pour back their treasures; as the sparkling waters of the fountain fall back into the same spring from whence they rose: social, domestic, individual conduct, benevolence, charity, every human virtue, are included in obedience to the second verse. In the third, the ten commandments are recalled to rest on our hearts, that we may remember them to do them. In the fourth, the duty of religious instruction, of strengthening our inward thoughts on this momentous subject by conversation, and of encouraging the spirit of piety to pervade even those amusements which we may deem profane, all are strongly inculcated. And lastly, lest the spirit thus enforced should fade away and die in our wavering hearts, adherence and obedience to instituted form are positively commanded. We cannot fail to perceive by the arrangement of this brief, yet perfect portion of our law, how closely and firmly the spirit is *united* with the form; and that, would we be Israelites indeed, not merely such in name, the command, implied in the *arrangement* as well as *precept*, MUST be obeyed. The *heart* must be wholly given to the Lord; yet still the instituted form *must* be obeyed, as strictly and steadily as our scattered state will permit. As both are here indivisibly connected: so is it evident, the religion of no Hebrew is perfect, unless the form be hallowed by the spirit, the SPIRIT quickened by the FORM.

When this is done, when we behold the union of religion and morality, as the God of heaven intended; when all that is here comprised is indeed obeyed; when we behold Hebrew parents bringing up their children in the fear of the Lord, and according to the law of Moses,—the Bible read, studied, alike in English, as in our own language, and *believed* by every Israelite, male or female; when the Sabbath-day is hallowed, the love of interest and money, giving place to the pure love of God; worldly ambition set at nought, when it can only be gratified at the expense of Judaism; when the Jewish nation glories in her captive state as a proof, she *is* the chosen of the Lord, and hails the fulfilment of these awful threatenings as convincing evidence, that the glorious promises will be with equal truth fulfilled; when such things are: then indeed may be hope that the peri-

From THE WOMEN OF ISRAEL

"Introduction"

Among the many valuable works relative to woman's capabilities, influence, and mission, which in the present age are continually appearing, one still seems wanting. The field has, indeed, been entered; detached notices of the women of Israel, the female biography of Scripture, have often formed interesting portions of those works, where woman is the subject; but all the fruit has not been gathered: much yet remains, which, thrown together, would form a history as instructive as interesting, as full of warning as example, and tending to lead our female youth to the sacred volume, not only as their guide to duty, their support in toil, their comfort in affliction, but as a true and perfect mirror of themselves.

To desert the Bible for its commentators; never to peruse its pages without notes of explanation: to regard it as a work which of itself is incomprehensible, is, indeed, a practice as hurtful as injudicious. Sent as a message of love to our own souls, as written and addressed, not to nations alone, but as the voice of God to individuals—whispering to each of us that which we most need; thus it is we should first regard and venerate it. This accomplished, works tending to elucidate its glorious and consoling truths, to make manifest its simple lessons of character, as well as precept; to bring yet closer to the youthful and aspiring heart, the poetry, the beauty, the eloquence, the appealing tenderness of its sacred pages, may prove of essential service. In this hope, to bring clearly before the women of Israel all that they owe to the word of God, all that it may still be to them, the present task is undertaken.

We are far from asserting that this has not been attempted, and for the larger portion of the sex, accomplished before. Religion is the foundation and mainspring of every work which has been written for the use and improvement of women. Female biographers of scripture have, we believe, often appeared; though the characters of the Old Testament are so briefly and imperfectly sketched, compared to those of the New, that but little pleasure or improvement could be derived from their perusal. Yet still, with the writings of Sandford, Ellis, and Hamilton before us, each exhibiting its authoress so earnest, so eloquent in her cause, with "woman's mission" marked so simply, yet so forcibly, in the little volume of that name, has not woman of every race, and every creed, all sufficient to teach her her duty and herself?[1]

We would say she had; yet for the women of Israel something still more is needed. The authors above mentioned are Christians themselves, and write for the Christian world. Education and nationality compel them to believe that "Christianity is the sole source of female excellence." To Christianity alone they owe their present station in the world: their influence, their equality with man, their spiritual provision in this life, and hopes of immortality in the next. Nay more, that the value and dignity of woman's character would never have been known, but for the religion of Jesus; that pure, loving, self-denying doctrines, were unknown to woman; she knew not even her relation to the Eternal; dared not look upon Him as her Father, Consoler, and Saviour, till the advent of Christianity.[2] We grant that the Gentiles knew it not, till the Bible became more generally known, till the Eternal, in His infinite mercy, permitted a partial knowledge of Himself to spread over the world—alike to prepare the Gentile for that day, when we shall all know Him as He is, and to render the trial of His people's faith and constancy yet more terribly severe. We feel neither anger nor uncharitableness towards those who would thus deny to Israel those very privileges which were ours, ages before they became theirs; and which, in fact, have descended from us to them. Yet we cannot pass such assertion unanswered, lest from the very worth and popularity of those works in which it is promulgated, the young and thoughtless daughter of Israel may believe it really has foundation, and look no further than the page she reads.

How or whence originated the charge that the law of Moses sank

---

1 Elizabeth Sanford, *Woman, in Her Social and Domestic Character*, 6th ed. (London: 1839); Sarah Stickney Ellis, *Women of England* (London: 1838); Elizabeth Hamilton, *Letters on the Elementary Principles of Education* (London: 1837); and *Letters, addressed to the Daughter of a Nobleman, on the Formation of Religious and Moral Principle*, 3rd ed. (London: 1814).

2 The negative sentiments regarding Judaism's treatment of women alluded to here and in the following paragraphs are typical, not only of the women's conduct manuals of Sandford, Ellis and Hamilton, but also of the literature of the Evangelical movement with a mission to convert Jews to Christianity.

the Hebrew female to the lowest state of degradation, placed her on a level with slaves or heathens, and denied her all mental and spiritual enjoyment, we know not: yet certain it is that this most extraordinary and unfounded idea obtains credence even in this enlightened age. The word of God at once proves its falsity; for it is impossible to read the Mosaic law without the true and touching conviction, that the female Hebrew was even more an object of the tender and soothing care of the Eternal than the male. The thanksgiving in the Israelite morning prayer, on which so much stress is laid, as a proof how little woman is regarded, is but a false and foolish reasoning on the subject; almost, in truth, too trivial for regard.[1]

The very first consequence of woman's sin was to render her in physical and mental strength, inferior to man; to expose her to suffering more continued, and more acute; to prevent her obtaining those honors and emoluments of which man thinks so much; to restrain her path to a more lowly and domestic, though not a less hallowed sphere; and, all this considered, neither scorn towards the sex, nor too much haughtiness for themselves, actuate the thanksgiving by which our opponents is brought forward against us. It was but one of those blessings in which the pious Israelite thanks God for all things, demanding neither notice nor reproof.

To the Gentile assertion that the Talmud has originated the above-mentioned blessing, and commanded or inculcated the moral and mental degradation of woman, we reply that even if it do, which we do not believe it does, its commands are wholly disregarded, and its abolishment is not needed to raise the Hebrew female to that station assigned her in the word of God, and which through many centuries she has been permitted, without reproof or question, to enjoy. The Eternal's provision for her temporal and spiritual happiness is proved in His unalterable word; and therefore no Hebrew can believe that He would issue another law for her degradation and abasement. If, indeed, there are such laws, they must have been compiled at a time when persecution had so brutalized and lowered the intellect of man that he partook the savage barbarity of the nations around him, and of the age in which he lived; when the law of his

---

1 Aguilar alludes to the blessing traditionally recited each morning by Jewish men upon first awakening, which offers thanks to God "Who has not made me a woman."

God had, as a natural consequence, become obscured, and the Hebrew female shared the same rude and savage treatment which was the lot of all the lower classes of women in the feudal ages. The protection, the glory, the civilizing influence of chivalry extended, in its first establishment, but to the baronial classes. We see no proofs of the humanizing and elevating influence of Christianity, either on man or woman, till the reformation opened the BIBLE, the whole BIBLE, to the nations at large; when civilization gradually followed. If, then, the situation of even Christian women was so uncertain, and but too often so degraded, for nearly fourteen centuries after the advent of Jesus, who his followers declare was the first to teach them their real position—was it very remarkable that the vilified and persecuted Hebrew should have in a degree forgotten his nationality, his immortal and glorious heritage, and shared in the barbarity around him? Granting for the moment that such was the case (but we by no means believe it was), if the degradation, mentally and morally, of the Hebrew female, ever did become part of the Jewish law, it was when man was equally degraded, and the blessed word of God hid from him.

The situation of many of the Hebrews at the present day proves this. In but too many parts of the world the Israelites are still the subjects of scorn, hatred, and persecution: and their condition is, in consequence, the lowest and most awfully degraded in the scale of man. But it is not to woman that degradation and slavery are confined; as, were it a portion of the law of Moses, would inevitably be the case. It is the consequence of cruelty, of abasement in social treatment; yet even here, when mind, principle, honor, all seem overthrown from such brutalizing influence, the affections retain their power.

Whatever of spiritual hope, of human privileges, the word of God bestows on man, and to which the mind, darkened and despairing from the horrors of persecution, may yet be open, are shared by the Hebrew wife, and imparted by the Hebrew mother.

Were it a portion of the law of Moses to enslave and degrade us, how is it that we do not see this law adhered to and obeyed, as well as others claiming the same divine origin? Neither Christianity nor civilization would alter or improve our condition, were it indeed such as it has been represented. The Hebrew ever loves, protects, and reverences his female relative; and if, indeed, he do not—if he deny her all share in immortality, and, in consequence, thinks she has no need of religion now, nor hope hereafter, it is because the remnants of barbarism, ignorance, and superstition remain, to have blinded both his spiritual and mental eye; yet whatever he may be accused of believing, his acts deny the belief. Why is he so anxious that his wife and daughters should adhere to every law, attend to every precept which he believes the law of God? If they have no soul, no portion in the world to come, it surely cannot signify how they act, or what they believe in this? Why are they blotted from the minds and hearts of their relatives, if, as it may sometimes happen, they intermarry with the stranger? If they have no spiritual responsibility, no claim, no part in the law of God, why should they be blamed and shunned, if they desert it for another? But it is idle to follow the argument further. The charge is either altogether false, or based on such contradictory and groundless report, as to render it of little consequence, save as it affects us in the eyes of those who uphold, that till Christianity was promulgated woman knew not her own station either towards God or man.

Simply to deny this assertion, to affirm, that instead of degrading and enslaving, the Jewish law exalted, protected, and provided for woman, teaching her to look up to God, not as a severe master and awful judge, but as her Father, her Defender, her Deliverer when oppressed, her Witness in times of false accusation, her Consoler and Protector when fatherless, widowed—aye, as the tender and loving Sovereign, who spared the young bride the anguish of separation from her beloved: merely to affirm, that with such laws woman was equally a subject of divine love as she is now, would not avail us much. The women of Israel must themselves arise, and prove the truth of what we urge—by their own conduct, their own belief, their own ever-acting and ever-influencing religion, prove without doubt or question that we need not Christianity to teach us our mission—prove that our duties, our privileges, were assigned to us from the very beginning of the world, confirmed by that law to which we still adhere, and will adhere for ever, and manifested by the whole history of the Bible.

A new era is dawning for us. Persecution and intolerance have in so many lands ceased to predominate, that Israel may once more breathe in freedom; the law need no longer be preached in darkness, and obeyed in secret; the voice of man need no longer be the vehicle of instruction from father to son, mingling with it unconsciously human opinions, till those opinions could scarcely be severed from the word of God, and by degrees so dimmed its lustre, as to render its comprehension an obscure and painful task. This need no longer be. The Bible may be perused in freedom; the law may be publicly explained and preached to all who will attend. A spirit of inquiry, of patriotism, of earnestness in seeking to know the Lord, and obey Him according to His word, is springing up in lieu of the stagnating darkness, the appalling indifference, which had reigned so long. Persecution never decreased our numbers. As the bush which burned without consuming, so was Israel in those blood-red ages of intolerance and butchery. In the very heart of the most Catholic kingdom—amongst her senate, her warriors, her artisans—aye, even her monks and clergy—Judaism lurked unconsumed by the fires ever burning round.[1] The spirit was ever awake and active, ready to endure martyrdom, but not to forswear that God whose witnesses they were. Persecution was a crisis in our History; prosperity the reaction; and from that reaction the natural consequence was the gradual rise, growth, and influence of indifference. Indifference, however, has but its appointed time: and Israel is springing up once more the stronger, nobler, more spiritually enlightened, from his long and waveless sleep. Free to assert their right as immortal children of the living God, let not the women of Israel be backward in proving they, too, have a Rock of Strength, a Refuge of Love; that they, too, have a station to uphold, and a "mission" to perform, not alone as daughters, wives, and mothers, but as witnesses of that faith which first raised, cherished, and defended them—witnesses of that God who has called them His, and who has so repeatedly sanctified the emotions peculiar to their sex, by graciously comparing the love he bears us, as yet deeper than a mother's for her child, a wife's for her husband, having compassion for his people, as on a "woman forsaken and grieved in spirit." "Can a woman forget her sucking child, that she should not have compassion on the son of her travail; yea,

1 Aguilar refers to the crypto-Jews in Spain and Portugal during the Inquisition. See p. 61, note 1, above.

she may forget, yet will I not forget thee." "As a mother comforteth her children, so will I comfort thee."[1]

Were not these relations holy and sanctified in the sight of the Lord, would He use them as figurative of His long suffering love? Many terms, similar to those above quoted, prove, without a shadow of doubt, the tender compassion with which He regarded woman long before He used such terms to figure His compassionating love towards Israel, when sinfulness called forth His long averted wrath.

Let us then endeavor to convince the nations of the high privileges we enjoy, in common with our fathers, brothers, and husbands, as the first-born of the Lord, by the peculiar sanctity, spirituality, and inexpressible consolation of our belief. Let us not, as women of Israel, be content with the mere performance of domestic, social, and individual duties, but vivify and enlighten them by the rays of eternal love and immortal hope, which beam upon us from the pages of the Bible. A religion of love is indeed necessary to woman, yet more so than to man. Even in her happiest lot there must be a void in her heart, which ever-acting piety alone can fill; and to her whose portion is to suffer, whose lot is lonely, O what misery must be hers, unless she can lean upon her God, and draw from His word the blessed conviction that His love, His tenderness, are hers, far beyond the feeble conception of earth; and that whatever she may endure, however unknown to or scorned by man, it is known to Him who smites but in love, and has mercy even while He smites.

To realize this blessed conviction, the Bible must become indeed the book of life to the female descendants of that nation whose earliest history it so vividly records; and be regarded, not as a merely political or religious history, but as the voice of God speaking to each individual, giving strength to the weak, encouragement to the desponding, endurance to the patient, justice to the wronged, and consolation as unspeakable as unmeasurable to the afflicted and the mourner. Do we need love? We shall find innumerable verses telling us, that the Lord Himself proclaimed His attribute as "merciful and gracious, long-suffering, abundant in goodness and truth, keeping mercy for thousands, forgiving iniquity and sin;" that "as far as the Heaven is above the earth so great is His mercy, extending from

1 Isa. 54.6; 49.15; 66.13.

everlasting to everlasting."[1] We have but to read those appeals of the Eternal to Israel, alike in Jeremiah and Isaiah, and many of the minor prophets—and if our hearts be not stone, they must melt before such compassionating love, such appealing tenderness, and feel we cannot be lonely, cannot be unloved, while such deep changeless love is ours. Do we need sympathy? Shall we not find it in words similar to these, "In all their afflictions He was afflicted, and the angel of His presence saved them? In His love and in His pity He redeemed them, and He bare them, and carried them all the days of old."[2] Do we need patience and strength? Shall we not exercise it, when we have the precious promise, "*Wait* on the Lord, be of good courage, and He shall strengthen thine heart?"[3] Shall we droop and grieve beneath the wrongs and false judgments of short-sighted man, when we are told the ways of God are not those of man—that He knoweth our frame, and readeth our thoughts—that not a bodily or mental pang is ours which He does not know and compassionate—aye, and in His own good time will heal![4]

To throw together all those verses which confirm and prove the loving-tenderness borne towards us by the Eternal, would be an endless and a useless task. We can but point to that ever-flowing fount of healing waters, and assure those who have once really tasted, and will persevere in the heavenly draught, that it will never fail them, never change its properties, but each year sink deeper and deeper into their souls, till at length it becomes indeed all they need; and they themselves will cling to it, despite of occasional doubt and darkness, inseparable from our souls while denizens of earth.

Nor is it only the verses containing such gracious promises, which will yield us comfort and assistance. We may glean the glad tidings of Eternal Love from the biographies and narratives with which the sacred book abounds—there may be some meek and lowly spirits amongst the female youth of Israel, who would gladly clasp the

---

1 The first allusion is to Exod. 34.6–7. The second combines Ps. 103.11 and 17. Verse 11: "For as the heavens are high above the earth, so great is his steadfast love toward those who fear him." Verse 17: "But the steadfast love of the Lord is from everlasting to everlasting on those who fear him."

2 Isa. 63.9–10.

3 Ps. 27.14.

4 Alludes to Ps. 103.13–14.

strength and guidance which we proffer them from the Bible, could they believe that God, the great, the almighty, the tremendous and awful Being (as which they have perhaps been accustomed to regard Him), can have love and pity for themselves, or give comfort and aid to trials, which appear even too trivial to ask, or to excite the sympathy of man. We would lead them to look earnestly and believingly into the history of every woman in the Bible, and trace there the influence of God's holy and compassionating love. We are not indeed placed as the women of Israel before their dispersion, or as the wives of the patriarchs before the law was given; yet their God is our God. It was not to a race so perfect, so gifted, so hallowed, as to be free from all the present faults and failings of the sex that the Lord vouchsafed His love. No, it was to woman, even as she is now. The women of the Bible are but mirrors of ourselves. And if the Eternal, in His infinite mercy, extended love, compassion, forbearance, and forgiveness unto them, we may believe He extends them equally unto us, and draw comfort, and encouragement, and faith from the biographies we read.

In a work entitled "The Women of Israel," some apology, perhaps, is necessary for commencing with the wives of the patriarchs, who may not lay claim to such holy appellation.[1] Yet, as the chosen and beloved partners of those favored of God, from whom Israel traces his descent, and for the sake of whose faith and righteousness we were selected and chosen as a peculiar people, and the law given to be our guide through earth to heaven, we cannot consider our history complete without them; more particularly as their lives are so intimately blended with their husbands; and that in them, even yet more vividly than at a later period, we may trace the Lord's dealings with His female children, and derive from them alike warning and support.

Eve, indeed, may not have such national claim, but if we believe that her history, as every other part of Genesis, was penned by the same inspired law-giver—that Moses recorded only that which had been—we shall find much, indeed, to repay us for lingering a while

1 Technically, the matriarchs—Sarah, Rebecca, Rachel, and Leah—were not Israelites, since the Israelite people only came into existence after Jacob's wrestling match with the angel, as a result of which he and his descendants were renamed Israel.

on her character and life. To the scepticism, the cavils, the doubts, and (but too often unhappily) the direct belief in the Mosaic account of the first disobedience of man, we give no heed whatever. We must either believe in the Pentateuch or deny it. There can be no intermediate path. The whole must be true or none. It is not because much may appear obscure, or even contradictory in the sacred narrative, that we are to pronounce it false, or mystify and poetize it as an allegory.

We are simply to believe, and endeavor to act on that belief. So much is there ever passing around us that we cannot solve; our thoughts, in their furthest flight, are so soon checked, can penetrate so little into the wonders of man and nature, that it appears extraordinary how man can doubt and deny, because he cannot understand. In this case, however—the history of Eve—truth is so simple and clear, that we know not how it can supply such an endless fund of argument and doubt. To remove this groundless disbelief, to endeavor to render the narrative clear and simple to the female youth of Israel, and, even through Eve's sad yet consoling history, to prove to them the deep love borne towards us from the very first of our creation by our gracious God, must be our apology, if apology be needed, for commencing a work entitled "The Women of Israel," with our general mother.

Beginning, then, from the very beginning, some degree of order is requisite in the arrangement of our subject. Our aim being to evince to the nations and to our own hearts, the privileges, alike temporal and eternal, which were ours from the very commencement—to prove that we have no need of Christianity, or the examples of the females in the Gospel, to raise us to an equality with man—to demonstrate our duties and secure us consolation here or salvation hereafter—the word of God must be alike our groundwork and our guide. From the past history which that unerring guide presents, our present duties and responsibilities, and our future destiny, will alike be revealed. In a simple biography each life is a sufficient division; but, with the exception of the wives of the patriarchs and one or two more, we have scarcely sufficient notice of individuals to illustrate our design by regarding them separately. There appear, therefore, seven periods in the history of the women of Israel, which demand our attention.

First Period—the Wives of the Patriarchs, including Eve, Sarah, Rebecca, Leah, and Rachel.

Second Period—the Exodus, and the Law considered as affecting the condition and establishing the privileges of women.

Third Period—Women of Israel between the establishment of the Law and the authority of the Kings, comprising sketches of Miriam, Deborah, the wife of Manoah, Naomi, and Hannah.

Fourth Period—Women of Israel during the continuation of the Kingdom, comprising, amongst other sketches, Michal, Abigail, the Shunammite, and Huldah.

Fifth Period—Babylonish Captivity, including the life of Esther.

Sixth Period—the War and Dispersion, and their effects on the condition and privileges of women in Israel.

Seventh Period—Women of Israel in the Present time, as influenced by the history of the Past.

For five of these periods, then, we perceive the word of God can be our only guide, and this at once marks our history as sacred, not profane. If, therefore, there should be parts which resemble more a religious essay than female biography, we reply, that to inculcate religion, the vital spirit of religion, is the sole intention of these pages.

We wish to infuse the spirit of truth and patriotism, of nationality, and yet of universal love, in the hearts of the young daughters of Israel; and we know of no means more likely, under the divine blessing, to accomplish this, than to bring before them, as vividly and engagingly as we can, the never-ending love, the compassionating tenderness, the unchanging sympathy, alike in our joys and in our sorrows, manifested by the Eternal so touchingly and simply in the history of our female ancestors,—to lead them to know Him and love Him, not only through the repeated promises, but through the narratives of His word, and to glory in those high privileges which as children, retainers and promulgators of His holy law, are ours, over and above every other nation, past or present, in the history of the world!

"Sarah"

So varied and so important are the incidents comprised in the life of Eve, that, on a mere superficial view, Sarah's biography appears somewhat deficient in interest. Yet, as the beloved partner of Abraham, she ought to be a subject of reverence and love to her female descendants; and we will endeavor to bring her history forward, that such she may become. Much of the Eternal's love and pity towards His female children is manifested in her simple life, and also in the life of her bondwoman, Hagar, which is too closely interwoven with hers to be omitted [...].

The first notice we have of Sarai is her accompanying her husband and Lot from the home of her kindred to a strange country, among all strange people, in simple obedience to the word of God.[1] Holy writ is silent on the youth of Abram; but it is the opinion of our ancient fathers, that his earnest desire after divine knowledge—his pure and holy life—his affectionate and virtuous conduct, attracted towards him the blessing of the Lord, and caused him to be selected as the promulgator of the Divine Revelation. That Abram was exposed to many dangers on account of his loving obedience to the one sole invisible God, instead of acknowledging the idols of his race, is indeed very possible, and probably originated the first removal of his family to Charran, where also his father accompanied him. At Charran they seem to have dwelt in peace and prosperity, secured from former persecutors, so that it must have been no little trial to go forth again, more particularly without any definite cause for the removal.

To Sarai the trial must have been more severe than to her husband. She was to go forth with him indeed; but it is woman's peculiar nature to cling to home, home ties, and home affections—to shrink from encountering a strange world, teeming with unknown trials and dangers. Rather than the parting from a husband, indeed, all other partings may seem light; but yet they are trials to a gentle woman: and the heart that can leave the home and friends of a happy youth—the associations of years—without regret, proves not that its affections are so centred on one object as to eschew all others; but that it is too often wrapped in a chilling indifference, which prevents strong emotions on any subject whatever. We have enough of Sarai in the Bible to satisfy us that such is not her character [...].

---

1 For the Biblical account of Sarah, see Gen. 11.27 – 23.20.

The extent of the patriarch's household may be imagined by the fact, that at his word, no less than three hundred and eighteen servants, born in his house and trained to arms, accompanied him to the rescue of his nephew. Those who were left to attend to his flocks and herds, which he possessed in great numbers, must have been in equal proportion; and over these, during his absence, Sarai, assisted by the steward, had unlimited dominion.

The beautiful confidence and true affection subsisting between Abram and Sarai, marks unanswerably their *equality*; that his wife was to Abram friend as well as partner; and yet, that Sarai knew perfectly her own station, and never attempted to push herself forward in unseemly counsel, or use the influence which she so largely possessed for any weak or sinful purpose. Some, however, would have found it difficult to preserve their humility and meekness, situated as was Sarai. A coarser and narrower mind would have prided herself on the promises made her husband, imagining there must be some superlative merit, either in herself or Abram, to be so singled out by the Eternal. There is no pride so dangerous and subtle as spiritual pride, no sin more likely to gain dominion in the early stages of religion—none so disguised, and so difficult to be discovered and rooted out. But in Sarai there was none of this; not a particle of pride, even at a time when, of all others, she might have been *almost* justified in feeling it. She was, indeed, blessed in a husband whose exalted, yet domestic and affectionate character must ever have strengthened, guided, and cherished hers; but it is not always the most blessed and distinguished woman who attends the most faithfully to her domestic duties, and preserves unharmed and untainted that meekness and integrity which is her greatest charm [...].

It was after these things, that we have the first allusion to the patriarch's being childless. And by the words in which the Lord addressed him—"Fear not, Abram, I am thy shield, and exceeding great reward,"[1] we are led to suppose that some anxious thoughts, and perhaps doubts, natural to humanity, were occupying his mind. *We*, weak and frail as himself, might exclaim, What, still doubting, still fearing, when he has had so many proofs of the Eternal's provi-

1 Gen. 15.1.

dence and care! But God, whose "thoughts are not as our thoughts,"[1] instead of *reproving*, addresses him in terms of the tenderest love and encouragement, for He knew the nature of His creatures, and that faith could *not* be perfectly attained without years of watchfulness and prayer; that if it were, man would cease to be man, and this life be no longer what it was intended—a life of trial. Abram's instant reply reveals the painful thoughts which had engrossed him:—"Lord God, what wilt thou give me? seeing I go childless, and the steward of my house is this Eliezer of Damascus. Behold, to me thou hast given no seed, and lo, one born in my house is mine heir."[2] God had promised that the land should be his and his *seed's*, but Abram in sorrow beheld years pass, and still he had no child. Sarai had long passed the ages when, humanly speaking, she could be a mother. It was much more natural—truly pious and faithful as he was—that Abram should be harrassed with contradictory fears and doubts, than that he should have had none. God had promised, but how was that promise to be fulfilled?—unless, indeed, not his own child, but "one born in his house" was to be his destined heir. This appeared perhaps the most probable, though it was painfully disappointing; and to soothe this fear and remove it, the Lord addressed him as we have said. The gracious and most blessed promise directly followed—that not one born in his house, but his own son should be his heir; and, bidding him look up at the stars—as countless and numberless they gemmed the clear, bright heavens—promised, that "so should his seed be."[3] And then it was, that—all of doubt and mist and fear dissolving in the heart of the patriarch, before the words of the Lord, as snow before the sun—HE BELIEVED: and that pure FAITH was accounted to him as RIGHTEOUSNESS. How blessed are those words! In every station of life, however tried, and sad, and mourning, and deprived of all power to *serve* the Lord as our hearts dictate, we may yet BELIEVE, and Faith is still accounted RIGHTEOUSNESS [...].

Great must have been Sarai's joy when this gracious promise was

1 Isa. 58.8: "For my thoughts are not your thoughts, neither are your ways my ways, saith the Lord."

2 Gen. 15.2.

3 Gen. 15.5.

made known to her. If to Abram the being childless was a source of deep regret, it must have been still more so to her. Loving and domestic, as her whole history proves she was, how often may she have yearned to list the welcome cry of infancy; to feel one being look up to her for protection and love, and call her by that sweet name—Mother. But this joyful anticipation could only have been of short duration. Sarai's, as is woman's nature, in all probability imagined the *fulfilment* would immediately follow the *promise.* The most difficult of all our spiritual attainments is to *wait* for the Lord: to believe still, through long months, perhaps years, of anticipation and disappointment, that as He has said it, so it *will be*, so it *must be*, though our finite wisdom cannot pronounce the *when.* Did the Eternal fulfil His gracious promises on the instant, where would be the trial of our faith, and of our confidence and constancy in prayer?

Finding still there was no appearance of her becoming a mother, we are led to suppose, by the events which follow, that all Sarai's joyous anticipations turned into gloomy fears, not merely from the belief that she herself would not be blessed with a child, but that Abram might, as was and is the custom of Eastern nations, take another wife; an idea excited, perhaps, by the recollection that *her* name had not been mentioned as the destined mother of the promised seed, but precisely the most painful which could find entrance in a heart affectionate and faithful as her own. To prevent this misfortune, and yet to further (as she supposed) the will of the Eternal, Sarai had recourse to human means.

All women in her position, and influenced as she was by the manners and customs of the East, would have both felt and acted as she did, but few, we think, would have waited so long. It was ten years after Abram had left Egypt to fix his residence in Canaan, before Hagar became his wife. The separation of himself and Lot appears to have taken place in the first year after their settlement in Canaan, the expedition against the kings in the second or third year following. And we are expressly told, that it was *soon after these occurrences* that the Lord appeared unto the patriarch, and promised him an heir in his own child; the Hebrew word, אחר (after), signifying, according to Rashi, that the event about to be related took place *soon after* the period of the former narration; but when a *long period* has intervened, the expression אחרי is used.[1]

According to this reckoning, then, full five, or at the very least three, years must have elapsed between the promise made to Abram and his taking Hagar, at Sarai's own request, to be his wife; and few women would have beheld year after year pass, each year increasing the probability of her becoming a mother, and yet so believed as to adopt no human means for the furtherance of her wishes. In perusing and reflecting on the blessings promised, and revelations made to the favored servants of the Lord, we are apt to suppose that their lives were preserved from all trouble, all trial of delay, from the fearful sickness of anticipation disappointed, and hope deferred; whereas, a more intimate study of the holy Scriptures would convince us, that though indeed most *spiritually* blessed, their *mortal* lives were not more exempt from labor, and all the sorrows proceeding from human emotions, than our own. We only see those periods on which the broad light of sunshine falls. The darker shades of human doubt, the often supposed blighting of hope, the struggles and terrors of the spirit alternating with the rest and confidence which it sometimes enjoys; these we see not, and, therefore, pronounce them unknown to our forefathers; whereas, did we examine more closely, we should not find severer trials in our own lives than in theirs: nor cease to believe, for a single moment, that the God who guided them through the dark shadows of human trials, and strengthened them with the light of His presence, does not equally guide and reveal Himself to us.

The first human evidence that Sarai's scheme would be productive of vexation and sorrow, as well as of joy, was her disappointment with regard to Hagar's continued humility and submission. Forgetful that it was to her mistress, humanly speaking, she owed the privileges now hers, the Egyptian so far forgot herself, as to feel and make manifest that Sarai "was despised in her eyes." Alas, how mournfully does that brief sentence breathe of woman's fallen nature! How apt are we to exalt ourselves for imaginary superiority—to look down

1 Aguilar's note: "See 'The Sacred Scriptures, Hebrew and English,' translated by the Rev. D. A. De Sola." In 1844, De Sola managed to complete and publish a translation of Genesis, two years after Aguilar had called publically for an English translation of the Hebrew Bible in *Spirit of Judaism*. No more of the translation was published.

on those who have served us, when God has bestowed on us privileges of which they are deprived. We forget, often through thoughtlessness, that those very things of which we are so proud, come not from ourselves, but from Him who might equally have vouchsafed them to others. We may not indeed have the same incitement to pride and presumption as Hagar, but have we *never* despised others for the want of those accomplishments, those advantages, that beauty, and other gifts from God, which we ourselves may possess? Aye, sometimes, though we trust such emotions as rare as they are sad, the parents who have toiled and labored to give us advantages of dress and education far above what they possessed themselves—the elder sister, who is contented and rejoiced to remain in the background, that younger and fairer ones, whom she loves with almost a mother's love, may come forward—the homely and older-fashioned aunt, to whom, perhaps, a sister's orphan family owe their all—these are the beings whom the young and thoughtless but too often secretly despise, as if their superior advantages had come from themselves, not from God, through loving relatives and friends.

And this was the case with Hagar. A superficial reading of the Bible often causes Sarai to be most unjustly blamed for undue harshness. We think only of Hagar's wanderings in the wilderness, and pity her as cruelly treated, and suppose, that as the Most High relieved her through His angel, she had never been in any way to blame. Now, though to sympathize with the sorrowing and afflicted be one of our purest and best feelings, it must not so blind us as to prevent our doing justice to the inflictor of that affliction. We candidly avow, that until lately we too thought Sarai harsh and unjust, and rather turned from than admired her character: but we have seen the injustice of this decision, and, therefore, without the smallest remaining prejudice, retract it altogether: retract it, simply because the words of the angel are quite sufficient proof that Hagar had been *wrong*, and Sarai's chastisement *just*, or he would not have commanded her, as Sarai's *bondwoman*, to return and submit herself to her mistress's power, without any reservation whatever.[1]

It must indeed have been a bitterly painful disappointment to Sarai, that instead of receiving increased gratitude and affection from one whom she had so raised and cherished, she was despised with an

1 See Aguilar's depiction of Sarah in her poem "The Wanderers," above.

insolence that, unless checked, might bring discord and misery in a household which had before been so blessed with peace and love. Sarai's was not a character to submit tamely to ingratitude. There was neither coldness nor indifference about her. In no part of the Bible, either in character or precept, do we perceive the necessity or the merit of that species of cold indifference, which is by some well-meaning religious persons supposed to be the self-control and pious forgiveness of injuries most acceptable to God. The Patriarchal and Jewish history alike prove, that natural feelings were not to be trampled upon. The Hebrew code was formed by a God of love for the nature of *man*, not angels—formed so as to be *obeyed*, not to be laid aside as impracticable. The passions and feelings of the East were very different to those of the calmer and colder North; and nowhere in Holy Writ are we told that those feelings and emotions must be annihilated. *Subdued* and *guided* indeed, as must be the consequence of a true and strict adherence to the law of God, and impartial study of His word; but in the sight of a God of love, indifference can never be, and never was, religion.

Yet even this, an affair of feeling entirely between herself and Hagar, could not urge Sarai to any line of conduct unauthorized by her husband. Naturally indignant, she complained to him, perhaps, too, with some secret fear that Hagar, favored so much above herself by the hope of her giving him a son, might be unduly justified and protected. But it was not so. Abram's answer at once convinced her that Hagar had not taken her place; nay, that though Abram could not do otherwise than feel tenderness and kindness towards her, he at once recognised Sarai's supremacy, both as his wife and Hagar's mistress, and bade her "do with her what seemeth good to thee."[1] We have so many proofs of Abram's just, affectionate, and forgiving character, that we may fully believe he would never have said this, if he had not been convinced that it was no unjust accusation on the part of Sarai. He knew, too, that she was not likely to inflict more punishment than was deserved, particularly on a favorite slave; and, therefore, it was with his full consent "Sarai afflicted her, and she fled from her presence."

Whatever the nature of this affliction, it could not have been very

---

1 The quotations relating to Hagar's treatment by Sarai and the Angel allude to Gen. 16.6-9.

severe—neither pain nor restraint—for Hagar had the power to fly. Reproof to an irritable and disdainful mind is often felt as intolerable, and given too, as it no doubt was, with severity, and at a time when Hagar felt exalted and superior to all around her, even to her mistress, her proud spirit urged flight instead of submission, and not till addressed by the voice of the angel did those rebellious feelings subside.

There was no mistaking the angelic voice, and his first words destroyed the proud dreams which she had indulged. "Hagar, Sarai's bondwoman!" he said, and the term told her in the sight of God she was still the same, "whence camest thou, and whither art thou going?" It was not because he knew not that he thus spoke. The messengers of the Lord need no enlightenment on the affairs of men, but their questions are adapted to the nature of men, to awaken them to consciousness, to still the tumult of human passion, and by clear and simple questioning *compel* a clear and true reply. Had his command to return been given without preparation, Hagar's obedience would have been the effect of fear, not conviction. But those simple questions, "whence camest thou? whither art thou going?" startled her from the tumultuous emotions of rebellion and presumption. Whence had she come? From a happy, loving home, where she had been the favorite of an indulgent and gentle mistress; a home which would speedily be to her yet dearer, as the birthplace of her child; that child who was to be the supposed heir to her master and all his sainted privileges; from friends, from companions, all whom she had loved: and she had left them! And whither was she going? How might she answer when she knew not? Was she about to resign all of affection, privilege, joy, to wander in the wilderness, helpless and alone? How idle and impotent now seemed her previous feelings. Those simple questions had flashed back light on her darkened heart, and humbled her at once; and simply and truthfully she answered, "I flee from the presence of my mistress Sarai;" thus meekly acknowledging that Sarai was still her mistress, and that her derision had indeed been wrong. Reproof, therefore, followed not; but the angel bade her, "Return to thy mistress, and submit thyself to her power." And, perceiving that her repentance was sincere, and would lead to obedience, he continued graciously to promise that her seed should be multiplied, so that it should not be numbered for multitude; that her son should bear a name which would ever remind her that God had heard her affliction, with other promises concerning that son, *yet none* which might lead her to the deceitful belief that he would be Abram's promised seed.

Inexpressibly consoled, in the midst of her bitter self-reproach, and convinced, by his supernatural voice and disappearance, that it was indeed an angel direct from the Lord with whom she had spoken, it is evident from the context, although not there mentioned, that Hagar must have unhesitatingly obeyed, and returned to her mistress—convinced of her error—submissive and repentant, and been by Sarai received with returning confidence and full forgiveness.

In due course of time the promise was fulfilled, and Hagar, to the great joy of Abram, had a son, whom *Abram* called Ishmael, thus proving that Hagar must have imparted the visit of the angel, and the command as to the name of her son.[1]

Before we proceed, we would entreat our younger readers to pause one moment on the simple facts we have related; and so take it to their hearts, that the first words of the angel may become theirs as well as Hagar's. We have not indeed the direct communings with the messengers of the Lord, as is recorded in the Bible; but we are not left unguided and unquestioned. We have still an angelic voice within us, that, would we but encourage it to speak—would we but listen to it—can, even as the angel's, still the wild torrent of passion, awaken us to our neglected duty, and lead us, repentant and sorrowing, to those whom we may have offended. God has not left us without His witness. The VOICE OF CONSCIENCE may be to us what angel visits were to our ancestors of old. There is no period of our lives in which it is wholly lost; but in youth it is strongest and most thrilling. In youth it is, that we awake from the (often) stagnant sleep of earlier years;—we awake to a consciousness of bright, glowing, beautiful existence;—we become conscious of a deep yearning after the *good*, and at the same time sorrowfully feel, that it is not quite as easy to attain as we believed it. As our emotions and feelings spring into life, so does conscience. We become aware of a peculiar thrilling sense of joy, when we have accomplished good, either in conquering

---

1 Ishmael: Hebrew for "God has heard."

ourselves—in giving up a selfish inclination—or in showing kindness, affection, and respect to others. There is a glowing sense of joy, when conscience tells us we have done well, unlike the joy proceeding from any other cause; and as it approves, with an angel voice that *will* be heard, so does it disapprove. We may stifle it—we may refuse to listen to its still small tones—yet we cannot shake off the depression and the sadness which it leaves. We may *refuse* to know wherefore we thus feel; but it is *conscience* still [...].

It may be that Sarai's correction of Hagar was unduly harsh, although we have no warrant in the Scripture for so believing; but it is evident, as there is no further mention of contention and disagreement between them, that she received her submission with gentleness, and restored her to favor. It is well when forgiveness is thus recorded: many and many a young meek spirit would obey the voice of the angel and return, in humility and love, could they but be sure that submission would be gently and lovingly received; and shrink from it only because the chilling reception, the *uttered* but not *felt* reconciliation, falls upon their still quivering hearts with a pain and degradation which they feel that as yet they cannot bear. The spirit of that healing and consoling love which has its birth in religion, must guide both the offended and the offender, or reconciliation can never be complete; nor the latter be securingly and convincingly led back to that better path to which the angel points. The pang of unrequited confidence, chilled affection, and all the bitterness of unnecessary degradation, will be stronger at first than the approving glow of conscience; while a contrary reception, even though it may heighten the pang of self-reproach, will soothe and encourage, for the inward voice whispers—we have done well; and, from that moment, the heavenly messenger assumes her mild dominion in the heart, never to be lured thence again.

For thirteen years Abram and Sarai must have looked upon Ishmael as the promised seed; for though, not actually so said, there was neither spiritual sign nor human hope of the patriarch having any other child. At the end of that period, however, the Most High again appeared unto Abram, proclaiming Himself as the ALMIGHTY,—a fit introduction to the event He was about to foretell; and bidding

His favored servant, "Walk before me, and be thou perfect,"[1] perfect in trust, in faith, without any regard to human probabilities, for, as Almighty God, all things were possible with Him. The name of the patriarch was then changed, as a sign of the many nations over whom he was appointed father—the land again promised him—and the covenant appointed him which was to mark his descendants as the chosen of the Lord, the everlasting inheritors of Canaan; and bear witness, to untold-of ages, of the truth of the Lord's word, and the election of His people. This proclaimed and commanded, the Eternal commenced His information of the miracle He was about to perform, by desiring Abraham to call his wife no longer Sarai שרי but Sarah שרה:—a change which our ancient fathers suppose to mean the same as from Abram to Abraham. "Sarai, signifying a lady or princess in a restricted sense, imported that she was a lady, or princess, to Abram only; whereas the latter name signifies princess or lady absolutely, indicating that she would thus be acknowledged by many, even as Abraham was to become the father of many nations."[2] A meaning perfectly reconcilable with the verse which follows: "And I will bless her, and give thee a son also of her: yea, I will bless her, so that she shall be a *mother of nations; kings of people* shall be of her." She was, therefore, no longer a princess over Abraham's household, but a princess in royal rank, from whom *kings* should descend. Joy must have been the first emotion of Abraham's heart at this miraculous announcement, mingled with a feeling of wonder and astonishment how such a thing could be; but then, in his peculiarly affectionate heart, came the thought of his first-born Ishmael, and with earnestness he prayed, "Oh! that Ishmael could live before thee!" And though the Eternal could not grant this prayer, for the seed of Abraham, from whom His chosen people would spring, must be of pure and unmixed birth, He yet, with compassionating tenderness, soothed the father's anxious love, by the gracious promise that, though Sarah's child must be the seed with whom His covenant should be established, yet Ishmael also should be blessed and multi-

---

1 Gen. 17.1.

2 Aguilar's note: "See note to Gen. xvii. 15, in the Rev. D.A. De Sola's translation of the Bible." The following discussion of God's promises to Sarah and Ishmael alludes to Gen. 17.15-22.

plied exceedingly, and become, even as Isaac, the father of a great nation. "And for Ishmael I have also heard thee." How blessed an encouragement for us to pour forth our prayers unto the Lord, proving, how consolingly, that no prayer is offered in vain; for if He cannot grant us as our infinite wishes would dictate, He will yet hear us—yet fulfil our prayer far better for our welfare, and the welfare of our beloved ones, than our own wishes could have accomplished, had they been granted to the full.

The acceptance of the covenant throughout Abraham's household, and the change in her own name, must, of course, have been imparted by Abraham to his wife, with the addition of the startling promise, that she too, even at her advanced age, should bear a son. Yet by her behavior, when the promise was repeated in the following chapter, it would appear that, though informed of it, she had dismissed it from her mind as a thing impossible.[1] Accustomed to regard Ishmael as the only seed of Abraham—to suppose her scheme had been blessed, more particularly as she had never been named before as the mother of the chosen seed—the hope of being so had long since entirely faded; and, not having attained the simple questionless faith of her husband, she, in all probability, dismissed the thought, as recalling too painfully those ardent hopes and wishes, which she had with such difficulty previously subdued. Engaged, as was her wont, in her domestic duties, she was one day interrupted by the hasty entrance of her husband, requiring her "quickly to prepare three measures of fine meal, knead it, and make it into cakes." Patriarchal hospitality was never satisfied by committing to hirelings only the fit preparations for a hearty welcome. We see either Sarah herself making the desired cakes, or closely superintending her domestics in doing so; and the patriarch hastening, in the warmth of his hospitality, himself to fetch a calf from the herd, to give it to a young man to dress it, though he had abundance of servants around him to save him the exertion. Yet both Abraham and Sarah were of the nobility of the Eternal's creating. He had raised them above their fellows, and bestowed on them the patent of an aristocracy, with which not one of the nations could vie, for it came from God Himself. He had

1 When Sarah hears the angel say she will bear a child in her old age, she laughs. The incident of her laughter is described in Gen. 18, to which the following paragraphs allude.

changed their names to signify their royal claims—to make them regarded in future ages as noble ancestors of a long line of prophets, kings, princes, and nobles; and there was a refinement, a nobleness, a magnanimity of character in both the patriarch and his wife, which, breathing through their very simplicity, betrayed their native aristocracy, and marked them of that princely race which has its origin in the favor and election of the King of kings [...].

Yet noble, even princely, as were Abraham and Sarah, it was no sign of rank, with them, to be cold and restrained by false artificial laws. In the Bible, nobility was nature and *heart*, simplicity and benevolence, cordiality and warmth; no coldness, no indifference, no folding up the affections and the impulses of feeling in the icy garment of pride and fashion, which so often turns to selfishness, and so utterly prevents all of benevolence and social good. Abraham knew not, at his first invitation, the rank or mission of his visitors. His address was one of the *heart's respect*, not the mere politeness of the lip; and the warmth of his welcome would not permit of his sitting idly down while hirelings prepared their meal—nay, we find that, even while they sat down to partake of it, their host stood,—a mark of profound respect, which a further consideration of their majestic aspect prompted, by the supposition that they were more than ordinary mortals.

Sarah joined not her husband or his guests. The modest and dignified customs of the East prevented all intrusion, or even the wish to intrude. Unless particularly asked for, the place of the Eastern and Jewish wife was in the retirement of home; not from any inferiority of rank, or servitude of station, but simply because their inclination so prompted. The strangers might have business with Abraham, which, if needed, he would impart to her; there was no occasion for her to come forward. But, while seated in the inner tent, engaged in her usual avocations, she heard her own name, "Where is Sarah, thy wife?" and her husband's reply, "She is in the tent," followed by words that must indeed have sounded strange and improbable, "Sarah, thy wife, shall bear a son;" yet, improbable as they might have seemed, there is no excuse for the laugh of incredulity with which they were received. Already prepared by the previous promise of the Lord, the words should at once have revealed the heavenly nature of those who spake, and been heard with faith and thankfulness; but Sarah thought only of the human impossibility. Strange as it is, that such unbelief should be found in the beloved partner of Abraham, yet her laugh proves that even she was not exempt from the natural feelings of mortality—the looking to human means and human possibilities alone; forgetting that with God all things are possible.

Yet, to us, the whole of this incident is consoling. It proves that not even Sarah was utterly free from human infirmities; and yet that the Eternal, through His angel, deigned graciously to *reprove*, not to *chastise*. It proves that God has compassion on the nature of His erring children; for he knows their weakness. *Man* would have been wroth with the laugh of scorn, and withdrawn his intended favor; but "the Lord said unto Abraham, Wherefore did Sarah laugh, saying, Shall I, who am old, indeed bear a child? Is anything too mighty for the Lord? At the time appointed I will return unto thee, and Sarah shall indeed have a son." The gracious mildness of the rebuke—the blessed repetition of the promise—must, to one so affectionate as Sarah, have caused the bitterest reproach; but, weakly listening to fear instead of repentance, she denied her fault, seeking thus mistakenly to extenuate it. But He said, "Nay, but thou didst laugh," proving that her innermost thoughts were known; and, silenced at once, left to the solitude of her own tent, for Abraham accompanied his guests on the road to Sodom, we know quite enough of Sarah's character to rest satisfied that repentance and self-abasement for unbelief, mingled with, and hallowed the burst of rejoicing thankfulness with which she must have looked forward to an event so full of bliss to her individually, and so blessed a revelation of the Lord's deep love for Abraham and herself. Nearly twenty years had passed since the first promise of an heir in his own child had been given. Years, long, full of incident and feeling, seeming in their passing an interval long enough for the utter forgetfulness of the promise, save as it was supposed fulfilled in the birth of Ishmael; but now, in the retrospect, the promise flashed back with a vividness, a brightness, as if scarce a single year had passed ere it had been given: and Sarah must have felt self-reproached in the midst of her joy, that she had not waited, had not trusted, had not believed unto the end. And many a one, ere life has closed, will feel as she did; not indeed, from the same cause—but often and often a prayer has been offered up, a promise given from the word of God, and both have been forgotten, neglected, mistrusted, through long weary years—as vainly prayed and vainly answered—and yet, ere life has closed, recalled as by a flash of sudden light, by the divine answer to the one, and gracious fulfilment of the other [...].

[A]t the appointed time "God visited Sarah as He had said;"[1] and the promised seed—the child of rejoicing—Isaac was born. What must have been the emotions of Sarah on beholding him? Not alone the bliss of a mother; but that in him the infant claimer of a love and joy which she had never so felt before, she beheld a visible and palpable manifestation of the wonderful power and unchanging love of the Most High God. Devoted, as Sarah had been, to the service and love of the Lord, how inexpressibly must those emotions have been heightened as she gazed upon her babe, and held him to her bosom as her *own*, her granted child! To those who really love the Lord, joy is as dear, as bright, as close a link between the heart and its God, as grief is to more fallen natures. We find the hymn of rejoicing, the song of thanksgiving, always the vehicle in which the favored servants of the Lord poured forth their grateful adoration, thus proving that the thought of the beneficent Giver ever hallowed and sanctified the gift; and therefore we believe with our ancient fathers, that though *not translated metrically*, Sarah expressed her joy in a short hymn of thanksgiving.[2] The peculiar idiom of the Hebrew text confirms this supposition, and we adopt it as most natural to the occasion. Her age had had no power, even before she became a mother, to dull her feelings, and her song of thanksgiving well expresses every emotion natural, not alone to the occasion, but to her peculiar situation. As a young mother, full of life, of sentiment, of affection, she felt towards her babe—giving him his natural food from her own bosom—tending his infant years—guiding him from boyhood to youth—from youth to manhood, and lavishing on him the full tide of love which had been pent up so long. The very character of Isaac, as is afterwards displayed—meek, yielding, affectionate almost as a

1 Gen. 21.1.

2 See Gen. 21.6-7: "6 And Sarah said, God hath made me to laugh, so that all that hear will laugh with me. 7 And she said, Who would have said unto Abraham, that Sarah should have given children suck? for I have born him a son in his old age." Aguilar cites De Sola for this interpretation.

woman—disinclined to enterprise—satisfied with his heritage—all prove the influence which his mother had possessed, and that his disposition was more the work of her hand than of his father's.

"The child grew and was weaned," Holy Writ proceeds to inform us; "and Abraham made a great feast the day Isaac was weaned,"[1]—a feast of rejoicing that the Eternal had mercifully preserved him through the first epoch of his young existence. He was now three years old, if not more—for the women of the East, even now, do not wean their children till that age. The feast, however, which commenced in joy, was, for the patriarch, dashed with sorrow ere it closed. Educated with the full idea that he was his father's heir—though the words of the angel before his birth gave no warrant for the supposition—to Ishmael and his mother, the birth of Isaac must have been a grievous disappointment. And we find the son committing the same fault as his mother previously had done—deriding, speaking disrespectfully of Sarah and her child. The youth of Ishmael, and Sarah's request that the bond-woman might also be expelled, would lead to the supposition that it was Hagar who had instigated the affront. The age of Sarah, and the decidedly superhuman birth of Isaac, must, to all but the patriarch's own household, have naturally given rise to many strange and perhaps calumniating reports. In the common events of life all that is incomprehensible is either ridiculed, disbelieved, or made matter of scandal; and, therefore, in a case so uncommon as this, it is more than probable reports very discreditable both to Sarah and Abraham were promulgated all around them. Hagar, indeed, and Ishmael must have known differently:—that it was the hand of God which worked, and therefore all things were possible; but it was to Ishmael's interest to dispute or deny the legitimacy of Isaac; and therefore it was not in human nature to neglect the opportunity. No other offence would have so worked on Sarah. We are apt to think more poetically than justly of this part of the Bible. Hagar and her young son, expelled from their luxurious and happy home, almost perishing in the desert from thirst, are infinitely more interesting objects of consideration and sympathy, than the harsh and jealous Sarah, who, for seemingly such trifling offence, demanded and obtained such severe retribution.

---

1 Gen. 21.8.

We generally rest satisfied with one or two verses; whereas, did we look further and think deeper, our judgment would be different. In a mere superficial reading we acknowledge Sarah does appear in rather an unfavorable light; as if her love for Isaac had suddenly narrowed and stagnated every other feeling; and, jealous of Ishmael's influence over his father, she had determined on seizing the first opportunity for his expulsion. That this, however, is a wrong judgment is proved by the fact, that the Eternal Himself desires Abraham to hearken to the voice of Sarah in all that she shall say; for in Isaac was to be the promised seed, though of Ishmael also would he make a nation, because he was Abraham's son. That Sarah's advice was not to be displeasing to him, because of the lad and his mother.

Now, had Sarah's advice proceeded from an undue harshness, a mean and jealous motive, the Most High would, in His divine justice, have taken other means for the fulfilment of His decrees. He would not have desired His good and faithful servant to be so guided by an evil and suspicious tongue. There are times when we feel urged and impelled to speak that which we are yet conscious will be productive of pain and suffering to ourselves. All such impulses are of God; and it must have been some such feeling which actuated Sarah, and compelled her to continue her solicitation for the expulsion of Hagar and Ishmael, even after the moment of anger was passed. We know that Hagar had ever been her favorite slave; it was impossible for one affectionate as was Sarah, to have regarded Ishmael as her son for thirteen or fourteen years and yet not have loved him, though of course with less intensity than his father. The birth of Isaac naturally revealed yet stronger emotions; still Ishmael could not have been excluded from her affections as to render her separation from him void of pain. And still she spoke, still urged the necessity, conscious all the time she was inflicting pain not only on her husband but on herself. This appears like contradiction; but each one who has attentively studied the workings of his own heart, will not only feel but pronounce it *truth*. Anger caused the demand: "Expel this bondwoman and her son; for the son of this bondwoman shall not inherit with my son, even with Isaac;"[1] and calmer reflection continued to see the necessity. Abraham's possessions were suffi-

1 Gen. 21.10.

cient for the heritage of both his sons; but as the course of nature was changed, and the younger, not the elder, was to be the heir of promise, confusion and discord would have ensued, and the brothers continually have been at war. Sarah's penetration appears to have discovered this; and as it was necessary for Ishmael to form a separate establishment, it was an act of kindness, not of harshness, to let him depart with Hagar, instead of going forth alone. From her own feelings she now knew the whole extent of a mother's love; and therefore, though Ishmael had been the sole offender, and the only one whose claims were likely to clash with Isaac's, she would not separate the mother from the son, and so urged Abraham to separate from both.

There is something touchingly beautiful in the patriarch's love for his elder son, and yet his instant conquest of self at the word of the Lord. His deep affection had blinded him to the probable discomforts which might ensue from his sons remaining together. His gentle and affectionate nature shrank from the pang of separation, causing even displeasure against Sarah for the first time in their long and faithful intercourse. Yet when God spake there was neither complaint nor murmur, nor one word of supplication that the heavy trial might be averted from him. It was enough that the Most High had spoken; and though all was dark before his son, to the fond anxious gaze of parental affection, he knew even from that darkness God *could* bring forth light, and *would* do so, for He had promised.

We are sometimes surprised at the small provision with which Abraham endowed his son at his departure. The riches of the patriarchs consisted of land, flocks, herds, and servants; nothing which could easily be bestowed. Besides which, Ishmael was to become the ancestor of a nation, through *the direct agency of the Lord*, not from any provision made him by his earthly father. Had Abraham endowed him, the interposition of the Eternal would not have been so clearly and unanswerably demonstrated. There would have been many to have traced his riches and the princely rank of his descendants from the gifts and power of Abraham, and denied altogether any interposition of the Lord; whereas, set forth as he was, with nothing but sufficient provision to sustain him till he reached his appointed resting, it was impossible even for the greatest sceptic to trace his future prosperity and wealth to any earthly power alone. The bread and water must not be supposed as meaning only what we now regard them. In the language of the Bible bread is used indiscriminately for every kind of food, and the bottle of water signifies a skinful, such being used by Eastern travellers even now, and containing much more than we imagine is comprised by the term "bottle." Yet even these were to fail, that the miraculous power and compassionate love of the Eternal might still more startlingly be proved. It was as easy for the Most High to have guided Ishmael and his mother at once to prove His love to them, and to give future ages, through his unerring word, comfort in their darkest hours; for as He relieved Hagar, so will He them. The God of the bondwoman is ours still; no time, no change can part us from Him.

The narrative of Hagar's wanderings in the wilderness, her maternal suffering and miraculous relief, is one of the most beautiful and most touching amongst the many beauties of the Bible. Hagar was not of Abraham's race, but one of a heathen and benighted nation, a bondwoman and a wanderer, a weak and lonely female, exiled from a home of love, overwhelmed with anxious fears for her child, perhaps, too, with self-reproaches for the unguarded words which she encouraged her boy to speak, and which she regarded as the sole cause of her banishment; yet was this poor sufferer the peculiar care of the great and mighty God. He caused the clouds of densest darkness to close around her—from them to bring forth the brightest, most enduring light. He deigned, by His angel, to speak comfort and hope, and even for her human wants provided the necessary aid. He did not guard from sorrow; for it was not until "the water was spent in the bottle, and she cast the child under one of the shrubs, and she went and sat down over against him, a good way off, for she said, Let me not see the death of the child; and she sat over against him, and lifted up her voice and wept"—not till her trial was thus at its height, that the angelic voice descended from heaven in such pitying and sympathizing accents: "What aileth thee, O Hagar? Fear not, for God hath heard the voice of the lad whence he is. Arise, lift up the lad, and hold him in thine hand, for I will make him a great nation." And the promise was fulfilled.[1]

The whole history of Hagar is fraught with the deepest comfort.

---

1 See Gen. 21.10-21.

She was one of the many in individual character; possessing alike women's engaging and faulty characteristics: feeling and affectionate at one time, overbearing and insolent at another—loving Ishmael with impetuous and clinging love, which could not bear to see his supposed heritage become the property of another, though she knew it was the decree of God—reverencing and loving Abraham alike as her master and the father of her child, but unable always to preserve the submission and respect due to Sarah as her mistress and indulgent friend; for, though the mother of Abraham's child, she was still Sarah's maid;—such was Hagar. Neither in character superior, nor in station equal, to the daughters of Israel now; yet was she the peculiar charge of the Most High, and twice did He deign, in closest communion, to instruct and console. Her life had its trials, in no way inferior in severity or in deep suffering to the trials of the present day. Yet God was with her in them all; and, in His own appointed time, permitted them to give place to prosperity and joy. And as He worked then, so He worketh now. It is no proof of His dearest love, when life passes by without a cloud—when sorrow and trial are strangers to our path. His word reveals that those whom He loved the *best*, alike male or female, endured the severest trials—that His love, His guiding word, were not given to the children of joy. To become His servant, His loved, His chosen, was to suffer and to labor. We see this throughout His word; and shall we, dare we, expect their exemption now? Oh! no, no! Would we love the Lord, would we truly be loved by Him, would we pray for and seek His paths, would we struggle on to the goal of immortal love and bliss, we must nerve both heart and frame to *bear*; strengthen and arouse every faculty to *endure* and *suffer*; for so did His chosen, His best beloved, and so too must we. We have still His word to be to us as the angelic whisper was to our ancestors. Their hope is ours, and their *reward*.

Few other events mark the life of Sarah. The Most High had brought her forth from the trials, anxieties, and doubts of previous years. He had, in His infinite mercy, fulfilled His word, and bestowed on her the blessed gift for which, in the midst of happiness, she had pined. Continuing His loving kindness, He lengthened her days much beyond the usual sum of mortality, that she might rear her child to manhood, and receive all the blessed fruit of her maternal care in Isaac's deep love and reverence for himself. In a mere superficial perusal of the life of Sarah, as read in our Sabbath portions, we are likely to overlook much of the consoling proofs of the Eternal's compassionating love for His female children, which it so powerfully reveals. Sarah was ninety years of age when Isaac was born. In this course of nature, ten or twelve years more would either have closed her mortal career, or rendered it, from the infirmities of so great an age, a burden to herself and all around her. There was no need of her preservation to forward the decrees of the Lord. In giving birth to the child of promise, her part was fulfilled, and at the age of ten or twelve the boy might have done without her. But God is LOVE, and the affections of His children are, in their strength and purity, peculiarly acceptable to Him. He never bestoweth happiness to withdraw it; and, therefore, to perfect the felicity of Sarah and her child, His tenderness preserved her in life and vigor seven and thirty years after she had given him birth. In this simple fact we trace the beneficent and tender Father, sympathizing not alone in every grief and pang, but in every joy and affection of His creatures. We feel to our heart's core the truth of the words of Moses, "Who hath God so near to him" as Israel?[1] What nation can so trace, so claim the love of the Eternal?

Nor was the preservation of Sarah the *only* proof of our Father's loving tenderness towards her, and of His condescending sympathy with the love she bore her child. The trial of faith in the sacrifice of his son was given to the *father*; but the *mother* was spared the continuing agony which must have been her portion, even had her faith continued strong. God had compassion on the feebler, weaker nature of His female servant. He demanded not from her that which He knew the mother could not bear. He spared her, in His immeasurable love, the suffering which it pleased Him to inflict upon the father,—suffering and temptation *not* to satisfy the Lord, for His omniscience knew that His faithful servant would not fail; but to prove to future ages the mighty power of spiritual faith and love, even while in the mortal clay [...].

1 No such speech occurs in the Bible, but Israel's nearness to God is a constant theme. See Ps. 148.14: "He also exalteth the horn of his people, the praise of all his saints; even of the children of Israel, a people near unto him. Praise ye the Lord." See also Deut. 30.14.

As the ancestor of His beloved, we find Sarah's death and age particularly recorded; being the first woman of the Bible whose death and burial are mentioned. The deep grief of her husband and son are simply but touchingly betrayed in the brief words, "And Abraham came to mourn for Sarah, and to weep for her;"[1] and, at a later period, not till his marriage with Rebekah, "and Isaac was comforted after his mother's death."[2] Words that portray the beauty and affection of Sarah's domestic character, and confirm our belief that, although perhaps possessing many of the failings of her sex, she was yet a help meet for Abraham—a tender and judicious parent to her son—and a kind, indulgent friend to the large household of which she was the mistress. Her noble or rather princely rank, received as it had been direct from the Lord, is still more strongly proved by the intercourse between Abraham and the sons of Heth, when seeking from them a place to bury his dead: "Hear us, my Lord," is their reply, "thou art a *mighty prince of God* amongst us; in the choicest of our sepulchres bury thy dead;"[3] and it was with difficulty Abraham could elude the offered gift, and procure the cave as a purchase. His princely rank, however, and in consequence that of his wife, we see at once acknowledged, even by strangers, and the promise of the Lord, expressed in changing the name of *Sarai* into *Sarah*, clearly fulfilled.

The grief of Isaac appears to have lasted yet longer than that of his father, and beautifully illustrates the love between the mother and son. Abraham, advanced in years and spiritual experience, felt less keenly the mere emotions of humanity; he was convinced that Sarah had only gone before him to that world in which, from his great age, he would no doubt speedily join her. His many duties—his close communion with the Eternal—enabled him to rouse himself sooner from the grief, which at first was equally severe; but Isaac was, according to the patriarchal reckoning of time, still a very young man, at the age when feeling is keener, less controlled than at any other; and when, though spiritual comfort is great, human emotions will have full vent. Except the three days' journey to Mount Moriah with his father, Isaac does not appear to have been separated a single

---

1 Gen. 23.2.

2 Gen. 24.67.

3 Gen. 23.6.

day from his mother; and her care, her guiding and fostering love, had so entwined her round his heart, that for three years after her death her son could find no comfort. How exalted and lovely must have been that mother's character to demand such a term of mourning from her son; whose youth and sex would, in some, have speedily roused him from sorrow, or urged its forgetfulness in scenes of pleasure!

We have little more to add on the spiritual lesson and divine consolation which Sarah's life presents to her female descendants, than those hints already given. Differently situated as we are, with regard to station, land, and customs, we may yet imitate her faithfulness in all her household duties—her love and reverence to her husband—her tenderness to her child—her quiet, unpretending, domestic, yet dignified fulfilment of all which she was called upon to do. We may learn from her to set no value on personal charms, save as they may enhance the gratification of those who love us best; or of rank and station, save as they demand from us yet deeper gratitude towards God, and more extended usefulness towards man. We may learn too from her history that it is better to wait for the Lord—to leave in His hands the fulfilment of our ardent wishes—than to seek to compass them by human means. We may trace and feel that nothing, in truth, is too wonderful for the Lord; that He will do what pleaseth Him, however we may deem it hopeless and in vain. Direct revelations, as vouchsafed to Sarah, indeed we have not, but God has, in His deep mercy, granted us His word—the record of all HE HAS DONE—that we may feel He is still OUR God; and though He worketh now in *secret*—for our sins have hid us from His ways—yet He worketh for us still, and hath compassion and mercy and love for each of us individually, even as He had for Sarah, and her bondwoman Hagar. All these to us, as women, her history reveals: as women of Israel, oh! yet more. It is of no stranger in race, and clime, and faith we read. It is of OUR OWN—of one from whom Israel hath descended in a direct, unshadowed line—of one—the beloved and cherished partner of that chosen servant and beloved friend of the Eternal, for whose sake revelation was given to mankind—Israel made not alone the nation, but the FIRST-BORN of the Lord; and that law bestowed, which revealed a God of "love, long-suffering and gracious, plenteous in mercy and truth;"[1]—instructed us how to tread our earthly path, so as to give happiness to ourselves and fellow-creatures—to be acceptable to Him;—and pointed with an angel-finger to that immortal goal, where man shall live for ever!

Is it nothing to be the lineal descendants of one so favored—nothing to hold in our hands and shrine in our hearts, the record of her life from whom the race of promise sprang? Nothing, to peruse the wonderful manifestations of the Lord's love to her—to feel that from Him direct was Sarah's patent of nobility, and yet possess the privilege of being her descendant? Will the women of Israel feel this as nothing? Will they disdain their princely birth, their heavenly heritage? Will they scorn to look back on Sarah as their ancestor, and yet long for earthly distinctions, earthly rank? No! oh, no! Let us but think of these things, of those from whom we have descended, and our minds will become ennobled, our hearts enlarged. We shall scorn the false shame which would descend to petty meannesses to hide our faith, and so exalt us in the sight of a Gentile world. Humbled, cast off for a little moment as we are—liable to persecution, scorn, contumely—to be "despised and rejected" of men—to bear the burden of affliction from all who choose to afflict—still, still we cannot lose our blessed heritage unless we cast it off; we cannot be deprived of our birthright unless, like Esau, we exchange it for mere worldly pelf, and momentary (because *earthly*) gratification. We are still Israelites—still the chosen, the beloved, the ARISTOCRACY of the Lord.

"Miriam"

Having now considered the law of God under all its various bearings relative to woman, it only remains to prove, from the female characters of Scripture, in what matter that law was obeyed; and whether it be possible to discover any trace of statutes, which, in direct contradistinction to the changeless law of the Eternal, tend to degrade, instead of to elevate, the female character; or whether we cannot

---

1 One of Aguilar's favorite quotations in its many biblical forms, this version is from Ps. 86.15.

bring forward some sufficiently convincing arguments in favor of our deeply studied theory, that the law of the Eternal is explained, by its practical illustration, through the whole history of the Bible.

To the oralist, or non-oralist, this consideration ought to be of equal weight.[1] Keeping aloof entirely from the discussion which has of late too painfully agitated the whole Jewish nation, we would yet present to both parties the simple fact, that the supposed degradation of the women of Israel can have no existence whatever in the Oral Law, or we must find some trace of this abasement in this and the succeeding periods of our history. If both were given at the same time, the women of Israel whom we are about to bring forward, must have lived under the jurisdiction of both; and as their lives, feelings, and actions, are all in exact accordance with the spirit and the form of the written law, it is clearly evident, that the modern accusation against us can have *no* foundation whatever in the Oral Law, or we must have discovered it in the female characters of Scripture. Nor will the groundless assertion of our individual inferiority and social abasement find confirmation in the writings of our ancient fathers, whose beautiful parables and tales will tend to illustrate alike the spirit of our law, and the axiom of our wise man, "Who can find a virtuous woman, for her price is far above rubies?"[2]

We will proceed, then, without further introduction, to our his-

---

1 Oralists and non-oralists were Jews who took different sides on the question of whether the Oral Law, consisting of the laws, moral exempla, and legends in the Talmud and its commentaries, had the status of sacred scripture. Traditionalists argued that the Oral Law was indeed sacred because it had been given to Moses on Sinai (around 1200 B.C.E.) and had been passed down orally from generation to generation until finally collected, first in the Mishnah around 200 C.E., then in the Talmud around 700 C.E, and then in the commentaries on the Talmud that had been generated ever since. Traditionalists argued that the Oral Law had equal status with the Written Law (i.e., the Pentateuch, the Prophets, and the Writings) as a guiding force in Jewish life. For them, both Oral and Written Law were considered "Torah" and were to be implicitly trusted and followed. By contrast, reformers argued that the Oral Law was a human compilation that had been corrupted by foreign influences, and thus did not have sacred status. Reformers sought to remove the kernel from the husk—i.e., they sought to save what they saw as the true and reasonable parts of the Oral Law, with its many strictures on Jews' lives, while excising the rest. Individuals could choose which portions of the Oral Law were still relevant. The Written Law was what was meant by "Torah." In 1841, a group of reformers seceded from the existing synagogues and formed the West London Synagogue of British Jews. They were excommunicated by the Chief Rabbi for being non-oralists.

2 The first line of the praise of the "woman of valor" from Proverbs 31, traditionally chanted by Jewish husbands to their wives on Friday night.

tory, convinced that were the word of the Eternal more deeply studied, the love and peace it breathes must infuse themselves unconsciously in every human heart, and strife and discord melt away before the inspired transcript of the love and mercy of our God.

The character of Miriam is one of the most perfect delineations of woman in her mixed nature of good and evil which the Bible gives. Her first introduction we have already noticed—a young girl, watching, at the command of her mother, the fate of the ark which held her baby brother, and boldly addressing the princess of Egypt in the child's behalf.[1]

Her next mention is her sharing the holy triumph of that brother, and responding, with apparently her whole heart, to the song of praise bursting forth from the assembled Israelites on the shores of the Red Sea. "And Miriam the prophetess, the sister of Aaron, took a timbrel in her hand, and all the women went out after her, with timbrels, and with dances. And Miriam answered them, Sing, sing ye to the Lord, for he hath triumphed gloriously, the horse and his rider hath he thrown into the sea."[2]

The Hebrew word, נביאה, here used, and translated prophetess, means also, a *poetess*, and the wife of a prophet, and is applied sometimes to a singer of hymns. In this latter meaning, and perhaps, also, as a poetess, it must be applied to Miriam, as she was neither the wife of a prophet, nor, as in the case of Deborah, and afterwards Huldah, endowed by the Eternal with the power of prophecy itself. She appears to have been one of those gifted beings, from whom the words of sacred song flow spontaneously. The miracles performed in their very sight were sufficient to excite enthusiasm in a woman's heart, and awaken the burst of thanksgiving; and Miriam might have fancied herself at that moment as zealous and earnest in the cause of God as she appeared to be. But for true piety, something more is wanted than the mere enthusiasm of the moment, or the high-sounding religion of flowing verse. By Miriam not being permitted to enter the promised land, it is evident that she "had not followed the Lord fully,"[3] but had probably joined in the rebellions and mur-

---

1 Exod. 2.4.

2 Exod. 15.20-21.

3 Cf. 1 Kings 11.6: "And Solomon did evil in the sight of the Lord, and went not fully after the Lord, as did David his father."

murings which characterized almost the whole body of the Israelites during their wanderings in the wilderness. The very next mention of her after her song of praise, is her presumptuous attack upon Moses, and daring insult to the power of the Lord, contained in the twelfth chapter of Numbers. Some chronologists believe this incident occurred only one year after the passage of the Red Sea, a period not sufficiently long for circumstances to have changed the character of Miriam so completely, had not jealousy and presumption been secretly inmates of her heart before; unknown, perhaps, even to herself, for how few of us know our "secret sins," until they are roused into action by some unlooked-for temptation in an unguarded moment, and we are startled at ourselves.

The feelings of Miriam, recorded in this chapter, are so perfectly accordant with woman's nature, that surely no woman of Israel will turn from it, believing the length of time which has elapsed removes all the warning which it should inculcate. One of the most prominent of female failings is secret jealousy, quite distinct, however, from the fearful passion so called. We allude simply to that species of secret and unconfessed jealousy, which is the real origin of *detraction*, so often, unhappily, practised by woman upon woman. We are not now writing of any class, or creed, or people in particular, but of women in general. There never yet was gossip, without some species of detraction spoken or implied; and never yet has detraction been probed candidly and fairly (disregarding the pain of so doing) to its root, without being traced to either jealousy or envy of some quality, or possession, of the more favored being so unkindly unjudged.

Women, and single women more especially, are more liable to petty failings than men, simply because they have less to engross their minds, and less of consequence to employ their hands. Unless taught from earliest years to find and take pleasure in resources *within*, they must look *without*, and busy themselves with the characters, and conduct, and concerns of their neighbors. Now acknowledged merit to such characters gives very little food for cosy chat; it wants *esprit*, and so they are never content, till something doubtful or suspicious is discovered, or supposed to be, and then the lovers of gossip may be found in full conclave, marvelling, and wondering, and turning, and twisting, and blaming, and pitying, till the very object of such animadversion might find it difficult to trace of whom they speak, and know infinitely less of her own concerns, intentions, and feelings, than her reporters.

As Miriam acted, so would most women, unenlightened by the pure spirit of religious love, which alone can conquer the natural inclination towards detraction, and subdue secret jealousy, by making us aware of its existence. "And Miriam and Aaron spake against Moses, *because of the Ethiopian woman whom he had married*."[1] The very thing to arouse jealousy and disturbance in an unenlightened woman's mind.

Miriam had never been thrown in contact with her sister-in-law till within the last few months: Moses having sent his wife for safety, with his two sons, to her father Jethro, during the troubles in Egypt and their subsequent redemption. From the silence with regard to Zipporah, we are led to infer that she was a woman of meek and retiring habits, but of course, as the wife of their great leader Moses, held in higher repute by the people than his sister. And this, trifling as it seems, is now, as it always has been, a trial to some of our sex. Few single women there are who can't look upon the elevation of a brother's wife without some secret feelings of pain, which will be subdued and changed into warmest affection, or gain ascendancy and violence, finding vent in petty malice or half-concealed detraction, according as religion, and candor, and self-knowledge are, or are not, predominant in the sister's character. Perhaps it is hard, in some cases, to see one younger and fairer, and only known but a few years or months, as the case may be, usurp entire possession of a beloved brother's heart; wherein we, who have been his hand-in-hand companions from earliest infancy, must now be content with but a very secondary place; but such is one of the many trials peculiarly woman's,—permitted, that from her very loneliness below, she may look above for that fulness of love and tenderness for which she yearns. And thrice happy is that woman who, conscious of this, can yet be content with, and value as before, the love her brother has still to spare for her; who will so subdue natural feeling as to find in very truth a friend and sister in a brother's wife, and subjects of deepest interest in her children.

Miriam, as we may infer from her punishment, was not one of

---

1 Num. 12.1. The next paragraphs refer to Num. 12.1-16.

these. That an Ethiopian should be raised above herself, who was a daughter of Israel, was, to one of her evidently proud spirit, unendurable. Unable, however, to discover aught in Zipporah herself for a publicly-avowed scorn, she sought to lessen the holiness and greatness of her brother, by daring to declare that the Lord had spoken through her and Aaron also. That this jealousy arose because of the "Ethiopian woman whom he had married," Holy Writ itself informs us; and from Miriam's name being mentioned before that of Aaron, and yet more, from the wrath of the Lord being manifested towards her alone, it is evident that hers was the greater sin. Her individual assumption of prophetic power, she knew, would avail her nothing, but, uniting Aaron in the declaration, she sought to make it appear that God had breathed His spirit into every member of Amram's family. She had too much policy to endeavor to deprive Moses of all his granted and allowed privileges. Her only wish was, to decrease the value and spirituality of those privileges to him individually, and elevate herself and Aaron on his descent; emboldened so to do by the excessive meekness and forbearance of Moses, which she knew would shield her from all *human* reproof. She might, perhaps, have so dwelt upon her own imaginary importance, as really to believe what she asserted, and so feel more and more galled at the little account in which she was held.

It is quite possible for woman so to feel and so to act, and for all to proceed from the petty feelings of jealousy and malice, first excited by the higher grade and more considered position of a brother's wife. "Hath the Lord indeed spoken only by Moses? hath he not spoken also by us?" were the words they said; brief, and perchance of little weight considered by themselves, but in a people ever ready to revolt and murmur, more than likely to kindle sedition and disturbance. "And the Lord heard it, and the Lord spake suddenly unto Moses, and unto Aaron, and unto Miriam, Come out ye three unto the tabernacle of the congregation: and they three came out, and the Lord came down in the pillar of the cloud, and stood in the door of the tabernacle, and called Aaron and Miriam; and they both came forth."

Where now could have been the presumptuous self-importance of Miriam, called thus by Him at whose word might be annihilation? With what fearful terror must she have heard that summons, and listened to the reproving words of the Eternal?—exalting Moses above even His inspired prophets; for to them He declared He would make Himself known in a vision, and speak unto them in a dream, "but my servant Moses is not so, who is faithful in all mine house. With him will I speak mouth to mouth, even apparently, and not in dark speeches; and the similitude of the Lord shall he behold: wherefore then were ye not afraid to speak against my servant Moses? And the anger of the Lord was kindled against them; and He departed. And the cloud departed from off the tabernacle; and, behold, Miriam was leprous, as snow: and Aaron looked upon Miriam, and, behold, she was leprous."

It is from this awful chastisement, inflicted by the Lord Himself, that we must judge of the heinousness of her sin; that presumption and arrogancy are no small crimes in His sight, and that God Himself was insulted in the insult offered to His chosen servant. "My servant Moses," He ever designated him; implying the severest reproof in those simple words. Even were they endowed with prophetic power, He tells them they would be less than Moses; for to Moses alone would He deign to speak mouth to mouth. Had Miriam's sin been but the impulse of the moment, the reproof would have been sufficient, as we see in other cases in Scripture; but, effectually to root out the sinful presumption which probably had lain dormant for months, the Eternal, in His perfect justice, inflicted such chastisement as would cause her to be shunned and loathed by the very people whom she had sought to impress with her individual importance. Human reproof, indeed, she had not; for Moses, "meek above all the men which were on the faith of the earth," had not even answered the detracting words, conscious that his power was not his own, and that He who gave it, would, if needed, appear in his defence. Had Miriam's heart been perfect towards God, neither her sin nor her punishment would have taken place. Pride and presumption *cannot* exist with true piety; and we are therefore justified in supposing, that the awful infliction was not only a chastisement for present sin, but to awaken her to all the neglectfulness and presumption dividing her from the Lord in years long past. She was now not only to feel His stupendous power, but the true forgiving meekness and piety of the brother she had scorned and spoken against, only "because of his Ethiopian wife."

Stunned and appalled with the suddenness of the infliction, and dumb perhaps from awakening shame, Miriam herself stood silent before Moses: and Aaron therefore appealed for her.

"Alas, my Lord, I beseech thee, lay not the sin upon us, wherein we have done foolishly, and wherein we have sinned. Let her not be as one dead, of whom the flesh is half consumed as in the moment of his birth." And Moses, without pause, without one word of reproof, or just indignation at being thus appealed to by the very persons who had sought to injure him, lifted up his voice in earnest prayer unto the Lord, saying, "Heal her now, O God, I beseech thee." And God heard the prayer, and in His infinite goodness so answered it, as to temper justice with mercy, promising to withdraw His hand after seven days, during which time, in obedience to the already instituted laws for lepers, she was to be shut out from the camp. "And the people journeyed not till she was healed."

As there is no further mention of Miriam, except her death, in Numbers xx., [v. 1], we may infer that her chastisement had its effect, and that her haughty and seditious spirit was sufficiently subdued. We learn, from her brief history, much to guide us as women in general, and much to support our position as women of Israel. In the former, we see in what light presumption is regarded by the Lord—that would we retain His favor, we must be content with our own position, and in no way interfere, or seek to depreciate those whom, even in our own families, it may have pleased Him to set above us; that even from so small a beginning as jealousy of a brother's wife, simply because she was the daughter of a stranger, sin gained such powerful ascendancy, as to demand the most awful punishment for its subjection. We learn, that according to the nature of our transgression, so will be its chastisement. Miriam sought to raise herself not only above her brother's wife, but to an equality with that brother himself; and, by the infliction of a loathsome disease, she sank at once below the lowest of her people. No one dared approach her; she was cut off even from employment, from every former object of interest, banished from the camp; and she would have thus remained till her death, had not Moses interfered to beseech and obtain forgiveness.

The direct interposition of the Lord in punishing sin, and rewarding virtue, is no longer visible; but few who study His word, their own hearts, and the face of the world, both past and present, will not acknowledge that He is still the same, retributing and rewarding as when His ways were made manifest to all. By the example of Scripture characters, He reveals to us now that which is still acceptable or unacceptable to Him. Presumption, jealousy, the scorn of individual blessings, in the coveting others, may no longer be punished by leprosy, but "the Lord's arm is not shortened," and He may afflict us in a variety of ways, and through the very feelings which we so sinfully encourage. Let us beware, then, of detraction, of jealousy, of presumption; for our Father in Heaven abhors these things. Let us look only for the blessings granted us individually, in our inward and outward lot, and comparing them with the sorrowing and afflicted, bless God for what He has given us; not insult Him, by looking with an eye of envy only on those to whom His wisdom has given more. There is not a thought, not a feeling, unknown to Him; and oh! let us so guard our hearts, that we may be aware of the first whispering of sin, and banish it, even if it be in seeming but a thought.

As women of Israel, the history of Miriam is fraught with particular interest, from its so undeniably proving that woman must be quite as responsible a being as man before the Lord, or He certainly would not have deigned to appear Himself as her judge. Were woman unable of herself to eschew sin, Miriam's punishment would have been undoubtedly unjust. Nay, were she not responsible for *feelings*, as well as acts, God would not thus have stretched forth His avenging hand. Her feelings had only been formed into words, *not* yet into *actions*; still the Lord punished. And would He have done so, did he not wish to make manifest, in the sight of the whole people, that both sexes were alike before Him? Were woman in a degraded position, Miriam, in the first place, would not have had sufficient power for her seditious words to be of any consequence; and, in the next, it would have been incumbent on man to chastise—there needed no interference of the Lord. We see, therefore, the very sinfulness of Jewish women, as recorded in the Bible, is undeniable evidence of their equality, alike in their power to subdue sin, and in its responsibility before God.

That the Eternal graciously pardoned at the word of Moses, is no proof that Miriam *needed* the supplication of man to bring her cause before the Lord, but simply that forgiveness and intercession from the *injured* for the *injurer*, are peculiarly acceptable to Him, and will ever bring reply. Miriam had equal power to pray and be heard, [like] Rebekah, Hannah, and other female characters of Scripture; but her punishment was no doubt to be increased by the painful feelings which, if she were not quite hardened, must have been excited by the appeal of Moses in her favor, and in receiving the remission of her sentence through him. It at once proclaimed his power with the Lord, which she had sought to depreciate, and his still continued affection for herself. That the whole camp of Israel should halt in its march seven days for her alone,—that she should suffer less than were she shut out from her fellows in the act of travelling, argues pretty strongly, that her being a woman in no degree lessened her importance, or rendered the men of Israel less careful for her comfort. They could not have done more, had the chastised been Aaron in her stead.

"Deborah"

The promised land was gained, deeds of extraordinary valor and military skill and prowess marked its conquest and subdivision; but God's express command was disobeyed; and, in consequence, the tribes, even after they had settled in their respective territories, were continually "doing evil in the sight of the Lord," and at war, as a chastisement, with their idolatrous neighbors.[1] God had ordained the extermination of the former inhabitants of Palestine, because of their fearful state of idolatry, and various abominations. He had deferred bringing in the seed of Abraham to their appointed land, because "the iniquity of the Amorites was not yet full."[2] He might in

---

1 The story of Deborah occurs in chapters 4-5 of Judges, the most anarchic book of the Hebrew Bible. In the book of Joshua (immediately preceding Judges), the Israelites take the land of Canaan by force, but as of Judges they have not settled on any permanent governance structure. As a consequence, the people constantly become rebellious and "do evil in the sight of the Lord," for which God punishes them by permitting the surrounding Canaanite peoples to attack them. During such crises, natural leaders (the so-called judges, although they are also warriors, political leaders, prophets, and poets) rise up to protect the people. Along with Deborah, these include figures such as Samson, Jephthah, and Gideon.

2 Gen. 15.16. The Amorites were one of the seven Canaanite peoples that God commanded the Israelites to destroy, but according to the text they failed to do so. The Bible depicts the Amorites as evil giants who denied the wandering Israelites passage through their land

His wisdom have exterminated them by fire, water, or disease; but He appointed the swords of the Israelites as the instruments of His wrath, simply to try their faith and obedience, and bid them *earn* the rest, peace, spiritual and temporal glory, which he had held forth as the recompense of perfect obedience.

This fact is very frequently disregarded in a mere superficial reading of the history of Canaan. There are those even to doubt and cavil at the ways of their God, because He commanded His people to obtain possession of the promised land at the edge of the sword; forgetting that so doing was at once a punishment for those who had insulted Him by their awful iniquities (having full power to subdue sin, and keep in the straight path, as did the inhabitants of Mesopotamia even without direct revelation), and also to try the obedience of His people. Disease, fire, or flood, would have accomplished the first of these designs equally with the plan adopted; but not the second. Yet the former would at once have been recognised as the hand of God; no one questioning the agency of either the deluge, the destruction of Sodom, or the earthquake and the plague, punishing the rebellion of Korah. Why then should not the sword of slaughter be traced to the same Divine ordination, whence alone in fact it proceeded?

The Israelites, however, failed in their commanded obedience. Instead of exterminating, they entered into friendly leagues with the enemies and insulters of their God; and the Eternal, in His just anger, permitted them, in consequence, to remain as "thorns, and pricks in their sides, and their false gods as a snare unto them."[1] And so it was: "They took their daughters to be their wives, and gave their daughters to their sons, and served their gods; and the children of Israel did evil in the sight of God, and forgot the Lord their God, and served Baalim and the groves."[2] And this fearful state of things occurred repeatedly; rousing the anger of the Lord each time to sell them into the hands of their enemies, and yet whenever they cried unto Him in returning faith and repentance, His infinite mercy raised up deliverers in whom He put His spirit, and saved them.

---

and were defeated in battle (See Amos 2.9, Num. 21.21-23). They became proverbial enemies of Israel, much as one might say today that this or that group is "a bunch of Nazis."

1 Combines Num. 33.55 and Judg. 2.3.

2 Judg. 3.6.

Othniel, the nephew and son-in-law of Caleb, [as well as] Ehud, and Shamgar, had each in his turn been thus selected by the Lord; and during their respective sways Israel was at rest and obedient. But between each, they had relapsed into idolatry and rebellion; and after the deaths of Ehud and Shamgar, who appear contemporaries, falling anew into evil, the Eternal sold them into the hands of Jabin, king of Hazor, who mightily oppressed them twenty years, and caused them again to cry unto the Lord.

But even in these periods of anarchy and rebellion, all were not idolatrous. There must still have been many "seven thousands who had not bowed the knee to Baal,"[1] else would not the Lord have thus repeatedly compassionated and relieved them. Amongst these faithful few, the law was of course followed, and the people judged according to the statutes given through Moses. Had there been the very least foundation for the supposition of the degrading and heathenizing the Hebrew female, we should not find the offices of prophet, judge, military instructor, poet, and sacred singer, all *combined* and all *perfected* in the person of a woman; a fact clearly and almost startlingly illustrative of what must have been their high and intellectual training, as well as natural aptitude for guiding and enforcing the statutes of their God, to which at that time woman could attain.

"And Deborah, a prophetess, the wife of Lapidoth, she judged Israel at that time. And she dwelt under the palm tree of Deborah, between Ramah and Bethel, in Mount Ephraim: and the children of Israel came under her for judgment."[2] This simple description evinces that the greatness of Deborah consisted not at all in outward state, in semblance of high rank, or in particular respect or homage outwardly paid her; but simply in her vast superiority of mental and spiritual acquirements which were acknowledged by her countrymen, and consequently revered. The office of judge in Israel was not hereditary. It only devolved on those gifted to perform it: and, by the example before us, might be held by either sex: rather an *unsatisfactory* proof of the degradation of Jewish women. We are expressly

---

1 1 Kings 19.18. "Baal" was a generic name for any of several different Canaanite deities, described as false idols in the Bible.

2 Judg. 4.4-5.

told that Deborah was a prophetess, and "the wife of Lapidoth." Now, by the arrangement of this sentence, confirmed by the context, it is very evident that Deborah was a prophetess in her own person, wholly and entirely distinct from her husband, who was a mere cypher in public concerns. The Eternal had inspired her, a WOMAN and a WIFE in Israel, with His spirit expressly to do His will, and make manifest to her countrymen how little is He the respecter of persons; judging only by hearts perfect in His service, and spirits willing for the work: heeding neither the weakness nor apparent inability of one sex, compared with the greater natural powers of the other.

Yet so naturally are her public position and personal gifts described, that we cannot possibly believe her elevation to be an extraordinary occurrence, or that her position as a wife forbade her rising above mere conjugal and household duties. We never hear of a slave, or leper, or heathen, being intrusted with the prophetic spirit of the Eternal, simply because the social condition of such persons would and must prevent their obtaining either the respect, obedience, or even attention of the people. For the same reason, had woman really been on a par with these, as she is by some declared to be, she would never have been intrusted with gifts spiritual and mental, which Deborah so richly possessed. She never could have been a prophetess, for her words would only have been regarded as idle raving. She could never have been a judge, from the want of opportunities to train and perfect her intellect, and to obtain the necessary experience. Now it is clear that instead of this, her natural position must have been so high, that there needed not even adventitious state and splendor to make it acknowledged; and her intellect and judgment so cultivated, as not only to bring the people flocking to her for judgment, but to occasion Barak's refusal to set out on a warlike expedition unless she accompanied them.

We find the first recorded instance of her using her prophetic power in Judges iv. 6: "And she sent and called Barak the son of Abinoam out of Kedesh Naphtali, and said unto him, Hath not the Lord God of Israel commanded, saying, Go and draw toward Mount Tabor, and take with thee ten thousand men of the children of Naphtali and the children of Zebulun? And I will draw unto thee Sisera, the captain of Jabin's army, and his chariots and his multitudes;

and I will deliver him into thine hand. And Barak said unto her, *If thou wilt go with me*, then I will go: but if thou wilt not go with me, then will I not go. And she said, I will surely go with thee: notwithstanding the journey shall not be for thine honor; for the Lord will send Sisera into the hand of a woman."

We should be at a loss to understand the feeling in Barak, which impelled his reply, might we not infer it from Deborah's rejoinder. It would appear that, like many of his countrymen, while he obeyed, he was still wanting in the perfect faith which would have given him a glorious triumph in his own person. The presence of Deborah could in no way give him greater increase of safety and glory, than had he gone without her. She was but the instrument of the Lord, making His will known to her fellows. The words were not hers, but God's; and Barak should have acted on them without either reservation or doubt. Instead of which we find him making a *condition* to his obedience; and refusing to obey, if that condition were not complied with. What could the presence of a woman avail him? Her being a prophetess gave him no more assurance of conquest than the word of the Lord had already done; and *because he trusted more in the woman than in her God*, the journey would not be to his honor; a *woman's* hand should accomplish that complete downfall of Sisera, which would otherwise have accrued to his individual glory. It is evident that this is the real rendering of this rather obscure sentence, else we should not have it so expressly stated that the "journey would not be for his honor."

Deborah however arose, and went with Barak, first to collect the necessary troops from Zebulun and Naphtali, and then to Mount Tabor, where Sisera and his immense armament of nine hundred chariots of iron, besides infantry, marched to meet them. Still we find Barak but secondary, doing nothing without the word of the Lord through Deborah. And Deborah said, "Up! for this is the day in which the Lord hath delivered Sisera into thine hand: is not the Lord gone out before thee? So Barak went down from Mount Tabor, and ten thousand men after them;"[1] and the Lord gave them

1 Judg. 4.14. Sisera, the Canaanite general, dies when he comes to Jael, an Israelite woman, thirsty for water; she gives him milk and, after he falls asleep, drives a tent spike through his head. Judg. 4.18-21.

such complete victory, that but Sisera escaped, to receive his death at the hand of a woman, according to the Eternal's word. Nor was it a single victory, for "the hand of the children of Israel prospered and prevailed against Jabin, king of Canaan."[1]

We find next Deborah exercising that glorious talent of extempore poetry only found amongst the Hebrews; and by her, a woman and a wife in Israel, possessed to an almost equal degree with the Psalmists and prophets, who followed at a later period. Her song is considered one of the most beautiful specimens of Hebrew poetry, whether read in the original, or in the English version. We find her taking no glory whatever to herself, but calling upon the princes, and governors, and people of Israel, to join with her in "blessing the Lord for the avenging of Israel."[2] In the fourth and fifth verses, she alludes, by a most beautiful figure, to the power of the Eternal. That before Him "the earth trembled, and the heavens dropped, and the clouds dropped water. And the mountains trembled, even Sinai, before the Lord God of Israel," thus manifesting that his power, not man's, had brought delivery to Israel. Then in the sixth and eighth verses she describes the condition of the people before she arose a mother in Israel; that they were compelled to travel in by-paths, because of the high roads all being occupied by their foes; and from the villages all the inhabitants had ceased, from their being continually exposed undefended to the enemy. Nor was there a shield or spear seen in the forty thousand of Israel. The simplicity and lowliness of the prophetess's natural position, is beautifully illustrated by the term she applies to herself—neither princess, nor governor, nor judge, nor prophetess, though both the last offices she fulfilled—"until that I, Deborah, arose, until I arose a MOTHER in Israel."[3] She asked no greater honor or privilege for herself individually, than the being recognised as the mother of the people whom the Lord alone had endowed her with power to judge. "My heart is towards the governors of Israel," she continues, "that offered themselves willingly among the people. Bless ye the Lord,"[4] meaning those who, rising from the idolatry and sloth which had encompassed the people,

---

1 Judg. 4.24.

2 Judg. 5.2.

3 Judg. 5.7.

4 Judg. 5.9.

offered themselves willingly for the service of the Lord. She bids them speak,—all classes of people,—from those princes who rode on white asses, and those who sat in judgment, and those who walked by the way, to even the drawers of water who had before been harassed by the noise of the archers coming forcibly to disturb their domestic employments; and all were to rehearse the righteous acts of the Lord, for to Him alone they owed their preservation. "The Lord made ME have dominion over the mighty,"[1] she says, in verse thirteen, thus retaining her own dignity and power in Israel, yet tracing it to the Eternal, not to herself. The poetry describing the downfall of their foes, calling forth the imagery of nature to give it force and life; the death of Sisera, and the waiting and watching of his mother at her lattice—"Why is this chariot so long in coming? why tarry the wheels of his chariots?"[2] and the answer, alike from her ladies, and her own heart, "Have they not sped? have they not divided the prey; to every man a damsel or two; to Sisera a prey of divers colors, a prey of divers colors of needlework, meet for the necks of them that take the spoil?"[3] as if to fail with his mighty armament were impossible; and thus sung by the lips of the conquerors, infused with a species of satire, giving indescribable poignancy to the strain; and then the glorious conclusion, "So let all thine enemies perish, O Lord: but let them that love thee be as the sun when he goeth forth in his might;"[4] form altogether one of the sublimest strains of spiritual fervor in the Bible; and mark forcibly, by her conduct, both as prophetess and judge, that in Deborah, even as in Gideon, David, and the prophets of later years, God disdained not to breathe His spirit, but made a WOMAN His instrument to judge, to prophesy, to teach, and to redeem.

"And the land had rest forty years," we are told at the conclusion of Deborah's song; words which, as no other judge is mentioned, would lead us to infer that Deborah continued "a mother in Israel" all that time, retaining the people in fidelity, and consequently in temporal and spiritual peace. Even if she did not live herself to gov-

---

1 Judg. 5.13.

2 A paraphrase of Judg. 5.28.

3 A paraphrase of Judg. 5.30.

4 This and the following quotation refer to Judg. 5.31.

ern all those years, it is evident that her influence and instructions were remembered and acted upon, for it was not till *after* these forty years that "Israel again did evil in the sight of the Lord,"[1] and so again required a redeemer, which was granted in the person of Gideon.

The silence preserved regarding the subsequent life and death of Deborah, is a simple confirmation of the meekness and humility with which we found her judging Israel under her own palm-tree, before being called to a more stirring scene. The land was at peace, the power of prophecy and foresight in military matters was no longer needed, and Deborah resumed her personally humble station, evidently without any ambitious wish, or attempt to elevate her rank or prospects. It was enough that she was useful to her countrymen; that she was a lowly instrument in the Eternal's hand to work them good. What, now, did she need to satisfy the *woman nature*, which she still so evidently retained? Her judgments, her works, are covered with the veil of silence, but we learn their effects by the simple phrase, that "the land had rest forty years"—the land, the whole land, not merely that which was under her direct superintendence. Virtue, holiness, and wisdom, though the gifts of but one lowly individual, are not confined to one place, when used, as were Deborah's, to the glory of God, and the good of her people. Silently, and perhaps unperceived, they spread over space and time; and oh! how glorious must be the destiny of that woman, who, without one moment quitting her natural sphere, can yet by precept, example, and labor produce such blessed effects as to give the land peace, and bring a whole people unto God!

In a *practical* view, perhaps, the character of Deborah cannot now be brought home to the conduct of her descendants, for woman can no longer occupy a position of such trust and wisdom in Israel; but, *theoretically*, we may take the history of Deborah to our hearts, both *nationally* and individually. With such an example in the Word of our God, it is unanswerably evident that neither the Written nor the Oral Law could have contained one syllable to the disparagement of women.[2]

---

1 Judg. 6.1.

2 For the distinction between Written and Oral Law, see p. 282, note 1.

Men were in no condition to have permitted the influence of woman, had they not been accustomed, by the constant and emphatic enjoinments of the law, to look on her with respect, consideration, and tenderness. Mentally and spiritually, Deborah was gifted in an extraordinary degree, leading us to infer that the women of Israel must have had the power to cultivate both mind and spirit, and to delight in their resources, for we have the whole Bible to prove that the Eternal never selected for the instruments of His will, any but those whose hearts were inclined towards Him, even before He called them—witness the history of Abraham, Joseph, Moses, David, and others. All and every talent comes from God, but will not work and influence by His sole gift alone. They are given to be improved, persevered in, perfected, by those to whom they are intrusted, and then used in the service of their Giver. It is evident, then, that Deborah had the *inclination* and the *power* to cultivate, perfect, and use the gifts of her God; and this would have been quite impossible, had her social condition been such as the enemies of *scriptural* and *spiritual* Judaism declare. With the history of Deborah in their hands, the young daughters of Israel need little other defence or argument, to convince their adversaries that they require no other creed, nor even a denial of the Oral Law, to teach them their proper position, alike to themselves and their fellows, and in their relative duties towards God and man.

Deborah being a wife, confirms this yet more strongly. There must not only have been perfect freedom of *position*, but of *action*; even more than is found in the history of any modern nation, for we do not find a single instance of a wife being elected to any public office requiring intellect and spirituality, secular and religious knowledge, so completely distinct from her husband. Yet the history of Deborah in no way infers that she was neglectful of her conjugal and domestic duties. There is an unpretending simplicity about her very greatness. The very fact of those she judged coming to her under her own palm-tree, supposes her quiet and required mode of living. She never leaves her home, except at the earnest entreaty of Barak, which urges her to sacrifice domestic retirement for public good. To a really great mind, domestic and public duties are so perfectly compatible, that the first need never be sacrificed for the last.[1] And that Lapidoth in no manner interfered with the public offices of his wife, called as she was to them by God Himself through His gifts, infers a noble confidence and respectful consideration towards her, evidently springing at once from the national equality and freedom tendered to Jewish women; and from a mind great enough to appreciate and value such talents even in a woman; a greatness not very often found in modern times.

To follow in the steps of our great ancestress is not possible, now that the prophetic spirit is removed from Israel, and the few public offices left us fall naturally to the guardianship of man; yet many and many a Jewish woman is intrusted with one or more talents direct from God; and if she can stretch forth a helping hand to the less enlightened of her people, let her not hold back, from the false and unscriptural belief that woman cannot aid the cause of God, or in any way attain to religious knowledge. His word is open to her, as to man. In Moses' command to read and explain the Law to all people, woman was included by name. And now the whole Bible, Law, Historical books, Psalms, and Prophets, are open to her daily commune, and shall it be said that she has neither the right nor the understanding to make use of such blessed privilege? Shame, shame on those who would thus cramp the power of the Lord, in denying to any one of His creatures the power of addressing and comprehending Him, through the inexhaustible treasure of His gracious word!

Every married woman is judge and guardian of her own household. She may have to encounter the prejudices of a husband, not yet thinking with her on all points; but if she have really a great mind, she will know how to *influence*, without in any way *interfering*. She will know how to serve the Lord in her household without neglecting her duty and affection towards her husband; and by domestic conduct influence society at large, secretly and unsuspectedly indeed, but more powerfully than she herself can in the least degree suppose.

To unmarried women, even as to wives, some talent is intrusted,

---

1 The compatibility of women's domestic and public duties is also the subject of Aguilar's short story, "The Authoress," from *Home Scenes and Heart Studies*. As a poet and public persona, Deborah is a figure for the woman writer, much like Aguilar herself.

which may be used to the glory of its Giver. Life is not lent us to be frittered away in an unmeaning little satisfactory run of amusements, or often in their mere fruitless search. There surely is some period in a single woman's existence, when the hopes, ambition, and even favorite amusements, of girlhood must come to an end. Because unmarried, is woman still to believe herself a girl, hoping for, and looking for, a change in her existence, which will in reality never come? Would it not be wiser and better, aye, and incalculably happier, if woman herself withdrew from the sphere of exciting hopes and pleasures which she had occupied in girlhood? If she sought perseveringly and prayerfully some new objects of interest, affection, and employment, which she might justly hope would become a stay and support in rapidly advancing years, and thus entirely prevent the ennui, and its attendants, love of gossip, frivolity, and often sourness and irritability, which are too generally believed to be the sole characteristics of single (and so of course supposed disappointed) women? Have we not all some precious talent lent us by our God, and for the use of which He will demand an account? Is there not the whole human family from which to select some few objects of interest, on whom to expend some of our leisure time, and draw our thoughts from all-engrossing self? Were there but one object on whom we have lavished kindness, and taught to look up to God and heaven, and to walk this earth virtuously and meekly—but one or two whom, had we the pecuniary means, we have clothed and fed—a sick or dying bed that we have soothed—a sorrowing one consoled—an erring one turned from the guilty path—the repentant, or the weak, strengthened and encouraged—we shall not have lived in vain; or, when we come to die, look shudderingly back on a useless life and wasted gifts; on existence lost in the vain struggle to arrest the flight of time, and still seek hope and pleasure in thoughts and scenes, whose sweetness has been too long extracted for aught to remain but bitterness and gall. Deborahs in truth we cannot be; but each and all have talents given, and a sphere assigned them, and, like her, all have it in their power, in the good performed towards man, to use the one, and consecrate the other to the service of their God.

1845

From THE JEWISH FAITH

"Introduction"

[...] Our youth indeed need help and guidance, or they are likely to be lost in the fearful vortex of contending opinions around them. To rest indifferent and unenquiring, always unnatural to youth, would actually be impossible now; and more than ever, books are needed on which the mind and heart may rest: and more especially for our FEMALE YOUTH. For them, there is literally no help in the way of vernacular religious literature. For our young men, there are the works of our ancient sages; there are ministers and teachers to instruct in their obsolete and difficult languages, and explain their often puzzling and metaphysical sense. There is a vast fund of Hebrew learning and theology open to them. Their larger intellect, deeper reasoning, greater intensity and power of concentrating thought, will enable them to enter into, and master them; but this to woman is utterly impossible. Destined for home and home duties; to enliven and rejoice all the members of that home, be they parents, brothers and sisters, husband and children; to be ever ready to come out of self for others, and willingly sacrifice her leisure whenever called upon to do so, even for such apparently trifling duties as entering into and sharing others' *pleasures and amusements*, as well as smoothing their difficulties, and soothing their sorrows, how could she (granting she has the requisite mental powers, which we do not deny, if circumstances would allow her to concentrate them) find the time requisite for such absorbing employment, without neglecting duties of infinitely more importance?

But that our huge tomes of Hebrew wisdom and learning are inaccessible to woman, is no reason that she is to have no aid in the acquirement of her religion—no guide as to spiritual aspirations, and no comfort in her need. Metaphysics and speculative theories, indeed, are not for her. All she requires, is to understand the unspeakable comfort of her Bible, and the religion she follows, so as to obey its dictates from the calm conviction of the mind, as well as the impulse of the heart. Many suppose that this comes intuitively, and requires neither instruction nor sympathy. It may be so with some: but the generality of our youth demand it, yearn for it with such an intensity of longing, that, finding no books of their own, they are compelled to seek the works of Christian writers—and then we are astonished, if they are more Christian than Jewish in their thoughts. A charge, by the way, incomprehensible to us individually, as we know not, and never could discover, the distinction between Jewish and Christian *spirituality,* on which some good, but prejudiced persons, lay so great a stress. The distinction of creeds is, indeed, very clearly to be understood and defined, as also the difference in their respective ordinances and modes of thought; but spirituality is common to every creed and to every nation who earnestly seek to know and love the Lord, according to the dictates of the Laws that each believe that He has given, and so observe. And if this be the case with every creed, how much more in common ought those to have, who acknowledge the same Book, and the same foundation?

But if the imbibing of Christian spirituality will do our young sisters no harm whatever, for it is Jewish spirituality as well, the imbibing of the peculiar creed of the Christian undoubtedly will, and this is the great evil to be counteracted in the indiscriminate perusal of Christian books. Liberal as their writers may be, they must infuse their works with the doctrine in which they believe, and, in fact, they would be little worth to their own if they did not. Religion is the only subject in which prejudice in favour of one's own is a positive virtue; for it is a widely distinct sentiment to prejudice against another, contradictory as the assertion may at first sight appear. All who have at all studied human nature, will allow, that the heart most honest, most faithful, and most clearly comprehending its own, is endowed with the greatest charity and liberality towards the religion of another.

As an humble help in supplying the painful want of Anglo-Jewish literature, to elucidate for our female youth the tenets of their own, and so remove all danger from the perusal of abler and better works by spiritual Christians, not to attempt to vie with them the present work is undertaken. The familiar and appealing form of letters is chosen, as more likely to touch the heart, and to convince the understanding, than in the graver form of essays or chapters. No learned dissertation is attempted, the author merely wishing to reply as simply, affectionately and concisely, as is compatible with the weighty subject, to the doubts and questions which she has observed to rise in the minds of youth; and, especially, on the Jewish belief in Immortality. Youth, in its high aspirations and eager thoughts, will never be satisfied with the vague and fanciful belief in immortality, which it has imbibed in childhood. It must have something to rest on: something wherewith to guide its aspirings—and oh! who would not aid in giving these, when we look on the youthful being standing in such beauty and joy and hope on the threshold of life, about to enter a world, which, without the belief in and knowledge of another, must too soon seem so dark and woe-fraught, as to bewilder the mind with doubt and fear, and fling a dense cloud between the aspiring heart, and the consoling attributes of its God? Trials of sickness, or care, or sorrow, or bereavement, must sooner or later be the portion of our youthful charge, seeming, in their early freshness, as if neither sorrow nor care could ever approach to sadden them. And shall we fail to provide them with the strength and comfort which, for such alternations, a God of Love has provided, when we can? Should we not think that parent strangely unwise and cruel, who would send her child to a country of cold and snow, provided only with summer clothing? And is it not the same, if our experience teaches us, that trials must assail our cherished ones, and yet we provide them with nothing which would soften its suffering, strengthen to endure; and infuse a hope and faith in that better life, which will last for ever; and so shine, as even in the darkest hours to invigorate and bless?

The trial supposed to have been encountered by the young girl to whom the letters are addressed, is indeed an extreme case, but unhappily, far from being one without a parallel. Many of my young sisters may feel, and with perfect justice, that they are infinitely more spiritual, and must know a great deal more of their religion, than she does, for they already know and feel the truth of what she is doubting and questioning. But even to them, we hope sympathy will not be wholly unacceptable, though we acknowledge our letters are intended far more for those, whom circumstances have deprived of a decidedly religious education; who from the ages of sixteen to twenty-one, are beginning to think for themselves; and whose peculiar disposition compels them to seek, and find the Rock of Refuge and Shield of Salvation, whose infinite love and exhaustless mercy is proffered unto all His creatures, without any distinctions of age or sex.

For those of my own faith the following pages are written, and to them they are addressed. Young Christian women have such advantages and privileges in following the religion of the Land, in having teachers and guides without number, male and female—that it would be indeed a presumptuous hope to interest them in the subject under discussion; yet even to them it may not be entirely useless. Christianity in all, save its actual doctrine of belief, is the offspring of Judaism; and as one of our most enlightened and purest feeling Divines very lately said, "The differences between Christianity and Judaism, however *great and weighty in their speculative doctrines,* disappear in the *moral truths and principles alike upheld by both.*"[1] And the more we know of each other's faith and practice, the more clear and striking becomes this fact. Works then, tending to elucidate the religion of another, must ever be welcome to the candid and liberal mind; and though to my young Christian sisters the following letters may proffer nothing in the way of religious instruction, they will at least prove that the Hebrew faith is not one of spiritless form, meaningless observances, and comfortless belief, which some suppose it, not from wilful illiberality, but from actual ignorance. They may perhaps discover, that the foundation of all spiritual religion is the same—that from Judaism and the Bible all *their* privileges spring—and that if they deny the divinity of the one, that of the other falls to the ground; and then what becomes of Christianity? These are, or ought to be, important considerations to every Christian; and we trust, therefore, in this age of advanced enlightenment, and more especially in our own free, happy, sheltering England, that no work tending to explain and elevate the Jewish religion will be pronounced useless, or, if not regarded as controversial, merely considered as interesting only to the Jews. We have been charged as having exhibited in a former work an intolerant spirit—a charge to a heart filled with love for all its kind, be their creed what it may, more exquisitely painful than any other censure.[2] It may be, that in earnest defence of our own, we may not have been as careful or as charitable

1 Aguilar's note: "Rev. M.J. Raphall. See Jewish Chronicle of 9th January, 1846."

2 See the review of *The Women of Israel* in *The Athenaeum*, in Appendix B below.

in words, as God knows we are in heart—that the warmth of defence may have merged into attack; but if so, it was as unintentional at the time, as deeply regretted when pointed out afterwards. We shrink from all controversy. We would give every man that liberty of conscience which we ask for ourselves. We would simply instil the beauty, the holiness, the comfort, and the eternal duration of the religion God gave to Moses, into the inmost hearts of our own; and if, in the earnestness of this attempt, we *appear* to judge harshly of others, it is wholly and utterly opposed to the sentiments of either heart or mind.

We beg our readers of either denomination to remember, ere we proceed, that, written expressly for *youth* just beginning to think and inquire for themselves, the various subjects are more minutely examined, and entered upon, than had we been writing for adults; and this fact must therefore be our excuse, if we have treated too much at length subjects of religion generally, and the Jewish religion in particular, which are supposed, and may be, universally known.

"LETTER XXX."

FROM THE SAME TO THE SAME

My last communication was shorter than usual, dearest Annie; because I rather wished you to bring forward yourself the further questions, to which our lengthened examination of this important subject [i.e., Immortality] may have given rise, than start them myself. Correctly, as I perceive by your letter, I have surmised them.

I did not add Mendelssohn's Phaedon to my list of authorities, as to the Jewish opinion of the Immortality of the soul because, bold as the declaration may seem, the work disappointed me.[1] As the supposed opinions of a Heathen philosopher, reasoning from analogy, from acute perception, from the extraordinary power of a mind

---

1 Aguilar refers to the work of Moses Mendelssohn, the "enlightened" eighteenth-century German-Jewish philosopher best known for his work, *Jerusalem*, in which he attempted to prove that Jewish law could be derived strictly from reason. Aguilar probably refers to Charles Cullen's English translation of *Phædon; or, the Death of Socrates (in imitation of the Phædon of Plato)*, (London, 1789), translated from the original German edition of 1767. With this reference, Aguilar places her own interpretation next to that of the founder of Germany's Jewish Enlightenment.

unusually gifted, but unenlightened by revelation; the work is perfect. We feel that reason alone, is sufficient for conviction, that the soul cannot be annihilated, and must have a separate existence. As the work of a Jewish believer, to whom the Holy Scriptures, in their original tongues and all their commentators, were open, it is incomplete and disappointing. He could not, indeed, have put into the mouth of Socrates, allusions to a Divine revelation. He could not have infused the spirit of a Heathen with the spirit of a Jew; but when the Phaedon was accomplished, when he had concluded his imaginary conversation, which proved so clearly, that even to the unenlightened by religion, the soul's immortality was a realised and accepted fact, he should have proved that, though reason was a guide of the Heathen, FAITH was enough for the Hebrew; and that God's revealed attributes taught him in a few brief words, what the Heathen needed argument on argument to prove. Had he done this, he would indeed have left us a debt no after-ages could repay; he would have provided strength and consolation for the young and weak amongst his own, and checked at once the charge of Immortality being no part of Judaism. His book, whose widely spread popularity has brought such honour to his name, would have evinced not merely the sound reasoning of the philosopher, but the pure faith of a Scriptural Jew, and done more for the honour and glory of his holy religion, than any modern Hebrew had accomplished. There are merely individual opinions, my dearest Annie, and I am very bold, perhaps, to put them forward; but the feeling of disappointment with which I laid down the book was absolutely painful. There was no evidence of the Hebrew within its pages; the follower of any creed might have compiled it. It could not teach the Christian the immortal hope and spiritualised faith of the Jew; and therefore, though it may bid us venerate the genius of the philosopher, we cannot quote or lean upon it, as a witness of the faith of a believer [...].

1846

From SABBATH THOUGHTS AND SACRED COMMUNINGS

"Preface"

THE following Meditations and Prayers, were written by my beloved daughter, for her own use, and they would never have been published, but in compliance with the earnest solicitations of several friends, who, many years ago, had requested her to write and publish some for individual use. She constantly declined doing so. I have selected a few which I trust will be kindly received, more particularly by her young co-religionists, who may learn from them, to turn to their Heavenly Father on all occasions, with a firm religious humble trust in His love and mercy; likewise to encourage and foster sentiments of love and charity to all mankind, whatever their creed. Should their perusal induce the young daughters of Israel to reflect, and endeavour to walk in the path of one, who at the early age of fifteen began to seek to know how to love and serve her Creator with all her heart, soul, and mind, I shall indeed be fully repaid for the anxiety and hesitation which I felt, before I could resolve to publish my dear child's *private* meditations and prayers.

SARAH AGUILAR.
June 17th, 1853.

"Morning Meditation"

WITH a glowing and a grateful heart do I hail the return of the sunny morn. The Lord in His mercy hath held me up during the dark and fearful night, and hath permitted me once more to hail the glad and glorious approach of the day. I will seek the Lord in the early morning when all is silent around me, when there is a holy calm in the stillness of nature, that softens every tumultuous feeling and calms the weary spirit, and fills the soul with adoration, then will I seek the Almighty, ere the cares, thoughts, and desires of this world have entered my heart; and He will bend His gracious ear to the prayers and praises of a child of sin; if offered up in love, in reverence, and in adoration. I will awake from sleep, and arise early to seek my Creator, and offer Him the homage of a sinful, yet contrite heart, and in His infinite mercy He will deign to listen to my prayers. O how I love the Lord for all his mercies towards me! In sorrow have I sought Him, and He hath answered me, for the prayers of the young are acceptable to our Beneficent Creator, if offered up in lowliness and humbleness of heart. Think then, O my soul, how can I repay the manifold blessings I receive from the hand of my God; in what way dare I hope to evince the gratitude that gloweth in my heart. Think of all thy imperfections, thy follies, and thy sins. How difficult I sometimes find it, to give up the inclinations of my heart. Think on all this, O my soul, and know that fervent prayer alone can obtain pardon for my sins, and strength to guard against them. And what good do I do? Satisfy not thyself, my soul, with the thought, that thou hast no opportunities of doing good: many there are, but, careless and impatient, they are overlooked. Be on thy guard then, my soul, and let this day be passed in a manner acceptable to the Almighty, and pleasing to thyself. Beware, not to fall into the snares of temper and impatience. Lord, give me strength that I may walk in Thy ways, and become a good and faithful servant of Thy law. Amen.

"Prayer for the Government of the Thoughts"

TEACH me, O Almighty Father, so to govern my wild thoughts, that the inclinations of my heart may not gain too great an ascendancy over them. I am a weak and helpless being, O my God, and every day I feel, that without Thy merciful goodness upholding me, I should sink and be no more. O add to Thy manifold blessings, my Heavenly Father, and show me the means of governing my thoughts, and grant me strength to resist when they dwell too much on the wishes and desires of this world. Without Thy divine aid, O my God, I know not how to govern my ever-varying thoughts, I know not how to lead them in the right way, nor can I turn them from their favourite objects. O teach me how to govern them so as to enable me to prevent them from following too much the wishes and inclinations of my heart, and then trifling sorrows and disappointments will be less often mine, for I am but a weak and sinful child of

Earth, and my wild thoughts will become wild desires, if I know not how to govern them. Grant me, O my God, so to guide them in the right way, that they may be free from guilt or even folly, and that could my heart be open to the eye of man as it is to Thee, O God, I might not be ashamed of the thought contained therein. Hear me, O my God, for I put my trust in Thee, for I know, weak, sinful as I am without Thy divine assistance I shall have no light to guide me in my dark and difficult path, and my strength will fail me ere I reach that destined spot where peace and joy will be my blest reward. Then through Thine infinite mercy hear me, O most merciful and Almighty God. Hear me, and answer me from Thy throne of resplendent brightness, and for the sake of Thy Holy and Awful Name O grant my prayer! Amen.

From "The Prophecies of Isaiah"

> "Therefore the Lord Himself shall give you a sign; Behold, a virgin shall conceive, and bear a son, and shall call his name Immanuel."
>
> *Isaiah*, vii. 14.

THE prophecy contained in the 7th chapter of Isaiah—"Behold, a virgin shall conceive," etc., is one that is generally supposed to *favour* the Christian doctrine, if not to be its foundation. The last few years, however, even Christian divines acknowledge that the assertion will not bear strict examination, and have, I believe in many cases, given up these verses as alluding to their messiah.

The Jewish explanation of the chapter is very simple.[1] In the reign of Ahaz, king of Judah, Rezin, king of Syria, and Pekah (son of Remaliah), king of Israel, leagued together to make war against Jerusalem. This confederacy so terrified Ahaz, as to deprive him and his house of all spirit to undertake the war, and also of all faith in the Eternal. Notwithstanding this, the Lord, in His great mercy, bade Ahaz neither be faint-hearted nor cast down; as the league "should neither stand, nor their intentions come to pass" (by Ephraim, throughout the chapter, the kingdom of Israel is designated). Still Ahaz doubted, though God had said, "*If ye will not believe me, ye shall*

---

1 In this paragraph, Aguilar refers to events detailed in Isa. 7.1-17.

not be established."[1] And the Lord desired him to ask a sign of the Lord his God, "either in the depth beneath, or the height above."[2] Even this, Ahaz refused to do still from want of sufficient faith. God reproved him, and promised Himself to give a sign—"Behold, a virgin shall conceive and bear a son, and shall call his name, *God is with us*: butter and honey shall he eat, that he may know to refuse the evil and choose the good: and before the child shall know to refuse the evil and choose the good, the land that thou abhorrest shall be forsaken of both her kings."

Now, even granting that the Hebrew word translated *virgin* means *virgin* and nothing else, and that the sign was to be the birth of a child in a supernatural manner, it has, and can have *nothing* to do with Jesus, as it was to, and *did*, take place in the *reign of Ahaz*, king of Judah, several hundred years before the Christian era. The word, however, does not only signify *virgin*, but a *young woman*; and, as such, most probably indicates the wife of Isaiah, who bore a son as a sign, *before the usual time*, and was commanded, by the words, "Butter and honey shall he eat," etc., to rear him from his birth as a Nazarite (the laws for which are in the 6th chapter of Numbers: and their *practical* illustration in Judges, xiii. 2, to 6).[3] By being set apart, from his birth, to the service of his God, and kept from all strong drink and exciting meats, he was more easily to be able to "refuse the evil and choose the good."[4] But even before this was attained, by the child being sufficiently old to do this, the land which Ahaz abhorred and dreaded, Syria and Ephraim, should be forsaken by both her kings, Rezin and Pekah; whose confederacy had so terrified Judah. And this took place exactly as prophesied, as is written in 2 Kings xvi, 5-10, and xv. 30, also in 2 Chron. xxviii. 1-26. The remaining verses of Isaiah vii., will be found to prophesy and agree exactly with these chapters in the historical books above mentioned, as also the whole of Isaiah viii.

Not satisfied with the grant of *one sign*, the infinite mercy of the Eternal granted another, in the promise of the birth of a second son

---

1 Isa. 7.7,9.

2 Isa. 7.11.

3 In the Bible, the Nazirite is an Israelite child specially set apart from birth for divine service. Nazirites are not permitted to drink wine or cut their hair. The story of Samson is the practical illustration to which Aguilar refers.

4 Isa. 7.15-16.

by the *Prophetess* (the wife of Isaiah).[1] Witnesses were selected to bear testimony to the prophecy that before the promised child had knowledge "to cry 'My father, and my mother,' the riches of Damascus and the spoil of Samaria shall he take away before the king of Assyria:" Isaiah viii., 4.

And so it was—the child was born (not now miraculously): and by comparing this verse with the historical chapters before mentioned, its fulfilment is evident.

Again, the strong proof that both these promised signs were the children of Isaiah by his wife (however the birth of the first might have been attended with something unusual), is found in the 18th verse of this same 8th chapter: "Behold, *I* and *the children* whom the Lord hath given me are *for signs* and *for wonders* in Israel, from the Lord of hosts, which dwelleth in Mount Zion." Does not this agree exactly with verse 14 of the 7th chapter, and verses 3 and 4 of the 8th chapter? If the first child—who received the name of Immanuel, in his very name to reiterate the promise that God is with us—were the child of a virgin living thousands of years *afterwards*, or even of a virgin unconnected with Isaiah, what can the Prophet mean by saying, "*I* and the *children* whom the Lord hath given me are for signs and wonders," etc.? If only Maher-shalal-hash-baz had been his son, he would have said *child*, not *children*; but by the use of the word *children*, and *signs*, and *wonders*, instead of a sign and a wonder, it is as clear as if it had been written in direct words, that Immanuel and Maher-shalal-hash-baz were *both* the Prophet's sons, and both given as signs to a people sunk in iniquity—to prove that God was with them still, however they might disobey and disbelieve Him. That something miraculous attended the birth of Immanuel *might be*; but that his mother was, or became the wife of Isaiah, and her son acknowledged to be also the Prophet's, is proved by Isaiah's own words: "*I* and the *children* whom the Lord hath given *me*." The verse, therefore, however often quoted, has nothing whatever to do with the foundation or support of Christianity. It is a simple incident in Jewish history, confined to the reign of Ahaz and the people of Judah—the children of the prophet sinking into insignificancy as

---

1 Isa. 8.1-4. The second son is Maher-shalal-hash-baz, whose name means "The spoil speeds, the prey hastens." The name of the first son, Immanuel, means "God is with us."

soon as the prophecy connected with them was fulfilled: nor will the 8th verse of chapter viii. contradict this.[1] The end of verse 10 may just as well be translated "O Immanuel" as the end of verse 8; "for God is with us" is the meaning of both, and so ought both to be translated. "And he shall pass through Judah; he shall overflow and go over, he shall reach even to the neck; and by stretching out of his wings shall fill the breadth of thy land, for God is with us" [...].

(1840s?), 1853

1 Isa. 8.7-10 are translated in the King James Version as follows: "7 Therefore, behold, the Lord bringeth up upon them the waters of the river, strong and many, even the king of Assyria, and all his glory: and he shall come up over all his channels, and go over all his banks: 8 And he shall pass through Judah; he shall overflow and go over, he shall reach even to the neck; and the stretching out of his wings shall fill the breadth of thy land, O Immanuel. 9 Associate yourselves, O ye people, and ye shall be broken in pieces; and give ear, all ye of far countries: gird yourselves, and ye shall be broken in pieces; gird yourselves, and ye shall be broken in pieces. 10 Take counsel together, and it shall come to nought; speak the word, and it shall not stand: for God is with us."

"HISTORY OF THE JEWS IN ENGLAND"

THE Hebrew nation, as is well known, has been for ages scattered over the face of the earth, and now exists in different portions in every civilised country; retaining, however, in all situations, the religion, manners, and recollections of its ancestry—almost everywhere less or more oppressed, yet everywhere possessing the same unconquerable buoyancy of spirit and the indomitable industry. It would be a very long and dismal story to tell of the settlement and sufferings of the Jews in the various countries of Europe, and we propose, therefore, to confine ourselves to a brief narration principally concerning their residence and treatment in Great Britain.

Whence or by what route the exiles of Judea found their way to this island, cannot now be satisfactorily traced; but, scattered as they were over the extensive domains of their Roman conquerors, it is not unlikely that they originally crossed the Channel whilst England also was under imperial sway, their numbers increasing as centuries rolled on, and as the gradual desertion of the island by the Romans gave them a more peaceful and secure retreat than was enjoyed by their brethren scattered nearer the seat of empire.

During the struggles between the Britons and Saxons, and afterwards between Saxons and Saxons, till the Heptarchy was finally established, the Hebrew strangers remained unnoticed; but when Christianity was introduced, and monks and priests obtained supreme ecclesiastical authority, decrees were issued as early as 740 by Egbert, archbishop of York, and again in 833 by the monks of Croyland, prohibiting Christians from appearing at Jewish feasts. From these decrees we infer that the Jews must have become both numerous and influential, and their feasts and ceremonies attractive to the people, who in the early stages of Catholicism might have found a puzzling similarity in the outward ceremonies of the two religions—gorgeousness and splendor being at that time characteristic of the rites of both. The distinctions of actual creed were too subtle and too carefully made the study of churchmen alone to be understood or cared for by the multitude, and the priests must have feared some danger to their new and simple-minded converts from a too close intimacy with the Hebrews, or these prohibitions need not have been made.

No further allusion being made to the Jews during the monarchy, the decrees of the priests were probably obeyed, and no excuse given for persecution. When Canute of Denmark conquered England, however, the Jews shared the servitude of their Saxon brethren; and in 1020, without any assigned cause but the will of the sovereign, were banished from the kingdom. They crossed the Channel, and took refuge in the dominions of William, Duke of Normandy, where they were so kindly received that, on his conquest of England and assumption of her crown [in 1056-1087], they returned, increased in numbers, to their old homes, and purchased from William the right of settlement in the island.

The sons of the Conqueror pursued their father's kindly policy towards them. Under William Rufus [1087-1100] they established themselves in London and Oxford, erecting in the latter town three halls or colleges—Lombard Hall, Moses Hall, and Jacob Hall—where they instructed young men of either persuasion in the Hebrew language and the sciences. Until this reign the only burial-ground allowed them in all England was St. Giles, Cripplegate, where Jewen Street now stands; but under Rufus they obtained a place of interment also at Oxford, now the site of part of Magdalen College.[1] Indeed Rufus, from what is narrated to us by the chroniclers, would appear to have respected the feelings of the Jews more than those of the Christian portion of his subjects. "He appointed," says Milman, "a public debate in London between the two parties, and swore, by the face of St. Luke, that if the rabbins defeated the bishops, he would turn Jew himself. He received at Rouen the complaint of certain Jews, that their children had been seduced to the profession of Christianity. Their petition was supported by a liberal offer of money. One Stephen offered sixty marks for his son's restoration to Judaism, but the son had the courage to resist the imperious monarch. Rufus gave still deeper offence by farming to the Jews the vacant bishoprics."[2]

During this breathing-time from persecution their opulence naturally increased, and with it their unpopularity. The civil wars

1 place of interment: a burial-ground.

2 Henry Hart Milman (Dean of St. Paul's), *The History of the Jews*, 3 vols. (London: John Murray, 1829).

between Matilda and Stephen [1135-1154] had drained the royal coffers; money became more and more imperatively needed; and, following the example of the continental nations, charges the most false, but from their very horror and improbability eagerly credited by the ignorant populace, were promulgated against the Jews, and immense sums extorted from them to purchase remission from suffering and exile. Those who refused acceptance of the royal terms were mercilessly banished, and their estates and other possessions confiscated to the crown.

During the reigns of Stephen and Henry II [reigned 1154-1189], these persecutions continued with little intermission, yet still they remained industrious and uncomplaining, eager on every occasion to testify their loyalty and allegiance.

In the last year of Henry II's reign (1188), a parliament was convened at Northampton to raise supplies for an expedition to the Holy Land. The whole Christian population were assessed at £70,000, while the Jews alone, in numbers but a very small fraction of the king's native subjects, were burdened with a tax of £60,000; £3330 having been during this one reign already tortured from them. The abandonment of the project, followed as it was by the king's death, prevented this illegal extortion; and it was perhaps from joy at this unexpected relief that the Hebrews thronged in crowds to Westminster to witness the coronation of Richard, sumptuously attired, and bearing rich offerings, to testify their eager desire to conciliate the king.

This, however, was not permitted. The nobles and populace—whose strongest link of union in those days was jealous hatred of a people whose only crime was wealth—resolved on their exclusion. The presence of such ill-omened sorcerers at the coronation, it was declared, would blight every hope of prosperity for the reign, and commands were peremptorily issued that no Jews should be admitted to witness the ceremony. Some few individuals dared the danger of discovery, and made their way within the church. Their boldness was fatal; and not to themselves alone. Insulted and maltreated almost to death, they were dragged from the church, and the signal given for universal outrage. The populace spread through every Jewish quarter, pillaging without pause, setting even the royal commands at defiance; for avarice and hatred had obtained sole obsession of their hearts. For a day and a night these awful scenes continued in London, and not a Jewish dwelling in the city escaped. England was at that time thronged with friars preaching the Crusade; and, as had previously been the case on the continent, they urged the sacrifice of the unbelieving Jews as a fit commencement for their holy expedition. The example of London was held forth as an exhibition of praiseworthy enthusiasm; and at Edmondsbury, Norwich, and Stamford the same scenes of blood and outrage were enacted. At Lincoln the miserable Hebrews obtained protection from the governor. At York, after a vain attempt to check the popular fury, a great number retreated to the castle with their most valuable effects. Those not fortunate or expeditious enough to reach the temporary shelter were all put to the sword, neither age nor sex spared, their riches appropriated, and their dwellings burnt to the ground.

For a short time the castle appeared to promise a secure retreat, but gradually the suspicion spread that the governor was secretly negotiating for their surrender, the price of his treachery being a large portion of their wealth. Whether this suspicion were correct or not was never ascertained, but it worked so strongly on the minds of the Jews, that they seized the first occasion of the governor's absence from the castle, on a visit to the town, to close the gates against him. They then themselves manned the ramparts, and awaited a siege. It happened that the sheriff of the county (without whose permission no measures to recover the castle could be taken) was passing through York with an armed force; the incensed governor instantly applied to him and demanded the aid of his men. Recollecting the king's attempt to keep peace between his Christian and Jewish subjects in London, the sheriff at first hesitated but, urged on by the indignant representations of the governor, he at length permitted the assault.

The frantic fury with which the shouting rabble rushed to the attack, the horrid nature of the scenes which he knew must inevitably ensue, caused him, even at that moment, to revoke the order; but it was too late. License once given, the passions of the surging multitude could not be assuaged. The clergy fanned them into yet hotter flame, by encouraging their mad fury as holy zeal, promising salvation to all who shed the blood of a Jew; and themselves, in strange contradiction to the professions signified by the garbs they wore, joining in the affray, and often heading the attack. The unshrinking courage, the noble self-denial and heroic endurance of the hapless Hebrews, could little avail them against the wild excitement and immense multitude of their assailants; yet still they resisted with vigour. Accused as they were of never handling the weapons or experiencing emotions of the warrior, it was now shown that circumstances and not character were at fault. The spirit of true heroism peculiar to their race in the olden time might indeed *appear* crushed and lost beneath the heavy fetters of oppression, but it burned still, ready to burst into life and energy whenever occasion demanded its display.[1]

Notwithstanding the bold defence of the besieged, resistance was too soon seen to be hopeless, and in stern unbending resolution they assembled in the council-room. Their rabbi (a Hebrew word signifying chief or elder), a man of great learning and eminent virtue, rose up, and with mournful dignity thus addressed them: — "Men of Israel, the God of our ancestors is omniscient, and there is no one who can say, 'What doest thou?' This day he commands us to die for his law — that law which we have preserved pure throughout our captivity in all nations, and for which, for the many consolations it has given us, and the belief in eternal life which it communicates, can we do less than die? Posterity shall behold its solemn truths sealed with our blood; and our death, while it confirms our sincerity, shall impart strength to the wanderers of Israel. Death is before our eyes; we have only to choose an easy and an honourable one. If we fall into the hands of our enemies, which fate you know we can not elude, our death will be ignominious and cruel; for these Christians who picture the Spirit of God in a dove, and confide to the meek Jesus, are athirst for our blood, and prowl like wolves around us. Let us escape their tortures, and surrender, as our ancestors have done before us, our lives with our own hands to our Creator. God seems to call for us; let us not be unworthy of that call."

It was a fearful counsel, and the venerable elder himself wept as he ceased to speak; but by far the greater number declared that he had

---

1 Here Aguilar attempts to refute the idea, commonly espoused during the period, that in ancient times Jews were powerful and sublime, but since their dispersion from Israel in 70 C.E. they have become abjectly powerless and morally degraded.

spoken well, and they would abide by his words. The few that hesitated were desired by their chief; if they approved not of his counsel, to depart in peace; and some obeyed. It was night ere the council closed, and during the hours of darkness not a sound betrayed the awful proceedings within the castle to the besiegers. At dawn the multitudes furiously renewed the attack, falling back appalled for the minute by the sight of flames bursting from all parts of the citadel. A few miserable objects rushing to and fro on the battlements also became visible, with wild cries intreating mercy for themselves, imploring baptism rather than death, and relating with groans and lamentations the fate of their companions. The men had all slain their wives and children, and then fallen by each others' hands, the most distinguished receiving the sad honour of death from the sword of their old chief, who was the last to die. Their precious effects were burnt or buried, according as they were combustible or not; so that, when the gates were flung open, and the rabble rushed in eager to appropriate the wealth which they believed awaited them, they found nothing but heaps of ashes. Maddened with disappointment, all pledges of safety to the survivors, if the gates were opened, were forgotten, and every human being that remained was tortured and slain. Five hundred had already fallen by their own hands, and these voluntary martyrs were mostly men forced by persecution into such mean and servile occupations as to appear incapable of a lofty thought or heroic deed.

No punishment followed the atrocious proceedings at York. The laws of England never interfered in behalf of the king's Jewish subjects, though they would have been somewhat rigidly obeyed had the sufferers been the offenders. On King Richard's return from captivity, the Hebrews were under certain statute, acknowledged as the exclusive property of the crown. John commenced his reign with a semblance of extreme lenity towards them. The privileges formerly granted to them by Henry I [1100–1135] were confirmed. They might settle in any part of England, instead of being confined to certain quarters of certain towns; hold lands, and receive mortgages. Their evidence might be taken in courts of justice. All English subjects were commanded to protect their persons and possessions as they would the especial property of the king. Other laws equally lenient were issued; and, misled by such favourable appearances, many of the Continental Hebrews flocked to England. This increase of Jewish population of course materially increased Jewish wealth; the hatred of the people was anew excited, and several indignities were perpetrated against the Jews. The king wrote a rebuke to the perpetrators; and then, at the very time that Jews were rejoicing at this undeniable proof of his sincerity, and their own security, completely changed his policy, and from the extreme of lenity proceeded to the extreme of rigour. He had, in fact, only favoured them to multiply their wealth, and then revelled in its seizure; glad that there were now some possessions he could appropriate without any interference from the pope. The unhappy Israelites were imprisoned, tortured, murdered, and their treasures all confiscated to the crown. A Jew of Bristol having refused to betray his hoards, was condemned to have a tooth pulled out every day until he should yield. The man suffered seven of his teeth to be extracted before he complied: the king gained 10,000 marks by his cruel device. In the war between John [reigned 1199-1216] and his barons they were persecuted by both parties—by the king for their wealth; by the barons, because, they were vassals of the king. Even the stern and noble assertors of liberty, the heroes of the Magna Charta, seeking justice and freedom for all classes of Englishmen, had no pity for the wretched Jews; seizing their possessions, and demolishing their homes, to repair the walls of London, which had been injured in the civil war.[1]

The guardians of England during the reign of Henry III [reigned 1216-1272] sought in some degree to meliorate the condition of the Jews. Twenty-four burgesses of every town, where they resided, were appointed to protect their persons and property; but the protection even of royalty could avail little when every class of men conspired to detest and oppress them. The merchants were jealous of the privileges permitting the Jews to buy and sell. The people hated them, from the idle tales of horrible crimes attributed to them, which had no foundation whatever in truth, but which ignorance and prejudice not only believed, but so magnified and multiplied as to cause them

---

1 Magna Charta: The closest thing to a written English constitution, the Magna Carta was a guarantee of basic liberties granted under pressure of rebellion by King John in 1215. Many phrases in the American Constitution and Bill of Rights can be traced to the Magna Carta.

to be inseparably associated with the word Jew. The clergy—men who, both professors and preachers of a religion of peace, should have been the first to protect the injured, and calm the turbulent passions of the populace—were the constant incitors to persecution and cruelty, believing, by a most extraordinary hallucination, that to maltreat the Jew was the surest evidence of Christian zeal.

The guardians of the young king had, however, so guided him, that for a brief interval after attaining his majority, the royal protection shielded the Jews in some measure from popular oppression. But this was only until the king's coffers became impoverished: when these were empty, the only means of refilling them was to follow the example of his predecessors, and by fair means or foul, extort money from the Jews. In this reign alone, the enormous sum of 170,000 marks was, under various pretences and various cruelties, wrung from them; and when all other means of extortion seemed exhausted, all extraordinary spectacle was displayed in the convention of a Jewish parliament. The sheriffs of the different towns had orders to return six of the wealthiest and most influential Jews from the larger cities, and two from the smaller. In those times almost the only function of a parliament was to *vote supplies*; this Jewish parliament, therefore, in being informed by the sovereign that he must have 20,000 marks from the Jews of England, served for the Jewish part of the population pretty nearly the same purpose as the ordinary parliament served for the rest of the community. The assembled members were probably left to decide the amount of assessment which the various ranks of Jews should pay, so as to make up the total sum required; and as this right of proportioning the assessment was generally the only right exercised by ancient parliaments, properly so called, the particular hardship of the Jews, as compared with their fellow-subjects, consisted not in having no liberty of refusal—for that is a liberty which only modern parliaments have acquired—but in the enormous sum demanded from them, and in the rigours which they knew would be employed to enforce its speedy collection. Assembled, and made aware of the demand which was made upon them, the unfortunate Jewish representatives were dismissed to collect the money from their own resources as speedily as possible; and because it was not forthcoming as quickly as was requisite for the royal necessities, all their possessions were seized, and their families imprisoned.

Believing, at length, that their wealth must be exhausted by such demands, or weary of the trouble of extortion, Henry consummated his acts of oppression by actually selling his Jewish subjects, their persons and effects, to his brother Richard, Earl of Cornwall, for 5000 marks. The records of this disgraceful bargain are still preserved; and that the king had power to conclude it, marks the oppressed and fearful position of this hapless people more emphatically than any lengthened narrative. Yet the barbarity of the sovereign met with universal approbation; the wretchedness of the victims with neither sympathy nor commiseration.

On the election of Richard of Cornwall as king of the Romans, the Jews became again the property of the Crown, and were again sold by Henry. This time their purchaser was the heir to the throne, Prince Edward, by whom they were sold, to still better advantage, to the merchants of Dauphine; and this traffic was actually the sale and purchase of human beings, in all respects like ourselves, gifted with immortal souls, intelligent minds and the tenderest affections. Husbands, fathers, sons, wives, mothers, innocent childhood, and helpless age. The sufferers were inoffensive and unobtrusive, seeking no vengeance, patient, and even cringing under all their injuries. Of all the crimes imputed to them, and some of these were of the most horrible nature, not one appears ever to have been really proved against them, except, perhaps, that of clipping the coin of the realm; and even on this point the evidence is not clear. And yet, had all the accusations against them been true, one could hardly have wondered, considering their treatment.

After the battle of Lewes, reports became current that the Hebrews at Northampton, Lincoln, and London had sided with the king against the barons.[1] This of course roused the latter in their turn to plunder and destroy; while Henry annulled his bargain with

1 The "battle of Lewes" took place in 1264, and was an important moment in the civil war between followers of Henry III and the barons, led by Simon de Monfort, whom the king desired to deprive of land and office. The barons defeated the king's forces at Lewes but were subsequently conquered by forces led by the king's son, Prince Edward.

his son, and for a while treated them with lenity. But again one of the usual excuses for persecution—insult offered by the Jews to some symbol reverenced by the Catholics—found voice, and not only were extortions renewed, but a solemn statute was passed, disqualifying the Jews from possessing any lands or even dwellings. They might not erect any new habitations, only repair their present homes, or rebuild on the same foundations.

All lands and manors already in their hands were violently wrested from them; and those held in mortgages returned to the owners without any interest on the bonds. All arrears of charges were demanded, and imprisonment threatened if payment were postponed.[1] An extortion apparently more oppressive than all the rest, as we find the distress it occasioned amongst the Jews actually moved the pity of their rivals, the Caorsini bankers, and of the friars, their deadliest foes.[2]

The death of Henry [in 1272] was so far a reprieve that the above-named extortion was suspended; but the accession of Edward I [reigned 1272-1307] only aggravated their social bondage. Laws as severe, if not more severe in some respects than those of previous sovereigns, were issued against them, followed by an act of parliament prohibiting all usury, and desiring the Jews to confine themselves to pursuits of traffic, manufactures, and agriculture; for which last, though they could not hold, they might hire farms for fifteen years. But how could men, debarred so long from similar positions, so debased by oppression, with minds so disabled, as to render it difficult for them to commence any new pursuit, obey so violent a decree? Had they received the fit education for traffic, manufactures, and agriculture *before* the laws commanding such employments were passed, there would have been many glad and eager to obey them; but, as it was, obedience was impossible. That usurers and Jews in the dark ages were synonymous, and that the Jews in their capacity of money-lenders did exhibit an extraordinary spirit of rapacity and extortion, cannot be denied. But although this spirit of money-

1 I.e., The Jews were required to pay immediately any extortionate taxes that had previously been demanded of them.

2 "Caorsini bankers": probably a reference to the Corsini family, distinguished merchants in thirteenth-century Florence who were among the English Jews' principal rivals in trade.

making, even by methods esteemed dishonourable, characterising, as it did, the Jews of the Roman empire, as well as those of Europe in the middle ages, must be referred partly to an inherent national bent; there can be no doubt that much of the meanness and criminality displayed by the Jews of the middle ages, in their quest of wealth, is attributable to the binding oppression which absolutely fettered them to that one pursuit. Even if there were times when a Shylock pressed for his pound of flesh, when it would have been nobler to show mercy, was it unnatural?[1] Can we expect oppression to create kindness—social cruelty to bring forth social love?

After eighteen years of persecution, little varied in its nature and its causes from the persecutions of previous reigns, the seal was set on Jewish misery by an edict of total expulsion, issued in 1290. All their property was seized except a very scanty supply, supposed sufficient to transport them to other lands. No reason was given for this barbarous proceeding. The charge previously brought against them of clipping and adulterating the coin of the realm, for which 280 had been executed in London alone was never fully proved; nor, as might naturally have been expected, had the charge been really true, was it made the cause of their expulsion. A people's unfounded hate, and a monarch's cruel pleasure, exposed 16,511 human beings to all the miseries of exile. There were very few countries which were not equally inhospitable; for edicts of expulsion had gone forth from many of the continental kingdoms. Even if they could find other homes, the confiscation of all their property before they left England exposed them to multiplied sufferings which no individual efforts could assuage; and the loss of life ever attendant on these wholesale expulsions is fearful. The greater number probably never lived to reach another shore; and to what retreats those who were more fortunate betook themselves, history does not say. From this date (1290), therefore, all trace of the English Jews, properly so called, is lost.

Their great synagogue, situated in Old Jewry, was seized by an

1 Cf. Shakespeare's *The Merchant of Venice*, in which Shylock, a Jewish moneylender, agrees to lend 3000 ducats to Antonio, a Christian "merchant of Venice," on condition that, if Antonio fails to repay the loan on time, Shylock will take a "pound of flesh" as repayment. The term "Shylock" was subsequently used as shorthand for the stereotype of the stingy, usurious, and unmerciful Jew.

order of friars, called Fratres de Sacra or De Pententia, who had not been long established in England. In 1305, Robert Fitzwalter, the greater banner-bearer of the city, and whose house it adjoined, requested, we are told by the old chroniclers, that it aught be assigned to him; a request no doubt complied with in return for a good round sum of money. During the fifteenth century it belonged to two or three successive mayors, and was ultimately degraded into a tavern, known by the sign of the Windmill. The locality of this early Jewish house of worship, however, still retains its name and associations as Old Jewry.

Their valuable libraries at Stamford and Oxford were appropriated by the neighbouring monasteries. From that at Oxford, fifty years previous to their expulsion, Roger Bacon is said to have derived much of that chemical and astronomical information which enabled him to startle the age in which he lived by the boldness and novelty of his views.[1] The Babylonian Talmud, a series of gigantic tomes, of which, [along with] lesser works compiled from them, the Jewish libraries were composed, contained elaborate treatises on the various sciences which occupied the attention of the learned in the middle ages; including of course magic and astrology; and as it was to the Franciscan convent at Oxford, by which the Hebrew library had been appropriated, that Roger Bacon retreated on his return to England from Paris, it is by no means improbable that he may have been indebted to the Hebrew books thus placed within his reach.

From the year 1290 to 1655 the shores of Great Britain were closed against the Jews. No attempt ever appears to have been made on their part to revoke the order of expulsion. Oppression, perhaps, had left too blackened traces on their memories for England to be regarded with that strong feeling of local attachment which bound them, even after expulsion [in 1492], so closely to Portugal and Spain. In France they were once and again recalled after being expelled. In the German and Italian states they were constantly persecuted and murdered by thousands, but never cast forth from the soil. In Spain and Portugal they had always held the highest offices, not only in the schools, but in the state and the camp; nay, royalty

---

1 Roger Bacon (1220–ca. 1292): medieval proponent of experimental science, the first European to describe the process of making gunpowder.

itself, in more than one instance, was closely connected with Jewish blood. Oppressive exactments and degrading distinctions were frequently made, but never interfered with the positions of trust and dignity which the larger portion of the nation enjoyed; so that when the edict of their universal expulsion from the peninsula came in 1492, there was no galling remembrance of debasing misery to conquer the love of fatherland, so fondly fostered in every human heart. Notwithstanding the danger from the constant dread of death, if discovered, secret Jews peopled the most Catholic kingdoms of Portugal and Spain. The extraordinary skill and ingenuity with which these Spanish and Portuguese Jews preserved their secret, and their numerous expedients for the strictest adherence to their ancient religion under the semblance of most orthodox Catholicism, constitute a romance in history.[1] If ever exposed to the suspicion of the Inquisition, however, the love of land was sacrificed to security; the suspected individuals taking refuge either in Holland, or in some of the newly-discovered East and West India Islands, and there making public profession of their ancient faith.

Joseph Ben Israel was one of these fugitives. He was a Portuguese Jew, and a resident of Lisbon. Suspicion of secretly following Judaism having fallen upon him, he was twice incarcerated by the Inquisition, and twice released, from the impossibility of proving the charge against him. When confined within those dangerous precincts a third time, he would not wait another examination, but succeeded in scaling the walls of his prison, and secretly flying from Portugal bearing with him his young son Menasseh. At Amsterdam, where Ben Israel settled, both father and son received the peculiar covenant of their faith, and publicly avowed and confessed it. In the Jewish college of that city Menasseh Ben Israel received his education; and so remarkable was his progress in the difficult studies of the Hebrew Accolyte, that when only seventeen he exceeded his master, Isaac Uzieli, as preacher in the synagogue and expounder of the Talmud, and commenced the then difficult task of arranging and amplifying the scanty rules of the Hebrew language in the form of a grammar—a work obtaining him much fame; not only from the extreme

---

1 For an example of such romances, see Aguilar's *Records of Israel*, including "The Escape," reprinted in this volume.

youth of the writer, but also for the assistance it rendered to the learned men of all countries in the attaining of a language so little known, yet so much valued. The grammar was speedily followed by numerous other works, written both in Spanish and Latin. Their subject is mostly theology; but Ben Israel's own learning was not confined to sacred subjects alone. Well versed in Hebrew, Greek, Arabic, Latin, Spanish, and Portuguese, he not only wrote these languages with ease and fluency, but was well acquainted with the literature of each, and had thus, by extensive culture and thought on a great variety of subjects, acquired larger views and sentiments than were possessed by the generality of his race.

The confiscation of all his paternal property at Lisbon compelled him to resort to commerce—an interruption to his literary pursuits which he would have gladly eluded; but, already a husband and a father, he met the necessity cheerfully, and soon became as influential and as highly respected in commercial affairs as in literature; in which, notwithstanding the many and pressing calls of business, he never allowed his labours to relax. After the marriage of his daughter, he visited, partly for pleasure and partly on business, the Brazils, where his brother-in-law and partner resided. It was a very unusual thing in those days for any Hebrew to travel: the minute and numerous ordinances of the Talmud interfering too closely with daily life, and rendering it difficult to obey them anywhere save in cities, where there were communities of Jews.

But Menasseh Ben Israel, while he gloried in being inwardly a follower of the Hebrew faith, had a mind capable of distinguishing between the form and the spirit.[1] The death of his eldest son, a youth of great promise, occurred soon after his return from Brazil, and caused him such intense grief, as, according to his own acknowledgement, to render him incapable of the least mental exertion. His only comfort and resource was the perusal of that Holy Book which had been the origin and end of all his studies. It did not fail him in his grief; and after some severe struggles, energy returned.

His literary fame had procured him the intimacy and friendship of the most eminent and learned men throughout Europe. Amongst

---

1 For an extended discussion of the form/spirit distinction, see the selections from *The Spirit of Judaism*, above.

these was John Thurloe, who, in the year 1651, had gone to the Hague as secretary to St. John and Strickland, ambassadors from England to the States of the United Provinces.[1] During his stay in Holland he became acquainted with Ben Israel, and with his earnest but then apparently fruitless wishes for the readmission of his nation into England. In 1653, Thurloe became secretary of state to Cromwell; and, discovering the enlarged and liberal ideas which the Protector individually entertained, he ventured, on his own responsibility, to invite Menasseh Ben Israel to the court of England, and introduced him to Cromwell in 1655. The independence, the amiable qualities and the great learning of the Jewish stranger, obtained Cromwell's undisguised friendship and regard. Three hundred and sixty-five years had elapsed since a Jew had stood on British ground; and during that interval many changes and improvements, national and social had taken place. The Reformation had freed England from the galling fetters of ignorance and superstition which must ever attend the general suppression of the word of truth. Increase of toleration towards the Jews was already visible in those parts of the continent which were under Protestant jurisdiction; and it was therefore extremely natural in Menasseh Ben Israel to regard England as one of those favourite countries of Providence, where his brethren might enjoy security and rest.

Whether or not a formal act of readmission was passed during the Protectorship, is to this day a question. On the 4th of December 1655 a council was held at Whitehall, composed of the Lord Chief-Justice Glynn, Lord-Chief Baron Steele; the Lord mayor and sheriffs of London, and sundry merchants and divines, to consider the proposals of Menasseh Ben Israel, which may be condensed into the following:—1. That the Hebrew nation should be received and admitted into the commonwealth under the express protection of his highness, who was intreated to command all generals and heads of armies, under oath, to defend them as his other English subjects on all occasions. 2. That public synagogues, and the proper observance

1 John Thurloe (1616-1668), here the secretary to the Parliamentary leader Oliver St. John, later became the secretary of state during Oliver Cromwell's protectorate. The Hague: one of the principal cities in Holland, a country which was at this time uniquely tolerant of Jews. The Jewish philosopher Baruch Spinoza, whose philosophy sparked the radical Enlightenment throughout Europe, lived in seventeenth-century Amsterdam.

of their religion, should be allowed the Jews, not only in England, but in all countries under English jurisdiction. 3. That a cemetery, or grave-yard out of the town should be allowed them, without hindrance from any. 4. That they should be permitted to merchandise as others. 5. That a person of quality should be appointed to receive the passports of all foreign Jews who might land in England, and oblige them by oath to maintain fealty to the commonwealth. 6. That license should be granted to the heads of the synagogue, with the assistance of officers from their own nation, to judge and determine all differences according to Mosaic law, with liberty to appeal thence to the civil judges of the land. 7. That in case there should be any laws against the nation still existing, they should, in the first place, and before all things, be revoked, that by such means the Jews might remain in greater security under the safeguard and protection of his serene highness.

The council met again on the 7th, 12th, and 14th of December, on the last of which days, according to some authorities, the laws were formally admitted; but, according to others, the council reassembled on the 18th and dissolved without either adjournment or decision, the judges only declaring that there was *no* law prohibiting the return of the Jews. Burton, in his History of Oliver Cromwell, relates that the divines were divided in opinion; but on some asserting that the Scriptures promised their conversion, the Protector replied, "that if there were such promise, means must be taken to accomplish it, which is the preaching of the gospel; and that cannot be had, unless they were admitted where the gospel was publicly preached."[1]

Thomas Violet, a goldsmith, drew up a petition in 1660 to Charles II and his parliament, intreating that the Jews might be expelled from England, and their property confiscated and in this petition he asserts that, in consequence of the decided disapproval of the clergy in the celebrated council of 1655, the proposal for their readmission had been totally laid aside. Bishop Burnet, in his "History of his own Times," refutes this assertion, and declares that, after attentively hearing the debates, Cromwell and his council freely

1 Thomas Burton, *Diary of Thomas Burton, Esq. member in the Parliaments of Oliver and Richard Cromwell, from 1656 to 1659*, ed. John Towill Rutt, 4 vols. (London: Henry Colburn, 1828).

granted Ben Israel's requests;[1] and this appears really to have been the case, for the very next year, 1656, a synagogue for the Spanish and Portuguese Jews erected in King's Street, Duke's Place, and a burial-ground at Mile End, now the site of the hospital for the same congregation, taken on a lease for nine hundred and ninety-nine years.

Leaving the question, then, as to whether or not an act of readmission really passed, it is evident that the deed of toleration, granted from the Protector individually, did as much for the real interests of the Jews as any formal parliamentary enactment. From that time the Jewish nation have found a secure and peaceful home, not in England alone, but in all the British possessions. We shall perceive, as we proceed, that prejudice was still often and violently at work against them; but though it embittered their social position, it did not interfere with their personal security, or prevent the public observance of their faith.

The pen of Menasseh Ben Israel had not been idle during this period of solicitation and suspense. Under the title of "Vindiciae Judaeorum" ("Defense of the Jews"), he published a work in which he ably and fully refuted the infamous charges which in darker ages had been levelled against his brethren.[2] He had received, too, his degree as physician; and thus united the industry and information requisite for three professions—literature, commerce, and medicine. "He was a man," we are told, "without passion, without levity, and without opulence." Preserving and independent, full of kindly affection, and susceptible of strong emotion, with all the loftiness of the Spanish character, tempered, however, with qualities which gained for him the regard of the best and most learned men of his age. He did not continue in England—though it has been said he was solicited to do so by Cromwell—but rejoined his brother at Middleburg in Zealand, where he died in the year 1657.

The reign of Charles II [reigned 1660-85] beheld the Jews frequently attacked and seriously annoyed by popular prejudice; but

1 Gilbert Burnet, the Bishop of Salisbury during the rise and fall of Cromwell, published the multivolume work *A History of His Own Time* in 1724. Aguilar probably refers to a new edition published in London in 1838.

1 Menasseh Ben Israel, *Vindiciæ Judæorum* (London: 1656). The author of the quotation that follows is unknown.

their actual position as British subjects remained undisturbed. Thomas Violet's petition we have already noticed; but its vindictive spirit did harm only to its originator. Four years afterward, the security of their persons and property being threatened, they appealed to the king, who declared in council, that as long as they demeaned themselves peaceably, and with submission to the laws, they should continue to receive the same favours as formerly. At Surinam, the following year, the British government, by proclamation, confirmed all their privileges, guaranteed the full enjoyment and free exercise of their religion, rites, and ceremonies; adding, that any summons issued against them on their Sabbaths and holidays should be null and void; and that, except on urgent occasions, they should not be called upon for any public duties on those days. That civil cases should be decided by their elders, and that they might bequeath their property according to their own law of inheritance. All foreign Jews settling there were recognised as British-born subjects and included in the above-enumerated privileges. As a proof how strongly the affections of the Hebrews were engaged towards England by this exhibition of tolerance, we may mention that when Surinam was conquered by, and finally ceded to the Dutch, although their privileges were all confirmed by the conquerors, they gave up their homes, synagogues, and land; and braved all the discomforts of removal, and settled in Jamaica and other English colonies, rather than live under a government hostile to Great Britain.[1]

In 1673 we find prejudice again busy, in an indictment, charging the Jews with unlawful meeting for public worship. They again unhesitatingly appealed to the king, petitioning that, during their stay in England, they might be unmolested, or that time might be allowed them to withdraw from the country. Charles, pursuing his previous policy, peremptorily commanded that all proceedings against them should cease; and during the remainder of his reign no further molestation occurred.

On the accession of James II [reigned 1685-88] old prejudices

---

1 Aguilar's note: "Surinam, or Dutch Guiana, situated on the northeastern coast of South America, is still peopled with Jews; but they are emigrants from the Dutch possessions in Europe, not descendants of the former Anglo-Jewish settlers." The Jewish settlers in Surinam were often wealthy plantation owners.

were renewed, and thirty-seven Jewish merchants were arrested on the Exchange for no crime or fault, but simply from their non-attendance on any church. Certain writs in statute 23 of Elizabeth, instituted, probably, to suppress innovations in Protestantism, were the pretext for this aggression. James, as his brother had done, befriended the Jews; and summoning a council composed of the highest dignitaries of his realm, both church and laymen, declared "that they should not be troubled on this account, but should quietly enjoy the free exercise of their religion as they behaved themselves dutifully and obediently to the government."

The foregoing was the last public annoyance to which they were subjected in England. In 1690, indeed, a petition was sent to King William III [reigned 1689-1702] from the council of Jamaica, that all Jews, should be made to quit the island; but it was positively refused. And we infer that King William's sentiments towards the Israelites must have been even more favourable than those of his predecessors, from the circumstance that a great increase of Jews took place in England during his reign. Until this reign, one synagogue had sufficed; the service and laws of which were conducted according to the principles of the Spanish Jews. In 1692 the first German synagogue was erected in Broad Court, Duke's Place; and from that time two distinct bodies of Jews, known as Spanish and Portuguese, German and Dutch, have been naturalised in England.[1] No new privileges were granted them, however, during the reigns of either William or Anne [reigned 1702-1714].

It is not till the ninth year of George I, 1723, [reigned 1714-1727] that we can discover a parliamentary acknowledgment of their being British subjects; granting them a privilege, which, in the present age, it would appear meagre enough, but which, at the time of its bestowal, marked a very decided advance in popular enlightenment. "Whenever any of his *majesty's subjects*, professing the *Jewish religion*, shall present themselves to take the oath of Adjuration, the words on *the faith of a Christian* shall be omitted out of the said oath; and the taking of it by such persons professing the Jewish religion without

1 The Spanish and Portuguese Jews are known as *Sephardim*, the German, Dutch, and Polish as *Ashkenazim*. During this period, the *Sephardim* and *Ashkenazim* functioned as entirely separate communities.

the words aforesaid, in the Manner as Jews are admitted to be sworn to give evidence in the courts of justice, shall be deemed a sufficient taking."[1]

In the reign of George II [1727-1760], 1740, another act of parliament passed, recognising all Jews who resided in the American colonies, or had served as mariners during the war two years in British ships, as "natural born subjects, without taking the sacrament." Thirteen years afterwards, the naturalisation bill passed, but was repealed the year following, according to the petitions of the city of London, and other English towns. Since then the Jews have gradually gained ground in social consideration; but all attempts to place them on an exact equality with other British subjects of all religious denominations by removing the disabilities which the more fondly they cling to the land of their adoption, the more heavily oppress them, have as of yet been unavailing.

By the multitudes, the Jews are still considered aliens and foreigners; supposed to be separated by an antiquated creed and peculiar customs from sympathy and fellowship—little known and still less understood. Yet they are, in fact, Jews only in their religion—Englishmen in everything else. In point of fact, therefore, the disabilities under which the Jews of Great Britain labour are the last relic of religious intolerance. That which they chiefly complain of is, being subjected to take an oath contrary to their religious feelings when appointed to certain offices. In being called to the bar, this oath, as a matter of courtesy, is not pressed, and a periodical act of indemnity shelters the delinquent. Jews, therefore, now practise at the bar, but only by sufferance. The same indulgence has not been extended to entering parliament, and consequently no Jew is practically eligible as a member of the House of Commons. Is it not discreditable to the common sense of the age that such anomalies should exist in reference to this well-disposed and, in every respect, naturalised portion of the community?

---

1 The Oath of Abjuration, which asked subjects to swear non-allegiance to the Stuarts and their descendants "on the true faith of a Christian," was a necessity for joining Parliament. These words were not finally removed from the Oath until 1858. See Salbstein.

Social Arrangements of the English Jews

In externals, and in all secular thoughts and actions, the English naturalised Jew is, as already mentioned, an Englishman, and his family is reared with the education and accomplishments of other members of the community. Only in some private and personal characteristics and in religious belief, does the Jew differ from his neighbours. Many of the British Jews are descended from families who resided some time in Spain; others trace their origin to families from Germany. There have always been some well-defined differences in the appearance, the language, and the manners of these two classes. The Spanish Hebrews had occupied so high a position in Spain and Portugal, that even in their compulsory exile their peculiarly high and honourable principles, their hatred of all meanness, either in thought or act, their wealth, their exclusiveness, and strong attachment to each other, caused their community to resemble a little knot of Spanish princes, rather than the cowed and bending bargain-seeking individuals usually known as Jews.

The constant and enslaving persecution of the German Hebrews had naturally enough produced on their characters a very different effect. Nothing degrades the moral character more effectually than debasing treatment. To regard an individual as incapable of honour, charity, and truth, as always seeking to gratify personal interest, is more than likely to make him such. Confined to degrading employment, with minds narrowed, as the natural consequence—allowed no other pursuit than that usury, with its minor branches, pawnbroking and old clothes selling—it was not very strange, that when the German Hebrews did make their way into England, and were compelled, for actual subsistence, still to follow these occupations, that their brethren from Spain should keep aloof, and shrink from all connexion with them. Time, however, looks on many curious changes: not only are the mutual prejudices of the Jews subsiding, but the position of the two parties is transposed. The Germans, making good use of peace and freedom, have advanced, not in wealth alone (for that even when oppressed, they contrived to possess), but in enlightenment, influence, and respectability. Time, and closer connexions with the Spanish Jews, will no doubt produce still further improvements.

These distinguishing characteristics, which we have just pointed out, belong, with some modifications, to the poor as well as the rich of these two Jewish sects. The faults of the poor Spanish and Portuguese Jews are so exactly similar to those of the lower orders of the native Spaniards, that they can easily be traced to their long naturalisation in that country. Pride is their predominant and most unhappy failing, for it not only prevents their advancing themselves, either socially or mentally, but renders powerless every effort made for their improvement. The Germans, more willing to work, and push forward their own fortunes, and less scrupulous as to the means they employ, are more successful as citizens, and as a class are less difficult to guide. Both parties would be improved by the interchange of qualities. And comparing the present with the past, there is some reason to believe that this union will be effected on British ground, and that the idle distinctions of Spanish and Portuguese, Dutch and German, will be lost and consolidated in the proud designation of British Jews.

The domestic manners of both the German and the Spanish Jews in Great Britain, are so exactly similar to those of their British brethren, that were it not for the observance of the seventh day instead of the first, the prohibition of certain meats, and the celebration of certain solemn festivals and rites, it would be difficult to distinguish a Jewish from a native household. The characteristics so often assigned to them in tales professing to introduce a Jew or a Jewish family, are almost all incorrect, being drawn either from the impressions of the past, or from some special case, or perhaps from attention to some Pole, Spaniard, or Turk, who may just as well be a Polish or Spanish Christian, or Turkish Mussulman, as a Jew.[1] These great errors in delineation arise from the supposition, that because they are Hebrews they must be different from any other race. They *are* distinct in feature and religion, but in nothing else. Like the rest of the human race, they are, as individuals, neither wholly good nor wholly bad; as a people, their virtues very greatly predominate. Even in the lowest and most degraded classes, we never find those awful crimes with which the public records teem. A Jewish murderer, adulterer, burglar, or even petty thief is actually unknown. This may

1 Mussulman: a Muslim.

perhaps arise from the fact, that the numerous and well-ordered charities of the Jews prevent those horrible cases of destitution, and the consequent temptations to sin, from which such a mass of crime proceeds. A Jewish beggar by profession is a character unheard of; nor do we ever find the blind or deformed belonging to this people lingering about the streets. The virtues of the Jews are essentially of the domestic and social kind. The English are noted for the comfort and happiness of their firesides, and in this loveliest school of virtue, the Hebrews not only equal, but in some instances surpass, their neighbours. From the highest classes to the most indigent, affection, reverence, and tenderness mark their domestic intercourse. Three, sometimes four generations, may be found dwelling together—the woman performing the blended duties of parent, wife, and child; the man those of husband, father, and son. As members of a community, they are industrious, orderly, temperate, and contented; as citizens, they are faithful, earnest, and active; as the native denizens of Great Britain, ever ready to devote their wealth and personal services in the cause of their adopted land.

Both the Spanish and German congregations have their respective charities, either founded by benevolent individuals, or supported by voluntary contributions and annual subscriptions. There are schools for poor children of both sexes and all ages, from the infant too young to walk, to the youth or maiden ready for apprenticeship; orphan asylums and orphan societies for clothing, educating, maintaining, and apprenticing both male and female orphans; hospitals for the sick, comprising also establishments for lying-in women, and an asylum for the aged; societies, far too numerous to specify by name, for clothing the poor; for relieving by donations of meat, bread, and coals; for cheering the needy at festivals; for visiting and relieving women, when confined, at their own dwellings, and enabling them to adhere to the rites of their religion in naming infants; for allowing the indigent blind a certain sum weekly which they forfeit if ever seen begging about the streets; granting loans to the industrious poor, or gifts if needed; for outfitting boys who are to quit the country, and granting rewards for good behaviour to servants and apprentices; for furnishing persons to sit up with the sick poor, and granting a certain sum for the maintenance of poor families during the seven days' mourning for the dead, a period by the Jews always kept sacred;

for relieving distressed aliens of the Jewish persuasion; and, amongst the Portuguese, for granting marriage-portions, twice in the year, to one or more fatherless girls, and for giving pensions to widows. There are also almshouses for twenty-four poor women annexed to the Spanish and Portuguese synagogue, and others in Globe Lane for ten respectable poor families of the same congregation; and not many years ago, a philanthropic individual (A. L. Moses, Esq. of Aldgate) erected almshouses for twelve poor families of the German congregation, with a synagogue attached, in Bethnal Green Road, at his own sole expense.

When we remember how small is the number of Jewish denizens in the great city of London, compared with its Christian population, and observe the variety and number of these charities, we are surely borne out in our assertion, that benevolence is a very marked characteristic of the Jews. Nor is it a virtue confined to the rich. Beautiful is that charity which is shown by the poor to the poor, and it is in this that the Jews excel. To relieve the needy, and open the hand wide to their poor brother, is a repeatedly enforced command of their religion, which they literally and lovingly obey. On the eve of their great festival, the Passover, the door of the poorest dwelling may be found open, an extra plate, knife, and fork laid on the frugal table; and whoever needs food, or even lodging, for that holy festival, may freely enter and appropriate to himself the reserved seat. That he may be quite a stranger is of little consequence; he is a Hebrew, and needy, and is therefore welcome to the same fare as the family themselves partake.

Nor are these charities confined only to their own race; they never refuse assistance, according to their means, whatever may be the creed. Neither prejudiced nor penurious in calls of philanthropy, their heart is open as their hand; and if they amass gold too eagerly, the fault is in some degree atoned by the use to which it is applied. Nor can it be doubted that as time rolls and even the remembrance of persecution is lost in the peace and freedom which will be secured them, the mind as well as the heart will be enlarged; and that while they shall still retain their energy and skill on the Exchange and in the mart, literature and art will enliven and dignify their hours at home. We may mention as a hopeful symptom the recent establishment of the "Jews' and General Literary and Scientific Institution" (the Sussex Hall of Leadenhall Street).[1] Here Spanish and German meet on common ground; classes, lectures, and an excellent library are open alike to the artisan, the tradesman, the merchant, the professor, and the idler; and from the eagerness with which all classes avail themselves of the advantages afforded the institution, it would appear that its value is duly appreciated.

The domestic government of the Hebrews is very simple. Each synagogue is, as it were, a little independent state, governed by a sort of parliament, consisting of *parnassim* or wardens, *gaboy* or treasurer, and elders, with an attendant secretary, the congregation of the synagogue being like the members of a state. The wardens have the general superintendence of all the affairs of the congregation: the treasurer, the charge of all the sums coming into his hands for the use of the congregation, and their expenditure. These officers are elected yearly—two wardens being chosen about Easter, which is generally the time of the Jewish Passover; and two more, and the treasurer, about Michaelmas, at the conclusion of the Jewish feast of Tabernacles. Four wardens, or *parnassim*, therefore, act together, each performing the part of president three months alternately, and during the time of his presidency, considered as the civil head of the little community, and receiving certain honours accordingly.

The wardens and treasurer, attended by the secretary, whose business it is to take note of their proceedings, and bring cases before them for their consideration, meet once or twice a week in a large chamber adjoining the synagogue, to make grants of monies, distribute relief and endeavour, by strict examination and impartial judgment, to settle all causes and disputes according to the laws, institutions, and penalties of the Jewish state (that is, synagogue), and so prevent the scandal of bringing petty offences and domestic differences before the English law. If however, they cannot succeed in making peace, or the offence is of so grave a nature as to interfere with the British laws the offender is indicted before the Lord Mayor, and must take his trial as any other English subject.

When questions of general importance are agitated, the *gaboy*, or treasurer, summons the elders to monthly meetings; where, in con-

---

1 Established in 1844 by reform-leading Jews, the Institute sponsored discussions on a wide variety of topics.

junction with the wardens, the subject is discussed, and decided by a majority. If the votes are equal, the president is allowed the casting vote in addition to his own; but all resolutions passed at one meeting must be confirmed in the next, to be considered valid.

No member of the synagogue can be an elder, unless he has served or been elected a warden or treasurer; but there are some meetings to which, in the Spanish congregation, all the members of the synagogue are summoned, women as well as men; all, in short, of either sex who pay a tax to the synagogue; the paying of which tax, or *finta*, as it is called, constitutes a member. There is no fixed assessment but each member is taxed according to his means.

These remarks, however, refer principally to the Spanish and Portuguese congregation; the Dutch and German differs in some minor points, such as having three wardens instead of four, who serve sometimes two years instead of one. And in addition to the wardens and treasurer, they have an overseer of the poor and seven elders, who are annually elected from the members of the vestry, and regularly attend at monthly or vestry meetings; forming, with the honorary officers, wardens, &c. a committee, who deliberate on all matters essential to the congregation. The vestry of the Germans, like the elders of the Portuguese, consists of such members as have previously been elected to the honorary offices. Their duty is to attend all special and quarterly meetings for the general government of synagogue.

In both synagogues, Spanish and German, all members residing within twelve miles of the synagogue are eligible for either of the honorary offices, and are elected by ballot; the president in this, as in other cases, having the casting vote. No election is considered valid without a majority of seven votes. The individual elected may or may not accept, but is subject to a fine if he refuse, unless incapacitated for the duties of the office by ill health or old age. Persons above seventy years of age are exempted from the fine.

In London, we might almost say in England, there is but one Spanish and Portuguese synagogue; that founded by Menasseh Ben Israel in the time of Cromwell. The Germans have so multiplied, that not only have they four or five synagogues in London, but form a congregation in almost every provincial town. It is a rare occurrence to find a family of Spanish or Portuguese extraction established elsewhere than in London; but wherever the Germans can discover an opening for business, they will be found active and persevering, self-satisfied and happy; ever on the alert for the increase of wealth, and not over-scrupulous as to the means of its acquirement. The synagogues and Jewish congregations, therefore, in the provincial towns, it should be remembered, all belong to this body, and must not be considered as representatives of *all* the British Jews. Each synagogue belonging to the Germans has its own government of honorary officers, &c. who superintend the affairs of their own congregations, rich and poor. Formerly they were all considered tributary to the great synagogue of Duke's Place; but they are now independent, and the bond of union being of amity and not of restraint, their individual and several interests have been preserved in mutual harmony.

In addition to the already-mentioned officers, each synagogue has two or more deputies, elected every seven years, as representatives of the Jewish nation to the British government.[1] Their duty is to take cognisance of all political and statistical matters concerning the Hebrew communities throughout the British empire. In cases of general national importance, they meet together, consult, and then reporting the result of their deliberations to their elders and constituents, for such in fact are the several congregations by whom they are elected, and, receiving their assent, they proceed to act on the measures proposed. On all occasions of public rejoicing, as in the accession of a sovereign or national victory, &c. it is the office of the deputies to address the sovereign in the name of all their brethren; and in cases of petitions for increased privileges for themselves, or relief for their oppressed nation in other lands—as at the time of the Damascus persecution, or the recent Russian *ukase*—it is their duty to wait upon the premier, or any of the ministers in office, and request their interference.[2]

1 Aguilar refers to the Board of Deputies of British Jews, formally established in 1817 as the body through which Jews could advocate for their interests to the British government. The Board of Deputies is still active today.

2 On the Russian *ukase*, see p. 200, note 1, above.

Jews of Continental Europe

In the treatment of the Jews, Great Britain at present occupies a position between the United States of North America, France, and Belgium, on the one hand, and Germany and Russia, with some other countries, on the other. In the United States, Jews are eligible to all civil offices; and there it is far from uncommon to find Jews performing the functions of judges of the higher courts, sheriffs, and members of congress. All this is exactly as it should be. In France, Jews are likewise eligible for civil offices without violation of conscience; and also in Belgium, the Jews are not proscribed in the manner they too frequently have been.

Religious toleration cannot be said to extend farther in continental Europe than through France and the Netherlands. As respects the treatment of Jews, most continental nations are still less or more floundering in the darkness of the middle ages. In many nations the Jews are still liable to insults, oppressions, banishment, and even at intervals to torture and massacre. The same charge of kidnapping and murdering Christian children is in Poland, Prussia, and many parts of Germany, constantly fulminated against them—rousing the easily-kindled wrath and hate of the more ignorant, and occasioning such assaults as frequently demand the interference of the military to subdue—and the subsequent discovery that the supposed victim of Jewish bloodthirstiness has fled from the cruelty of Christian masters, found refuge, and kindness, and food in the Jewish households, to which he may have been tracked, and escaped thence, with their friendly aid, into the open country, where, happily for the release of his benefactors from unsparing slaughter, he is discovered and brought back.[1] Repeatedly, however, as this occurs, and not only the innocence but the benevolence of the Jews publicly established, it has no power to prevent the repetition of the same charges whenever a Christian child disappears: a perseverance in prejudice and perversion of humanity scarcely credible in the present day, but proved only too true by the constant witness of the continental press.

---

1 Aguilar refers to the "blood libel," the charge periodically made since the Middle Ages that Jews ritually murdered Christian boys and used their blood in the Passover bread. Chaucer's "Prioress' Tale" from *The Canterbury Tales*, is an example of a literary use of the blood libel.

It is very difficult to obtain a just and correct view of the domestic history of the Jews on the continent: scarcely possible, in fact, except by a residence of some weeks in the midst of them. Travellers notice them so casually, and these notices are so coloured with the individual feelings with which they are viewed, that we can glean no satisfactory information except as to their social position, which has been always that of a people apart. The less privileges they enjoy, the more marked of course this separation becomes. The prejudice on both sides is strengthened; and to penetrate the sanctuary of domestic life and their national government, is impossible. In France and Belgium, as we have seen in England, they are only Jews in the peculiar forms and observances of their religion: in everything else of domestic, social, or public life, they are as completely children of the soil as their Christian brethren. Elsewhere on the continent, they are so marked by degrading ordinances, even to their modes of their dress, and the localities of their dwellings, that their individual social identity is known at once, and they are shunned and hated as possessors of the plague. In Rome, the Jews are still confined to one quarter of the town, called the Ghetto, which several months in the year is so completely inundated, as only to permit egress and ingress by means of boats. In the other towns of Italy, though the quarters of the towns assigned them may be somewhat less unhealthy, their social position is the same. In Austria, though Francis I, and after him Joseph II, sought to meliorate their condition, the endeavour does not appear to have been continued; for the humiliating and distressing liabilities to which they are subject in the empire have degraded them to the lowest ebb, and, except in a very few instances, utterly prevent their raising themselves, either socially or mentally. It so chanced, however, that a wealthy Jew did obtain favour from the emperor, in return for some weighty service, as to be offered a patent of nobility, which, with a nobleness of soul needing no empty title to make it more distinguished, he refused, asking in its stead freedom of the city for his sons-in-law (he had no sons, and his daughters were then unmarried). It was granted; and the gift of his daughters obtained for their fortunate possessors a privilege granted to none other: for the sons-in-law of this honourable Jew are the only free Jewish citizens and merchants of Vienna.

In the time of Napoleon, several of the smaller German sovereignties befriended the Jews, issuing ordinances admitting them to many civil rights, exempting them from oppressive imposts,[1] and permitting them to pursue trade and obtain professorships. In gratitude for these unusual privileges, several entered the armies of the allies, formed in 1813 to break the galling yoke of Napoleon, and so distinguished themselves, as to receive as many medals and decorations of honour as their more naturally warlike compatriots. It was only reasonable that, as they performed all the duties of patriots and citizens to their respective states, they would demand and expect the abolition of all the oppressive enactments made against them in more barbarous times. And we find, in 1815, the Germanic Confederation assembled at Vienna, declaring in their sixteenth article, "The diet will take into consideration in what way the civil melioration of the Jews may best be effected, and in particular how the enjoyment of all civil rights, in return for the performance of all civil duties, may be most effectually secured to them in the states of the Confederation. In the meantime the professors of this faith shall continue to enjoy the rights already extended to them."

From the present condition of the Jews in Germany, however, this would appear mere words. With the cessation of the call for their patriotism from the general amnesty, the recollection of their services also ceased, and no decided means ever seem to have been taken to secure to them the promised privileges. The great trading towns, Hamburg, Lubec, Bremen, and especially Frankfort-on-Maine, never showed even the profession of friendliness towards them. The jealousy awakened by that spirit of commercial enterprise, so peculiarly a Jewish characteristic, continues still, and effectually retards their social consideration; rivalry in commerce being unhappily as great a fosterer of prejudice as the ignorance of former years. In Frankfort, until a very few years ago, so heavily were they oppressed, that if any Jew, even of the most venerable age, did not take off his hat to the mere children of Christian parents, he was pelted with stones, and insulted by terms of the grossest abuse, for which there was neither redress nor retaliation; and this was but one of those social humiliations, the constant pressure of which must at length degrade their subjects to the narrow mind, closed-up heart,

1 Imposts: taxes.

and sole pursuit of self-interest of which they are accused. The impoverished condition of the nobles and princes of the soil, during the late war, frequently compelled them to part with their estates to the only possessors of ready money—the Jews. When the immediate pressure of want had subsided, it was naturally galling to men, as proud as they were poor, to behold the castles and lands, the heritage of noble German families through many centuries, enjoyed by men of neither rank nor education, and whose sole consideration was great wealth. The very means by which that wealth was obtained—contracts entered into with the French emperor—increased the dislike of all classes towards them, heightened by the presumption and ostentation they displayed. In 1820 riots broke out against them at Meiningen, at Wurtzburg, and extended along the Rhine. Hamburg, and still farther northward, as far as Copenhagen, caught the infection; and so serious were the disturbances, so sanguinary the intentions of aroused multitudes, that it demanded the utmost vigilance of the various governments to prevent the nineteenth century from becoming a repetition of the twelfth, thirteenth, and fourteenth centuries. The very cry which was the signal for the old massacres, and which, once heard, was as certain doom to the hapless Jew as if the sword was already at his throat—"Hep! hep!" from the initials of the old Crusade cry, "Hierosolyma est perdita!" ("Jerusalem is lost!")—was revived on this occasion; a curious fact, as full four centuries had elapsed since it had last been heard. Nine years later, we are told that "when the states of Wirtemberg were discussing a measure which extended civil rights to the Israelites, the populace of Stuttgart surrounded the Hall of Assembly with savage outcries of 'Down with the Jews!' The states, however, calmly maintained their dignity, continued their sittings, and eventually passed the bill."[1]

When we remember that this fanatical outbreak of prejudice took place scarcely twenty years ago, we may have some idea of the social position of the Jews in Germany. Notwithstanding its humiliating nature, however, they have shared the advancement of the age in the zealous cultivation of intellect and art. The extraordinary genius of their great countryman, Moses Mendelssohn, who flourished in the eighteenth century—the boldness with which he had flung aside

1 Milman, *History of the Jews*.

the trammels of rabbinism, and the prejudices arising from long ages of persecution, making himself not only a name amongst the first of German literati, but forming friendships with Lessing, Lavater, and other great spirits of the age, completely destroying in his own person the unsocial spirit of his nation—had given an impulse to the Jews which even the excitement of the war, and its vast resources for amassing wealth, had not the power to diminish.[1] German, and the other modern languages, which, until the master-mind of Mendelssohn appeared, had been considered profane, and therefore neglected, are now zealously cultivated, the literature of each appreciated and studied. They attend the universities, and have greatly advanced in all the departments of mental and physical science; thus proving that when the Jews appear so devoted to interest alone, as to neglect all the higher and more, intellectual pursuits, it is position, not character, that is at fault. In the earlier ages we find them, in the brief intervals of peace, not merely merchants of splendour and opulence, but the sole physicians, sole teachers, sole ministers of finance in their respective realms to nobles and princes. Their superior intelligence and education at a period when it was rare for nobles and kings, and even the clergy, to write their names, marked them out for offices of trust, which they never failed to execute with ability and skill. And it is notorious that the ambassador between the Catholic Emperor Charlemagne, and the no less famous Mohammedan potentate Haroun al Raschid, holding in his sole trust the political interests of Europe and Asia—for at that time the princes we have named might be justly considered the representatives of the two continents—was neither knight, noble, nor prince, but simply Isaac, a Jew! But when these breathing-times had passed, when kings and princes needed wealth, and their exhausted coffers could only be replenished by the treasures of the Jews—when the

---

1 Moses Mendelssohn: German-Jewish philosopher responsible for initiating the modernization of Jews in Germany and throughout Western Europe. G.E. Lessing: an enlightened eighteenth-century playwright, known throughout Europe for *Nathan Der Weise* (*Nathan the Wise*, 1779), his dramatic plea for Christian toleration of Jews. The character Nathan was modeled on Moses Mendelssohn. Johann Caspar Lavater was a Protestant minister in Zurich, who challenged Mendelssohn either to refute the truth of Christianity publicly or convert. Mendelssohn responded in 1769 with a famous letter to Lavater defending Judaism, and later published a sustained refutation in his major work, *Jerusalem, Or on Religious Power and Judaism* (1783).

multitude asked but a rumour to fan suppressed hatred to a flame—the horrors of persecution recommenced; the services of the Jews were forgotten; and statute after statute, each more degrading than the last, hound them to such a position, such pursuits, that they became ignorant of their own power themselves, and made no effort to prove themselves other than they were believed. But the power was quenched—not lost; and it is bursting forth again with renewed vigour whenever it has scope for development and growth.

There is a street in Frankfort-on-Maine called the Juden Strasse, or Jews Street, in which the houses look so aged and poverty-stricken, that to walk down it almost seems to transport one to the middle ages, and recalls all the painful stories of the Jews of that time, and the marvellous tale of the lavish splendour and great wealth which these hovel-like entrances concealed; the affectation of poverty and abject misery assumed, not from any miserlike propensities in themselves, but to deceive their cruel foes, to whom the scent of wealth was always the signal for blood. In this street, during the late war, dwelt an honest, hardworking Jew, little regarded by his fellows of his own or the Christian faith; he was poorer than the generality of his brethren, and there was nothing in his appearance or manner to denote a more than common mind. How it happened that he was selected as the guardian of certain monies and treasures belonging to a German prince, whom the fate of war had caused to fly from his possessions, does not appear; but certain it is that the trust was willingly accepted and nobly fulfilled. The confusion and alarm of the French invasion, and the various revolutions in Germany thence proceeding, extended to Frankfort. Many of the Jews were pillaged; for wealth being imagined synonymous with the word Jew, they were less likely to escape than any. The Jew we have mentioned was amongst the number, but so effectually were the prince's treasures concealed, that their existence was not even suspected. And when the tumult had ceased, and Frankfort was again left to its own quiet, the Jew's own little property had greatly diminished, but his *trust* was untouched. Some few years passed; the pillaging of Frankfort had reached the ears of the dispossessed prince, and he quietly resigned himself to the belief that his own treasures had shared the common fate, or at least had been appropriated by the Jew to atone for his own losses. As soon as he could, he returned to his country, but he was so fully possessed with the idea that he was utterly impoverished, that he made no effort at first even to inquire after the fate of his property. His astonishment—which, however, admiration and gratitude equalled—may be conceived when he received from the hands of the Jew the whole untouched; some assert with the full interest of certain sums which his necessities had compelled him to use; but this is traditional. We can only vouch for the truth as far as the immediate undiminished return of the whole property as soon as claimed. The *effects* of this honourable conduct can be traced to this day in the whole financial world.

The prince was not of that easy nature to be satisfied with the mere expressions of gratitude. He spread the tale—which, regarded as an utter contradiction to the imagined characteristic practices of the Jews, appeared far more extraordinary than it really was— over all the courts of Germany. From them it spread to other kingdoms: the Jew found himself suddenly withdrawn from obscurity, and all his talents for financial enterprise— of the extent of which, perhaps, he had been ignorant himself till the *hour* found the *man*—called into play. Not only did he amass such wealth himself as perhaps sometimes to cause a smile at the treasures which had seemed of such moment to their owner, but his family, ennobled, accomplished, prince-like in their establishments and position, may be found scattered in most every European court, and acknowledged on every Exchange as the great movers of the money market of the world. But the widow of their founder; now nearly a century old, refuses all state or grandeur: she receives the visits of her descendants, but in the same lowly dwelling that beheld the rise of her husband's fortunes—in the old dilapidated Juden Strasse of Frankfort.[1]

While Poland was an independent sovereignty, the Jews there had greater privileges than in any other European kingdom except Spain; and in fact many Spanish and Portuguese refugees fled to that country when expelled from their own. A charter is still extant, made by Duke Bodislas, who flourished in the thirteenth century, protecting them from oppressions of every kind, and breathing a spirit of toleration and benevolence strangely contrasting with the cruel enactments of contemporary sovereigns. The love said to be

1 These paragraphs pay homage to the Rothschilds, the wealthy family of Jewish bankers based in Germany but with connections in many European cities, including London.

borne by Casimir, the great-grandson of Bodislas, for a Jewish girl, occasioned the confirmation of this deed. And even when, at a later period, and in the first heat of the controversy between the Catholics and Protestants, the latter faith was prohibited, the Jews still remained unmolested. They formed the only middle class of the kingdom, and, as such, were the sole engrossers of traffic, constituting in several towns and villages nearly the whole of the population. They had numerous academies, where, however, the rabbinical, more than general learning, was made a first object. Poland might at that time have been termed the seat of rabbinism, for nowhere were the traditions more considered, nor its teachers revered. Jewish parents from all quarters sent their sons to the Polish schools, satisfied that there they must attain all necessary knowledge.

With the dismemberment of Poland, the privileges of the Jews ceased.[1] Prussia and Austria have often made professions of toleration, but there is little evidence in the condition of the Jews under either government. Nor was it likely that the Polish Jews should be the favoured portion of the emperor of Russia's Polish subjects, to be excluded from oppression. Mr. Herschel has thus graphically delineated their miserable condition:—"They are driven from place to place, and not permitted to live in the same street where the so-called Christians reside. It not unfrequently happens that one or more wealthy Jews have built commodious houses in any part of a town not hitherto prohibited: this affords a reason for proscribing them. It is immediately enacted that no Jew must live in that quarter of the city; and they are forthwith driven from their houses, without any compensation for their loss. They are oppressed on every side, yet dare not complain; robbed and defrauded, yet obtain no redress. In the walk of social life, insult and contempt meet them at every turning. The very children in the streets often throw stones at the most respectable Jews, and call them the most opprobrious names, unchecked and unrebuked."[2]

---

1 Between 1772 and 1795, Prussia, Austria, and Russia partitioned Poland three times, dividing the territory among themselves and changing the balance of power among European states. Many of the Jews ended up in Russia, where they were subject to increasingly severe imperial *ukases*, or decrees. See p. 200, note 1.

2 Attribution unknown, but this might be from a lost speech delivered by Solomon Hirschel, a Victorian Jewish synagogue functionary and historian of London synagogues in the 1830s.

The late *ukase*, which, for the fault of one or two individuals, condemned 50,000 Jews to a doom far worse than the famous edict of expulsion from Spain in 1492, but too fearfully confirms this account. Banished from their dwellings, cast out from all trade, all employment, even from the poor occupation of breaking stones on the highway, by which three hundred families earned scarcely dry bread—not permitted to leave the kingdom; but sentenced to inhabit not only the most unhealthy part of the interior, but a space of ground not large enough to accommodate half their number, they perished by thousands; and the misery of the survivors it needs a powerful pen to picture. There was no escape, no hope, no remedy. The decree of a single individual sentenced 50,000 of his harmless subjects to a fate than which the slaughters and massacres of the middle ages were almost merciful. And this horrible *ukase* is of so late a date that neither its execution nor its misery can yet be looked on as the past.

We would gladly turn from this melancholy picture: but the history of the continental Jews is almost all the same. In the Mohammedan kingdoms, indeed, they have enjoyed a toleration which might shame many a Christian sovereignty; the extreme indolence of the Mussulmen assisting in permitting them to obtain the almost exclusive trade of the Levant. Subject as they are to the oppression of individuals—sultans and pashas—needing wealth or excitement, still these are but temporary misfortunes. Their general position in the Ottoman provinces, both of Europe and Asia, is one of more security, peace, and consideration, in contemporary and more enlightened kingdoms.

Scattered as they are all over the world, literally from north to south, and east to west, and in all the corners and islands of the globe, forming colonies, or being already domiciled in every newly-discovered land, yet America now seems their continental central home. They have there privileges and freedom in common with any and every other faith; they are debarred from no social advantages; can enjoy public honours, and perform public duties. Professions, military, naval, and civil, are open to them, and all the various branches of commerce and trade. It is rather a remarkable coincidence, the very year in which the Jews were expelled from Spain—the country which had been to them a second Judea—Christopher

Columbus discovered America, the land which was to be to those persecuted people a home of security and freedom, such as they then could never have even hoped to enjoy. The edict of expulsion from Spain was never recalled; but yet, though outwardly and professedly the most rigidly Catholic kingdom of Europe, it was actually peopled with Jews, though with great secrecy.

Many families now naturalised in England trace their descent, and in no very remote degree, from individuals whose history in Portugal or Spain have all the elements of romance. About the middle of the eighteenth century, a merchant, whom we will call Garcias, though that was not his real name, resided in Lisbon, commanding the respect and consideration of all classes from his upright character, lavish generosity, and great wealth.[1] He conducted his family, consisting of a wife, two young daughters, and a large establishment of domestics, so exactly in accordance with the strictly orthodox principles of Catholicism, that for years all suspicion had been averted. How he contrived, with so many jealous eyes upon him, to adhere to the rigid essentials of the Jewish faith—keeping the festivals and sabbaths, never touching prohibited meats, and celebrating the solemn fast once a year—must now and for ever remain a mystery. We only know that it was done, and not only by him, but by hundreds of other families. At length suspicion was aroused. It was the eighth birthday of his younger daughter, celebrated with music and dancing, and all the glad festivities which such occasions call forth in an affectionate and generously-conducted household. His elder daughter, a young girl of sixteen, was engaged to the son of a friend, also in prosperous business in Lisbon, and life had never smiled more hopefully on Garcias than it did that night.

In the midst of the festive scene, the merchant was called out to speak with some strangers, who waited on business—important business they said—which could not be delayed. He descended to the hall of entrance; the strangers threw off their cloaks and appeared in the garb and with the warrant of the Holy Office, authorised to demand and enforce the surrender of his person. From the very midst of his family, friends, and household, he was borne to the

---

1 The story of Garcias that follows bears resemblance in many details to Aguilar's story "The Escape," and is no doubt the incident on which the story is based.

prisons of the Inquisition, and there remained without any communication with the outer world, without even knowing the fate of his family, for an interval of eight years. He was several times examined—a word in the present instance synonymous with torture, always applied to impell a confession of Judaism, which confiscated the whole property of the accused to the use and pleasure of his accusers; but Garcias was as firm and unflinching as his examiners. Neither torture nor imprisonment could succeed in obtaining one word which could betray the real truth, and condemn him as a secret Jew.

The devices to which he resorted to beguile his imprisonment might fill a moderate-sized volume; we have only space to mention one or two. His peculiarly gracious and winning manner, his courteous and gentle speech, which never changed, tried as he must have been by a variety of sorrows and anxieties in this weary interval, won him so far the regard of his jailor as to permit his employments to pass unnoticed, when otherwise they would undoubtedly have been forbidden. Undoing with some degree of care one of his own knitted socks gave him not only the materials but the knowledge how, if he could but contrive the necessary implements, to knit a smaller pair from it. By excessive patience and perseverance he so sharpened the lid of a metal snuff-box as to serve for a knife, and with this he contrived to fashion a pair of knitting-needles from the bones of a chicken which had served him for dinner. With these he knitted socks for children, and presented them to his jailor for the use of his family. His next wish was for the implements of writing, which, more rigidly than anything else, were denied him. His urbanity and his presents, however, permitted him the secret acquirement of some paper, the jailor quieting his conscience perhaps by the idea that no evil could come of it, as pen and ink it was quite impossible for the prisoner to make, and equally impossible, unless he wished to lose his situation, for him to grant. But Garcias' was not a mind to rest quiet without some effort for the accomplishment of his wishes. The snuff-box, knife, and chicken bones were again in requisition, and a pen was successfully formed. The ink, or at least its substitute, was rather more difficult, but necessity is always a sharpener of intellect, and even this was accomplished. He made a hole in the brick flooring of his prison, and supplied it regularly with lamp-black, procured from the lamp, which, as an unusual indulgence, was permitted him every evening. With these rough materials, carefully secreted even from his friend the jailor, he beguiled his confinement with writing several plays and dramas, mostly on Scriptural subjects, which are still in the possession of his family, and display the elastic and versatile mind of the man as strongly as his urbane and gracious manner; his humorous gaiety, which never failed him even in prison, and his enduring patience, evince his calm and collected dignity of character. In the seventh or eighth year of his imprisonment, the great earthquake of 1755, which almost destroyed the whole of Lisbon, took place. The confusion and ruin extending to the prisons of the Inquisition, caused the guards and officials hurriedly to disperse, and left the gates open to the several prisoners. Many fled, but in so doing sealed their own doom; for they were mostly all retaken, and their flight pronounced sufficient evidence of their guilt to condemn their persons, and confiscate their whole property. Garcias knew, or suspected this, and quietly abode in his prison, attempting no escape, and apparently regardless of the dangers round him. After this, all attempts to compel a condemnation of himself appear to have ceased, and he was restored to his family. So little had his danger and various trials affected him, that he would have continued calmly to pursue his business in Lisbon as before, if his elder daughter had not besought him on her knees, and with tears, to fly from such a city of horror. The unknown destiny of her father had of course prevented all thought of the fulfilment of her marriage engagement: and not long after Garcias' summons, the parents of her betrothed were in the Inquisition likewise, and Podriques, the man himself, compelled to fly. So much secrecy and caution were necessary effectually to conceal all trace of such fugitives, that no communication could pass between the betrothed. She had not even an idea of the country which had given him refuge, nor of his means of subsistence. His mother, not herself an actual prisoner, was an inmate of the Holy Office, a voluntary attendant on her husband, and twice herself exposed to imminent danger, both times foreshadowed by an extraordinary dream. Once she fancied herself in the arena of a bull-fight, exposed to all the horror of an attack from one of these savage animals, without any means of defence. The bull came roaring and foaming towards her; death seemed inevitable, and in its most fearful shape, when suddenly the infuriated animal stopped in its mad career, and laid itself quietly as a pet-dog at her feet. She awoke with the strong feeling of thankfulness, as if some real danger had been averted, and the impression of this strange and peculiarly vivid dream remained till its foreshadowing seemed fulfilled. She was summoned to the "question," by her evidence to condemn her husband; the instruments of torture were produced, and actually about to be applied, when the surgeon interfered with the assertion that she was not in a state of health to bear them, and she was remanded, and not recalled. In her second dream, she was alone on the summit of a high tower, which suddenly seemed to give way beneath her, having nothing but space between the battlements where she stood and the ground several hundred yards below, causing the fearful dread of immediate precipitation and death, yet still as if the doom were averted by her being upheld by some invisible power, and aid and a safe descent permitted, the means of which the vagary of her dream seemed utterly to prevent her ascertaining. Not long afterwards, the great earthquake already mentioned took place. She was in one of the upper chambers of the Inquisition at the time of the first shock, and rushing out on the landing with her infant in her arms, found, to her horror and consternation that the staircase had disappeared, and nothing but space lay between her and the basement storey, her only means of escape into the open air. While gazing with horror on her terrible position, the recollection of her dream returned to her, and she felt strengthened by faith that she and her child would both be preserved, though how, she could not indeed imagine. A few minutes passed, and then came a second shock, *restoring the staircase to its place*; and in little more than a minute the awe-struck but grateful woman was in safety.

Incredible as this story seems, we have neither added nor diminished one item of the real truth, and our romance of real life is not quite concluded. Garcias and his family went to England, and not long afterwards the release of Podriques permitted him and his wife, the heroine of the above escape, to do the same. There they were joined by their son, and a brief interval beheld the nuptials of the long-betrothed, long-severed, whose children still survive. It would be wrong to dismiss the anecdote without mentioning it as our belief that all intelligent Roman Catholics of the present day disclaim the propriety of perpetrating such acts of oppression, and as earnestly sympathise with the Jews as any class of the community.

Such is the history of a people who, though for so many years denizens and subjects of this free and happy land, are yet regarded as aliens and strangers; and still, unhappily too often, as objects of rooted prejudice and dislike. To trace this prejudice to its origin might be difficult; for it would be hard to say it proceeded from ignorance, when it is so often found amongst the educated classes. Yet ignorance in reality it is. The peculiar religion of the Hebrews, and their habit of worshipping apart, keeps them strangers in a great degree to the community at large. But whenever it so happens that the interdicted circle of a Jewish family is entered, and its inmates known, prejudice is sure to give way. The faults of the Hebrews, such as they are, may be traced, in a great measure at least, to the degrading influences of long-continued persecution, which they suffered from the bigotry of ancient barbarism in this and in other countries. Now, however, the British empire has given the exiles of Judea a home of peace and freedom, and that they feel towards her an affection and reverence as strong and undying as any of her native sons, it is to be hoped that the prejudice against the Jews will ultimately disappear with the dawn of an era in which all Englishmen, however differently they may pray to the Great Father of all, shall yet, so long as they fail not in duty to their country and to each other, be regarded as the common children of one soil.

1847

Appendix A: Victorian Tributes

[Aguilar received numerous tributes both during her lifetime and after death. Just prior to leaving on what was to be her final journey, to Frankfurt, in 1847, Aguilar was presented with a testimonial by a number of middle-class Anglo-Jewish women, which is reprinted here.

Aguilar received memorial tributes from Jewish and Christian writers in Britain, France, the U.S., and Jamaica. This section includes the obituaries from *The Jewish Chronicle*, *The Occident*, and *The Athenaeum*; literary tributes from the Anglo-Jewish poet Marion Hartog, and the popular Christian domestic novelist Anna Maria Hall; a tribute from a women's auxiliary in Charleston, South Carolina; and excerpts from letters in which the American Jewish educator Rebecca Gratz discusses Aguilar's work.]

1. Testimonial from the Misses Levison and Isaacs, accompanied by some other admirers, 14 June 1847.

TO GRACE AGUILAR

THE HEARTFELT ADDRESS OF A FEW "WOMEN OF ISRAEL"

DEAREST SISTER,—Our admiration of your talents, our veneration for your character, our gratitude for the eminent services your writings render our sex, our people, our faith, in which the sacred cause of true religion is embodied: all these motives combine to induce us to intrude on your presence, in order to give utterance to sentiments which we are happy to feel and delighted to express. Until you arose, it has, in modern times, never been the case, that a Woman in Israel should stand forth the public advocate of the faith of Israel; that with the depth and purity of feelings which is the treasure of woman, and with the strength of mind and extensive knowledge that form the pride of man, she should call on her own to cherish, on others to respect, the truth as it is in Israel.

You, dearest Sister, have done this, and more. You have taught us to know and to appreciate our own dignity; to feel and to prove that no female character can be more worthy than the Hebrew mother; none more pure than that of the Jewish maiden; none more pious than that of the woman in Israel. You have vindicated our social and spiritual equality with our brethren in the faith; you have, by your own excellent example, triumphantly refuted the aspersion, that the Jewish religion leaves unmoved the heart of the Jewish woman. Your writings place within our reach those higher motives, those holier consolations, which flow from the spirituality of our religion, which urge the soul to commune with its Maker, and direct it to His grace and His mercy, as the best guide and protector here and hereafter. Many a gay votary of pleasure your writings have led to think; many a worldly-minded sister your writings reclaim; many a stricken heart your writings guide and conduct to the never-failing source of consolation, of the strength which sustaineth, the hope which faileth not—God's holy law and word.

Sister! You wrote not for fame, nor to obtain the admiration and thanks of mankind, yet they are yours. Your task was less to delight than to instruct, yet you do both. Alike heart and mind treasure your words and assent to your teaching. Then continue what you have so well begun. Still persevere as the instructress, the friend, the champion of your sisters. Accept their thanks; they are sincere. Disdain not their friendship's offering, though they who present it be young and few. Their fervent prayers call down upon you the protection of the All-bounteous Father; and their children's children will bless your name.

June 14, 1847. Sivan 30, 5607.

[Aguilar was then presented with an inkstand, inscribed as follows:]

A testimonial of respect
To Miss Grace Aguilar,
Presented by a few of the "Women of Israel"
Of Great Britain,
On Monday, June 14th, 1847, corresponding to Sivan 30th, 5607,
In appreciation of her pious and able Productions in the
Cause of Religion and Virtue

2. Abraham Benisch, Obituary, *Jewish Chronicle*, 1 and 8 Oct. 1847.

To communicate evil tidings privately is one of the most painful tasks we have to perform in the course of our lives. But to be the medium of announcing to the public a heavy national loss is a duty so sad and heart-rending, the extent of which can only be felt by the messenger of the mournful event. Such, we lament to say, is our duty this day, in recording the death of Miss Grace Aguilar, at the age of 32. We do not in the least degree exaggerate the loss in calling it a *national* one, as the numerous literary productions of that lady were not only appreciated in England but also in America, Germany, and France. Indeed, we may go so far as to state, that her works were much more appreciated by the Jews on the continent than by those in this country. Her "Women of Israel," a work every page of which is stamped with the most ardent zeal and fervent piety—in every line of which breathes that national sense and true patriotism which is the great characteristic of all her writings; her "Women of Israel," which are teeming with powerful lessons to her own sex, and eloquent exhortations to the opposite one—parts of that work have been translated into German, propagated by her true friend the Rev. Mr. Leeser of Philadelphia, on the other side of the Atlantic; but, alas, our Jewish brethren in England have not appreciated its value. Had it not been for the kindness of an excommunicated philanthropist,[1] her works would hardly have become known much less disseminated, among the Jews of England. Her "Spirit of Judaism," "Jewish Faith," &c., are likewise works of great merit, and full of that pious fervor and filial affection which carries the reader along with her alike in sympathy with the writer and conviction of the argument. The "Jewish Faith" betrays signs of no mean acquaintance with Jewish and Christian philosophers and divines, and its logical reasoning is far from betraying the sex of the author.

3. Isaac Leeser, Obituary, *Occident* 5 (Nov. 1847): 419-420.

We know that our simple announcement that GRACE AGUILAR is dead, will send a thrill of pain though the hearts of nearly all our readers, who, with us, have had cause to admire the sweet thoughts of devotional piety which breathe through her many writings [...]. [H]er dying couch was watched by her mother, brother, and her friend Miss Samuda. But even if all these had been absent, Grace Aguilar would not have been among strangers; for the fame of her works had gone before her [...].

Probably during her lifetime, Miss Aguilar was not sufficiently appreciated [...]. But even so was she enabled to accomplish so much more than one could have expected from her youth and bodily infirmity, and by this standard only must her works be judged [...]. [T]here has not arisen a single Jewish female in modern times who has done so much for the illustration and adornment of her faith as Grace Aguilar. So, then, if she was early called to appear in the assembly of saints above, she has been permitted long enough on earth to be enrolled amidst the noble Women of Israel, who have shed a lustre around their ancient race [...].

---

1 Isaac D'Israeli, father of Benjamin Disraeli and author of *Curiosities of Literature*. He was excommunicated from London's Spanish and Portuguese Synagogue in Bevis Marks for refusing to pay a fine. Aguilar's correspondence with him reveals his importance in securing the publication of her works in England.

4. Obituary, *Athenaeum*.[1]

[...] Graceful as were her works, they were yet more full of promise than of performance [...].

5. Tribute by the Ladies Of the Society for the Religious Instruction Of Jewish Youth, Charleston, 23 Nov 1847, in *Occident* 5 (Jan 1848): 510-511.

[...] At the announcement of her departure, the whole house of Israel rises up to honor the memory of our spiritual kinswoman; whose soul seemed divinely commissioned to execute Truth's righteous embassy [...]. Her devotional offering was more costly than the oblation of the temple builder—a life consecrated to sacred culture; until ceaseless labour laid its fragile framework in ruins! The sinews of her mind shrank not even while she wrestled with the angel of death [...]. Where shall that other be found who can properly fill the station of this moral governess of the Hebrew family? [...]. [P]ages pure as hers might form a fitting preface to the book of peace and perfect faith [...]. "[We] Resolve, unanimously, that the death of our gifted Sister Grace Aguilar, must be regarded as a national calamity [...]."

6. Marion Hartog, "Lines Written on the Death of Grace Aguilar."[2]

Awhile the harp of Judah sadly slumbers,
  Its soothing chords neglected and forsaken,
For she whose gifted hand awoke its numbers
  Sleeps that long sleep from which none e'er awaken.

O who shall tell, high heart, how thou hast pined,
  In the drear world, with cold neglect away,
Till the pure soul by that frail form enshrined
  Consumed in its own light the shell of clay.

Not thine the thoughts that burn in words of fire
  And, flashing, flame into the heart their way:
Thou best could'st wake the sweet domestic lyre,
  That o'er the home-affections holds its sway.

---

1 Qtd. from Athenaeum in the *Grace Aguilar* MSS.

2 *JC*, 10 Nov. 1854. Hartog's poem appeared just as she was beginning to gather subscriptions for a new literary effort, *The Jewish Sabbath Journal*.

Thine were the soft notes of the turtle-dove,
   That breathes a sweetness o'er the desert waste;
And shall thy lessons of religious love
   Die with the brain that thought, the hand that traced?

No; Israel long shall cherish Grace's name,
   All apathetic though her children be;
Though living they neglected thee, O shame!
   In death they'll twine a myrtle wreath for thee.

How long shall Israel's thoughtless great ones—say—
   (Who to be learning's patrons should be proud)
Let living genius hopeless pine away,
   And waste their empty honours on a shroud.

7. Anna Maria Hall, from "Pilgrimage to the Grave of Grace Aguilar."

[...] At our first introduction to Grace Aguilar, we were struck, as much by the earnestness and eloquence of her conversation, as by her delicate and lovely countenance. Her person and address were exceedingly prepossessing; her eyes of the deep blue that look almost black in particular lights; and her hair dark and abundant. There was no attempt at display; no affectation of learning; no desire to obtrude "me and my books" upon any one, or in any way; in all things she was graceful and well-bred. You felt at once that she was a carefully educated gentlewoman, and if there was more warmth and cordiality of manner than a stranger generally evinces on a first introduction, we remember her descent, and that the tone of her studies, as well as her passionate love of music and high musical attainments had increased her sensibility. When we came to know her better, we were charmed and astonished at her extensive reading; at her knowledge of foreign literature, and actual learning—relieved by a refreshing pleasure in juvenile amusements. Each interview increased our friendship, and the quantity and quality of her acquirements commanded our admiration. She had made acquaintance with the beauties of English nature during a long residence in Devonshire; loved the country with her whole heart, and enriched her mind by the leisure it afforded; she had collected and arranged conchological and mineralogical specimens to a considerable extent; loved flowers as only sensitive women can love them; and with all this was deeply read in theology and history. Whatever she knew she knew thoroughly; rising at six in the morning, and giving to each hour its employment; cultivating and exercising her home affections, and keeping open heart for many friends. All these qualities were warmed by a fervid enthusiasm for whatever was high and holy. She spurned all envy and uncharitableness, and rendered loving homage to whatever was great and good. It was difficult to induce her to speak of herself or of her own doings. After her death it was deeply interesting to hear from the one, of all others who loved and knew her best (her mother), of the progress of her mind from infancy to womanhood; it proved so convincingly how richly she deserved the affection she inspired [...].

It is a beautiful picture to look upon—this young and highly endowed Jewish maiden, nurtured in the bosom of her own family, the beloved of her parents, themselves high-class Hebrews—gifted with tastes for the beautiful in Art and in Nature, and a sublime love for the true; leaving the traffic of the busy city, content with a moderate competence, soothed by the accomplishments, the graces, and the devotion, of that one cherished daughter, whose high pursuits and purposes never prevented the daily and hourly exercise of those domestic duties and services which the increasing indisposition of her father demanded more and more.

[...] Grace Aguilar prayed fervently to God that she might be enabled to do something to elevate the character of her people in the eyes of the Christian world and—what was, and is, even more important—in their own esteem. They had, she thought, been too long satisfied to go on as they had gone during the days of their tribulation and persecution, content to amass wealth, without any purpose beyond its possession; she panted to set before them "The Records of Israel," to hold up to their admiration "The Women of Israel," those heroic women of whom any nation might be justly proud. Here was a grand purpose,—a purpose which made her heart beat high within her bosom [...]. The young Jewish girl, with few, if any, literary connections, with limited knowledge as to how she could set those things before the world, treasured up her intention for a while, and then imparted it to that mother who, she felt assured would support her in whatever design was high and holy. Her mother exulted in her daughter's plan, and had faith in that daughter's power to work it out; she believed in her noble child, and thanked the God of Israel, who had put the thought into her mind [...].

[T]o those who really knew Grace Aguilar, all eulogium falls short of her deserts; and she has left a blank in her particular walk of literature, which we never expect to see filled up! Her loss to her own people is immense, she was a golden link between the Christian and the Jew; respected and admired alike by both, she drew each in charity closer to the other; she was a proof, living and illustrious, of Jewish excellence and Jewish liberality, and loyalty, and intelligence. The sling of the son of Jesse was not wielded with more power and effect against the scorner of his people, than was her pen against the giant Prejudice.

We have dwelt more than may be thought necessary on Grace Aguilar's championship of her own people, because *that* distinguishes her from all other female authors of our time; and when writing of the "fold of Judah," there is a tone of feeling in all she has published which elevates and sustains her in a remarkable manner. In conversation, the mention of her people produced the same effect. Sometimes she seemed as one inspired; and the intense brightness of her eyes, the deep tones of her voice, the natural and unaffected eloquence of her words, when referring to the past history of the Jews, and the positive radiance of her countenance when she spoke of the gathering of the tribes at Jerusalem, could never be forgotten by those who knew this young Jewish lady [...].

Grace Aguilar had earnestly desired that we should have met her at Frankfurt [...]. This was, however, impossible; but when we knew that we should see her no more in this world, we promised ourselves a pilgrimage to her grave; and over all the plans which mingled with our dreams of the splendid churches and vast cathedrals we were to see in Germany, would come a vision of Grace Aguilar's quiet grave in the Jewish burying-ground of Frankfort-on-the-Maine [...].

Mrs. Aguilar had told us that HER grave was near the wall of the Protestant burying-ground,—and there we found it.

[...] Our pilgrimage was accomplished. It was, though in a foreign city, a pilgrimage to an English shrine, for it was to the grave of an English Woman, pure and good. On the 16th of September, 1847, at the early age of thirty-one, Grace Aguilar was laid in that cemetery, far from the England she loved so well—the bowl was broken, the silver cord was loosed!

8. Excerpts from letters, Rebecca Gratz to Miriam Gratz Cohen.[1]

June 3, 1845

[...] Miss Aguilar's Women of Israel is a delightful book and will raise her reputation as an author and as an Israelite, Mr Leeser has sent on the work to Mr Cohen I have obtained a copy from him, when you write to her present my affectionate and admiring regards to her, I wish she would send you a vol. of domestic worship—we want devotional exercises for every day in the week—and could print an edition that would yield her some profit, and be cheap enough to suit the smallest means [...]

God bless you,

---

1 From Southern Historical Collection #2639, Series 1, Folder 8, [UNC].

Decr 18th—1845

I have [...] been applied to for more copies of Miss Aguilar's "Women of Israel" than Mr Leeser can supply if your husband has any unsold copies to spare I should be glad if he would entrust them to her Agent here, in order that Mrs Lee of Ball and Miss Peters could be gratified—The last copy Mr Leeser had I obtained for Mrs Sullivan last week, I am glad she has become so popular and hope her future writing may be equally successful.—do you not think the Occident improves under the patronage of our fair country-women? [...].

Philadelphia, Jany 16th—1847

[...] Have you heard lately from Miss Aguilar is it not time for her new work to be forth coming I am constantly lending her books to my Christian friends—for tho' they will sometimes read, very few will buy them—

I took the liberty of giving Mr David a letter of introduction to her, and recommended him as a friend of yours—

Mr S. Solis a year ago went to England and took letters to her—she received him so kindly and talked freely of her books to him—he has not half the good breeding or intelligence of Mr D—and therefore I thought it might gratify them both to meet—She is entitled to the homage of Israelites for the great good she has done for the [...] efforts she is making to spiritualize their minds and hearts in the cause most important to individuals as well as to communities—and she should not be surprised if she is frequently intruded on with expressions of gratitude—or visits of thanks [...]

Feby 2nd—1847.

[...] Miss Aguilar stands at the head of the present tree of literary Jews. The Miss Moss' are also very agreeable writers and we have some very fair authoresses on this side the water [...].

Oct. 24th 1847

[...] The last arrivals brought letters containing heavy news for us all my dear Miriam—heavy news for the literary world—most heavy for the Jewish Nation in the death of Miss Aguilar which occurred on the 16th Sept. at Frankfort—at her brother's house, where you knew she went with her Mother in the summer [...].

I do lament her more than I can express—no such an Israelitish pen has been consecrated to the service of religion for ages. Her works will "preserve her in the gale," and live to enlighten generations to come.

Novr 8th 1847

[...] The death of Miss Aguilar is truly a national calamity. I realize your feeling of sorrow as if she had been a personal friend, for we feel as if she were identified with her works and they took possession of our minds and hearts raising them above the earth and its cares and fixed them on the way that leads to heaven—she read the scriptures understandingly and drew inspiration from its pages—She illustrated the beauties and virtues of character and brought them so naturally out as telling examples that all your sympathies were engaged: you could mourn with Eve in her fall, and Leah in her loneliness, while her lofty heroines carried you along with them in their enthusiasm—every thing Miss Aguilar has written makes you love her—and it is sad to think that her very zeal in a holy cause shortened her stay on earth—she wore out a feeble frame, by constant and intense labor [...]. I cannot help regretting that she wrote her last novel I would rather have had all her works dedicated to the holy cause on which she so early in life embarked but she did more than any writer of modern times to sanctify her faith and every Jewish worshiper must hold her memory dear [...].

Appendix B: Victorian Criticism

[Aguilar's writings were reviewed widely within both the Jewish and Christian communities in Britain and the Jewish community in the U.S. Her work was read and commented on by traditional and reforming Jews, men as well as women, conversionists as well as anti-conversionist liberal Christians. The reviews selected for inclusion offer the reader a range of responses to her work.

The earliest is Jacob Franklin's review of *The Spirit of Judaism* in the orthodox Anglo-Jewish periodical *The Voice of Jacob*. It makes for interesting reading next to Isaac Leeser's "Editor's Preface" to *Spirit of Judaism*. Aguilar's reception among Christian readers can be gauged by reviews of *Women of Israel* from the conservative *Athenaeum*, and *Home Influence* from the liberal *Howitt's Journal*. Finally, letters from Aguilar's mother, Sarah, indicate the unusual circumstances under which she compiled and edited *Sabbath Thoughts and Sacred Communings* after Aguilar's death.]

1. Isaac Leeser, Editor's Preface to *The Spirit of Judaism*.

It is with a high degree of gratification that I am enabled to introduce to our religious public a new labourer in the elucidation of our time-honoured faith, in the person of Miss Aguilar, the author of the present publication [...].

My first published sermons having attracted the kind attention of Miss A., she requested me to undertake the editorial supervision of her MS. work on the "Spirit" of our religion. I shall readily be believed when asserting, that I felt truly happy that such a demand had been made upon me; and I accordingly offered my services to do as I was desired [...]. I assure my friends that they cannot afford me a greater pleasure than to receive kindly and favourably the offering on the shrine of our religion so beautifully offered by our distant sister, distant only in body, because though residing in another hemisphere, her spirit is linked to ours by the ties of national consanguinity and the bonds of one belief in the same kind and omnipotent God, whose are the sea and the dry land.

It would not become me to speak of the merits of this work, as it might be supposed that I were but offering the usual and fulsome adulation, which it is only too much the fashion to bestow on an author. Yet I may say without hesitation, that our females will find in it many passages peculiarly calculated to win and arrest their attention by their elegant imagery and truly delicate portraiture. Few indeed, whether male or female, but must rise refreshed and invigorated by a new feeling of religious hopefulness called forth by the pious aspirations which are scattered throughout these pages [...].

The chief points of difference between Miss Aguilar and myself are her seeming aversion to the *tradition*, and her idea that the teaching of mere formal religion opens the door to the admission of Christianity. The reader will easily perceive from my notes to various passages, that I believe the traditions of our fathers of vital importance in elucidating the words of Scripture and regulating our course of action. And I insist, in concert with all who have duly weighed the subject, that, without claiming infallibility for the sayings and decisions of our Rabbins, they are nevertheless entitled to be listened to with profound respect and to be obeyed as holy ancestral customs, unless indeed they flatly contradict the text of Scripture and the legitimate common-sense deductions therefrom. It is too evident for denial by the most prejudiced, that a discretionary power was conferred by the law of Moses upon the various chief tribunals for the time being, (see Deut. xvii. 10;) and their decisions, together with the oral traditions delivered by Moses himself to the elders, always constituted our customs, and are what we term the oral law, or tradition. That many things may have crept in in process of time, neither warranted by the strict letter of the law nor necessary for any useful purpose, I will neither deny nor affirm, for this is not the place to do so; but this much may be asserted without fear of contradiction, that without traditional authority there could be no Jewish conformity; since others use the Bible as well as we do, and still their conduct is so totally different from ours. Now what constitutes this difference, but our mode of interpretation? And whence is this derived, but from tradition? I regret that the small space I am necessarily limited to in this preface prevents me from enlarging on the subject [...].

2. Jacob Franklin, Review of *The Spirit of Judaism*, from *The Voice of Jacob.*

This is truly becoming a printing age among our people; the spirit of former times is reviving, and an imperious sense of duty is impelling many to step forth from the ranks, to enquire, and to inform. From the ranks—and wherefore?—On all sides we find an eagerness to be instructed, and guided:—and where are our *leaders*?

But this is a review, and we owe it to the pious spirit which conceived the work before us, to explain how the above queries have intruded. Their best apology is the frequent notes of her own editor; a series of comments and corrections, forced upon him by the necessity of counteracting the erroneous impressions which the text would else produce on the ordinary reader. The deeper research, the wider, experience, and, therefore, sounder judgment of the Rev. Editor, impels him to break through the stricter line usually observed, with an author's concurrence, and to protect his own reputation, by frequent protests against the views he helps to disseminate.—We sincerely hope that these strictures will be construed as courteous as they are candid. No offence can be reasonably entertained at the institution of a comparison between the qualifications of an editor, thus elected by herself, and the author from whom he differs. A lady, and that too a young lady, whatever the advantages of quick perception conceded to her sex, is, by the iron rule of custom, limited to fewer opportunities of acquiring that information and experience, which might restrict a too apt disposition to generalize from few facts. The notions which many form of Talmudical study, or of traditional doctrine, are founded not on what they sift from them, but on what they are told concerning them. The book before us bears evident traces of the peculiar readings of its fair writer, not designedly or even avoidably peculiar, so far as she is concerned; the peculiarity is at once an evidence of an activity on the part of others, and a supineness on the part of those responsible, among ourselves. The traces referred to are conspicuous—in Miss Aguilar's frequent refutations of Anti-Jewish sophistries—her rather overstated estimate of the part to be played by a Messiah in our religious system—and her occasionally exaggerated apprehensions, of the success of those who would apostatize us.

We will now turn to the more agreeable task of pointing out the many beauties which the work contains [...].

3. Review of *The Women of Israel*, *Athenaeum*, August 2, 1845, 829-30.

To criticize a work like this is a task of some delicacy, if not difficulty. The author being a Jewess, enthusiastically attached to her ancient faith, and entertaining no great respect for the Nazarenes, or, perhaps, we should say the religion of the Nazarenes, the critic's first duty is to suppress feelings which, however natural, must not bias him in the exercise of his judgement. His next, is to make all reasonable allowances for the influences of education on her mind—the authoress would say on his own—and, consequently, for the power of prejudices which, though often unperceived by herself, creep forth in several passages of her book. He must, indeed, do more than this: he must elevate himself to such a position that he can look down with calmness on the growth of such prejudices, on their ever active energy, and on the circumstances which rendered them an inevitable result. There are prejudices, which all may lament, but which, at the same time, every honest mind must respect—not in, or for, themselves, but purely in consideration of the circumstances to which we allude.

Divesting ourselves then (at least as far as possible) of the feelings which "have grown with our growth, and strengthened with our strength," and become a part of our moral nature, we do not hesitate to characterize this work as a delightful contribution to the stock of our sacred literature. It is, in the best sense of the word, a woman's production. Dictated by feelings at once pure and fervent; eloquent, sometimes impassioned; glowing with the warmest spirit of devotion; entering with unspeakable and intuitive delicacy into the motives and conduct of the female characters of the Old Testament, it is even more creditable to the heart than to the head. It will be read by no person, whatever his difference of creed, without respect for the author.

But while awarding her this high and just praise, we must regret that she has allowed herself the use of expressions in regard to Christianity which, though few in number, and evidently the result rather of temporary feeling than of design, will be fatal to the success of her book. We put it to herself whether (supposing that she intended the book for Christian no less than Jewish reading) she has acted either discreetly or considerately in the censure of tenets and of writings which, though she may consider them the offspring of prejudice, she cannot fail to respect as honest prejudice. She is much too enlightened not to know that in a subject so momentous as religion, no man would willingly err; and her own piety must have taught her that errors which God tolerates, ought also to be tolerated by mankind. She may, indeed, reply that the fanatical denunciations of the (so called) Christians in all ages, on her faith and people, have sometimes provoked expressions which she would not otherwise have used. But such conduct will only lead to the retort, that she furnishes another illustration of the truth of the charge against her community—of their returning evil for evil. Unfeignedly do we regret that religious asperity should for a moment have found its way into a work otherwise so excellent—so calculated to inspire every reader with respect for the female characters of Scripture. Would that the passages containing them (they are but few) were entirely erased from it! The general tenor of her observations proves that hers is not a controversial mind—that she has not much taste for censure, which, indeed, seems alien to her nature. But though the aggregate of all the expressions at which a Christian might take offence, would not fill half-a-dozen pages, still they are there; and unfortunately alike for herself and her book, they cannot fail to neutralize the good which she would otherwise have effected.

It may, in reply, be urged that truth is truth, let it come from whatever pen it may; and consequently that the general merit of "The Women of Israel" cannot, and ought not to be affected by the occasional display of prejudice, especially when that prejudice is so honest. Granted. Nobody more than ourselves deplores the bigotry which will not make allowance for education and circumstances. It is surely no part of wisdom to refuse the gold because it is combined with dross; especially when, as in the present case, the dross bears so insignificant a proportion to the whole. But alas! such is human nature, that the evil, however minute, is always admitted to counterbalance the greatest good! For our own parts, we do not think any worse either of the book or of the author from the blemish in question. But others will not exercise the same charity, though by neglecting to do so, they deprive themselves of the high and pure gratification the book is so capable of affording. A few minds will value truth, and feeling, and eloquence, wherever they may be found—in Jew or Christian, in Pagan or Mohammedan—and with the approbation of those few Grace Aguilar must be satisfied.

4. Review of *Home Influence: A Tale for Mothers and Daughters*, *Howitt's Journal* 1.18 (May 1, 1847): 251.

The works of Grace Aguilar prove of how little vital consequence are the differences of creed, where the heart is influenced by the spirit of true religion. In this spirit, the Jew and the Christian are one. Earnest faith in one God, the universal Father, makes us all brethren, and true brotherhood is love. In this spirit are the works of this young Jewish lady conceived; and we unhesitatingly recommend them to every Christian, be he young or old.

The work before us is the first which Miss Aguilar has written not immediately intended for "her own" people. To quote her preface, "in this simple, domestic story, the characters are all Christians, believing in and practicing the Christian religion; all doctrinal points, therefore, have been avoided, and the author has sought only to illustrate the spirit of true piety, and the virtues always designated as the Christian virtues thence proceeding"[...].

The work, as addressed to mothers, is intended to inculcate and illustrate sound principles of education [...].

Out of [...] simple materials a story of such deep interest is made up, that if we were inclined to find one little fault with the work, it would be that there are parts of the second volume, where the plot is deepest—if that may be called plot which is in itself so simple—which are almost too painful and exciting [...].

5. Abraham Benisch, Review of Hester Rothschild, trans., *Imrei Lev: Prayers and Meditations for Every Situation and Occasion in Life*, *Jewish Chronicle*, 1 Aug. 1856.

It is a remarkable phenomenon on the horizon of Anglo-Jewish literature that it is women, not men, that shine there as the principal stars. The translations of Miss Goldsmid and the original writings of the late Miss Aguilar and Mrs. H. Montefiore, are productions of which the community may well be proud. It is in vain that we seek for an explanation of this phenomenon. We cannot look for it in the nature of our literature, for its abstract character and gravity seem to hold out little attraction to the female mind, nor can we discover it in precedent, emulation, or example set elsewhere, for female authors have been comparatively rare in Jewish literature, nor is this field at all cultivated by continental Jewesses. Teeming as the modern German and French Jewish presses do with literary productions, we are not yet acquainted with one which proceeded from a female mind. This distinctive mark seems to be wholly and entirely reserved for the Anglo-Jewish literature [...]. If the works of the female writers should exhibit some of the defects under which productions of female minds are supposed to be apt to labour, such shortcomings [...] are amply compensated by beauties and excellencies which the minds of women generally elaborate in their greatest perfection.

6. Letters from Sarah Aguilar to Miriam and Solomon Cohen on the publication of *Sabbath Thoughts and Sacred Communings*.[1]

54 Gt Prescot Street
Goodman's Fields
23d May—1850

My dear Mrs Cohen

[...] I have frequently thought over Mr Cohen's kindly expressed wish, to publish a portion of the beautiful prayers written by my Angel Child for my benefit.—I think such a request had been made to her—but she seemed to shrink from it, fearing to be thought presumptuous—Had she met with the appreciation in England she has received from America, perhaps she might have been induced to publish some of them—. As she did not I cannot yet make up my mind to bring them before the Public—but present my very kind regards to Mr Cohen and tell him he has my full and

1 From Southern Historical Collection #2639, Series 1, Folder 8, [UNC].

entire permission to have published twenty or thirty copies of the manuscript in your possession for the benefit of those friends who would value and appreciate them as you and Mr Cohen do […].

54 Gt Prescot St
Goodman's Fields
16th Sept. [1851] My dear Sir

I accept your most kind and friendly offer in the same spirit in which it is given [...] I have got 4 vols. of Manuscript Prayers from which I will make selections, and send to you as soon as I have copied them […]. Mrs Cohen was much anxious to have the "Sabbath Thoughts on Family Prayer" made public, she knew so many Mothers who would gladly purchase it and who were quite grieved at not being able to obtain it—in fact she told me I *ought not* to withhold any of my dear child's religious thoughts, which would prove a blessing, perhaps even more to the generation to come than to the present—

54 Gt Prescot Street
Goodman's Fields
31st December—51

My dear Sir

I have at length finished copying the Prayers and Meditations, selected from my Angel Child's Books; but I still hesitate, and ask myself; "Have I any right can I be justified, thus to publish my Daughters private thoughts and prayers, which were written solely for her own use, many of them on various occasions, concerning only herself, and applying to her God for guidance and assistance in all things:" her Father, Mother, Brother never having seen them, ought I to bring them before the Public[?] [W]hen requested to compose and publish prayers for individual use my sweet child refused, she had not courage to comply, being aware that by many persons she had been considered presumtuous [sic], for writing at all on religious subjects that as a woman, and a very young one she could know little or nothing on the subject, and *one* individual told her Father that he *could* not purchase a copy of "the Jewish Faith" unless it were read and corrected by some man tho' he did [not] say who—*that* my child would not allow, saying that nothing should go forth to the world hers unless she could boldly and fearlessly write as she *felt and thought.* Had she been spared to have altered her opinion and at length to have complied with the wishes of our friends in America, she would have doubtless written some for the purpose, and not thus have brought her own private thoughts feelings, and imaginary feelings, before a severe harsh judging world, who may on reading her beautiful prayers, fancy she must have been very wicked and sinful, not knowing that the most pious are by far the most humble, and frequently accuse themselves of weaknesses and failings, whilst many who do not "know themselves" and study every thought and feeling of heart and mind as my dear Grace was in the habit of doing, may fancy they have not a sin, weakness, or failing to confess, and implore strength to guard against.—I do not say I can never send them but I must study this a little more and perhaps keep back some that I have copied.—

54 Gt Prescot Street
Goodman's Fields
26th Feby 1852 My dear Sir

I have at length determined to send you the Prayers &c of my Angel Child.—I have read them many times over and have taken the opinion of a Friend who was intimate with and truly loved my sweet Grace. She agreed with me that some of those I had copied had better be with-drawn, which I have done and which will account for the numbering of the pages being in many places altered, but which I hope will not cause any mistakes in the printing.—Mr B Cohen has kindly promised to forward the Parcel to you, by the same steamer that will take this letter tomorrow.—Give my kind love to Mrs Cohen and ask her to read them all through and if she thinks there are any that had better *not* be published, to take them away, beg her to act as if they were her own daughter's writings [...].

Appendix C: Romantic and Victorian Contexts

[Aguilar's literary education consisted largely of the popular literature published during the late Romantic and early Victorian periods when she was growing up. Many of these texts were concerned with the role of Jews in English history, society, and politics.

Byron's pervasive influence on Aguilar is felt everywhere: his invocation of the natural sublime in Canto IV of *Childe Harold's Pilgrimage*, his romanticization of the Wandering Jew in *Cain*, and his lyrics celebrating Biblical figures in *Hebrew Melodies* (1815) all shape Aguilar's work. His depiction of the Biblical figure of Jephthah's daughter (Judges 11) in *Hebrew Melodies* was perhaps especially important. Like many such poems of its day, Byron's poem recalls a woman killed because her father has taken an oath that, if God will make him victorious in war, he will sacrifice the first thing he sees upon returning home. The first thing he sees is his daughter. The conflict between Jephthah and his daughter in Byron's poem (like the conflict between the money-grubbing Isaac and his more compassionate daughter Rebecca in *Ivanhoe*) was often used to imply that Jewish women were the self-sacrificing and heroic victims of an antiquated, arbitrarily rule-bound, and materialist patriarchy. Although Aguilar chose not to discuss the tale of Jephthah's daughter directly in *The Women of Israel*, she nonetheless vigorously rejected Byron's implication that Jewish women were oppressed, either by Jewish law or Jewish men. She also rejected Byron's Romantic nationalism—displayed, for example, when he went to fight in the Greek war of independence. Instead of advocating a Byronic vision of an autonomous Jewish nation-state, Aguilar's novella *The Perez Family* depicts Jews as assimilated English citizens, productive members of a thriving diaspora harboring no aspirations for a nation-state of their own.

Some of Aguilar's most important influences were Walter Scott's historical romances of Scotland and his Jewish romance *Ivanhoe* (1819). She drew inspiration, positive and negative, from Scott's depiction of the beautiful but exotic "Jewess," agreeing that Jewish women were admirable like Scott's Rebecca, but disagreeing that Jews were too oriental and foreign to be accepted as full English citizens. In her historical romance *The Vale of Cedars*, she directly resisted Ivanhoe's claim—that a Jewish woman cannot understand chivalry because she is "no Christian"—by having her heroine, Maria, fall in love with the chivalrous Englishman, Arthur Stanley. (On the other hand, Maria refuses to convert to Christianity to marry Stanley, suggesting that Aguilar's Jews do not desire to be radically assimilated.) As Aguilar's story "The Escape" illustrates, she rejected *Ivanhoe*'s conclusion, in which Isaac and Rebecca exile themselves from England to Granada. In "The Escape," Almah and Alvar do just the reverse, migrating *from* the Iberian peninsula *to* England.

Wordsworth's poem, "A Jewish Family," depicts Jews as admirably romantic wanderers. This was perhaps somewhat more akin to Aguilar's view. No doubt she would have applauded Wordsworth's poetic attempt to "redeem" Jews from "scorn," but she would probably also have objected to the poem's intense focus on the family's aesthetic beauty, as though these Jews were figures from one of Raphael's paintings or throwbacks to the prophets of ancient Palestine, rather than being mundane modern human beings with all too human needs.

As much as her poetry was inspired by the Romantics, its form and content were perhaps more directly related to the sentimental poems, prophecies, and hymns of Felicia Hemans in books like *Records of Woman* (1828). In her mature poems, Aguilar developed a style and an ideology analogous to that of Hemans. Like Hemans, she idealizes motherhood, and uses maternal poetry to meditate on political events. In what is perhaps her most successful poem, "The Wanderers," she gives voice to the figure of Hagar, the mother of Ishmael whose name in Hebrew means "the stranger," and whose plea on behalf of her son is that the stranger should find acceptance. But as Cynthia Scheinberg as shown, Aguilar resisted Hemans' attempt in "The Song of Miriam," reprinted here, to use women's prophecy from the Hebrew Bible as a precursor to English Christian women's poetry.

Finally, Aguilar was influenced by the non-fiction prose writers of the period. She modeled her own prose style as well as the domestic ideology displayed in *The Women of Israel*, *Spirit of Judaism*, and *The Jewish Faith* on the conduct manuals popular in her day, represented here by Sarah Stickney Ellis in a selection from *Women of England* (1838). In Aguilar's polemics, she shared T.B. Macaulay's Whiggish view, in his speech to the House of Commons on Jewish civil disabilities (1831), that Jews should be permitted the full rights of citizenship. She disagreed, however, with Macaulay's conclusion that, once given full rights, Jews would eventually convert to Christianity.]

1. George Gordon, Lord Byron, "Jephthah's Daughter," from *Hebrew Melodies* (1815).

SINCE our Country, our God—Oh, my sire!
Demand that thy Daughter expire;
Since thy triumph was bought by thy vow—
Strike the bosom that's bared for thee now!

And the voice of my mourning is o'er,
And the mountains behold me no more:
If the hand that I love lay me low,
There cannot be pain in the blow!

And of this, oh, my Father! be sure—
That the blood of thy child is as pure
As the blessing I beg ere it flow,
And the last thought that soothes me below.

Though the virgins of Salem lament,
Be the judge and the hero unbent!
I have won the great battle for thee,
And my father and country are free!

When this blood of thy giving hath gush'd,
When the voice that thou lovest is hush'd,
Let my memory still be thy pride,
And forget not I smiled as I died!

2. Walter Scott, from *Ivanhoe* (1819).

CHAPTER XXVIII

The wandering race, sever'd from other men,
Boast yet their intercourse with human arts;
The seas, the woods, the deserts, which they haunt,
Find them acquainted with their secret treasures;
And unregarded herbs, and flowers, and blossoms,
Display undreamt-of powers when gather'd by them.

The Jew

OUR history must needs retrograde for the space of a few pages, to inform the reader of certain passages material to his understanding the rest of this important narrative. His own intelligence may indeed have easily anticipated that, when Ivanhoe sunk down, and seemed abandoned by all the world, it was the importunity of Rebecca which prevailed on her father to have the gallant young warrior transported from the lists to the house which, for the time, the Jews inhabited in the suburbs of Ashby.

It would not have been difficult to have persuaded Isaac to this step in any other circumstances, for his disposition was kind and grateful. But he had also the prejudices and scrupulous timidity of his persecuted people, and those were to be conquered.

'Holy Abraham!' he exclaimed, 'he is a good youth, and my heart bleeds to see the gore trickle down his rich embroidered haqueton, and his corslet of goodly price; but to carry him to our house! damsel, hast thou well considered? He is a Christian, and by our law we may not deal with the stranger and Gentile, save for the advantage of our commerce.'

'Speak not so, my dear father,' replied Rebecca; 'we may not indeed mix with them in banquet and in jollity; but in wounds and in misery, the Gentile becometh the Jew's brother.'

'I would I knew what the Rabbi Jacob ben Tudela would opine on it,' replied Isaac; 'nevertheless, the good youth must not bleed to death. Let Seth and Reuben bear him to Ashby.'

'Nay, let them place him in my litter,' said Rebecca; 'I will mount one of the palfreys.'

'That were to expose thee to the gaze of those dogs of Ishmael and of Edom,' whispered Isaac, with a suspicious glance towards the crowd of knights and squires. But Rebecca was already busied in carrying her charitable purpose into effect, and listed not what he said, until Isaac, seizing the sleeve of her mantle, again exclaimed, in a hurried voice—'Beard of Aaron! what if the youth perish! If he die in our custody, shall we not be held guilty of his blood, and be torn to pieces by the multitude?'

'He will not die, my father,' said Rebecca, gently extricating herself from the grasp of Isaac—'he will not die unless we abandon him; and if so, we are indeed answerable for his blood to God and to man.'

'Nay,' said Isaac, releasing his hold, 'it grieveth me as much to see the drops of his blood as if they were so many golden byzants from mine own purse; and I well know that the lessons of Miriam, daughter of the Rabbi Manasses of Byzantium, whose soul is in Paradise, have made thee skilful in the art of healing, and that thou knowest the craft of herbs and the force of elixirs. Therefore, do as thy mind giveth thee: thou art a good damsel—a blessing, and a crown, and a song of rejoicing unto me and unto my house, and unto the people of my fathers.'

The apprehensions of Isaac, however, were not ill founded; and the generous and grateful benevolence of his daughter exposed her on her return to Ashby, to the unhallowed gaze of Brian de Bois-Guilbert. The Templar twice passed and repassed them on the road, fixing his bold and ardent look on the beautiful Jewess; and we have already seen the consequences of the admiration which her charms excited, when accident threw her into the power of that unprincipled voluptuary.

Rebecca lost no time in causing the patient to be transported to their temporary dwelling, and proceeded with her own hands to examine and to bind up his wounds. The youngest reader of romances and romantic ballads must recollect how often the females, during the dark ages, as they are called, were initiated into the mysteries of surgery, and how frequently the gallant knight submitted the wounds of his person to her cure whose eyes had yet more deeply penetrated his heart.

But the Jews, both male and female, possessed and practised the medical science in all its branches, and the monarchs and powerful barons of the time frequently committed themselves to the charge of some experienced sage among this despised people when wounded or in sickness. The aid of the Jewish physicians was not the less eagerly sought after, though a general belief prevailed among the Christians that the Jewish rabbins were deeply acquainted with the occult sciences, and particularly with the cabalistical art, which had its name and origin in the studies of the sages of Israel. Neither did the rabbins disown such acquaintance with supernatural arts, which added nothing—for what could add aught?—to the hatred with which their nation was regarded, while it diminished the contempt with which that malevolence was mingled. A Jewish magician might be the subject of equal abhorrence with a Jewish usurer, but he could not be equally despised. It is, besides, probable, considering the wonderful cures they are said to have performed, that the Jews possessed some secrets of the healing art peculiar to themselves, and which, with the exclusive spirit arising out of their condition, they took great care to conceal from the Christians amongst whom they dwelt.

The beautiful Rebecca had been heedfully brought up in all the knowledge proper to her nation, which her apt and powerful mind had retained, arranged, and enlarged, in the course of a progress beyond her years, her sex, and even the age in which she lived. Her knowledge of medicine and of the healing art had been acquired under an aged Jewess, the daughter of one of their most celebrated doctors, who loved Rebecca as her own child, and was believed to have communicated to her secrets which had been left to herself by her aged father at the same time, and under the same circumstances. The fate of Miriam had indeed been to fall a sacrifice to the fanaticism of the times; but her secrets had survived in her apt pupil.

Rebecca, thus endowed with knowledge as with beauty, was universally revered and admired by her own tribe, who almost regarded her as one of those gifted women mentioned in the sacred history. Her father himself, out of reverence for her talents, which involuntarily mingled itself with his unbounded affection, permitted the maiden a greater liberty than was usually indulged to those of her sex by the habits of her people, and was, as we have just seen, frequently guided by her opinion, even in preference to his own.

3. William Wordsworth, "A Jewish Family, in a Small Valley Opposite St. Goar, Upon the Rhine" [composed July 1828;—published in *Yarrow Revisited*, Moxon, 1835.]

GENIUS of Raphael! if thy wings
Might bear thee to this glen,
With fanciful memory left of things
To pencil dear and pen,
Thou wouldst forego the neighbouring Rhine,
And all his majesty—
A studious forehead to incline
O'er this poor family.

The Mother—her thou must have seen,
In spirit, ere she came
To dwell these rifted rocks between,
Or found on earth a name;
An image, too, of that sweet Boy,
Thy inspirations give—
Of playfulness, and love, and joy,
Predestined here to live.

Downcast, or shooting glances far,
How beautiful his eyes,
That blend the nature of the star
With that of summer skies!
I speak as if of sense beguiled;
Uncounted months are gone,
Yet am I with the Jewish Child,
That exquisite Saint John.

I see the dark-brown curls, the brow,
The smooth transparent skin,
Refined, as with intent to show
The holiness within;
The grace of parting Infancy
By blushes yet untamed;
Age faithful to the mother's knee,
Nor of her arms ashamed.

Two lovely Sisters, still and sweet
As flowers, stand side by side;

Their soul-subduing looks might cheat
The Christian of his pride:
Such beauty hath the Eternal poured
Upon them not forlorn,
Though of a lineage once abhorred,
Nor yet redeemed from scorn.

Mysterious safeguard, that in spite
Of poverty and wrong,
Doth here preserve a living light,
From Hebrew fountains sprung;
That gives this ragged group to cast
Around the dell a gleam
Of Palestine, of glory past,
And proud Jerusalem!

4. Thomas Babington Macaulay, from "Speech on Jewish Disabilities" (1831).

[...] My honourable friend, the Member for the University of Oxford, began his speech by declaring that he had no intention of calling in question the principles of religious liberty. He utterly disclaims persecution, that is to say, persecution as defined by himself. It would, in his opinion, be persecution to hang a Jew, or to flay him, or to draw his teeth, or to imprison him, or to fine him; for every man who conducts himself peaceably has a right to his life and his limbs, to his personal liberty and his property. But it is not persecution, says my honourable friend, to exclude any individual or any class from office; for nobody has a right to office: in every country official appointments must be subject to such regulations as the supreme authority may choose to make; nor can any such regulations be reasonably complained of by any member of the society as unjust. He who obtains an office obtains it, not as matter of right, but as matter of favour. He who does not obtain an office is not wronged; he is only in that situation in which the vast majority of every community must necessarily be. There are in the United Kingdom five and twenty million Christians without places; and, if they do not complain, why should five and twenty thousand Jews complain of being in the same case? In this way my honourable friend has convinced himself that, as it would be most absurd in him and me to say that we are wronged because we are not Secretaries of State, so it is most absurd in the Jews to say that they are wronged because they are, as a people, excluded from public employment.

Now, surely my honourable friend cannot have considered to what conclusions his reasoning leads. Those conclusions are so monstrous that he would, I am certain, shrink from them. Does he really mean that it would not be wrong in the legislature to enact that no man should be a judge unless he weighed twelve stone, or that no man should sit in Parliament unless he were six feet high? [...]

My honourable friend has appealed to us as Christians. Let me then ask him how he understands that great commandment which comprises the law and the prophets. Can we be said to do unto others as we would that they should do unto us if we wantonly inflict on them even the smallest pain? As Christians, surely we are bound to consider, first, whether, by excluding the Jews from all public trust, we give them pain; and, secondly, whether it be necessary to give them that pain in order to avert some greater evil. That by excluding them from public trust we inflict pain on them my honourable friend will not dispute. As a Christian, therefore, he is bound to relieve them from that pain, unless he can show, what I am sure he has not yet shown, that it is necessary to the general good that they should continue to suffer.

But where, he says, are we to stop, if once you admit into the House of Commons people who deny the authority of the Gospels? Will you let in a Mussulman? Will you let in a Parsee? Will you let in a Hindoo, who worships a lump of stone with seven heads? I will answer my honourable friend's question by another. Where does he mean to stop? Is he ready to roast unbelievers at slow fires? If not, let him tell us why: and I will engage to prove that his reason is just as decisive against the intolerance which he thinks a duty, as against the intolerance which he thinks a crime. Once admit that we are bound to inflict pain on a man because he is not of our religion; and where are you to stop? Why stop at the point fixed by my honourable friend rather than at the point fixed by the honourable Member for Oldham, who would make the Jews incapable of holding land? And why stop at the point fixed by the honourable Member for Oldham rather than at the point which would have been fixed by a Spanish Inquisitor of the sixteenth century? When once you enter on a course of persecution, I defy you to find any reason for making a halt till you have reached the extreme point [...]. In truth, those persecutors who use the rack and the stake have much to say for themselves. They are convinced that their end is good; and it must be admitted that they employ means which are not unlikely to attain the end. Religious dissent has repeatedly been put down by sanguinary persecution. In that way the Albigenses were put down. In that way Protestantism was suppressed in Spain and Italy, so that it has never since reared its head. But I defy anybody to produce an instance in which disabilities such as we are now considering have produced any other effect that that of making the sufferers angry and obstinate. My honourable friend should either persecute to some purpose, or not persecute at all. He dislikes the word persecution, I know. He will not admit that the Jews are persecuted. And yet I am confident that he would rather be sent to the King's Bench Prison for three months, or be fined a hundred pounds, than be subject to the disabilities under which the Jews lie. How can he then say that to impose such disabilities is not persecution, and that to fine and imprison is persecution? All his reasoning consists in drawing arbitrary lines. What he does not wish to inflict he calls persecution. What he does wish to inflict he will not call persecution. What he takes from the Jews he calls political power. What he is too good-natured to take from the Jews he will not call political power. The Jew must not sit in Parliament: but he may be the proprietor of all the ten-pound houses in a borough. He may have more fifty-pound tenants than any peer in the kingdom. He may give the voters treats to please their palates, and hire bands of gipsies to break their heads, as if he were a Christian and a Marquess. All the rest of this system is of a piece. The Jew may be a juryman, but not a judge. He may decide issues of fact, but not issues of law. He may give a hundred thousand pounds damages; but he may not in the most trivial case grant a new trial. He may rule the money-market: he may influence the exchanges: he may be summoned to congresses of Emperors and Kings. Great potentates, instead of negotiating a loan with him by tying him in a chair and pulling out his grinders, may treat with him as with a great potentate, and may postpone the declaring of war or the signing of a treaty till they have conferred with him. All this is as it should be: but he must not be a Privy Councillor. He must not be called Right Honourable, for that is political power. And who is it that we are trying to cheat in this way? Even Omniscience. Yes, Sir; we have been gravely told that the Jews are under the divine displeasure, and that if we give them political power God will visit us in judgment. Do we then think that God cannot distinguish between substance and form? Does not He know that, while we withhold from the Jews the semblance and name of political power, we suffer them to possess the substance? The plain truth is that my honourable friend is drawn in one direction by his opinions, and in a directly opposite direction by his excellent heart. He halts between two opinions. He tries to make a compromise between principles which admit of no compromise. He goes a certain way in intolerance. Then he stops, without being able to give a reason for stopping. But I know the reason. It is his humanity. Those who formerly dragged the Jew at a horse's tail, and singed his beard with blazing furze-bushes, were much worse men than my honourable friend; but they were more consistent than he [...].

5. Sarah Stickney Ellis, "Modern Education," from *Women of England* (1838).

[...] In order to ascertain what kind of education is most effective in making woman what she ought to be, the best method is to inquire into the character, station, and peculiar duties of woman throughout the largest portion of her earthly career; and then ask, for what she is most valued, admired, and beloved.

In answer to this, I have little hesitation in saying,—For her disinterested kindness. Look at all the heroines, whether of romance or reality—at all the female characters that are held up to universal admiration—at all who have gone down to honoured graves, amongst the tears and the lamentations of their survivors. Have these been the learned, the accomplished women; the women who could speak many languages, who could solve problems, and elucidate systems of philosophy? No: or if they have, they have also been women who were dignified with the majesty of moral greatness [...].

Woman, with all her accumulation of minute disquietudes, her weakness, and her sensibility, is but a meagre item in the catalogue of humanity; but, roused by a sufficient motive to forget all these, or, rather, continually forgetting them, because she has other and nobler thoughts to occupy her mind, woman is truly and majestically great.

Never yet, however, was woman great, because she had great acquirements; nor can she ever be great in herself—personally, and without instrumentality—as an object, not an agent [...].

It is impossible that the teachers, or even the parents themselves, should always know the future destiny of the child; but there is an appropriate sphere for women to move in, from which those of the middle class in England seldom deviate very widely. This sphere has duties and occupations of its own, from which no woman can shrink without culpability and disgrace; and the question is, are women prepared for these duties and occupations by what they learn at school?

For my own part, I know not how education deserves the name, if it does not prepare the individual whom it influences, for filling her appointed station in the best possible manner. What, for instance, should we think of a school for sailors, in which nothing was taught but the fine arts; or for musicians, in which the students were only instructed in the theory of sound?

With regard to the women of England, I have already ventured to assert that the quality for which, above all others, they are esteemed and valued, is their disinterested kindness. A selfish woman may not improperly be regarded as a monster, especially in that sphere of life, where there is a constant demand made upon her services. But how are women taught at school to forget themselves [...?]

In what school, or under what system of modern education, can it be said that the chief aim of the teachers [...] is to correct the evil of selfishness in the hearts of their pupils? Improved methods of charging and surcharging the memory are eagerly sought out, and pursued, at any cost of time and patience, if not of health itself; but who ever thinks of establishing a *selfish* class amongst the girls of her establishment, or of awarding the honours and distinctions of the school to such as have exhibited the most meritorious instances of self-denial for the benefit of others?

6. Felicia Hemans, "The Song of Miriam," from *Works* (1839).

A song for Israel's God!—Spear, crest, and helm,
Lay by the billows of the old Red Sea,
When Miriam's voice o'er that sepulchral realm
Sent on the blast a hymn of jubilee;
With her lit eye, and long hair floating free,
Queen-like she stood, and glorious was the strain,
E'en as instinct with the tempestuous glee
Of the dark waters, tossing o'er the slain.
A song for God's own victory!—O, thy lays
Bright Poesy! were holy in their birth:—
How hath it died, their seraph note of praise,
In the bewildering melodies of earth!
Return from troubling bitter founts—return,
Back to the life-springs of thy native urn!

Appendix D: Victorian Jewish Writers

[Aguilar's contemporaries among Anglo-Jewish writers—especially Marion and Celia Moss, Judith Montefiore, Charlotte Montefiore, and Anna Maria Goldsmid—published poetry, fiction, and non-fiction prose that was distinguishable from Aguilar's in many different ways. For example, Celia Moss's "The Two Pictures" (1855) offered a "Sketch of Domestic Life" among Victorian Jews that was far less idealized than Aguilar's *The Perez Family*, and the Moss sisters' poems on Jerusalem in *Early Efforts* (1838), like their tales in *The Romance of Jewish History* (1840), endorsed Byron's Romantic nationalism, envisioning Jews as members of a nation who might ultimately return to their ancient homeland.

Anglo-Jewish journalism was both a spur and an obstacle to Aguilar's imagination. In the earliest Anglo-Jewish periodical, *The Hebrew Review and Magazine of Rabbinical Literature*, the editor, Morris Raphall, published many of the *midrashim* that had come down from Jewish tradition. In a community that had no belles lettres, these *midrashim* constituted the first Anglo-Jewish fiction. For example, Raphall published a version of the legend of "The Sun and the Moon" (1834). Aguilar subsequently rewrote the gender politics of Raphall's version in her tale, "The Spirit of Night" (included in this edition, pp. 180-85). Male editors of Anglo-Jewish journals also meditated incessantly on the changing roles of women in the community. A significant example was Abraham Benisch, the editor of *The Jewish Chronicle*, whose long editorial, "Our Women" (1861), called for women's greater participation in Jewish life and learning while at the same time lamenting that women were "the weakness in our camp."]

1. Morris Raphall, "The Sun and the Moon," *The Hebrew Review and Magazine of Rabbinical Literature* 2 (1835): 41-42.

From the council of the Eternal the creating decree went forth: "Two lights shall shine in the firmament. They shall rule the earth, and decide revolving times and seasons."

"He spoke and it was." The Sun arose, the first of lights. As a bridegroom comes forth from his chamber, as a hero rejoices in his victorious career, the glorious luminary proceeded on its course, robed in the radiant splendours of the Creator. A chaplet of all colours flowed round his head. Earth rejoiced; the herbs sent forth their fragrance; the flowers expanded in beauty.

The second light beheld the splendid sight, and its heart was filled with envy. It saw that its own splendour could not excel the effulgence of the orb of day.

Repining and complaints broke from the orb of night: "Why do two monarchs occupy One throne? Why must I be the second, and not the first?"

And, suddenly, expelled by its inward discontent, the splendid light of the moon vanished. Far it spread in the empyrean, and became the numerous host of stars.

Pale as death stood the moon, downcast and ashamed before the celestial hosts; weeping she prayed, "Have mercy, Father of all beings, have mercy on me!" And the angel of the Lord stood before the darkened luminary, and announced the irrevocable decree: "Because thou hast envied the splendour of the sun, thy radiance will henceforth be borrowed from his light; arid, when yonder earth passes thee, thou wilt stand, as now thou dost, deprived of thy light, and eclipsed either wholly or in part. But weep not, orb of the silent night. The All-merciful has pardoned thy repining and granted thy prayer. 'Go forth,' he commanded me, 'console the penitent moon. She too shall be a queen in her radiance. The tears of her repentance shall be a reviving balm to all that languish, imparting new force to all whom the noon-tide heat has exhausted.'"

The moon was consoled, and, behold, the pale radiance in which still she shines, flowed around her. She entered on her silent career, the queen of night, leader of the attendant stars. Weeping over her own fault, she commiserates the tears that are shed on earth: She sends forth her silvery rays to console those who mourn, to sympathise with those who suffer.

★ ★ ★ ★ ★ ★ ★ ★

Daughters of beauty, beware of envy. Envy has driven angels from heaven; it has quenched the splendour of the beauteous moon, the silent queen of the night.

2. Celia and Marion Moss, from *Early Efforts. A Volume of Poems by the Misses Moss, of the Hebrew Nation. Aged 18 and 16* (1839).

"Lament for Jerusalem."

Jerusalem, on thy ruin'd walls
  The sun yet sheds its glittering rays,
And shines amid thy lonely halls
  As once it shone in happier days:
And Judea's clime is still as fair,

Though Judah's sons are outcasts there.

How long shall pagan foot profane
  Jehovah's hallow'd shrine;
And memories alone remain
  Of all that once was thine:
How long shall we thy children roam
As exiles from our ancient home.

To weep o'er Salem's blighted fame,
  To gaze upon her strand,
'Tis all the heritage we claim
  Within our father land;
To mourn o'er our free parents' graves
That we their children are but slaves.

When will that glorious hour come,
  When shall we once more see
Thy temple rear its stately dome,
  Thy children with the free:
And thou, our fair, ill-fated land
Amongst the nations take thy stand?

"The Jewish Captive Song."

Gone is thine hour of might,
  Zion, and fallen art thou;
Thy temple's sacred height,
  Is desecrated now,
That I should live to see
  The ruins of that dome,
And Judah's children be
  Bondsmen and slaves to Rome.

When I saw heav'n's wrath descending,
  Why 'scap'd I from the grave,
While thousands died defending,
  The shrines they could not save,
But blest are those who sleep,
  In their quiet resting place,
That they did not live to weep
  O'er the scattering of their race.

"The Return from the Captivity."

Arise sons of Israel arise!
The days of thy liberties dawn,
The Lord hath relented his wrath,
The night of thy slavery's gone.

Let the hills in thy gladness rejoice,
That freedom now smiles upon thee,
Till the ocean's loud echoless voice,
Roars back to the vallies we're free.

They roar and the mountain replies,
In thy dwellings let joyfulness be;
Arise, sons of Israel, arise!
Raise the hymn of thanksgiving, thou'rt free.

3. Abraham Benisch, "Our Women," *Jewish Chronicle*, 8 and 15 Nov. 1861.

Some time ago a lively correspondence on our women was carried on in these columns. Ungallant men assailed the fair sex. Some grave writers assured us that our women were pleasure-hunters, spendthrifts, and card-players, the terror of bachelors anxious to renounce their single blessedness, and the ruin of husbands entrapped by them. Ungainly youths charged their sisters in faith with a preference for the society of the stranger, and querulous fathers of hopeful well-to-do-sons declared that it was they who dissuaded their offspring from linking their fate to those good for nothing, except show and extravagance. The presumed decrease of marriages in the community was laid to the charge of these convenient scapegoats. It is true, these unprotected females neither lacked nor required champions. Bold young ladies, just out of their 'teens, indignantly retorted upon their traducers, whilst challenging all their statements. Old maids, with great pertinacity, contended for the lawfulness of a quiet game, as a poor compensation for the exciting out-door pleasures, arrogated to themselves exclusively by the relentless Lords of creation; whilst staid matrons, with a sigh, admitted the increase of frivolousness among the females, contrasting it—of course to its disadvantage—with the greater restraint and austerity prevailing in their own younger days. The brave defence made by the women themselves, and its open or implied reproof to those whose duty and privilege it is to protect the weak, at last brought also male champions into the field. The faults attributed to our women were unhesitatingly denied by some, or palliated by others [...].

We dismiss at once, as devoid of all foundation, the assertion that our women are either less domesticated, fonder of pleasure, or more extravagant than their Christian neighbours. On this score, to say the least, they deserve no more censure than the females of the rest of the population [...]. If our females are open to any charge, it is a tasteless love of finery, perceptible in the humbler, and perhaps also in the middle classes. But this fondness of adornment, springing as it does from the innocent desire to please, if it leads to greater attention to personal appearance, and to neatness, is not without its redeeming points [...]. But this fault is more than outweighed by virtues in which our women excel. Their sobriety in general, their obedience to their parents when single, their sacred respect for the conjugal ties when married, their profound attachment to their offspring as mothers, mark them in every stage of life. We may have among us slatterns but not drunkards, fallen women but not adulteresses, foolish indulgers of their children but not heartless deniers of the necessaries of life. An honourable acquittal of all the charges urged by our correspondents against our women, must be the verdict [...].

Whilst in every other respect our women need not fear comparison with those of other communities, and may be pronounced to form the elements of our strength, they, in a religious point of view, unfortunately constitute the weakness of our camp [...]. Whilst in all denominations around us the females frequently form the broad arteries in which the religious life circulates, and always the capillary vessels through which it is carried into the households, and even to individuals, our own women, as a rule, are devoid of religious enthusiasm, and not rarely indifferent, if not absolutely hostile, to all religious aspirations. As a rule, the mass of our females is incapable of any exertion, or of any sacrifice, be it pecuniary or of time, for the promotion of any purely religious object. Just compare the number of female worshippers attending the synagogues on Sabbaths with those crowding the churches on Sundays. Just compare the amount of Biblical and religious knowledge possessed by our women with that acquired by our neighbours. Just compare the number of our ladies amidst our middle classes, with plenty of leisure on their hands, who devote themselves to works of charity, requiring time and personal exertion, with that of our neighbours [...]. Those acquainted with the communal history will have no difficulty in tracing many, if not most, of the losses sustained by the Jewish body to the pernicious influence exercised by women in their capacities as wives or mothers.

This is a phenomenon perceived only in modern time, for in the days of our fathers Israel's women were also Israel's heroines. They then constituted as much our religious strength as now our religious weakness [...]. When

Ferdinand and Isabella of Spain decreed the expulsion of their Jewish subjects from the kingdom, it was the women, who encouraged the desponding men, who confirmed the waverers, and who with a religious heroism rarely equalled, and never surpassed, spurred and cheered on those by whom they themselves ought to have been sustained. They, the physically weaker, were the spiritually stronger; they who knew that the hardships, the toil, and deprivations to be endured, must press upon them with double weight—they who knew that death was not the worst fate that could befall them—they who knew that they must fall the first sacrifices of the atrocious edict—these delicate, these fragile women, in the terrible hour of trial, when the stout hearts of their husbands, sons, fathers, and brothers, seemed to fail—when in the awful struggle between the present ease, safety, and domestic happiness, and the contemplation of the impending unutterable woes, their steps faltered, called upon their male relatives to stand firm, and prepare themselves for the bitterest lot, rather than ward it off by the renunciation of their religious convictions. The contrast between our women of then and of now is truly saddening, and the grave, very grave question arises, Whence this woeful degeneracy? [...] How is it that the mother, the confidant of her child, her guide and counselor—at all events, the earliest observer of the emotions of her heart, should, if not encourage the sinful affection, at least connive at it? [...].

The order of religious instruction to our women must be reversed [...]. We must begin by unrolling before the female mind the glorious principles upon which Judaism is based, must make clear to it the momentous importance of the belief in the strict unity of God, must point out Israel's heaven-appointed mission, evolve from it the special laws enjoined for this purpose on God's witnesses on earth, must with the thread of history in our hands show how this mission had at all times been discharged, what sacrifices were made for it, and what effect it had upon mankind's fate. We must fill the female heart with an ideal Israel which it can understand, after which it can aspire, and which it can venerate. There is a poetry, there is a grandeur, there is a sublimity in these religious principles and historical events which, whilst convincing the intellect, are well calculated powerfully to lay hold on the feeling. Once convince the intellect, once enlist the feelings, and enthusiasm is sure to come, and strictness in the observance of religious ceremonies is much more likely to follow than through mere mechanical injunction. Again, our endeavour must be to awaken in the female mind a sense of its religious dignity and independence, and to impress the imagination by some striking solemnity that shall bring these ideas vividly to its consciousness, and fix them for life. No solemnity is so well calculated to produce this effect as that known by religious confirmation, or rather initiation. By making it analogous to the *Bar Mitsvah* of our sons, and its counterpart, our females will feel themselves raised to the equals of men, and proud of the distinction of having been received into religious fellowship. And lastly, we must endeavour to create in the spirit of our age a popular religious literature in the vernacular, to replace that of former centuries, which has become unenjoyable. These are the remedies which may serve as efficient substitutes for the means employed by our forefathers, in order firmly to attach their daughters to the God of Israel [...].

Appendix E: Aguilar's Frankfurt Journal

[Aguilar set out for Frankfurt-am-Main for what would be her final journey on June 15, 1847. She died three months later on September 16, after unsuccessful treatment in the waters of Schwalbach, and was buried in the Frankfurt Cemetery. Until now, not much has been known about the circumstances of her journey or the final months of her life, beyond the few spare details that Sarah Aguilar relates in her "Memoir." The recent reappearance of Aguilar's last journal, detailing the experiences of her trip through Belgium to Frankfurt, and her final weeks in that city, is therefore of considerable interest.

Space considerations prevent inclusion of a full transcription of the journal, which runs to some 32,000 words. About a third of the journal is included here, highlighting the characteristic turns of thought and the variety of interests that captured Aguilar's attention during her final weeks. The journal begins in the vein of many middle class English travelogues of the period. Aguilar exhibits a Romantic interest in local folklore and customs, in gothic architecture and stories of the supernatural, in music, opera, and art criticism, and above all in viewing and describing natural landscapes. Her landscape descriptions vie with one another for superlatives, the most common words in the journal being "beautiful" and "luxuriant." She seems to say of each new landscape that it is the most arresting one she has ever seen.

This surfeit of praise seems to be a way of combating certain darker moods that well up throughout the journal. Constantly interrupting her paens to natural beauty are descriptions of the dinginess of the Judengasse (or Jews' street), laconic historical anecdotes detailing German persecution of Jews, and observations on the sometimes quite literal marks left by the recent Napoleonic wars on German villages, castles, people, and landscape. Political questions keep interrupting the natural idyll. She compares the electoral system of the Prussian towns to England's hereditary succession, and reflects on the dangers faced by social reformers. In a way that is both particular to Aguilar as a Jewish writer and typical of early Victorian travel writing, her historical sense constantly disrupts the Wordsworthian impulse to idealize nature.

But none of these anti-Romantic details unsettle the journal as much as its record of the rapid deterioration of Aguilar's body and the profound spiritual and creative crisis this engendered. Her illness not only incapacitated her to greater and greater degrees, but precipitated feelings of depression, severe guilt over these feelings, and despair that she had been abandoned by God. She describes the disease's destructive effects on her imagination. Like the ideal Victorian woman she described in her published works, she constantly strives here to remain cheerful and useful. She does not permit her spiritual crisis to take up the greater part of the journal. In fact, she rarely refers to herself in these pages, generally simply omitting the first person pronoun altogether when reporting on her observations. Likewise, although she makes passing mention to her recent reading (Schiller, Ruskin, Dickens, Dumas), she makes no mention whatever of her own career. There are only the most circumspect remarks about the people with whom she travels (her mother, her brother Emanuel, her friend, Anne Samuda), and very little of her circle in Frankfurt. In sum, the journal communicates a pervasive sense of isolation, even in the midst of friends. Michael Dugdale captures the experience of reading the journal when he writes that it is "desperately moving [...] as you read it you can almost feel her dying [...] it is tragically sad [...] until finally she is too unwell to write."[1]

One can often infer Aguilar's internal state from her external descriptions. For instance, she is repeatedly fascinated by the "spark" emanating from the German firefly, which she seems to identify with her own dwindling spark of life. At another point, in an otherwise lighthearted description of an opera (Carl Maria von Weber's *Oberon*), she suddenly shifts tone to describe the opera's principal singer, one Mrs. Tuszchek: "I never saw any one look so ghost like as Tuszchek—It was almost pain to me to look at her as if she could not live—her hands and throat were like those of a skeleton and her face white as death" (July 19, 1847). In Mrs. Tuszchek's face Aguilar seems to have found an object by which to contemplate her own impending demise.

For readers today, the journal's pathos is only heightened by its promise of a new direction in Aguilar's work. The observations here are sharper, the writing less sentimental and more truculent, than in almost any of her earlier prose. In its numerous forays into art and opera criticism, the journal continues the trend of Aguilar's later work toward cultural critique. One can only wonder how Aguilar might have absorbed and responded to the trends of the high Victorian period—especially realism—and whether in fact she would have pursued the kind of cultural criticism exhibited here on her way to becoming the nineteenth century's Jewish Ruskin.

Square brackets in the transcription indicate places when Aguilar's handwriting is illegible. A word in the brackets indicated the editor's best guess at the word.]

---

1 Michael Dugdale, email to Michael Galchinsky, Oct. 5, 2002.

Wed., June 16—The journal of an Invalid cannot be of the same value or information as when health permits the indulgence of inclination in visiting every spot worth seeing & making every movement of time tell—I can only mention things which have passed before me, leaving with regret much that is of much greater interest—

Thursday 17—E. & A. started for the Cathedral[1] at ½7—greatly regretted felt too exhausted to attempt even driving to it—more tired than last night [...]—Had breakfast of eggs rolls & tea in a private sitting room down stairs overlooking the street, where I amused myself with watching the women in their hooded cloaks—some with the hoods thrown over the head & others with caps—but none with bonnets[2]—The same stillness reigned in the morning as last night & the same air of age & of the Past—The little hostess came to wish us "bon voyage" as did the little waiter—our sleeping there seeming rather a novelty to them—Drove thoro' the Town to the cathedral which I could not resist trying to walk around—It was the first Catholic Cathedral I ever saw & I was struck & delighted by it—tho' I could not see it half long enough. On every pillar is a Statue—& between the pillars on the sides of the Aisles—having large paintings all of course in subjects from the Old & New Testaments—Before the high altar in the center of the choir was a bier in yellow & black—from which the corpse had only been removed the day before [...]—But the most striking object was the pulpit, which describes in the most exquisite oak carving the conversion of St. Paul—There is the frightened Horse falling on its haunches—& St. Paul half on the ground with the whole countenance turned in horror to the vision of the Crucifixion & an angel pointing to it which formed the left side of the Pulpit[3]—[...] The Aisles all open into shrines which particularly struck me especially that of the Virgin—by the Side are large cases containing a variety of silver offerings mostly in the shape of hearts, which have been brought by devotees, who have been cured by the intercession of the Virgin or Saint, to whom they have come—An Old Woman kneeling at the entrance of the Virgin's Shrine most devoutly telling her beads—was the complete realization of a picture—The absence of pews added so much to the grandeur [...] I could have lingered there for hours—recalling not only the past but agreeing with E's observations as to the Rise of the Arts in Religion,—Painting, Sculpture, & Architecture—inspiring so much greater perfection & higher efforts than since the era of Protestantism has forbidden decoration in

1 Aguilar is passing through Malines, Belgium.

2 Bonnets were in fashion in England at this time.

3 For Saul of Tarsus' conversion to become the apostle Paul, see Acts 9.

churches—I could only notice one touch of an Archbishop—very large—with a fresco of Death summoning him—Left it with the greatest regret, & proceeded to the Station where sat some time watching the concourse of people watching for the various trains—Saw one woman with a high case like the French. In our carriage was a young Priest—a particularly pleasing looking man especially when he spoke. Thought of Father Clement.[1]

Friday 18th [...] Andernach[2] containing a Cathedral or Dom—with four curious Towers of the beginning of the 12 century & a picturesque Tower close to the water's edge round below & eight sided above—of 1520—& a Jews' bath[3] of considerable antiquity—The Jews were expelled from Andernach in 1596 & have never settled there since.[...]

Coblenz—The whole course of this beautiful view from Bonn to Andernach especially was one view of Rock Valley Mountain & vineyards which last in this early season have merely the appearance of diagonal green lines in rows one above another [...] thus covering every inch of ground from the highest ledge where it seemed no foot could scale to plant them down to the very brink of the river—Sometimes the most beautiful valleys would run up between the rocks & hills—Then the mountains would as it were fall back from the brink of the river—& then a little while afterwards close upon it again—The effects of light & shadow from the clouds continually passing over the blue heavens were magnificent—Sometimes the whole back ground was a glowing flood of light & the foreground a mass of shade relieved here & there by patches of brilliant sunshine—then like the shifting of phantasmagoria the back ground would become dark as a thundercloud the midmost distance bright as a beam of sunshine & the nearest [ ] grey—& then all would change again—still tho' most beautiful & of more continued beauty than our little Island can display—I have seen as much of beauty in the Morwell Rocks & when rowing up the [ ][4]—I could not feel it *more* of loveliness—only that it continued up so many miles—& thoro' so many hours—The view of Ehrenbreitstein & the bridge & boats at Coblenz was more striking than any other point of that

---

1 A reference to the title character in Grace Kennedy's, *Father Clement: a Roman Catholic Story*, 9th ed. (Edinburgh: William Oliphant & Son, 1838), a romance about Roman Catholic integration in England, first published in 1823. Father Clement is an ideal and attractive young priest.

2 Along with Coblenz and Bonn named further in the paragraph, a principal town in the Rhineland area of the Prussian Territories near Frankfurt-am-Main.

3 A ritual bath, or *mikveh*, in which Jews immerse themselves for purposes of spiritual purification.

4 Presumably these are English locales.

day's voyage—The fortress & height of Ehrenbreitstein painting a view of grandeur one might gaze on long without any sensation of satiety—At Coblenz the Moselle [river] joins the Rhine & from any height they say the blue waters of the former are distinctly traceable in the more turbid stream of the latter—Mamma—E & A all saw it—I could not from the impossibility of walking—[...] We went thoro' the Jews' street one of the worst & most ancient parts of the Town.[...]

Saturday 19—Woke very weak—E & A went up to Ehrenbreitstein—Mama & I remained quietly at the Inn doing as much of our Sabbath duty as Time would allow At 12 started in the Rubens up the Rhine to Mayence.[...]

[...] Oberldreistein a walled Town with a red castle on the margin of the Rhine [...] standing at the foot of a high conical rock surrounded by the castle of Marksburg—which retains all the characteristics of a fortress of the middle ages—even with secret passages—vaults hewn in the rock a chamber of torture & every thing that could make me long to see it—[...]

A little above St. Goar—our vessel rocked & tossed as if on the sea instead of a calmly flowing river, & we found it was passing over a whirlpool & then a rapid formed by the stream making its way over a number of sunken rocks increased by a sudden bend [...]—The first object after the bend of the river is the town of Obervessel—with a very picturesque round tower by the waters edge—& a little chapel glen by the river consecrated to the memory of St. Werner—said to have been crucified by the Jews—& here thrown into the Rhine. The body instead of sinking, or even floating with the current[,] ascended the stream as far as Bacharach—where a beautiful chapel in the florid gothic style was erected to St. Werner's memory & over his relics in 1428 tho' demolished by the Swedes in the 30 Years War—it still remains an elegant fragment of the highest & most beautiful [Lancet] style existing—[...]

At the narrow pass below Rheinstein, was a Jews' toll & dogs were trained to single out the Jews from the passing crowd—[...]

[...]An hours railway took us to Frankfurt where we found lodgings & kind friends awaiting us—[....]

Tuesday 22—Too weak & languid to attempt walking took a drive—thoro' the ancient Juden Strasse[1]—transported me back to the dark ages when poverty & dirt around the entrances were adopted to conceal the riches within—Several times the doors & windows were open & revealed the inner depth of houses—allowing plenty of space for concealed

1 Jews' Street.

grandeur—Over the picturesque ancient looking bridge & passed on our left hand a very old looking building formerly the residence of the Knights Templars—thoro' Saxen Hausen which is the frontier of Frankfurt over the river—into beautiful country—superb fields of every variety of grain diversified by the blue cornflower & another beautiful variety of a violet hue—No ditches between the fields & road—therefore the latter is planted with beautiful trees, sometimes Lindens, sometimes fruit trees otherwise when the snow is thickly on the ground the road would be undistinguishable—The principal figure in the scene unlike England is the orchard within the cornfield & neither defended by fence or hedge—The rich straggling forms of the apple trees amongst the grain are very beautiful [—] We just entered the Forest not having time to go farther it is a very beautiful distant object in the scenery round tho' not very lofty—Home by the same way we came & an intense headache prevented my doing or being any thing more that day except enjoying some of E's music & making a cap—

Wednesday 23—Weakness & depression more painful than it has been for weeks. Dr. S's visit & examination of my spine tho' he assures me it has no disease—did not tend to cheer me—I believe the hope that change of air & scene would have been sufficient, had gained more dominion over me than I was aware of, & the [ ] that I am still out of health & must still have all the restrictions & disagreeables of Invalidism, increased to an overpowering degree the depression—which in itself is part of my illness—The weather was stormy & showery to go out until after tea—I did not regret it, for I felt too exhausted to wish to move—Walked in the promenades on the right side of the Bockenheim gate it is very pretty—E. played most exquisitely on our return—but that crushing pain on my heart would not leave me—becoming denser & denser, till it gave way to an hysterical emotion that afflicted my night & the next day as from a spasm of illness—

Thursday 24—Weakness & depression more exhausting than ever—preventing my doing anything tho' I tried to write journal—a visit from Konigswerter—The Dr came again examining my chest & heart with an instrument—continues his opinion that there is no disease but all my sufferings proceed from exhaustion of the nervous system, brought about by sorrow & mental excitement—& if this illness has indeed been coming on since the measles as I believe it has—he is right I have often & often turned to mental labour, to bear up against the pressure of internal sorrow—sorrow which none would understand, for it comes from my peculiar character, & things produced it that other natures would not comprehend—oh that the mystery of feeling could be explained!—I fancy [ ] Dr

May [ ] from his discovering that I was subject to swelled glands & other weaknesses in childhood—& that the gland under my arm proceeded from the same cause & was the same thing as my thumb at 3 years old—I could not understand why but was completely overcome for hours after he left me—from the bitter feeling of self-reproach—that I could not be cheerful—could not feel all the petty annoyances of this long long illness, as from my God—I could not wish my worst Job[,][1] if I had any, the agony of feeling which that strife of the spirit caused—[...]

Friday 25th—Still that exhausting depression—could do nothing worth recording—went with S. to a wool shop in the Zeil[2] to purchase some work, & had a drive round some of the promenades—but the air seemed only to add to the intense weight on the heart & frame—that I could not rouse myself for hours but could "look up" with more fervour & pray for strength to endure it—Went to the promenades—where we may take several walks without going over the same spot—& tried to converse, but the exhausting depression returned as intense as ever at night—

Saturday 26—Depression not quite so exhausting. Dr S. says it is the last symptom of my illness that will leave me—This gave me comfort & hope—When I can but realize it as illness I can bear it—but when it seems all mental, I feel so changed that self respect departs from me & I feel as a crushed worm—Read a very little, but could not realize any Sabbath feeling—Took a little walk down Bockenheimer chaussée—w/ Eml—Depression as dense at night—

Sunday 27—Tried to write journal, but compelled to cease from an intense headache—endeavoured to disperse it by sitting & walking in promenades, but only increased it & the exhausting depression which returned more than ever with all the feelings of irritation & misery that seemed to say my God had utterly turned His face away, for to pray was impossible Had I seen all I should endure the first week of my sojourn here, I believe I should never have had courage to come—my whole spirit seemed to yearn to England & the Friends I had left—Letters from them & from dear H. in a degree removed these feelings—Spent the Evening rationally & pleasantly at the L's—Depression somewhat less at night—but dreaded it—as any would the most terrible physical pain

---

1 In the Bible, an upstanding citizen whom God causes to experience enormous suffering as a test of his faith.

2 A broad commercial road in the middle of Frankfurt.

Monday 28—Rather less depressed—could write journal read & work with less pain Did not go out in morning because it was showery—but getting finer at four—[...] Went to the promenades from ½7 till ½9—sitting & walking—the air being so delicious & the evening lovely & noticed a species of fire fly—they called it a glow worm but glow worms of England do not fly—& this *was* flying about like a spark of fire—

Tuesday—29—One of the most lovely days we have had this summer—Wrote journal & to Aunt S.[1] Read Schiller's Maria Stuart—not a good translation—but a most beautiful play—[2] Started at ½3—a party of 8 in a delightful carriage for Wilhelmsbad—[...] consisting of a curious town—with moat & bridge, which thoro' the trees as we approach is a most interesting object appearing like an old ruin—a fine Kursale[3]—deserted Theatre & most extensive & beautiful gardens—The part of which opposite the Kursale has an orchestra, & innumerable tables laid under superb horse chestnut & Linden trees—We rambled about the gardens walking & sitting for full an hour—Noticing some fine beeches in full blossom which I never saw before—Limes or Lindens almost yellow with their exquisitely scented bloom several wild flowers transporting me back to Devonshire[4]—a wide tunnel running under a vegetation covered rock on which is a large merry go round, & leads on the right into [...] more lovely parts of the garden—The music sounding most thrillingly to my ear in the open air—drew us to the more frequented parts—heard some fine waltzes & overtures to Don Juan[5]—went & tasted the water which resembles that of Tunbridge Wells[6] in flavour but is not so powerful—Looked into the Kursale most elegant rooms, but their use is too repugnant to my feelings even for admiration It seems to me a marvelous invention—the temples to the most horrid, joy destroying vice gambling—always erected in the loveliest purest peace giving scenes of nature—[...] A narrow [ ] bridge led over the moat to the high road [ ]—our carriage awaited us—& the drive home was most enjoyable from the lovely stillness of tree covered

1 Sarah Aguilar, the sister of Grace Aguilar's father, Emanuel. From the Michael Dugdale Aguilar Family Tree, private collection of Michael Dugdale.

2 The edition is probably Johann Christoph Friedrich von Schiller, *Maria Stuart: A Tragedy in Five Acts*, trans. E.L. Percival (Munich, 1839).

3 A large concert or resort space, in this instance a gambling resort.

4 County in southwest England where Aguilar spent much of her childhood.

5 Wolfgang Amadeus Mozart's opera, *Don Giovanni* (K. 527), was first performed in Prague in Oct. 1787.

6 A popular middle-class resort southeast of London known for the healing effects of its spring waters.

prospect—Earth & Sky—To me poetry so dwells in deep repose—It is the first excursion I have enjoyed with something of the zest of former years, tho' the impossibility, to walk & go along as our companions do still a painful drawback—Before the Kursale is a double row of fine orange trees & on one side are [numerous] [beds] of flowers—rising from the floor almost to the height of a tree—

Wednesday 30th—Another most lovely day—Wrote my journal—interrupted by a visit from Miss Strauch with GS. There is nothing yet attractive to me in any of the Germans I have seen—The spirit of the country appears to me completely, [lying] & speculation—instead of Truth & Faith—that a residence in it would be to me most painful—My whole heart yearns at times to the kindly natures, & warm sympathies—& truthful hearts of some even of the most casual acquaintanceships in England—Continued with Monte Christo, which is one of the purest (as yet) French Books I have ever read, finely conceived & drawn—[1] The intense heat occasioned an almost painful feeling of languor—at five went to the Main Lust a tea garden on the bank of the Maine commanding a fine view of the opposite banks—The tables are laid before avenues of lime or Linden trees—& one avenue is left free for promenades—There is an excellent band & the scene was peculiarly German every table filled with tea drinking, or beefsteak eating parties—The ladies knitting the gentlemen stockings—The music was to my ear most beautiful—a fine band playing several airs I knew—from Sonnambula—Norma—Lucretia Borgia—& most inspiring waltzes[2]—In former days story after story would have risen in my mind under the influence of such sounds & scenes—Now Imagination feels quite dormant—& that is one reason why I am less capable of realizing enjoyment—The ladies dresses were much the same as in England—& some of the Germans very pretty looking girls The Lindens were completely covered with blossom—the exquisite scent of which when wafted by the air to us—seemed like some old strain of melody—[...] We were in the gardens till ½9—& going home—the exquisite clearness of the sky almost a pale green tint, struck me as more approaching holy than England—[...].

---

1 Aguilar's edition was probably Alexandre Dumas, Père, *The Count of Monte Christo* (London: Chapman and Hall, 1846), 2 vols.

2 Aguilar refers to three Italian operas: Vincenzo Bellini's *La Sonnambula* (*The Sleepwalker*), first performed at the Teatro Carcano, Milan, 6 March 1831; Bellini's *Norma*, first performed at Teatro alla Scala, Milan, 26 Dec. 1831; and Gaetano Donizetti's *Lucrezia Borgia*, first performed at Teatro alla Scala, 26 Dec. 1833.

Friday 2—A bad night following the enjoyment of the opera, rendered to day rather languid—read in the promenades—wrote journal—Dr S. came—& commended me constant excursions—& going to the opera if I can do so without being pushed & when I can sit on easy seats etc.—in short that I am to be a lady at large with regard to amusement—all that does not excite, or increase the beating of the heart—a very *very* little thing does that—even the receipt of a letter I have longed for—Went in the afternoon a drive to Millberge—crossed the bridge on which noticed a fine statue of Charlemagne, & an iron crucifix, on the top of which is a gold cock—the legend of which very much resembles the usual legends of Germany in the Devil assisting architects & the architects in their turn cheating the devil The old gentleman aids in the erection of the bridge demanding as fee the first life that passed across—The architect by the advise of the priest sent a cock across at which the devil in a great rage stamped a hole in the bridge, which hole has never been filled up but a crucifix erected over it with the cock in commemoration of the successful cheat—Went thoro' a good part of Saxon Hausen which seemed very old—up a hill commanding one of the finest views we have yet seen The Cathedral formed a fine object looking down on Frankfurt—& the Maine lay like a thread of silver beneath us—Our drive was in a path centre of the richest cultivation: fruit trees of every description growing in fields not only of grain but of vegetables—not an inch [of] ground is left uncultivated but there are no divisions in them—& no houses as there are in England to give evidence to whom they could belong—The distant views very much resemble those in Kent,[1] in the drive from Tunbridge Wells to Penshurst but not quite so rich—[...]. It was one of the hilliest drives we have taken & the air & skies most delicious & the country tho' exceedingly pretty around Frankfurt cannot compare in beauty & grandeur, to the scenery in Devonshire—The view of the Tannus Mountains from our drawing room window looked so exquisitely violet in the evening light, that we went up stairs into the servants' room to look at them & it was one of the most magnificent effects of sky I ever witnessed—The sun had gone down behind the highest mountain leaving on its edge a broad ridge of gold. From that gold was a splendidly shaped cloud of dark violet—to the right of which was another of the same hue with golden edges—There lay in a sky a most perfect blue becoming rose towards the horizon bathing the far mountains in violet & the mid & near distances in a sort of *flood* of liquid clearness—of exquisite blue—You seemed as the author of Modern Painters observes to be able to look thoro' & thoro' & in & in it

---

1 A county in southeast England.

as if there were no reaching its depths —[1] In the dark chatted & asked riddles—

Saturday 3rd—A letter I had longed to receive telling me news—of my dear friend so made my heart beat that I think Dr S. would have forbidden its receipt—but its effects made the day almost a happy one—did not go out—the weather was so hot that I did not go out but sat with all the windows open reading—Howitt's German experiences[2]—Spent the evening at Eschenheimer Strasse most pleasantly conversing & looking over some dried plants—talking principally with Solomon—[...].

Monday—5—The heat more intense than ever not only preventing my going out, but making [me] feel quite sick & faint all the afternoon till after tea —[...] After lying down, a little while after dinner, we heard Emanuel's beautiful concertante for piano & violin cello, by him & Mr Bochmuhl [?]. I never heard him play so beautifully nor liked his compositions more—It is thrilling—overpowering in the end—Those are the things which I believe I ought not to hear from the rapid palpitations of heart, & [ ] of the whole frame which generally attends *any* thing of his—Such strange sad thoughts came to me as I listened & looked on my gifted brother. Can all that genius end in the cold grave? or is it not rather but the commencement of perfected power—oh when will the mystery of Life be solved—They tell me not to think & when I am not writing, thought presses on me even from seemingly trifling & happy things, till I would give anything to escape from it—& nothing more, than the end & aim of Life—. After his own beautiful piece he played two of Beethoven's sonatas with no. 6—it was a real treat[3]—Afterwards we went a drive under Sol's—guidance; out at the Eschenheimer Gasse round the Grungebirge & looked in at the cemetery—passed several large farm yards very different & more aristocratic in appearance to the rural tree [ ] once of Devonshire & Kent—in one belonging to Rothschild[4]—there were turkey peacocks etc.—We

---

1 John Ruskin, *Modern Painters: their superiority in the art of landscape painting to all the Ancient Masters proved by examples of the True, the Beautiful, and the Intellectual from the works of modern artists, especially from those of J.M W. Turner Esq., R.A.* (London: Smith, Elder and Co., 1843).

2 William Howitt, *German Experiences: addressed to the English, both stayers at home and goers abroad.* (London, 1844). William and Mary Howitt were friends of Aguilar's.

3 Ludwig van Beethoven, *Sonata No. 6 in F*, composed 1796-97, published Vienna, 1798.

4 An allusion to the famous Jewish banking family whose founder, Mayer Amschel Rothschild, was the first Jew allowed to purchase property outside the Frankfurt *Judengasse*, or Jews' street. His purchase of 10 Bockenheimer Landstrasse in 1811 was a symbol of Jewish emancipation throughout Europe. See Niall Ferguson, *The House of Rothschild: Money's Prophets, 1798-1848* (New York: Viking, 1998), 164.

rode thoro' fields & etc. the wheat so full of grain, as actually to be on the ground impelled by its own weight, as if the wind had lain it there—some beautiful wild flowers were gathered for me by S & the coachman who was a complete character telling me how silver *schönes* neat beautiful flowers were which God Almighty planted, so superior to those planted by man—then he would [regale] us, in a strain so elevated, that a sad downfall to my ideas of enthusiasm in a character Our party pronounced him somewhat inclined to be in liquor—[...].

Thursday, 8—A day of bitter & complete exhaustion bodily & mental—Every nerve felt aching & yet powerless. Voice & swallow[ing] difficult & painful —[...]—the same pain as in the early part of my illness—could do nothing but lie down—& scarcely even read until quite the evening Wished to do several things but could do nothing; will & energy utterly gone—& depression as exhausting as ever. Eml's nocturne made the tears pour down without the power to stop them—It was in the dark, & no one knew it, which a comfort—If I could but [hide] this exhausting depression[,] could but hide from every eye irritation, & sadness—I could better bear this long continued trial—It is the utter loss of self esteem, the feeling God has in wrath stricken me with uselessness—from which I cannot rally—

Friday, 9th—Had little power for any thing in the morning except to write to H—compelled myself at four to go to the Kaiser Salle—compelled is a strange word to use when there is no *necessity* for me to go, but when illness has no palpable evidence—for weakness is known only to the individual who endures it—it is most painful to prevent a whole party going any where by refusal to accompany them The Kaiser Salle is one of the oldest houses in Frankfurt—& was the seat of the election of Emperors & of their banquets after their Coronation in the Cathedral which is visible from the windows of the Salle.[...] The next room we were shown was used formally for the elections—of the Emperors—it is now used for the sittings of the Senate—has a paneled ceiling—very much like those [...] in Hampton Court[1] & a broad gilt cornice—silver candle sticks of peculiar shape are affixed to the wall—but the modern chairs [...] etc. take away the appearance of the Past—I could not help thinking of how the fate of nations might have been once decided in that room & the election of individuals by their fellows—decide the misery or happiness of thousands—I have thought again & again on elections whether they are good or bad but still I cannot conquer original ideas, that hereditary successions are superi-

1 A palace on the north bank of the river Thames in the London borough of Richmond.

or—It is impossible for finite Judgment to decide—when the mere *outward beings* of the candidate can be visible—[....]

Monday, 12—The whole day until a six oclock tea felt one of such complete exhaustion, that I could do nothing scarcely even read—tried to write journal but could not—& even playing an easy duet seemed quite to tire me—After tea walked to a carriage, & had a delicious drive thoro' part of the Forest—over a bridge which crosses above a railroad & watched a train passing to Heidelberg. It looked just like a toy [ ] Walked a little in the Forest & drove thoro' what E called a complete tunnel of trees a long vista in the very thickest in the Forest—so that even at noon day it must be perfect shade & late[,] as it then was ½ 8[,] it presented an almost awful aspect of dense shade The flying glow worms or whatever they are, were glittery on the leaves & grass, or floating[,] for the movement is much more that of floating on the air than flying, by [ ] producing the most beautiful effect, I could not help fancying them some of the spirits of which [ ][1] says the atmosphere is filled, or fairies holding tiny lamps—Another beautiful effect was the glimmering light at the termination of the leafy vista, whose arms interlaced overhead & clustered on each side exactly like the pure gothic architecture of cathedrals—The principle trees of the Forest seemed Firs growing to an immense height—some lindens—birches—larches—very young oaks more like brush wood than full grown trees—& some fine birches, the silver stemmed bark & pendant leaves of which, are to me so very beautiful—Before we entered the Forest, we passed thoro' a complete avenue of immense birches almost as fine as our elms—We were not home until just tea & a longed for letter, crowned the pleasure of the excursion & made me feel lighter & happier tho' it took away my appetite.

Tuesday 13—Either the Forest or my letter, caused me to feel so much of former will to make the exertion of going to the picture gallery in the morning—but the exhausting feeling of weakness soon prevented any thing like true enjoyment—No one I believe, but sufferers themselves from weakness can tell the bitter alloy this powerlessness brings to every pleasure—I could not attempt to look at the pictures—some of which are very old but except Lessing's picture of Huss before the Council of Constance [...] none struck me very particularly [...].[2] The figures are all the size of life & every one a study—Huss himself stands nearly in the cen-

---

1 Name illegible.

2 Carl Friedrich Lessing, *Johann Huss und das Concilium zu Kostnitz* (1842). Huss was a fifteenth-century intellectual forerunner of the Protestant Reformation who was executed for heresy.

tre his right hand extended & his left resting on the open Bible—He is dressed in the black robes of the Rector of the University of Prague—bareheaded & the face is one on which we might gaze & gaze again & love & reverence almost to worship the mind, the calm pure elevated spirit which that pale worn face reveals[,] the very hands[,] the right pale, thin as the face—the left with rather more color from its fine pressure of the book whose doctrines he upholds, add to the expressiveness of the whole—To his extreme right (the left of the spectator) stands his friend Jerome of Prague in profile—a younger & perhaps prim looking man whose every thought is evidently absorbed in his friend—equally fine & as attractive—close to Huss's right sit three cardinals with their red hats cloaks etc. the one nearest him has his face opposite the spectator & the countenance actually haunts me, from its so completely embodying my idea of Torquemada[1] determined even in the face of conviction to persecute Huss, & denounce his doctrines—The next is a very old man—with a long white beard his eyes fixed on the book he holds—seeming to feel Huss' argument may satisfy himself, but cannot stand against his belief in the teaching of previous ages—The two bishops in the splendid robes of the Roman clergy even to the silk gloves with their rings outside the glove fill up the right of the picture all the back ground of which is filled with figures, every face of which is distinct & characteristic. The third cardinal whom I ought to have mentioned before is a much younger man with his eyes fixed on Huss—seeming to wish to express, that his argument would convince him, if he dared allow it—To the left of Huss, just below the desk on which his bible leans is another Bishop holding Sigismund's (the Emperor's) letter of safe conduct half open from which the golden seal falls negligently—His face, turned from the spectator, is directed to one of the civil councillors who leaning over him appears in that earnest conversation which would almost lead me to fancy the forfeiture of that safe conduct, & seizure of Huss was being agitated between them darkly even then—At the extreme left of the spectator is another fine head seeming an Italian & by the coronet some Italian bishop or prince It is a face so expressive as quite to haunt me either as one having been seen in life, or embodying some idea, the exact subject of which I try in vain to remember. There are several other heads & figures all exquisitely expressive & the workmanship, the exquisite spirit pervading the whole picture stamps it as one of the sublimest efforts of Genius—I never remember a picture that so fascinated me—The mighty emotions struggling in so many hearts, diverse as the individuals—yet such an aspect of still, stern calm pervading all—I did not

1 Tomás de Torquemada (1420–1498), Spain's first Grand Inquisitor, who burned Jews at the stake for heresy during the Spanish Inquisition.

know till I referred to the History *after* seeing the picture, that the safe conduct was really forfeited & Huss despite the Emperor's promise of protection [seized], imprisoned, & finally burnt—but the picture told it me.[...][1]

Whether going to the Gallery exhausted me or the heat I know not, but I was unfit for any thing else the remainder of the day. Tried to crawl to the promenades, but the exertion was too painful—breath & limbs all failing—Oh this exhausting weakness! What enjoyment is there without health? [....]

Friday 16 The day too intensely hot to move—received letters from London dated 2 & 4 July—I began an answer to Aunt S—Finished Monte Christo—many parts of which I like better than any French work I have yet read—There are sentences which fix themselves on one's mind compelling thought & had my mind been in a healthy state—I could have written a whole chapter upon it—The end is tame compared with the many exciting scenes in the work but it finely shows how incompetent is man to execute the work of vengeance[,] how impossible for him to hurl it on those who deserve it from him, without it recoiling in suffering & death on others comparatively innocent—even when he merely avenges, by causing his enemies' own crimes follies or passions, to bring their punishment—That is a fine idea—even tho' the working [out] it compels scenes of immorality & horror, poisoning & suicide peculiar to France—Mercedes reply to him when he quotes the Bible "The children shall bear the penalty of their Father's sins"—as an excuse for his seeking revenge contains a whole volume of exquisite Truth—

"Man has but *Time* God has Time & *Eternity*"

& his own acquired knowledge that with all his riches all his power—he cannot work as God—for with Providence there is no chance Evil nothing of Hazard to interfere with his judgments—& again Happiness & Misery, are more the creation of contrasts, than reality & we do not know the [ ] of the one till we know the other & can so compare them, & that man's motto should be "Attendez et Espirez—" all are things to think about[2]—

---

1 The history Aguilar refers to is probably François Paul Émile Boisnormand de Bonnechose, *The Reformers before the Reformation. The fifteenth century. John Huss and the Council of Constance*, (Edinburgh: W. Whyte & Co., 1844) Trans. Campbell Mackenzie.

2 In Dumas' *The Count of Monte Christo*, Edmond Dantès has been unfairly persecuted and imprisoned by four men. When he escapes years later, he dons a new identity as the Count of Monte Christo and begins taking revenge on his persecutors. His former fiancée, Mercédès, is the only one who recognizes him upon his return, and she warns him against

Saturday 18—[...] After tea—took a pretty drive to the Kircheweigh at Oberrad. The Kircheweigh is a village festival held in commemoration generally of the dedication of the church—[...] But the scene on the road was animated beyond description—Carriages of all sorts the lumbering poste & more elegant omnibus—open cabs—& almost all with young men & women the latter with their uncovered heads & gracefully hanging shawls—foot passengers—all eager—all happy looking, either returning from the scene of festivity or—pressing on to it—becoming more & more numerous as we neared the village, which seemed a complete fair—It appeared to consist principally of one long street—forming the large capacious looking dwellings peculiar to German villages—from all the Gasthofs inns or hotels on which were suspended fresh & tasteful wreaths & some few garlands. On each side of the street were booths filled with ginger bread—& toys, of every variety of description—The booths were shaped much like those in the fairs in England, but their contents seemed of quite different shape & kind—Had I had all my former strength & energy, I should have liked to have walked down to have examined the things—Music was issuing from one of the gardens, but our Coachman who had already told E. how well he danced & seemed quite touched with the spirit of the same, drove us into the Frankforter Hof—where we left the carriage & proceeded up a staircase (*outside* the house tho' covered,) into the dancing room where there appeared some hundreds of people. At first from the pipes & numbers, it felt so oppressing close, as sent M. & Mrs. L. quickly down—but E & G. remained with me—the whole scene amusing me exceedingly—The girls were all neatly dressed, no pretence of finery—the hair so brightly & smoothly done in bands on the temples & braids behind—in neat white dresses or pink & other colored chiffon The men most of them with the pipes in their mouths, but all dancing with such zeal & energy—the alternate polka, galop,[1] & waltz—as if their very lives depended on it The music was so spirited & inspiring, that weak as I am I felt as if I could have joined them—The orchestra is at the upper end of the room, & they waltz & galop completely round the room—without either confusion or shocks, or any of the contretemps, often met with in polished society, tho' above 20 or 25 couples were dancing together—My amusement was in our coachman a remarkably bright honest looking

---

taking vengeance on his enemy's daugther, Valentine. When he discovers that Valentine is the beloved of his own dear friend, Maximilien, he relinquishes vengeance, and counsels the lovers, "Attendez et Espirez"—wait and hope.

1 According to the *OED*, a galop is "A lively dance in 2/4 time, originally a separate and independent dance, but now also forming a portion of a set of quadrilles," popular in the nineteenth century.

young man, [his] hand seeking the prettiest girls & dancing con amore & exceeding well—The manners to each other are so extremely courteous that it would strike any stranger with surprise—The price for the whole evening's amusement is one florin ⅛—or 6 Kreutzers (2d) each dance—In the garden were a variety of groups, sitting at tables with the stone seltzer bottles—& Rhenish wine bottles [...] & pipes before them—several beautiful trees gave an air of great richness & shade to the aspect of the garden—On our way home the same air of bustle & gaiety pervaded—a soldier with his arm folded very lovingly round his companion a young girl, walked on as composedly as if no eyes were reproving him Our Coachman still more excited by his dance cracked his whip & made all the other out of the way moves peculiar to German coachmen—driving at a most tremendous rate, & jeering all the other coachmen that could not keep up with him, but all in a most goodhumoured way & laughing, greater part of the time—He was still more endearing at E giving him 12 Kreutzers 4 for himself, over & above his fare—There are some fine poplars, & some of the largest elms I have seen in Germany forming an avenue just after we cross the railing on our way to Muhllers & Oberrad—S. had caught a fire fly—& the light proceeds from a spot on the lower part of the body—nearly concealed when the wings are closed—It is a pale greenish phosphoric light—The fly itself is something like a moth—[...].

Tuesday, 20—The first day since we have left London that we have not been able to go out for a wet day—employed myself comfortably at home in writing journal, reading history of Germany, receiving a visit from my Dr—looking over Philip Augustus[1]—practicing working my bag—while listening to E—& reading Dumas' Albine a ghost story which fascinated me[2]—especially under the influence under E's beautiful music—not so depressed—but cannot realize elasticity—all my best & highest feelings seem so gone—I so long once more to realize that consoling devotion, that communing with a God of love, which has never deserted me for so long a time before—Will it ever return?

Wednesday, 21—The day was rather showery but clearing off & promising fine about four we started for Bergen—a little village famous for its magnificent view—[...].

---

1 George Payne Rainsford James, *Philip Augustus, or the Brothers in Arms* (London, 1837), a historical novel.

2 Alexandre Dumas, Père, *Albine* (Brussels: Alph. Lebègue et Sacré fils, 1843), Dumas' first attempt at a gothic romance. For details see Douglas Munro, ed., *Alexander Dumas Père: A Bibliography of Works Translated into English to 1910* (New York: Garland Publishing Inc., 1978), 59-60.

[…] Leaving Seckbach the road continued still hilly & winding, & more beautiful in itself & its distant views than any other ride we have taken—carts full of corn & drawn by cows, a large wagon drawn by four straggling horses harnessed in the most *un*english fashion curiously shaped corn sheaves quite unlike those in England or rather appearing to be formed of four or five English sheaves with a sixth turned downwards on the four, so as to thatch them & give them the appearance of a large beehive—[…] with one or two figures sitting by or lying under them—*women* cutting the corn with a sickle—or carrying large milk cans on their heads—were all objects unlike England. I cannot remember exactly whether it was at Seckbach, or at a few straggling houses & a larger [ ] & horse trough at which several country people were standing, that an old woman received the turnpike money—the head costume of whom was different to the women about Frankfurt—something like the caps of the broomgirls who come over to England but not exactly—[…].

Monday [26] & Tuesday [27] incessant wet days—& head too painful combined with an all overish feeling of illness—for any thing like satisfactory employment—or any realization of lightness & enjoyment Drove to Eschenheimer Gasse to tea on Tuesday—which in some degree removed the weight of head & [mind]

Wednesday 28—Beautifully fine, fresh feeling day but my head continued strangely painful, & the difficulty to write a few notes for an opportunity so unlike my former self as to overpower & depress me most exhaustingly—Tried to walk to a shop & home, & so faint & tired as scarcely to be able to get home […].

Thursday 29—Dr S. insists on my resting from writing even this amusement & letters—I do not cannot agree with him as to this treatment of the case—but

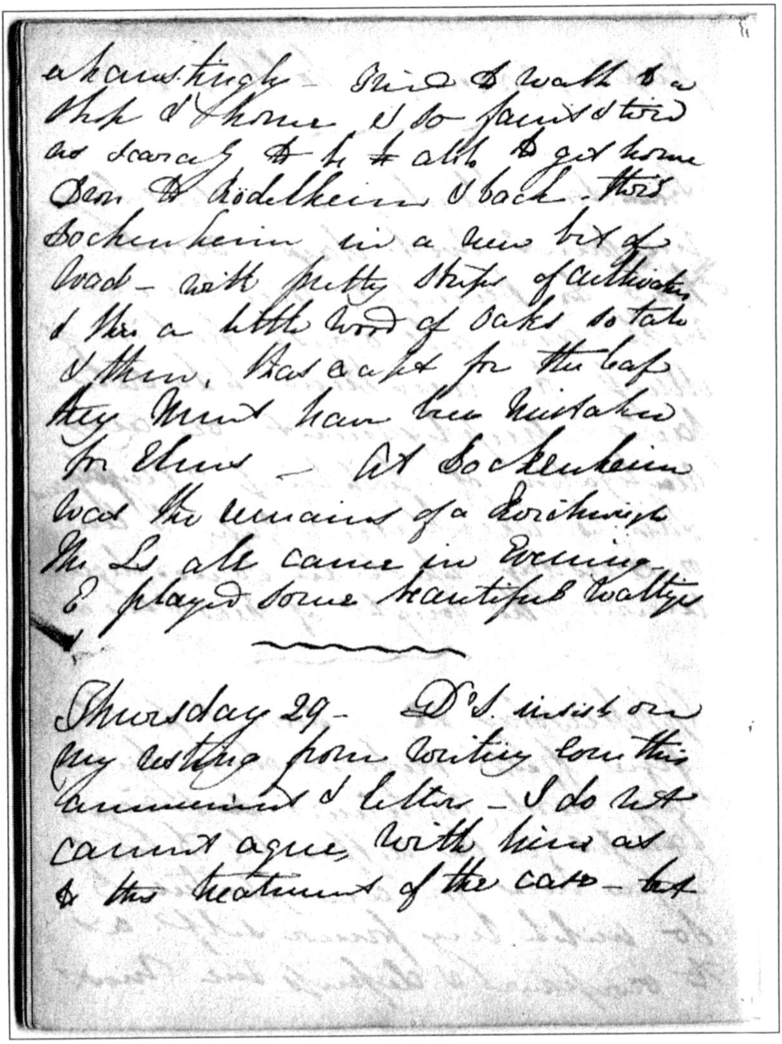

Figure 3. Aguilar's Frankfurt Journal, 29 July 1847. Photo: Michael Dugdale

Select Bibliography

Primary Documents

Aguilar's manuscripts, correspondence, published works, medical and legal documents, and effects are held in eight major libraries and archives:

Bod – Bodleian
BL – British Library
UPENN – University of Pennsylvania Center for Judaic Studies
UPENN-IL – University of Pennsylvania Center for Judaic Studies Isaac Leeser Archive
UCL-MSS – Grace Aguilar Manuscripts, University College London Manuscript Library
UNC – Manuscripts Department Library of the University of North Carolina, Chapel Hill
NLS – National Library of Scotland
HRO – Hertfordshire Record Office

MSS.

Aguilar, Grace. "Leila, A Poem in Three Cantos with Notes" UCL-MSS.
——. "Notes on Chonchology" UCL-MSS.
——. "Notes on Excursion" Oct. 1843 UCL-MSS.
——. Poems. 1834-1835 UCL-MSS.
——. "Sabbath Thoughts Lecture on Psalm 32 by Rev. R.A. Feb. 1837" UCL-MSS.
——. Frankfurt Journal. Private collection of Michael Dugdale. Available through www.graceaguilar.info.

Medical and Legal Documents, Tributes, and Obituaries

"The Late Miss Aguilar's Case." Translation of German doctor's description of the stages of her illness UCL-MSS.
"Proctor's Account of the Administration of the Estate of Grace Aguilar, Spinster" UCL-MSS.
Bowles, Caroline A. "Reminiscences of Grace Aguilar" Jan. 1848 UCL-MSS.
Female Hebrew Benevolent Society. Philadelphia. Nov. 3, 1847 UCL-MSS.
Hall, Mrs. S[amuel] C[arter]. *Art Union.* Nov. 1, 1847 UCL-MSS.

Hebrew Benevolent Society of Charleston, South Carolina. April, 1848 UCL-MSS.
Hyneman, Rebekah. Philadelphia. Nov. 1847 UCL-MSS.
Ladies of the Society for Religious Instruction of Jewish Youth, Charleston, South Carolina. Nov. 23, 1847 UCL-MSS.
Obituary. *Athenaeum*. Nov. 1847 UCL-MSS.
Obituary. *Voice of Jacob*. Nov. 1847 UCL-MSS.
Obituary and Leader. *Occident*. Nov. 1847 UPENN-IL.
Toulmine, Camilla. *La Belle Assemblée*. Nov. 1847 UCL-MSS.

Correspondence

Grace Aguilar to Miriam Gratz Moses Cohen and Solomon Cohen. Southern Historical Collection #2639, Series 1, Folder 8 UNC.
Sarah Aguilar to Miriam Gratz Moses Cohen and Solomon Cohen. Southern Historical Collection #2639, Series 1, Folder 8 UNC.
Grace Aguilar to Isaac D'Israeli. Dep. Hughenden 243/1, fols. 3-12 Bod.
Grace Aguilar to Edward Bulwer Lytton. D/EK C22/4 HRO.
Grace Aguilar to Robert Chambers. Dep. 341/96, letter 95; Dept. 341/94, letter 183 NLS.
Grace Aguilar to Isaac Leeser. Isaac Leeser Collection, Box 1, FF4; Box 8, FF2 UPENN-IL.
Grace Aguilar to Isaac Leeser. *Occident* 2 (Oct. 1844): 340-342 UPENN.

Published Texts and Selected Poetry

Aguilar, Grace. *Works*. 8 vols. London: Groombridge and Sons, 1869.
——. *The Days of Bruce: A Story of Scottish History*. London: Groombridge and Sons, 1852.
——. *Essays and Miscellanies: Choice Cullings from the Manuscripts of Grace Aguilar*. Ed. Sarah Aguilar. Philadelphia: A. Hart, Late Carey and Hart, 1853.
——. "History of the Jews in England." *Chambers' Miscellany* 18. 153 (1847): 1-32.
——. *Home Influence: A Tale for Mothers and Daughters*. London: R. Groombridge, 1847.
——. *Home Scenes and Heart Studies*. London: Groombridge and Sons, 1852.
——, trans. *Israel Defended* by Orobio de Castro. Brighton: 1838.
——. *The Jewish Faith*. London: 1846.
——. *The Magic Wreath of Hidden Flowers*. Brighton: 1839.

——. *A Mother's Recompense; a Sequel to Home Influence*. London: Groombridge and Sons, 1851.
——. *Records of Israel*. London: J. Mortimer, 1844.
——. *Sabbath Thoughts and Sacred Communings*. London: Groombridge and Sons, 1853.
——. *The Spirit of Judaism*. Ed. Isaac Leeser. Philadelphia: Jewish Publication Society of America, 1864.
——. *The Vale of Cedars; or, the Martyr*. London: Groombridge and Sons, 1850.
——. *Woman's Friendship: A Story of Domestic Life*. London: Groombridge and Sons, 1850.
——. *The Women of Israel*. 3 vols. London: Groombridge and Sons [?], 1845.
——. "A Poet's Dying Hymn." *Voice of Jacob* (18 February 1842): 87 BL.
——. "Communings with Nature. No. VII. Address to the Ocean." *Occident* 5 (Oct. 1847): 337-38 UPENN-IL.
——. "Sabbath Thoughts III." *Occident* 2 (Jun 1844): 141-42 UPENN-IL
——. "An Hour of Peace." *Occident* 1 (Sept. 1843): 287-88 UPENN-IL.
——. "Song of the Spanish Jews, During Their 'Golden Age.'" *Occident* 1 (Sep 1843): 289-90 UPENN-IL.
——. "The Hebrew's Appeal, On Occasion of the Late Fearful *Ukase* Promulgated by the Emperor of Russia." *Occident* 2 (Sep 1844): 292-93 UPENN-IL.
——. "The Wanderers." *Occident* 3 (Oct 1845): 330-32 UPENN-IL.
——. "A Vision of Jerusalem, While Listening to a Beautiful Organ in one of the Gentile Shrines." *Occident* 1 (Feb 1844): 541-43 UPENN-IL.
——. "Dialogue Stanzas" and "Rocks of Elim." *Spirit of Judaism*, ed. Isaac Leeser. Cincinnati: Jewish Publication Society of America, 1864, 242-43; 254-57.

Anthologized Work

Aguilar, Grace. "The Exodus—Laws for the Mothers of Israel," excerpt from *The Women of Israel*. *The Longman Anthology of Women's Literature*. Ed. Mary K. DeShazer. New York: Addison-Wesley 2001. 690-95.
——. "The Authoress." *Victorian Love Stories: An Oxford Anthology*. Ed. Kate Flint. New York: Oxford UP, 1996. 1-17.
——. Excerpt from *The Spirit of Judaism*. *Four Centuries of Jewish Women's Spirituality*. Ed. Ellen M. Umansky and Dianne Ashton. Boston: Beacon, 1992. 78-83.

Other Available Victorian Jewish Literature

Levy, Amy. *The Complete Novels and Selected Writings of Amy Levy, 1861-1889.* Ed. Melvyn New. Gainesville: UP of Florida, 1993.

Zangwill, Israel. *Children of the Ghetto: a Study of a Peculiar People.* Meri-Jane Rochelson, ed. Detroit: Wayne State UP, 1998.

Secondary Literature

Abrahams, Rachel Beth Zion Lask. "Grace Aguilar: A Centenary Tribute." *Transactions of the Jewish Historical Society of England* 16 (1952): 137-48.

Anderson, Benedict. *Imagined Communities.* New York: Verso, 1991.

Baskin, Judith, ed. *Jewish Women in Historical Perspective.* 2nd ed. Detroit: Wayne State UP, 1998.

Bitton-Jackson, Livia. *Madonna or Courtesan? The Jewish Woman in Christian Literature.* New York: Seabury, 1982.

Brantlinger, Patrick. "Nations and Novels: Disraeli, George Eliot, and Orientalism." *Victorian Studies* 35 (1992): 255-75.

Brooks, Joseph C. *New York Public Library, Aguilar Branch.* New York: Landmarks Preservation Commission, 1996.

Cesarani, David. *The Jewish Chronicle and Anglo-Jewry, 1841-1991.* New York: Cambridge UP, 1994.

——, ed. *The Making of Modern Anglo-Jewry.* Oxford: Blackwell, 1990.

Cheyette, Bryan. *Constructions of "the Jew" in English Literature and Society: Racial Representations, 1875-1945.* Cambridge: Cambridge UP, 1993.

——. "From Apology to Revolt: Benjamin Farjeon, Amy Levy and the Post-Emancipation Anglo-Jewish Novel." *Transactions of the Jewish Historical Society of England* (Jan. 1985): 253-65.

Dugdale/Mason Aguilar Family Tree. Private collection of Michael Dugdale. Available through www.graceaguilar.info.

Endelman, Todd. *The Jews of Georgian England: 1714-1830: Tradition and Change in a Liberal Society.* Ann Arbor: U of Michigan P, 1999.

——. *Radical Assimilation in English Jewish History, 1656-1945.* Bloomington: Indiana UP, 1990.

Feldman, David. *Englishmen and Jews: Social Relations and Political Culture, 1840-1914.* New Haven: Yale UP, 1994.

Felsenstein, Frank. *Anti-Semitic Stereotypes: A Paradigm of Otherness in English Popular Culture, 1660-1830.* Baltimore: Johns Hopkins UP, 1995.

Freedman, Jonathan. *The Temple of Culture: Assimilation and Anti-Semitism in Literary Anglo-America.* Oxford: Oxford UP, 2000.

Galchinsky, Michael. *The Origin of the Modern Jewish Woman Writer: Romance and Reform in Victorian England.* Detroit: Wayne State UP, 1996.

——. "Engendering Liberal Jews: Jewish Women in Victorian England." *Jewish Women in Historical Perspective*, 2nd ed. Ed. Judith Baskin. Detroit: Wayne State UP, 1999. 208-26.

——. "Grace Aguilar's Correspondence." *Jewish Culture and History* 2 (Summer 1999): 88-110.

——. "Otherness and Identity in the Victorian Novel." *Victorian Literary Cultures: A Critical Companion.* Eds. William Baker and Kenneth Womack. Westport, CT: Greenwood, 2002. 485-507.

——. "The New Anglo-Jewish Literary Criticism." *Prooftexts* 15 (Sept. 1995): 272-82.

——. "'Permanently Blacked': Julia Frankau's Jewish Race." *Victorian Literature and Culture* (1999): 171-184.

Harris, Daniel A. "Hagar in Christian Britain: Grace Aguilar's 'The Wanderers.'" *Victorian Literature and Culture* 27 (1999): 143-69.

Hertzberg, Arthur. *The French Enlightenment and the Jews: The Origins of Modern Anti-Semitism.* New York: Columbia UP, 1968.

Hyman, Paula. *Gender and Assimilation in Modern Jewish History.* Seattle: U of Washington P, 1995.

Isaacs, Abram Samuel. *Young Champion.* Philadelphia: Jewish Publication Society, 1913.

Kaplan, Marion A. *The Making of the Jewish Middle Class: Women, Family, and Identity in Imperial Germany.* New York: Oxford UP, 1991.

Kushner, Tony, ed. *The Jewish Heritage in British History.* London: Frank Cass, 1992.

Kuzmack, Linda Gordon. *Woman's Cause: The Jewish Woman's Movement in England and the United States, 1881-1933.* Columbus: Ohio State UP, 1990.

Modder, Montagu Frank. *The Jew in the Literature of England: To the End of the Nineteenth Century.* New York: Meridian, 1939.

Page, Judith W. "Jerusalem and Jewish Memory: Judith Montefiore's *Private Journal.*" *Victorian Literature and Culture* (1999): 125-41.

Ragussis, Michael. "The 'Secret' of English Anti-Semitism: Anglo-Jewish Studies and Victorian Studies." *Victorian Studies* (Winter 1997): 295-307.

——. *Figures of Conversion: "The Jewish Question" and English National Identity.* Durham, NC: Duke UP, 1995.

Rosenberg, Edgar. *From Shylock to Svengali: Jewish Stereotypes in English Fiction.* Stanford: Stanford UP, 1960.

Roth, Cecil, ed. *Magna Bibliotheca Anglo-Judaica: A Bibliographical Guide to Anglo-Jewish History*. London: Jewish Historical Society of England, 1937.
——. *History of the Jews in England*. London: Oxford UP, 1941.
——. "Evolution of Anglo-Jewish Literature." London: Edward Goldston, 1937.
Said, Edward. *Orientalism*. New York: Vintage, 1978.
Salbstein, M.C.N. *The Emancipation of the Jews in Britain: the Question of the Admission of the Jews to Parliament, 1828-1860*. Rutherford, NJ: Fairleigh Dickinson UP, 1982.
Scheinberg, Cynthia. "Introduction: Re-Mapping Anglo-Jewish Literary History." *Victorian Literature and Culture* (1999): 115-24.
——. "'Measure to Yourself a Prophet's Place': Biblical Heroines, Jewish Difference and Women's Poetry." *Women's Poetry, Late Romantic to Late Victorian: Gender and Genre, 1830-1900*. Ed. Isobel Armstrong and Virginia Blain. New York: St. Martin's Press, 1999, 263-91.
——. "Canonizing the Jew: Amy Levy's Challenge to Victorian Poetic Identity." *Victorian Studies* 39 (1996): 173-200.
——. "Recasting 'Sympathy and Judgment': Amy Levy, Women Poets, and the Victorian Dramatic Monologue." *Victorian Poetry* 35 (1997): 173-92.
——. *Women's Poetry and Religion in Victorian England: Jewish Identity and Christian Culture*. New York: Cambridge UP, 2002.
Shapiro, James S. *Shakespeare and the Jews*. New York: Columbia UP, 1996.
Sorkin, David. *The Transformation of German Jewry, 1780-1840*. Oxford: Oxford UP, 1987.
Trumpener, Katie. *Bardic Nationalism: The Romantic Novel and the British Empire*. Princeton, NJ: Princeton UP, 1997.
Valman, Nadia. "Speculating upon Human Feeling: Evangelical Writing and Anglo-Jewish Women's Autobiography." *The Uses of Autobiography*. Ed. Julia Swindells. London: Taylor & Francis, 1995. 98-109.
——. "Semitism and Criticism: Victorian Anglo-Jewish Literary History." *Victorian Literature and Culture* (1999): 235-248.
Viswanathan, Gauri. *Outside the Fold: Conversion, Modernity, and Belief*. Princeton: Princeton UP, 1998.
Weinberger, Phillip M. "The Social and Religious Thought of Grace Aguilar (1816-1847)." Diss. New York U, 1970.
West-Burnham, Joss. "Travelling Towards Selfhood: Victorian Religion and the Process of Female Identity." *Women's Lives into Print: The Theory, Practice, and Writing of Feminist Auto/Biography*. Ed. Pauline Polkey. New York: St. Martin's, 1999. 80-95.

Wolfreys, Julian. *Being English: Narratives, Idioms, and Performances of National Identity from Coleridge to Trollope.* Albany: State U of New York, 1994.
Zatlin, Linda Gertner. *The Nineteenth-Century Anglo-Jewish Novel.* Boston: G.K. Hall 1981.

FSC
www.fsc.org